T0312647

100
World's
Greatest
SHORT
STORIES

CLASSICS

Reprint 2024

FiNGERPRINT! CLASSICS
An imprint of Prakash Books India Pvt. Ltd

113/A, Darya Ganj,
New Delhi-110 002
Email: info@prakashbooks.com/sales@prakashbooks.com

Fingerprint Publishing
@FingerprintP
@fingerprintpublishingbooks
www.fingerprintpublishing.com

ISBN: 978 93 8881 054 8

For as long as people have existed, they have told each other stories. Being as old as language itself, short stories are brief narratives of varying kinds—fables, fairytales, parables, myths, legends, and many more. Even recollections that begin with 'you would not believe what happened to me today' are stories, so you too have been a storyteller at a point. You too have crafted how to tell a tale to your listener, selecting parts of your happenings and imbuing a particular emotion in your narrative.

Before the nineteenth century, short story as a literary form had not received much critical appreciation . . . but still, stories about anything and everything were concocted. Some such stories can be read in one sitting, others take days, sometimes even weeks to finish. But stories have a way of swooping you in their fantastic world. Their realism makes readers identify with their characters, and their fiction and larger-than-life scenarios are a means of escape. Some are splayed with humour, others get you teary; some make you all warm and fuzzy, while others leave you rattled.

Whether they are as short as a paragraph, or as long as a novel, short stories remain one of the most interesting written pieces to exist today. There are many well-known novelists and poets who have been unable to resist dipping their pen in ink to try their hand in writing a short story. *100 World's Greatest Short Stories* is an anthology bringing together such fine writers with their finest works of short fiction—from Aesop, the teller of fables, to the avant-garde and modernist Virginia Woolf. Here is a careful selection of stories that were written years ago, but are equally relevant and moving today—stories of servants and masters, of towns and pipers, of homes and hauntings, and many more that are unforgettable, rich, resonant, and unputdownable.

Contents

CHARLES DICKENS

CONFUCIUS

EDGAR ALLAN POE

FRANK STOCKTON

FYODOR DOSTOEVSKY

GEORGE ADE

Æsop

(c. 620-564 BC)

1

The Hare and the Tortoise

The Hare was once boasting of his speed before the other animals. "I have never yet been beaten," said he, "when I put forth my full speed. I challenge any one here to race with me."

The Tortoise said quietly, "I accept your challenge."

"That is a good joke," said the Hare; "I could dance round you all the way."

"Keep your boasting till you've won," answered the Tortoise. "Shall we race?"

So a course was fixed and a start was made. The Hare darted almost out of sight at once, but soon stopped and, to show his contempt for the Tortoise, lay down to have a nap. The Tortoise plodded on and plodded on, and when the Hare awoke from his nap, he saw the Tortoise just near the winning-post and could not run up in time to save the race.

Then the Tortoise said: "Slow but steady progress wins the race."

2

A Shepherd's Boy

There was once a young Shepherd Boy who tended his sheep at the foot of a mountain near a dark forest. It was rather lonely for him all day, so he thought upon a plan by which he could get a little company and some excitement. He rushed down towards the village calling out "Wolf, Wolf," and the villagers came out to meet him, and some of them stopped with him for a considerable time. This pleased the boy so much that a few days afterwards he tried the same trick, and again the villagers came to his help. But shortly after this a Wolf actually did come out from the forest, and began to worry the sheep, and the boy of course cried out "Wolf, Wolf," still louder than before. But this time the villagers, who had been fooled twice before, thought the boy was again deceiving them, and nobody stirred to come to his help. So the Wolf made a good meal off the boy's flock, and when the boy complained, the wise man of the village said:

"A liar will not be believed, even when he speaks the truth."

3

The Lion in Love

A lion once fell in love with a beautiful maiden and proposed marriage to her parents. The old people did not know what to say. They did not like to give their daughter to the Lion, yet they did not wish to enrage the King of Beasts. At last the father said: "We feel highly honoured by your Majesty's proposal, but you see our daughter is a tender young thing, and we fear that in the vehemence of your affection you might possibly do her some injury. Might I venture to suggest that your Majesty should have your claws removed, and your teeth extracted, then we would gladly consider your proposal again." The Lion was so much in love that he had his claws trimmed and his big teeth taken out. But when he came again to the parents of the young girl they simply laughed in his face, and bade him do his worst.

"Love can tame the wildest."

4

The Mountains in Labour

One day the Countrymen noticed that the Mountains were in labour; smoke came out of their summits, the earth was quaking at their feet, trees were crashing, and huge rocks were tumbling. They felt sure that something horrible was going to happen. They all gathered together in one place to see what terrible thing this could be. They waited and they waited, but nothing came. At last there was a still more violent earthquake, and a huge gap appeared in the side of the Mountains. They all fell down upon their knees and waited. At last, and at last, a teeny, tiny mouse poked its little head and bristles out of the gap and came running down towards them, and ever after they used to say:

"Much outcry, little outcome."

Ambrose Bierce

(1842—c.1914)

5

A Man with Two Lives

Here is the queer story of David William Duck, related by himself. Duck is an old man living in Aurora, Illinois, where he is universally respected. He is commonly known, however, as 'Dead Duck'.

"In the autumn of 1866 I was a private soldier of the Eighteenth Infantry. My company was one of those stationed at Fort Phil Kearney, commanded by Colonel Carrington. The country is more or less familiar with the history of that garrison, particularly with the slaughter by the Sioux of a detachment of eighty-one men and officers—not one escaping—through disobedience of orders by its commander, the brave but reckless Captain Fetterman. When that occurred, I was trying to make my way with important dispatches to Fort C. F. Smith, on the Big Horn. As the country swarmed with hostile Indians, I traveled by night and concealed myself as best I could before daybreak. The better to do so, I went afoot, armed with a Henry rifle and carrying three days' rations in my haversack.

"For my second place of concealment I chose what seemed in the darkness a narrow canon leading through a range of rocky hills. It contained many large bowlders, detached from the slopes of the hills. Behind one of these, in a clump of sage-brush, I made my bed for the day, and soon fell asleep. It seemed as if I had hardly closed my eyes, though in fact it was near midday, when I was awakened by the report of a rifle, the bullet striking the bowlder just above my body. A band of Indians had trailed me and had me nearly surrounded; the shot had been fired with an execrable aim by a fellow who had caught sight of me from the hillside above. The smoke of his rifle betrayed him, and I was no sooner on my feet than he was off his and rolling down the declivity. Then I ran in a stooping posture, dodging among the clumps of sage-brush in a storm of bullets from invisible enemies. The rascals did not rise and pursue, which I thought rather queer, for they must have known by my trail that they had to deal with only one man. The reason for their inaction was soon made clear. I had not gone a hundred yards before I reached the limit of my run—the head of the gulch which I had mistaken for a canon. It terminated in a concave breast of rock, nearly vertical and destitute of vegetation. In that cul-de-sac I was caught like a bear in a pen. Pursuit was needless; they had only to wait.

"They waited. For two days and nights, crouching behind a rock topped with a growth of mesquite, and with the cliff at my back, suffering agonies of thirst and absolutely hopeless of deliverance, I fought the fellows at long range, firing occasionally at the smoke of their rifles, as they did at that of mine. Of course, I did not dare to close my eyes at night, and lack of sleep was a keen torture.

"I remember the morning of the third day, which I knew was to be my last. I remember, rather indistinctly, that in my desperation and delirium I sprang out into the open and began firing my repeating rifle without seeing anybody to fire at. And I remember no more of that fight.

"The next thing that I recollect was my pulling myself out of a river just at nightfall. I had not a rag of clothing and knew nothing of my whereabouts, but all that night I traveled, cold and footsore, toward the north. At daybreak I found myself at Fort C. F. Smith, my destination, but without my dispatches. The first man that I met was a sergeant named William Briscoe, whom I knew very well. You can fancy his astonishment at seeing me in that condition, and my own at his asking who the devil I was.

"'Dave Duck,' I answered; 'who should I be?'

"He stared like an owl.

"'You do look it,' he said, and I observed that he drew a little away from me. 'What's up?' he added.

"I told him what had happened to me the day before. He heard me through, still staring; then he said:

"'My dear fellow, if you are Dave Duck I ought to inform you that I buried you two months ago. I was out with a small scouting party and found your body, full of bullet-holes and newly scalped—somewhat mutilated otherwise, too, I am sorry to say—right where you say you made your fight. Come to my tent and I'll show you your clothing and some letters that I took from your person; the commandant has your dispatches.'

"He performed that promise. He showed me the clothing, which I resolutely put on; the letters, which I put into my pocket. He made no objection, then took me to the commandant, who heard my story and coldly ordered Briscoe to take me to the guardhouse. On the way I said:

"'Bill Briscoe, did you really and truly bury the dead body that you found in these togs?'

"'Sure,' he answered—'just as I told you. It was Dave Duck, all right; most of us knew him. And now, you damned impostor, you'd better tell me who you are.'

"'I'd give something to know,' I said.

"A week later, I escaped from the guardhouse and got out of the country as fast as I could. Twice I have been back, seeking for that fateful spot in the hills, but unable to find it."

6

The Boarded Window

In 1830, only a few miles away from what is now the great city of Cincinnati, lay an immense and almost unbroken forest. The whole region was sparsely settled by people of the frontier—restless souls who no sooner had hewn fairly habitable homes out of the wilderness and attained to that degree of prosperity which today we should call indigence, than, impelled by some mysterious impulse of their nature, they abandoned all and pushed farther westward, to encounter new perils and privations in the effort to regain the meagre comforts which they had voluntarily renounced. Many of them had already forsaken that region for the remoter settlements, but among those remaining was one who had been of those first arriving. He lived alone in a house of logs surrounded on all sides by the great forest, of whose gloom and silence he seemed a part, for no one had ever known him to smile nor speak a needless word. His simple wants were supplied by the sale or barter of skins of wild animals in the river town, for not a thing did he grow upon the land which, if needful, he might have claimed by right of undisturbed possession. There were evidences of 'improvement'—a few acres of ground immediately about the house had once been cleared of its trees, the decayed stumps of which were half concealed by the new growth that had been suffered to repair the ravage wrought by the axe. Apparently the man's zeal for agriculture had burned with a failing flame, expiring in penitential ashes.

The little log house, with its chimney of sticks, its roof of warping clapboards weighted with traversing poles and its 'chinking' of clay, had a single door and, directly opposite, a window. The latter, however, was boarded up—nobody could remember a time when it was not. And none knew why it was so closed; certainly not because of the occupant's dislike of light and air, for on those rare occasions when a hunter had passed that lonely spot the recluse had commonly been seen sunning himself on his doorstep if heaven had provided sunshine for his need. I fancy there are few persons living today who ever knew the secret of that window, but I am one, as you shall see.

The man's name was said to be Murlock. He was apparently seventy years old, actually about fifty. Something besides years had had a hand in his ageing. His hair and long, full beard were white, his grey, lustreless eyes sunken, his face singularly seamed with wrinkles which appeared to belong to two intersecting systems. In figure he was tall and spare, with a stoop of the shoulders—a burden bearer. I never saw him; these particulars I learned from my grandfather, from whom also I got the man's story when I was a lad. He had known him when living nearby in that early day.

One day Murlock was found in his cabin, dead. It was not a time and place for coroners and newspapers, and I suppose it was agreed that he had died from natural causes or I should have been told, and should remember. I know only that with what was probably a sense of the fitness of things the body was buried near the cabin, alongside the grave of his wife, who had preceded him by so many years that local tradition had retained hardly a hint of her existence. That closes the final chapter of this true story—excepting, indeed, the circumstance that many years afterward, in company with an equally intrepid spirit, I penetrated to the place and ventured near enough to the ruined cabin to throw a stone against it, and ran away to avoid the ghost which every well-informed boy thereabout knew haunted the spot. But there is an earlier chapter—that supplied by my grandfather.

When Murlock built his cabin and began laying sturdily about with his axe to hew out a farm—the rifle, meanwhile, his means of support—he was young, strong and full of hope. In that eastern country whence he came he had married, as was the fashion, a young woman in all ways worthy of his honest devotion, who shared the dangers and privations of his lot with a willing spirit and light heart. There is no known record of her name; of her charms of mind and person tradition is silent and the doubter is at liberty to entertain his doubt; but God forbid that I should share it! Of their affection and happiness there is abundant assurance in every added day of the man's widowed life; for what but the magnetism of a blessed memory could have chained that venturesome spirit to a lot like that?

One day Murlock returned from gunning in a distant part of the forest to find his wife prostrate with fever, and delirious. There was no physician within miles, no neighbour; nor was she in a condition to be left, to summon help. So he set about the task of nursing her back to health, but at the end of the third day she fell into unconsciousness arid so passed away, apparently, with never a gleam of returning reason.

From what we know of a nature like his we may venture to sketch in some of the details of the outline picture drawn by my grandfather. When convinced that she was dead, Murlock had sense enough to remember that the dead must be prepared for burial. In performance of this sacred duty he blundered now and again, did certain things incorrectly, and others which he did correctly were done over and over. His occasional failures to accomplish some simple and ordinary act filled him with astonishment, like that of a drunken man who wonders at the suspension of familiar natural laws. He was surprised, too, that he did not weep—surprised and a little ashamed; surely it is unkind not to weep for the dead. "Tomorrow," he said aloud, "I shall have to make the coffin arid dig the grave; and then I shall miss her, when she is no longer in sight; but now—she is dead, of course, but it is all right—it must be all right, somehow. Things cannot be so bad as they seem."

He stood over the body in the fading light, adjusting the hair and putting the finishing touches to the simple toilet, doing all mechanically, with soulless care. And still through his consciousness ran an undersense of conviction that all was right—that he should have her again as before, and everything explained. He had had no experience in grief; his capacity had not been enlarged by use. His heart could not contain it all, nor his imagination rightly conceive it. He did not know he was so hard struck; that knowledge would come later, and never go. Grief is an artist of powers as various as the instruments upon which he plays his dirges for the dead, evoking from some the sharpest, shrillest notes, from others the low, grave chords that throb recurrent like the slow beating of a distant drum. Some natures it startles; some it stupefies. To one it comes like the stroke of an arrow, stinging all the sensibilities to a keener life; to another as the blow of a bludgeon, which in crushing benumbs. We may conceive Murlock to have been that way affected, for (and here we are upon surer ground than that of conjecture) no sooner had he finished his pious work than, sinking into a chair by the side of the table upon which the body lay, and noting how white the profile showed in the deepening gloom, he laid his arms upon the table's edge, and dropped his face into them, tearless yet and unutterably weary. At that moment came in through the open window a long, wailing sound like the cry of a lost child in the far deeps of the darkening woods! But the man did not move. Again, and nearer than before, sounded that unearthly cry upon his failing sense. Perhaps it was a wild beast; perhaps it was a dream. For Murlock was asleep.

Some hours later, as it afterward appeared, this unfaithful watcher awoke and lifting his head from his arms intently listened—he knew not why. There in the black darkness by the side of the dead, recalling all without a shock, he strained his eyes to see—he knew not what. His senses were all alert, his breath was suspended, his blood had stilled its tides as if to assist the silence. Who—what had waked him, and where was it?

Suddenly the table shook beneath his arms, and at the same moment he heard, or fancied that he heard, a light, soft step—another—sounds as of bare feet upon the floor!

He was terrified beyond the power to cry out or move. Perforce he waited—waited there in the darkness through seeming centuries of such dread as one may know, yet live to tell. He tried vainly to speak the dead woman's name, vainly to stretch forth his hand across the table to learn if she were there. His throat was powerless, his arms and hands were like lead. Then occurred something most frightful. Some heavy body seemed hurled against the table with an impetus that pushed it against his breast so sharply as nearly to overthrow him, and at the same instant he heard and felt the fall of something upon the floor with so violent a thump that the whole house was shaken by the impact. A scuffling ensued, and a confusion of sounds impossible to describe. Murlock had risen to his feet. Fear had by excess forfeited control of his faculties. He flung his hands upon the table. Nothing was there!

There is a point at which terror may turn to madness; and madness incites to action. With no definite intent, from no motive but the wayward impulse of a madman, Murlock sprang to the wall, with a little groping seized his loaded rifle, and without aim discharged it. By the flash which lit up the room with a vivid illumination, he saw an enormous panther dragging the dead woman toward the window, its teeth fixed in her throat! Then there were darkness blacker than before, and silence; and when he returned to consciousness the sun was high and the wood vocal with songs of birds.

The body lay near the window, where the beast had left it when frightened away by the flash and report of the rifle. The clothing was deranged, the long hair in disorder, the limbs lay anyhow. From the throat, dreadfully lacerated, had issued a pool of blood not yet entirely coagulated. The ribbon with which he had bound the wrists was broken; the hands were tightly clenched. Between the teeth was a fragment of the animal's ear.

Anton Chekhov

(1860-1904)

7

The Death of a Government Clerk

One fine evening, a no less fine government clerk called Ivan Dmitritch Tchervyakov was sitting in the second row of the stalls, gazing through an opera glass at the Cloches de Corneville. He gazed and felt at the acme of bliss. But suddenly . . . In stories one so often meets with this "But suddenly." The authors are right: life is so full of surprises! But suddenly his face puckered up, his eyes disappeared, his breathing was arrested . . . he took the opera glass from his eyes, bent over and . . ."Aptchee!!" he sneezed as you perceive. It is not reprehensible for anyone to sneeze anywhere. Peasants sneeze and so do police superintendents, and sometimes even privy councillors. All men sneeze. Tchervyakov was not in the least confused, he wiped his face with his handkerchief, and like a polite man, looked round to see whether he had disturbed any one by his sneezing. But then he was overcome with confusion. He saw that an old gentleman sitting in front of him in the first row of the stalls was carefully wiping his bald head and his neck with his glove and muttering something to himself. In the old gentleman, Tchervyakov recognised Brizzhalov, a civilian general serving in the Department of Transport.

"I have spattered him," thought Tchervyakov, "he is not the head of my department, but still it is awkward. I must apologise."

Tchervyakov gave a cough, bent his whole person forward, and whispered in the general's ear.

"Pardon, your Excellency, I spattered you accidentally . . ."

"Never mind, never mind."

"For goodness sake excuse me, I . . . I did not mean to."

"Oh, please, sit down! Let me listen!"

Tchervyakov was embarrassed, he smiled stupidly and fell to gazing at the stage. He gazed at it but was no longer feeling bliss. He began to be troubled by uneasiness. In the interval, he went up to Brizzhalov, walked beside him, and overcoming his shyness, muttered:

"I spattered you, your Excellency, forgive me . . . you see . . . I didn't do it to . . ."

"Oh, that's enough . . . I'd forgotten it, and you keep on about it!" said the general, moving his lower lip impatiently.

"He has forgotten, but there is a fiendish light in his eye," thought Tchervyakov, looking suspiciously at the general. "And he doesn't want to talk. I ought to explain to him . . . that I really didn't intend . . . that it is the law of nature or else he will think I meant to spit on him. He doesn't think so now, but he will think so later!"

On getting home, Tchervyakov told his wife of his breach of good manners. It struck him that his wife took too frivolous a view of the incident; she was a little frightened, but when she learned that Brizzhalov was in a different department, she was reassured.

"Still, you had better go and apologise," she said, "or he will think you don't know how to behave in public."

"That's just it! I did apologise, but he took it somehow queerly . . . he didn't say a word of sense. There wasn't time to talk properly."

Next day Tchervyakov put on a new uniform, had his hair cut and went to Brizzhalov's to explain; going into the general's reception room he saw there a number of petitioners and among them the general himself, who was beginning to interview them. After questioning several petitioners the general raised his eyes and looked at Tchervyakov.

"Yesterday at the Arcadia, if you recollect, your Excellency," the latter began, "I sneezed and . . . accidentally spattered . . . Exc . . ."

"What nonsense . . . It's beyond anything! What can I do for you," said the general addressing the next petitioner.

"He won't speak," thought Tchervyakov, turning pale; "that means that he is angry . . . No, it can't be left like this . . . I will explain to him."

When the general had finished his conversation with the last of the petitioners and was turning towards his inner apartments, Tchervyakov took a step towards him and muttered:

"Your Excellency! If I venture to trouble your Excellency, it is simply from a feeling I may say of regret! . . . It was not intentional if you will graciously believe me."

The general made a lachrymose face, and waved his hand.

"Why, you are simply making fun of me, sir," he said as he closed the door behind him.

"Where's the making fun in it?" thought Tchervyakov, "there is nothing of the sort! He is a general, but he can't understand. If that is how it is I am not going to apologise to that fanfaron any more! The devil take him. I'll write a letter to him, but I won't go. By Jove, I won't."

So thought Tchervyakov as he walked home; he did not write a letter to the general, he pondered and pondered and could not make up that letter. He had to go next day to explain in person.

"I ventured to disturb your Excellency yesterday," he muttered, when the general lifted enquiring eyes upon him, "not to make fun as you were pleased to say. I was apologising for having spattered you in sneezing . . . And I did not dream of making fun of you. Should I dare to make fun of you, if we should take to making fun, then there would be no respect for persons, there would be . . ."

"Be off!" yelled the general, turning suddenly purple, and shaking all over.

"What?" asked Tchervyakov, in a whisper turning numb with horror.

"Be off!" repeated the general, stamping.

Something seemed to give way in Tchervyakov's stomach.

Seeing nothing and hearing nothing he reeled to the door, went out into the street, and went staggering along . . . Reaching home mechanically, without taking off his uniform, he lay down on the sofa and died.

8

The Looking Glass

New Year's Eve. Nellie, the daughter of a landowner and general, a young and pretty girl, dreaming day and night of being married, was sitting in her room, gazing with exhausted, half-closed eyes into the looking-glass. She was pale, tense, and as motionless as the looking-glass.

The non-existent but apparent vista of a long, narrow corridor with endless rows of candles, the reflection of her face, her hands, of the frame—all this was already clouded in mist and merged into a boundless grey sea. The sea was undulating, gleaming and now and then flaring crimson . . .

Looking at Nellie's motionless eyes and parted lips, one could hardly say whether she was asleep or awake, but nevertheless she was seeing. At first she saw only the smile and soft, charming expression of someone's eyes, then against the shifting grey background there gradually appeared the outlines of a head, a face, eyebrows, beard. It was he, the destined one, the object of long dreams and hopes. The destined one was for Nellie everything, the significance of life, personal happiness, career, fate. Outside him, as on the grey background of the looking-glass, all was dark, empty, meaningless. And so it was not strange that, seeing before her a handsome, gently smiling face, she was conscious of bliss, of an unutterably sweet dream that could not be expressed in speech or on paper. Then she heard his voice, saw herself living under the same roof with him, her life merged into his. Months and years flew by against the grey background. And Nellie saw her future distinctly in all its details.

Picture followed picture against the grey background. Now Nellie saw herself one winter night knocking at the door of Stepan Lukitch, the district doctor. The old dog hoarsely and lazily barked behind the gate. The doctor's windows were in darkness. All was silence.

"For God's sake, for God's sake!" whispered Nellie.

But at last the garden gate creaked and Nellie saw the doctor's cook.

"Is the doctor at home?"

"His honour's asleep," whispered the cook into her sleeve, as though afraid of waking her master.

"He's only just got home from his fever patients, and gave orders he was not to be waked."

But Nellie scarcely heard the cook. Thrusting her aside, she rushed headlong into the doctor's house. Running through some dark and stuffy rooms, upsetting two or three chairs, she at last reached the doctor's bedroom. Stepan Lukitch was lying on his bed, dressed, but without his coat, and with pouting lips was breathing into his open hand. A little night-light glimmered faintly beside him. Without uttering a word Nellie sat down and began to cry. She wept bitterly, shaking all over.

"My husband is ill!" she sobbed out. Stepan Lukitch was silent. He slowly sat up, propped his head on his hand, and looked at his visitor with fixed, sleepy eyes. "My husband is ill!" Nellie continued, restraining her sobs. "For mercy's sake come quickly. Make haste . . . Make haste!"

"Eh?" growled the doctor, blowing into his hand.

"Come! Come this very minute! Or . . . it's terrible to think! For mercy's sake!"

And pale, exhausted Nellie, gasping and swallowing her tears, began describing to the doctor her husband's illness, her unutterable terror. Her sufferings would have touched the heart of a stone, but the doctor looked at her, blew into his open hand, and—not a movement.

"I'll come to-morrow!" he muttered.

"That's impossible!" cried Nellie. "I know my husband has typhus! At once . . . this very minute you are needed!"

"I . . . er . . . have only just come in," muttered the doctor. "For the last three days I've been away, seeing typhus patients, and I'm exhausted and ill myself . . . I simply can't! Absolutely! I've caught it myself! There!"

And the doctor thrust before her eyes a clinical thermometer.

"My temperature is nearly forty . . . I absolutely can't. I can scarcely sit up. Excuse me. I'll lie down . . ."

The doctor lay down.

"But I implore you, doctor," Nellie moaned in despair. "I beseech you! Help me, for mercy's sake! Make a great effort and come! I will repay you, doctor!"

"Oh, dear! . . . Why, I have told you already. Ah!"

Nellie leapt up and walked nervously up and down the bedroom. She longed to explain to the doctor, to bring him to reason . . . She thought if only he knew how dear her husband was to her and how unhappy she was, he would forget his exhaustion and his illness. But how could she be eloquent enough?

"Go to the Zemstvo doctor," she heard Stepan Lukitch's voice.

"That's impossible! He lives more than twenty miles from here, and time is precious. And the horses can't stand it. It is thirty miles from us to you, and as much from here to the Zemstvo doctor. No, it's impossible! Come along, Stepan Lukitch. I ask of you an heroic deed. Come, perform that heroic deed! Have pity on us!"

"It's beyond everything . . . I'm in a fever. . . my head's in a whirl . . . and she won't understand! Leave me alone!"

"But you are in duty bound to come! You cannot refuse to come! It's egoism! A man is bound to sacrifice his life for his neighbour, and you . . . you refuse to come! I will summon you before the Court."

Nellie felt that she was uttering a false and undeserved insult, but for her husband's sake she was capable of forgetting logic, tact, sympathy for others . . . In reply to her threats, the doctor greedily gulped a glass of cold water. Nellie fell to entreating and imploring like the very lowest beggar . . . At last the doctor gave way. He slowly got up, puffing and panting, looking for his coat.

"Here it is!" cried Nellie, helping him. "Let me put it on to you. Come along! I will repay you . . . All my life I shall be grateful to you . . ."

But what agony! After putting on his coat the doctor lay down again. Nellie got him up and dragged him to the hall. Then there was an agonizing to-do over his goloshes, his overcoat . . . His cap was lost . . . But at last Nellie was in the carriage with the doctor. Now they had only to drive thirty miles and her husband would have a doctor's help. The earth was wrapped in darkness. One could not see one's hand before one's face . . . A cold winter wind was blowing. There were frozen lumps under their wheels. The coachman was continually stopping and wondering which road to take.

Nellie and the doctor sat silent all the way. It was fearfully jolting, but they felt neither the cold nor the jolts.

"Get on, get on!" Nellie implored the driver.

At five in the morning the exhausted horses drove into the yard. Nellie saw the familiar gates, the well with the crane, the long row of stables and barns. At last she was at home.

"Wait a moment, I will be back directly," she said to Stepan Lukitch, making him sit down on the sofa in the dining-room. "Sit still and wait a little, and I'll see how he is going on."

On her return from her husband, Nellie found the doctor lying down. He was lying on the sofa and muttering.

"Doctor, please! . . . doctor!"

"Eh? Ask Domna!" muttered Stepan Lukitch.

"What?"

"They said at the meeting . . . Vlassov said . . . Who? . . . what?"

And to her horror Nellie saw that the doctor was as delirious as her husband. What was to be done?

"I must go for the Zemstvo doctor," she decided.

Then again there followed darkness, a cutting cold wind, lumps of frozen earth. She was suffering in body and in soul, and delusive nature has no arts, no deceptions to compensate these sufferings . . .

Then she saw against the grey background how her husband every spring was in straits for money to pay the interest for the mortgage to the bank. He could not sleep, she could not sleep, and both racked their brains till their heads ached, thinking how to avoid being visited by the clerk of the Court.

She saw her children: the everlasting apprehension of colds, scarlet fever, diphtheria, bad marks at school, separation. Out of a brood of five or six one was sure to die.

The grey background was not untouched by death. That might well be. A husband and wife cannot die simultaneously. Whatever happened one must bury the other. And Nellie saw her husband dying. This terrible event presented itself to her in every detail. She saw the coffin, the candles, the deacon, and even the footmarks in the hall made by the undertaker.

"Why is it, what is it for?" she asked, looking blankly at her husband's face.

And all the previous life with her husband seemed to her a stupid prelude to this.

Something fell from Nellie's hand and knocked on the floor. She started, jumped up, and opened her eyes wide. One looking-glass she saw lying at her feet. The other was standing as before on the table.

She looked into the looking-glass and saw a pale, tear-stained face. There was no grey background now.

"I must have fallen asleep," she thought with a sigh of relief.

9

Oh! The Public

"Here goes, I've done with drinking! Nothing . . . n-o-thing shall tempt me to it. It's time to take myself in hand; I must buck up and work . . . You're glad to get your salary, so you must do your work honestly, heartily, conscientiously, regardless of sleep and comfort. Chuck taking it easy. You've got into the way of taking a salary for nothing, my boy—that's not the right thing . . . not the right thing at all . . ."

After administering to himself several such lectures Podtyagin, the head ticket collector, begins to feel an irresistible impulse to get to work. It is past one o'clock at night, but in spite of that he wakes the ticket collectors and with them goes up and down the railway carriages, inspecting the tickets.

"T-t-t-ickets . . . P-p-p-please!" he keeps shouting, briskly snapping the clippers.

Sleepy figures, shrouded in the twilight of the railway carriages, start, shake their heads, and produce their tickets.

"T-t-t-tickets, please!" Podtyagin addresses a second-class passenger, a lean, scraggy-looking man, wrapped up in a fur coat and a rug and surrounded with pillows. "Tickets, please!"

The scraggy-looking man makes no reply. He is buried in sleep. The head ticket-collector touches him on the shoulder and repeats impatiently: "T-t-tickets, p-p-please!"

The passenger starts, opens his eyes, and gazes in alarm at Podtyagin.

"What? . . . Who? . . . Eh?"

"You're asked in plain language: t-t-tickets, p-p-please! If you please!"

"My God!" moans the scraggy-looking man, pulling a woebegone face. "Good Heavens! I'm suffering from rheumatism . . . I haven't slept for three nights! I've just taken morphia on purpose to get to sleep, and you . . . with your tickets! It's merciless, it's inhuman! If you knew how hard it is for me to sleep you wouldn't disturb me for such nonsense . . . It's cruel, it's absurd! And what do you want with my ticket! It's positively stupid!"

Podtyagin considers whether to take offence or not—and decides to take offence.

"Don't shout here! This is not a tavern!"

"No, in a tavern people are more humane . . ." coughs the passenger. "Perhaps you'll let me go to sleep another time! It's extraordinary: I've travelled abroad, all over the place, and no one asked for my ticket there, but here you're at it again and again, as though the devil were after you . . ."

"Well, you'd better go abroad again since you like it so much."

"It's stupid, sir! Yes! As though it's not enough killing the passengers with fumes and stuffiness and draughts, they want to strangle us with red tape, too, damn it all! He must have the ticket! My goodness, what zeal! If it were of any use to the company—but half the passengers are travelling without a ticket!"

"Listen, sir!" cries Podtyagin, flaring up. "If you don't leave off shouting and disturbing the public, I shall be obliged to put you out at the next station and to draw up a report on the incident!"

"This is revolting!" exclaims "the public," growing indignant. "Persecuting an invalid! Listen, and have some consideration!"

"But the gentleman himself was abusive!" says Podtyagin, a little scared. "Very well . . . I won't take the ticket . . . as you like . . .

Only, of course, as you know very well, it's my duty to do so . . . If it were not my duty, then, of course . . . You can ask the station-master . . . ask anyone you like . . ."

Podtyagin shrugs his shoulders and walks away from the invalid. At first he feels aggrieved and somewhat injured, then, after passing through two or three carriages, he begins to feel a certain uneasiness not unlike the pricking of conscience in his ticket-collector's bosom.

"There certainly was no need to wake the invalid," he thinks, "though it was not my fault . . . They imagine I did it wantonly, idly. They don't know that I'm bound in duty . . . if they don't believe it, I can bring the station-master to them." A station. The train stops five minutes. Before the third bell, Podtyagin enters the same second-class carriage. Behind him stalks the station-master in a red cap.

"This gentleman here," Podtyagin begins, "declares that I have no right to ask for his ticket and . . . and is offended at it. I ask you, Mr. Station-master, to explain to him . . . Do I ask for tickets according to regulation or to please myself? Sir," Podtyagin addresses the scraggy-looking man, "sir! you can ask the station-master here if you don't believe me."

The invalid starts as though he had been stung, opens his eyes, and with a woebegone face sinks back in his seat.

"My God! I have taken another powder and only just dozed off when here he is again . . . again! I beseech you have some pity on me!"

"You can ask the station-master . . . whether I have the right to demand your ticket or not."

"This is insufferable! Take your ticket . . . take it! I'll pay for five extra if you'll only let me die in peace! Have you never been ill yourself? Heartless people!"

"This is simply persecution!" A gentleman in military uniform grows indignant. "I can see no other explanation of this persistence."

"Drop it . . ." says the station-master, frowning and pulling Podtyagin by the sleeve.

Podtyagin shrugs his shoulders and slowly walks after the station-master.

"There's no pleasing them!" he thinks, bewildered. "It was for his sake I brought the station-master, that he might understand and be pacified, and he . . . swears!"

Another station. The train stops ten minutes. Before the second bell, while Podtyagin is standing at the refreshment bar, drinking seltzer water, two gentlemen go up to him, one in the uniform of an engineer, and the other in a military overcoat.

"Look here, ticket-collector!" the engineer begins, addressing Podtyagin. "Your behaviour to that invalid passenger has revolted all who witnessed it. My name is Puzitsky; I am an engineer, and this gentleman is a colonel. If you do not apologize to the passenger, we shall make a complaint to the traffic manager, who is a friend of ours."

"Gentlemen! Why of course I . . . why of course you . . ." Podtyagin is panic-stricken.

"We don't want explanations. But we warn you, if you don't apologize, we shall see justice done to him."

Certainly I . . . I'll apologize, of course . . . To be sure . . ."

Half an hour later, Podtyagin having thought of an apologetic phrase which would satisfy the passenger without lowering his own dignity, walks into the carriage. "Sir," he addresses the invalid. "Listen, sir . . ."

The invalid starts and leaps up: "What?"

"I . . . what was it? . . . You mustn't be offended . . ."

"Och! Water . . ." gasps the invalid, clutching at his heart. "I'd just taken a third dose of morphia, dropped asleep, and . . . again! Good God! when will this torture cease!"

"I only . . . you must excuse . . ."

"Oh! . . . Put me out at the next station! I can't stand any more . . . I . . . I am dying . . ."

"This is mean, disgusting!" cry the "public," revolted. "Go away! You shall pay for such persecution. Get away!"

Podtyagin waves his hand in despair, sighs, and walks out of the carriage. He goes to the attendants' compartment, sits down at the table, exhausted, and complains:

"Oh, the public! There's no satisfying them! It's no use working and doing one's best! One's driven to drinking and cursing it all . . . If you do nothing—they're angry; if you begin doing your duty, they're angry too. There's nothing for it but drink!"

Podtyagin empties a bottle straight off and thinks no more of work, duty, and honesty!

10

The Lottery Ticket

Ivan Dmitritch, a middle-class man who lived with his family on an income of twelve hundred a year and was very well satisfied with his lot, sat down on the sofa after supper and began reading the newspaper.

"I forgot to look at the newspaper today," his wife said to him as she cleared the table.

"Look and see whether the list of drawings is there."

"Yes, it is," said Ivan Dmitritch; "but hasn't your ticket lapsed?"

"No; I took the interest on Tuesday."

"What is the number?"

"Series 9,499, number 26."

"All right . . . we will look . . . 9,499 and 26."

Ivan Dmitritch had no faith in lottery luck, and would not, as a rule, have consented to look at the lists of winning numbers, but now, as he had nothing else to do and as the newspaper was before his eyes, he passed his finger downwards along the column of numbers. And immediately, as though in mockery of his scepticism, no further than the second line from the top, his eye was caught by the figure 9,499! Unable to believe his eyes, he hurriedly dropped the paper on his knees without looking to see the number of the ticket, and, just as though some one had given him a douche of cold water, he felt an agreeable chill in the pit of the stomach; tingling and terrible and sweet!

"Masha, 9,499 is there!" he said in a hollow voice.

His wife looked at his astonished and panic-stricken face, and realized that he was not joking.

"9,499?" she asked, turning pale and dropping the folded tablecloth on the table.

"Yes, yes . . . it really is there!"

"And the number of the ticket?"

"Oh, yes! There's the number of the ticket too. But stay . . . wait! No, I say! Anyway, the number of our series is there! Anyway, you understand . . ."

Looking at his wife, Ivan Dmitritch gave a broad, senseless smile, like a baby when a bright object is shown it. His wife smiled too; it was as pleasant to her as to him that he only mentioned the series, and did not try to find out the number of the winning ticket. To torment and tantalize oneself with hopes of possible fortune is so sweet, so thrilling!

"It is our series," said Ivan Dmitritch, after a long silence. "So there is a probability that we have won. It's only a probability, but there it is!"

"Well, now look!"

"Wait a little. We have plenty of time to be disappointed. It's on the second line from the top, so the prize is seventy-five thousand. That's not money, but power, capital! And in a minute I shall look at the list, and there—26! Eh? I say, what if we really have won?"

The husband and wife began laughing and staring at one another in silence. The possibility of winning bewildered them; they could not have said, could not have dreamed, what they both needed that seventy-five thousand for, what they would buy, where they would go.

They thought only of the figures 9,499 and 75,000 and pictured them in their imagination, while somehow they could not think of the happiness itself which was so possible.

Ivan Dmitritch, holding the paper in his hand, walked several times from corner to corner, and only when he had recovered from the first impression began dreaming a little.

"And if we have won," he said—"why, it will be a new life, it will be a transformation! The ticket is yours, but if it were mine I should, first of all, of course, spend twenty-five thousand on real property in the shape of an estate; ten thousand on immediate expenses, new furnishing . . . travelling . . . paying debts, and so on . . . The other forty thousand I would put in the bank and get interest on it."

"Yes, an estate, that would be nice," said his wife, sitting down and dropping her hands in her lap.

"Somewhere in the Tula or Oryol provinces . . . In the first place we shouldn't need a summer villa, and besides, it would always bring in an income."

And pictures came crowding on his imagination, each more gracious and poetical than the last. And in all these pictures he saw himself well-fed, serene, healthy, felt warm, even hot!

Here, after eating a summer soup, cold as ice, he lay on his back on the burning sand close to a stream or in the garden under a lime-tree . . . It is hot . . . His little boy and girl are crawling about near him, digging in the sand or catching ladybirds in the grass. He dozes sweetly, thinking of nothing, and feeling all over that he need not go to the office today, tomorrow, or the day after. Or, tired of lying still, he goes to the hayfield, or to the forest for mushrooms, or watches the peasants catching fish with a net. When the sun sets he takes a towel and soap and saunters to the bathing-shed, where he undresses at his leisure, slowly rubs his bare chest with his hands, and goes into the water. And in the water, near the opaque soapy circles, little fish flit to and fro and green water-weeds nod their heads. After bathing there is tea with cream and milk rolls . . . In the evening a walk or vint with the neighbours.

"Yes, it would be nice to buy an estate," said his wife, also dreaming, and from her face it was evident that she was enchanted by her thoughts.

Ivan Dmitritch pictured to himself autumn with its rains, its cold evenings, and its St. Martin's summer. At that season he would have to take longer walks about the garden and beside the river, so as to get thoroughly chilled, and then drink a big glass of vodka and eat a salted mushroom or a soused cucumber, and then—drink another . . . The children would come running from the kitchen-garden, bringing a carrot and a radish smelling of fresh earth . . . And then, he would lie stretched full length on the sofa, and in leisurely fashion turn over the pages of some illustrated magazine, or, covering his face with it and unbuttoning his waistcoat, give himself up to slumber.

The St. Martin's summer is followed by cloudy, gloomy weather. It rains day and night, the bare trees weep, the wind is damp and cold. The dogs, the horses, the fowls—all are wet, depressed, downcast. There is nowhere to walk; one can't go out for days together; one has to pace up and down the room, looking despondently at the grey window. It is dreary!

Ivan Dmitritch stopped and looked at his wife.

"I should go abroad, you know, Masha," he said.

And he began thinking how nice it would be in late autumn to go abroad somewhere to the South of France . . . to Italy . . . to India!

"I should certainly go abroad too," his wife said. "But look at the number of the ticket!"

"Wait, wait! . . ."

He walked about the room and went on thinking. It occurred to him: what if his wife really did go abroad? It is pleasant to travel alone, or in the society of light, careless women who live in the present, and not such as think and talk all the journey about nothing but their children, sigh, and tremble with dismay over every farthing. Ivan Dmitritch imagined his wife in the train with a multitude of parcels, baskets, and bags; she would be sighing over something, complaining that the train made her head ache, that she had spent so much money . . . At the stations he would continually be having to run for boiling water, bread and butter . . . She wouldn't have dinner because of its being too dear . . .

"She would begrudge me every farthing," he thought, with a glance at his wife. "The lottery ticket is hers, not mine! Besides,

46

what is the use of her going abroad? What does she want there? She would shut herself up in the hotel, and not let me out of her sight . . . I know!"

And for the first time in his life his mind dwelt on the fact that his wife had grown elderly and plain, and that she was saturated through and through with the smell of cooking, while he was still young, fresh, and healthy, and might well have got married again.

"Of course, all that is silly nonsense," he thought; "but . . . why should she go abroad? What would she make of it? And yet she would go, of course . . . I can fancy . . . In reality it is all one to her, whether it is Naples or Klin. She would only be in my way. I should be dependent upon her. I can fancy how, like a regular woman, she will lock the money up as soon as she gets it . . . She will hide it from me . . . She will look after her relations and grudge me every farthing."

Ivan Dmitritch thought of her relations. All those wretched brothers and sisters and aunts and uncles would come crawling about as soon as they heard of the winning ticket, would begin whining like beggars, and fawning upon them with oily, hypocritical smiles.

Wretched, detestable people! If they were given anything, they would ask for more; while if they were refused, they would swear at them, slander them, and wish them every kind of misfortune.

Ivan Dmitritch remembered his own relations, and their faces, at which he had looked impartially in the past, struck him now as repulsive and hateful.

"They are such reptiles!" he thought.

And his wife's face, too, struck him as repulsive and hateful. Anger surged up in his heart against her, and he thought malignantly:

"She knows nothing about money, and so she is stingy. If she won it she would give me a hundred roubles, and put the rest away under lock and key."

And he looked at his wife, not with a smile now, but with hatred. She glanced at him too, and also with hatred and anger. She had her own daydreams, her own plans, her own reflections; she

47

understood perfectly well what her husband's dreams were. She knew who would be the first to try and grab her winnings.

"It's very nice making daydreams at other people's expense!" is what her eyes expressed.

"No, don't you dare!"

Her husband understood her look; hatred began stirring again in his breast, and in order to annoy his wife he glanced quickly, to spite her at the fourth page on the newspaper and read out triumphantly:

"Series 9,499, number 46! Not 26!"

Hatred and hope both disappeared at once, and it began immediately to seem to Ivan Dmitritch and his wife that their rooms were dark and small and low-pitched, that the supper they had been eating was not doing them good, but lying heavy on their stomachs, that the evenings were long and wearisome . . .

"What the devil's the meaning of it?" said Ivan Dmitritch, beginning to be ill-humoured.

"Wherever one steps there are bits of paper under one's feet, crumbs, husks. The rooms are never swept! One is simply forced to go out. Damnation take my soul entirely! I shall go and hang myself on the first aspen-tree!"

11

A Chameleon

The police superintendent Otchumyelov is walking across the market square wearing a new overcoat and carrying a parcel under his arm. A red-haired policeman strides after him with a sieve full of confiscated gooseberries in his hands. There is silence all around. Not a soul in the square . . . The open doors of the shops and taverns look out upon God's world disconsolately, like hungry mouths; there is not even a beggar near them.

"So you bite, you damned brute?" Otchumyelov hears suddenly. "Lads, don't let him go! Biting is prohibited nowadays! Hold him! ah . . . ah!"

There is the sound of a dog yelping. Otchumyelov looks in the direction of the sound and sees a dog, hopping on three legs and looking about her, run out of Pitchugin's timber-yard. A man in a starched cotton shirt, with his waistcoat unbuttoned, is chasing her. He runs after her, and throwing his body forward falls down and seizes the dog by her hind legs. Once more there is a yelping and a shout of "Don't let go!" Sleepy countenances are protruded from the shops, and soon a crowd, which seems to have sprung out of the earth, is gathered round the timber-yard.

"It looks like a row, your honour . . ." says the policeman.

Otchumyelov makes a half turn to the left and strides towards the crowd.

He sees the aforementioned man in the unbuttoned waistcoat standing close by the gate of the timber-yard, holding his right hand in the air and displaying a bleeding finger to the crowd. On his half-drunken face there is plainly written: "I'll pay you out, you rogue!" and indeed the very finger has the look of a flag of victory. In this man Otchumyelov recognises Hryukin, the goldsmith. The culprit who has caused the sensation, a white borzoy puppy with a sharp muzzle and a yellow patch on her back, is sitting on the ground with her fore-paws outstretched in the middle of the crowd, trembling all over. There is an expression of misery and terror in her tearful eyes.

"What's it all about?" Otchumyelov inquires, pushing his way through the crowd. "What are you here for? Why are you waving your finger . . .? Who was it shouted?"

"I was walking along here, not interfering with anyone, your honour," Hryukin begins, coughing into his fist. "I was talking about firewood to Mitry Mitritch, when this low brute for no rhyme or reason bit my finger . . . You must excuse me, I am a working man . . . Mine is fine work. I must have damages, for I shan't be able to use this finger for a week, may be . . . It's not even the law, your honour, that one should put up with it from a beast . . . If everyone is going to be bitten, life won't be worth living . . ."

"H'm. Very good," says Otchumyelov sternly, coughing and raising his eyebrows. "Very good. Whose dog is it? I won't let this pass! I'll teach them to let their dogs run all over the place! It's time these gentry were looked after, if they won't obey the regulations! When he's fined, the blackguard, I'll teach him what it means to keep dogs and such stray cattle! I'll give him a lesson! . . . Yeldyrin," cries the superintendent, addressing the policeman, "find out whose dog this is and draw up a report! And the dog must be strangled. Without delay! It's sure to be mad . . . Whose dog is it, I ask?"

"I fancy it's General Zhigalov's," says someone in the crowd.

"General Zhigalov's, h'm . . . Help me off with my coat,

Yeldyrin . . . it's frightfully hot! It must be a sign of rain . . . There's one thing I can't make out, how it came to bite you?" Otchumyelov turns to Hryukin. "Surely it couldn't reach your finger. It's a little dog, and you are a great hulking fellow! You must have scratched your finger with a nail, and then the idea struck you to get damages for it. We all know . . . your sort! I know you devils!"

"He put a cigarette in her face, your honour, for a joke, and she had the sense to snap at him . . . He is a nonsensical fellow, your honour!"

"That's a lie, Squinteye! You didn't see, so why tell lies about it? His honour is a wise gentleman, and will see who is telling lies and who is telling the truth, as in God's sight . . . And if I am lying let the court decide. It's written in the law . . . We are all equal nowadays. My own brother is in the gendarmes . . . let me tell you . . ."

"Don't argue!"

"No, that's not the General's dog," says the policeman, with profound conviction, "the General hasn't got one like that. His are mostly setters."

"Do you know that for a fact?"

"Yes, your honour."

"I know it, too. The General has valuable dogs, thoroughbred, and this is goodness knows what! No coat, no shape . . . A low creature. And to keep a dog like that! . . . where's the sense of it. If a dog like that were to turn up in Petersburg or Moscow, do you know what would happen? They would not worry about the law, they would strangle it in a twinkling! You've been injured, Hryukin, and we can't let the matter drop . . . We must give them a lesson! It is high time . . . !"

"Yet maybe it is the General's," says the policeman, thinking aloud. "It's not written on its face . . . I saw one like it the other day in his yard."

"It is the General's, that's certain!" says a voice in the crowd.

"H'm, help me on with my overcoat, Yeldyrin, my lad . . . the wind's getting up . . . I am cold . . . You take it to the General's, and inquire there. Say I found it and sent it. And tell them not to let it out into the street . . . It may be a valuable dog, and if every

51

swine goes sticking a cigar in its mouth, it will soon be ruined. A dog is a delicate animal . . . And you put your hand down, you blockhead. It's no use your displaying your fool of a finger. It's your own fault . . ."

"Here comes the General's cook, ask him . . . Hi, Prohor! Come here, my dear man! Look at this dog . . . Is it one of yours?"

"What an idea! We have never had one like that!"

"There's no need to waste time asking," says Otchumyelov. "It's a stray dog! There's no need to waste time talking about it . . . Since he says it's a stray dog, a stray dog it is . . . It must be destroyed, that's all about it."

"It is not our dog," Prohor goes on. "It belongs to the General's brother, who arrived the other day. Our master does not care for hounds. But his honour is fond of them . . ."

"You don't say his Excellency's brother is here? Vladimir Ivanitch?" inquires Otchumyelov, and his whole face beams with an ecstatic smile. "Well, I never! And I didn't know! Has he come on a visit?"

"Yes."

"Well, I never . . . He couldn't stay away from his brother . . . And there I didn't know! So this is his honour's dog? Delighted to hear it . . . Take it. It's not a bad pup . . . A lively creature . . . Snapped at this fellow's finger! Ha-ha-ha . . . Come, why are you shivering? Rrr . . . Rrrr . . . The rogue's angry . . . a nice little pup."

Prohor calls the dog, and walks away from the timber-yard with her. The crowd laughs at Hryukin.

"I'll make you smart yet!" Otchumyelov threatens him, and wrapping himself in his greatcoat, goes on his way across the square.

Arthur Machen

(1863-1947)

12

The Bowmen

It was during the Retreat of the Eighty Thousand, and the authority of the Censorship is sufficient excuse for not being more explicit. But it was on the most awful day of that awful time, on the day when ruin and disaster came so near that their shadow fell over London far away; and, without any certain news, the hearts of men failed within them and grew faint; as if the agony of the army in the battlefield had entered into their souls.

On this dreadful day, then, when three hundred thousand men in arms with all their artillery swelled like a flood against the little English company, there was one point above all other points in our battle line that was for a time in awful danger, not merely of defeat, but of utter annihilation. With the permission of the Censorship and of the military expert, this corner may, perhaps, be described as a salient, and if this angle were crushed and broken, then the English force as a whole would be shattered, the Allied left would be turned, and Sedan would inevitably follow.

All the morning the German guns had thundered and shrieked against this corner, and against the thousand or so of men who held it. The men joked at the shells, and found funny names for them, and had bets about them, and greeted them with scraps of music-hall songs. But the shells came on and burst, and tore good Englishmen limb from limb, and tore brother from brother, and as the heat of the day increased so did the fury of that terrific cannonade. There was no help, it seemed. The English artillery was good, but there was not nearly enough of it; it was being steadily battered into scrap iron.

There comes a moment in a storm at sea when people say to one another, "It is at its worst; it can blow no harder," and then there is a blast ten times more fierce than any before it. So it was in these British trenches.

There were no stouter hearts in the whole world than the hearts of these men; but even they were appalled as this seven-times-heated hell of the German cannonade fell upon them and overwhelmed them and destroyed them. And at this very moment they saw from their trenches that a tremendous host was moving against their lines. Five hundred of the thousand remained, and as far as they could see the German infantry was pressing on against them, column upon column, a gray world of men, ten thousand of them, as it appeared afterwards.

There was no hope at all. They shook hands, some of them. One man improvised a new version of the battle-song, "Good-by, good-by to Tipperary," ending with "And we shan't get there." And they all went on firing steadily. The officer pointed out that such an opportunity for high-class fancy shooting might never occur again; the Tipperary humorist asked, "What price Sidney Street?" And the few machine guns did their best. But everybody knew it was of no use. The dead gray bodies lay in companies and battalions, as others came on and on and on, and they swarmed and stirred, and advanced from beyond and beyond.

"World without end. Amen," said one of the British soldiers with some irrelevance as he took aim and fired. And then he remembered—he says he cannot think why or wherefore—a queer vegetarian restaurant in London where he had once or twice eaten eccentric dishes of cutlets made of lentils and nuts that pretended to be steak. On all the plates in this restaurant there was printed a figure of St. George in blue, with the motto, *Adsit Anglis Sanctus Georgius*—'May St. George be a present

help to the English.' This soldier happened to know Latin and
other useless things, and now, as he fired at his man in the gray
advancing mass—three hundred yards away—he uttered the
pious vegetarian motto. He went on firing to the end, and at last
Bill on his right had to clout him cheerfully over the head to make
him stop, pointing out as he did so that the King's ammunition
cost money and was not lightly to be wasted in drilling funny
patterns into dead Germans.

For as the Latin scholar uttered his invocation he felt something
between a shudder and an electric shock pass through his body.
The roar of the battle died down in his ears to a gentle murmur;
instead of it, he says, he heard a great voice and a shout louder than
a thunder-peal crying, "Array, array, array!"

His heart grew hot as a burning coal, it grew cold as ice within
him, as it seemed to him that a tumult of voices answered to his
summons. He heard, or seemed to hear, thousands shouting: "St.
George! St. George!"

"Ha! Messire, ha! sweet Saint, grant us good deliverance!"

"St. George for merry England!"

"Harow! Harow! Monseigneur St. George, succor us!"

"Ha! St. George! Ha! St. George! a long bow and a strong
bow."

"Heaven's Knight, aid us!"

And as the soldier heard these voices he saw before him,
beyond the trench, a long line of shapes, with a shining about
them. They were like men who drew the bow, and with another
shout, their cloud of arrows flew singing and tingling through the
air towards the German hosts.

The other men in the trench were firing all the while. They had
no hope; but they aimed just as if they had been shooting at Bisley.

Suddenly one of them lifted up his voice in the plainest English.

"Gawd help us!" he bellowed to the man next to him, "but
we're blooming marvels! Look at those gray . . . gentlemen, look
at them! D'ye see them? They're not going down in dozens nor in
'undreds; it's thousands, it is. Look! look! there's a regiment gone
while I'm talking to ye."

57

"Shut it!" the other soldier bellowed, taking aim, "what are ye gassing about?"

But he gulped with astonishment even as he spoke, for, indeed, the gray men were falling by the thousands. The English could hear the guttural scream of the German officers, the crackle of their revolvers as they shot the reluctant; and still line after line crashed to the earth.

All the while the Latin-bred soldier heard the cry:

"Harow! Harow! Monseigneur, dear Saint, quick to our aid! St. George help us!"

"High Chevalier, defend us!"

The singing arrows fled so swift and thick that they darkened the air, the heathen horde melted from before them.

"More machine guns!" Bill yelled to Tom.

"Don't hear them," Tom yelled back.

"But, thank God, anyway; they've got it in the neck."

In fact, there were ten thousand dead German soldiers left before that salient of the English army, and consequently there was no Sedan. In Germany, a country ruled by scientific principles, the Great General Staff decided that the contemptible English must have employed shells containing an unknown gas of a poisonous nature, as no wounds were discernible on the bodies of the dead German soldiers. But the man who knew what nuts tasted like when they called themselves steak knew also that St. George had brought his Agincourt Bowmen to help the English.

Arthur Quiller-Couch

(1863-1944)

13

The Omnibus

It was not so much a day as a burning, fiery furnace. The roar of London's traffic reverberated under a sky of coppery blue; the pavements threw out waves of heat, thickened with the reek of restaurants and perfumery shops; and dust became cinders, and the wearing of flesh a weariness. Streams of sweat ran from the bellies of 'bus-horses when they halted. Men went up and down with unbuttoned waistcoats, turned into drinking-bars, and were no sooner inside than they longed to be out again, and baking in an ampler oven. Other men, who had given up drinking because of the expense, hung about the fountains in Trafalgar Square and listened to the splash of running water. It was the time when London is supposed to be empty; and when those who remain in town feel there is not room for a soul more.

We were eleven inside the omnibus when it pulled up at Charing Cross, so that legally there was room for just one more. I had travelled enough in omnibuses to know my fellow-passengers by heart—a governess with some sheets of music in her satchel; a minor actress going to rehearsal; a woman carrying her incurable complaint for the hundredth time to the hospital; three middle-aged city clerks; a couple of reporters with weak eyes and low collars; an old loose-cheeked woman exhaling patchouli; a bald-headed man with hairy hands, a violent breast-pin, and the indescribable air of a matrimonial agent. Not a word passed. We were all failures in life, and could not trouble to dissemble it, in that heat. Moreover, we were used to each other, as types if not as persons, and had lost curiosity. So we sat listless, dispirited, drawing difficult breath and staring vacuously. The hope we shared in common—that nobody would claim the vacant seat—was too obvious to be discussed.

But at Charing Cross the twelfth passenger got in—a boy with a stick, and a bundle in a blue handkerchief. He was about thirteen; bound for the docks, we could tell at a glance, to sail on his first voyage; and, by the way he looked about, we could tell as easily that in stepping outside Charing Cross Station he had set foot on London stones for the first time. When we pulled up, he was standing on the opposite pavement with dazed eyes like a hare's, wondering at the new world—the hansoms, the yelling news-boys, the flower-women, the crowd pushing him this way and that, the ugly shop-fronts, the hurry and stink and din of it all. Then, hailing our 'bus, he started to run across—faltered—almost dropped his bundle—was snatched by our conductor out of the path of a running hansom, and hauled on board. His eyelids were pink and swollen; but he was not crying, though he wanted to. Instead, he took a great gulp, as he pushed between our knees to his seat, and tried to look brave as a lion.

The passengers turned an incurious, half-resentful stare upon him, and then repented. I think that more than one of us wanted to speak, but dared not.

It was not so much the little chap's look. But to the knot of his sea-kit there was tied a bunch of cottage-flowers—sweet williams, boy's love, love-lies-bleeding, a few common striped carnations, and a rose or two—and the sight and smell of them in that frowsy 'bus were like tears on thirsty eyelids. We had ceased to pity what we were, but the heart is far withered that cannot pity what it has been; and it made us shudder to look on the young face set towards the road along which we had travelled so far. Only the minor actress dropped a tear; but she was used to expressing emotion, and half-way down the Strand the 'bus stopped and she left us.

The woman with an incurable complaint touched me on the knee.

"Speak to him," she whispered.

But the whisper did not reach, for I was two hundred miles away, and occupied in starting off to school for the first time. I had two shillings in my pocket; and at the first town where the coach baited I was to exchange these for a coco-nut and a clasp-knife. Also, I was to break the knife in opening the nut, and the nut, when opened, would be sour. A sense of coming evil, therefore, possessed me.

"Why don't you speak to him?"

The boy glanced up, not catching her words, but suspicious: then frowned and looked defiant.

"Ah," she went on in the same whisper, "it's only the young that I pity. Sometimes, sir—for my illness keeps me much awake—I lie at night in my lodgings and listen, and the whole of London seems filled with the sound of children's feet running. Even by day I can hear them, at the back of the uproar—"

The matrimonial agent grunted and rose, as we halted at the top of Essex Street. I saw him slip a couple of half-crowns into the conductor's hand: and he whispered something, jerking his head back towards the interior of the 'bus. The boy was brushing his eyes, under pretence of putting his cap forward; and by the time he stole a look around to see if anyone had observed, we had started again. I pretended to stare out of the window, but marked the wet smear on his hand as he laid it on his lap.

In less than a minute it was my turn to alight. Unlike the matrimonial agent, I had not two half-crowns to spare; but, catching the sick woman's eye, forced up courage to nod and say—

"Good luck, my boy."

"Good day, sir."

A moment after I was in the hot crowd, whose roar rolled east and west for miles. And at the back of it, as the woman had said, in street and side-lane and blind-alley, I heard the footfall of a multitude more terrible than an army with banners, the ceaseless pelting feet of children—of Whittingtons turning and turning again.

Bjørnstjerne Bjørnson
(1832-1910)

14

The Father

The man whose story is here to be told was the wealthiest and most influential person in his parish; his name was Thord Overaas. He appeared in the priest's study one day, tall and earnest. "I have gotten a son," said he, "and I wish to present him for baptism."

"What shall his name be?"

"Finn, —after my father."

"And the sponsors?"

They were mentioned, and proved to be the best men and women of Thord's relations in the parish.

"Is there anything else?" inquired the priest, and looked up.

The peasant hesitated a little.

"I should like very much to have him baptized by himself," said he, finally.

"That is to say on a week-day?"

"Next Saturday, at twelve o'clock noon."

"Is there anything else?" inquired the priest.

"There is nothing else;" and the peasant twirled his cap, as though he were about to go.

Then the priest rose. "There is yet this, however," said he, and walking toward Thord, he took him by the hand and looked gravely into his eyes: "God grant that the child may become a blessing to you!"

One day sixteen years later, Thord stood once more in the priest's study.

"Really, you carry your age astonishingly well, Thord," said the priest; for he saw no change whatever in the man.

"That is because I have no troubles," replied Thord.

To this the priest said nothing, but after a while he asked: "What is your pleasure this evening?"

"I have come this evening about that son of mine who is to be confirmed to-morrow."

"He is a bright boy."

"I did not wish to pay the priest until I heard what number the boy would have when he takes his place in church to-morrow."

"He will stand number one."

"So I have heard; and here are ten dollars for the priest."

"Is there anything else I can do for you?" inquired the priest, fixing his eyes on Thord.

"There is nothing else."

Thord went out.

Eight years more rolled by, and then one day a noise was heard outside of the priest's study, for many men were approaching, and at their head was Thord, who entered first.

The priest looked up and recognized him.

"You come well attended this evening, Thord."

"I am here to request that the banns may be published for my son; he is about to marry Karen Storliden, daughter of Gudmund, who stands here beside me."

"Why, that is the richest girl in the parish."

"So they say," replied the peasant, stroking back his hair with one hand.

The priest sat a while as if in deep thought, then entered the names in his book, without making any comments, and the men wrote their signatures underneath. Thord laid three dollars on the table.

"One is all I am to have," said the priest.

"I know that very well; but he is my only child, I want to do it handsomely."

The priest took the money.

"This is now the third time, Thord, that you have come here on your son's account."

"But now I am through with him," said Thord, and folding up his pocket-book he said farewell and walked away.

The men slowly followed him.

A fortnight later, the father and son were rowing across the lake, one calm, still day, to Storliden to make arrangements for the wedding.

"This thwart is not secure," said the son, and stood up to straighten the seat on which he was sitting.

At the same moment the board he was standing on slipped from under him; he threw out his arms, uttered a shriek, and fell overboard.

"Take hold of the oar!" shouted the father, springing to his feet and holding out the oar.

But when the son had made a couple of efforts he grew stiff.

"Wait a moment!" cried the father, and began to row toward his son.

Then the son rolled over on his back, gave his father one long look, and sank.

Thord could scarcely believe it; he held the boat still, and stared at the spot where his son had gone down, as though he must surely come to the surface again. There rose some bubbles, then some more, and finally one large one that burst; and the lake lay there as smooth and bright as a mirror again.

For three days and three nights people saw the father rowing round and round the spot, without taking either food or sleep; he was dragging the lake for the body of his son. And toward morning of the third day he found it, and carried it in his arms up over the hills to his gard.

It might have been about a year from that day, when the priest, late one autumn evening, heard some one in the passage outside of the door, carefully trying to find the latch. The priest opened the door, and in walked a tall, thin man, with bowed form and white hair. The priest looked long at him before he recognized him. It was Thord.

"Are you out walking so late?" said the priest, and stood still in front of him.

"Ah, yes! it is late," said Thord, and took a seat.

The priest sat down also, as though waiting. A long, long silence followed. At last Thord said:

"I have something with me that I should like to give to the poor; I want it to be invested as a legacy in my son's name."

He rose, laid some money on the table, and sat down again. The priest counted it.

"It is a great deal of money," said he.

"It is half the price of my gard. I sold it today."

The priest sat long in silence. At last he asked, but gently:

"What do you propose to do now, Thord?"

"Something better."

They sat there for a while, Thord with downcast eyes, the priest with his eyes fixed on Thord. Presently the priest said, slowly and softly:

"I think your son has at last brought you a true blessing."

"Yes, I think so myself," said Thord, looking up, while two big tears coursed slowly down his cheeks.

Charles Dickens

(1812-1870)

15

A Child's Dream of a Star

There was once a child, and he strolled about a good deal, and thought of a number of things. He had a sister, who was a child, too, and his constant companion. These two used to wonder all day long. They wondered at the beauty of the flowers; they wondered at the height and blueness of the sky; they wondered at the depth of the bright water; they wondered at the goodness and the power of God who made the lovely world.

They used to say to one another sometimes, Supposing all the children upon earth were to die, would the flowers, and the water, and the sky be sorry? They believed they would be sorry. For, said they, the buds are the children of the flowers, and the little playful streams that gambol down the hillsides are the children of the water; and the smallest bright specks playing at hide-and-seek in the sky all night, must surely be the children of the stars; and they would all be grieved to see their playmates, the children of men, no more.

There was one clear shining star that used to come out in the sky before the rest, near the church spire, above the graves. It was larger and more beautiful, they thought, than all others, and every night they watched for it, standing hand in hand at the window. Whoever saw it first, cried out, "I see the star!" And often they cried out both together, knowing so well when it would rise, and where. So they grew to be such friends with it, that before lying down in their beds, they always looked out once again, to bid it good night; and when they were turning around to sleep, they used to say, "God bless the star!"

But while she was very young, oh, very, very young, the sister drooped, and came to be so weak that she could no longer stand in the window at night; and then the child looked sadly out by himself, and when he saw the star, turned round and said to the patient, pale face on the bed, "I see the star!" and then a smile would come upon the face, and a little weak voice used to say, "God bless my brother and the star!"

And so the time came, all too soon! when the child looked out alone, and when there was no face on the bed; and when there was a little grave among the graves, not there before; and when the star made long rays down toward him, as he saw it through his tears.

Now, these rays were so bright, and they seemed to make such a shining way from earth to heaven, that when the child went to his solitary bed, he dreamed about the star; and dreamed that, lying where he was, he saw a train of people taken up that sparkling road by angels. And the star, opening, showed him a great world of light, where many more such angels waited to receive them.

All these angels who were waiting turned their beaming eyes upon the people who were carried up into the star; and some came out from the long rows in which they stood, and fell upon the people's necks, and kissed them tenderly, and went away with them down avenues of light, and were so happy in their company, that lying in his bed he wept for joy.

But there were many angels who did not go with them, and among them one he knew. The patient face that once had lain upon the bed was glorified and radiant, but his heart found out his sister among all the host.

His sister's angel lingered near the entrance of the star, and said to the leader among those who had brought the people thither—

"Is my brother come?"

And he said, "No."

She was turning hopefully away, when the child stretched out his arms, and cried, "O sister, I am here! Take me!" And then she turned her beaming eyes upon him and it was night; and the star was shining into the room, making long rays down toward him as he saw it through his tears.

From that hour forth the child looked out upon the star as on the home he was to go to, when his time should come; and he thought that he did not belong to the earth alone, but to the star, too, because of his sister's angel gone before.

There was a baby born to be a brother to the child; and while he was so little that he never yet had spoken word, he stretched his tiny form out on his bed and died.

Again the child dreamed of the opened star, and of the company of angels, and the train of people, and the rows of angels with their beaming eyes all turned upon those people's faces.

Said his sister's angel to the leader:—

"Is my brother come?"

And he said, "Not that one, but another."

As the child beheld his brother's angel in her arms, he cried: "O sister, I am here! Take me!" And she turned and smiled upon him, and the star was shining.

He grew to be a young man, and was busy at his books, when an old servant came to him and said:—

"Thy mother is no more. I bring her blessing on her darling son!"

Again at night he saw the star, and all that former company. Said his sister's angel to the leader:—

"Is my brother come?"

And he said, "Thy mother!"

A mighty cry of joy went forth through all the star, because the mother was reunited to her two children. And he stretched out his arms and cried: "O mother, sister, and brother, I am here! Take me!" And they answered him, "Not yet." And the star was shining.

He grew to be a man whose hair was turning gray, and he was sitting in his chair by the fireside, heavy with grief, and with his face bedewed with tears, when the star opened once again.

Said his sister's angel to the leader, "Is my brother come?"

And he said, "Nay, but his maiden daughter."

And the man who had been the child saw his daughter, newly lost to him, a celestial creature among those three, and he said, "My daughter's head is on my sister's bosom, and her arm is round my mother's neck, and at her feet there is the baby of old time, and I can bear the parting from her, God be praised!"

And the star was shining.

Thus the child came to be an old man, and his once smooth face was wrinkled, and his steps were slow and feeble, and his back was bent. And one night as he lay upon his bed, his children standing round, he cried, as he had cried so long ago:—

"I see the star!"

They whispered to one another, "He is dying."

And he said: "I am. My age is falling from me like a garment, and I move toward the star as a child. And, O my Father, now I thank thee that it has so often opened to receive those dear ones who await me!"

And the star was shining; and it shines upon his grave.

16

The Noble Savage

To come to the point at once, I beg to say that I have not the least belief in the Noble Savage. I consider him a prodigious nuisance, and an enormous superstition. His calling rum fire-water, and me a pale face, wholly fail to reconcile me to him. I don't care what he calls me. I call him a savage, and I call a savage a something highly desirable to be civilised off the face of the earth. I think a mere gent (which I take to be the lowest form of civilisation) better than a howling, whistling, clucking, stamping, jumping, tearing savage. It is all one to me, whether he sticks a fish-bone through his visage, or bits of trees through the lobes of his ears, or bird's feathers in his head; whether he flattens his hair between two boards, or spreads his nose over the breadth of his face, or drags his lower lip down by great weights, or blackens his teeth, or knocks them out, or paints one cheek red and the other blue, or tattoos himself, or oils himself, or rubs his body with fat, or crimps it with knives. Yielding to whichsoever of these agreeable eccentricities, he is a savage— cruel, false, thievish, murderous; addicted more or less to grease, entrails, and beastly customs; a wild animal with the questionable gift of boasting; a conceited, tiresome, bloodthirsty, monotonous humbug.

Yet it is extraordinary to observe how some people will talk about him, as they talk about the good old times; how they will regret his disappearance, in the course of this world's development, from such and such lands where his absence is a blessed relief and an indispensable preparation for the sowing of the very first seeds of any influence that can exalt humanity; how, even with the evidence of himself before them, they will either be determined to believe, or will suffer themselves to be persuaded into believing, that he is something which their five senses tell them he is not.

There was Mr. Catlin, some few years ago, with his Ojibbeway Indians. Mr. Catlin was an energetic, earnest man, who had lived among more tribes of Indians than I need reckon up here, and who had written a picturesque and glowing book about them. With his party of Indians squatting and spitting on the table before him, or dancing their miserable jigs after their own dreary manner, he called, in all good faith, upon his civilised audience to take notice of their symmetry and grace, their perfect limbs, and the exquisite expression of their pantomime; and his civilised audience, in all good faith, complied and admired. Whereas, as mere animals, they were wretched creatures, very low in the scale and very poorly formed; and as men and women possessing any power of truthful dramatic expression by means of action, they were no better than the chorus at an Italian Opera in England—and would have been worse if such a thing were possible.

Mine are no new views of the noble savage. The greatest writers on natural history found him out long ago. BUFFON knew what he was, and showed why he is the sulky tyrant that he is to his women, and how it happens (Heaven be praised!) that his race is spare in numbers. For evidence of the quality of his moral nature, pass himself for a moment and refer to his 'faithful dog'. Has he ever improved a dog, or attached a dog, since his nobility first ran wild in woods, and was brought down (at a very long shot) by POPE? Or does the animal that is the friend of man, always degenerate in his low society?

It is not the miserable nature of the noble savage that is the new thing; it is the whimpering over him with maudlin admiration, and the affecting to regret him, and the drawing of any comparison of advantage between the blemishes of civilisation and the tenor of his swinish life. There may have been a change now and then in those diseased absurdities, but there is none in him.

Think of the Bushmen. Think of the two men and the two women who have been exhibited about England for some years. Are the majority of persons—who remember the horrid little leader of that party in his festering bundle of hides, with his filth and his antipathy to water, and his straddled legs, and his odious eyes shaded by his brutal hand, and his cry of 'Qu-u-u-u-aaa!' (Bosjesman for something desperately insulting I have no doubt)—conscious of an affectionate yearning towards that noble savage, or is it idiosyncratic in me to abhor, detest, abominate, and abjure him? I have no reserve on this subject, and will frankly state that, setting aside that stage of the entertainment when he counterfeited the death of some creature he had shot, by laying his head on his hand and shaking his left leg—at which time I think it would have been justifiable homicide to slay him—I have never seen that group sleeping, smoking, and expectorating round their brazier, but I have sincerely desired that something might happen to the charcoal smouldering therein, which would cause the immediate suffocation of the whole of the noble strangers.

There is at present a party of Zulu Kaffirs exhibiting at the St. George's Gallery, Hyde Park Corner, London. These noble savages are represented in a most agreeable manner; they are seen in an elegant theatre, fitted with appropriate scenery of great beauty, and they are described in a very sensible and unpretending lecture, delivered with a modesty which is quite a pattern to all similar exponents. Though extremely ugly, they are much better shaped than such of their predecessors as I have referred to; and they are rather picturesque to the eye, though far from odoriferous to the nose. What a visitor left to his own interpretings and imaginings might suppose these noblemen to be about, when they give vent to that pantomimic expression which is quite settled to be the natural gift of the noble savage, I cannot possibly conceive; for it is so much too luminous for my personal civilisation that it conveys no idea to my mind beyond a general stamping, ramping, and raving, remarkable (as everything in savage life is) for its dire uniformity. But let us—with the interpreter's assistance, of which I for one stand so much in need—see what the noble savage does in Zulu Kaffirland.

The noble savage sets a king to reign over him, to whom he submits his life and limbs without a murmur or question, and whose whole life is passed chin deep in a lake of blood; but who, after killing incessantly, is in his turn killed by his relations and friends, the moment a grey hair appears on his head. All the noble savage's wars with his fellow-savages (and he takes no pleasure in anything else) are wars of extermination—which is the best thing I know of him, and the most comfortable to my mind when I look at him. He has no moral feelings of any kind, sort, or description; and his 'mission' may be summed up as simply diabolical.

The ceremonies with which he faintly diversifies his life are, of course, of a kindred nature. If he wants a wife he appears before the kennel of the gentleman whom he has selected for his father-in-law, attended by a party of male friends of a very strong flavour, who screech and whistle and stamp an offer of so many cows for the young lady's hand. The chosen father-in-law—also supported by a high-flavoured party of male friends—screeches, whistles, and yells (being seated on the ground, he can't stamp) that there never was such a daughter in the market as his daughter, and that he must have six more cows. The son-in-law and his select circle of backers screech, whistle, stamp, and yell in reply, that they will give three more cows. The father-in-law (an old deluder, overpaid at the beginning) accepts four, and rises to bind the bargain. The whole party, the young lady included, then falling into epileptic convulsions, and screeching, whistling, stamping, and yelling together—and nobody taking any notice of the young lady (whose charms are not to be thought of without a shudder)—the noble savage is considered married, and his friends make demoniacal leaps at him by way of congratulation.

When the noble savage finds himself a little unwell, and mentions the circumstance to his friends, it is immediately perceived that he is under the influence of witchcraft. A learned personage, called an Imyanger or Witch Doctor, is immediately sent for to Nooker the Umtargartie, or smell out the witch. The male inhabitants of the kraal being seated on the ground, the learned doctor, got up like a grizzly bear, appears, and administers a dance of a most terrific nature, during the exhibition of which remedy he incessantly gnashes his teeth, and howls:— "I am the original physician to Nooker the Umtargartie. Yow yow yow! No connexion with any other establishment. Till till till! All other Umtargarties are feigned Umtargarties, Boroo Boroo! but I perceive here a genuine and real Umtargartie, Hoosh Hoosh Hoosh! in whose blood I, the original Imyanger and Nookerer, Blizzerum Boo! will wash these bear's claws of mine. O yow yow yow!" All this time the learned physician is looking out among the attentive faces for some unfortunate man who owes him a cow, or who has given him any small offence, or against whom, without offence, he has conceived a spite. Him he never fails to Nooker as the Umtargartie, and he is instantly killed. In the absence of such an individual, the usual practice is to Nooker the quietest and most gentlemanly person in company. But the nookering is invariably followed on the spot by the butchering.

Some of the noble savages in whom Mr. Catlin was so strongly interested, and the diminution of whose numbers, by rum and smallpox, greatly affected him, had a custom not unlike this, though much more appalling and disgusting in its odious details.

The women being at work in the fields, hoeing the Indian corn, and the noble savage being asleep in the shade, the chief has sometimes the condescension to come forth, and lighten the labour by looking at it. On these occasions, he seats himself in his own savage chair, and is attended by his shield-bearer: who holds over his head a shield of cowhide—in shape like an immense mussel shell—fearfully and wonderfully, after the manner of a theatrical supernumerary. But lest the great man should forget his greatness in the contemplation of the humble works of agriculture, there suddenly rushes in a poet, retained for the purpose, called a Praiser. This literary gentleman wears a leopard's head over his own, and a dress of tigers' tails; he has the appearance of having come express on his hind legs from the Zoological Gardens; and he incontinently strikes up the chief's praises, plunging and tearing all the while. There is a frantic wickedness in this brute's manner of worrying the air, and gnashing out, "O what a delightful chief he is! O what a delicious quantity of blood he sheds! O how majestically he laps it up! O how charmingly cruel he is! O how he tears the flesh of his enemies and crunches the bones! O how like the tiger and the leopard and the wolf and the bear he is! O, row row row row, how fond I am of him!" which might tempt the Society of Friends to charge at a hand-gallop into the Swartz-Kop location and exterminate the whole kraal.

When war is afoot among the noble savages—which is always—the chief holds a council to ascertain whether it is the opinion of his brothers and friends in general that the enemy shall be exterminated. On this occasion, after the performance of an Umsebeuza, or war song, —which is exactly like all the other songs, —the chief makes a speech to his brothers and friends, arranged in single file. No particular order is observed during the delivery of this address, but every gentleman who finds himself excited by the subject, instead of crying 'Hear, hear!' as is the custom with us, darts from the rank and tramples out the life, or crushes the skull, or mashes the face, or scoops out the eyes, or breaks the limbs, or performs a whirlwind of atrocities on the body, of an imaginary enemy. Several gentlemen becoming thus excited at once, and pounding away without the least regard to the orator, that illustrious person is rather in the position of an orator in an Irish House of Commons. But, several of these scenes of savage life bear a strong generic resemblance to an Irish election, and I think would be extremely well received and understood at Cork.

In all these ceremonies the noble savage holds forth to the utmost possible extent about himself; from which (to turn him to some civilised account) we may learn, I think, that as egotism is one of the most offensive and contemptible littlenesses a civilised man can exhibit, so it is really incompatible with the interchange of ideas; inasmuch as if we all talked about ourselves we should soon have no listeners, and must be all yelling and screeching at once on our own separate accounts: making society hideous. It is my opinion that if we retained in us anything of the noble savage, we could not get rid of it too soon. But the fact is clearly otherwise. Upon the wife and dowry question, substituting coin for cows, we have assuredly nothing of the Zulu Kaffir left. The endurance of despotism is one great distinguishing mark of a savage always. The improving world has quite got the better of that too. In like manner, Paris is a civilised city, and the Theatre Francais a highly civilised theatre; and we shall never hear, and never have heard in these later days (of course) of the Praiser THERE. No, no, civilised poets have better work to do. As to Nookering Umtargarties, there are no pretended Umtargarties in Europe, and no European powers to Nooker them; that would be mere spydom, subordination, small malice, superstition, and false pretence. And as to private Umtargarties, are we not in the year eighteen hundred and fifty-three, with spirits rapping at our doors?

To conclude as I began. My position is, that if we have anything to learn from the Noble Savage, it is what to avoid. His virtues are a fable; his happiness is a delusion; his nobility, nonsense.

We have no greater justification for being cruel to the miserable object, than for being cruel to a WILLIAM SHAKESPEARE or an ISAAC NEWTON; but he passes away before an immeasurably better and higher power than ever ran wild in any earthly woods, and the world will be all the better when his place knows him no more.

Births. Mrs. Meek, of a Son

My name is Meek. I am, in fact, Mr. Meek. That son is mine and Mrs. Meek's. When I saw the announcement in the Times, I dropped the paper. I had put it in, myself, and paid for it, but it looked so noble that it overpowered me.

As soon as I could compose my feelings, I took the paper up to Mrs. Meek's bedside. 'Maria Jane,' said I (I allude to Mrs. Meek), 'you are now a public character.' We read the review of our child, several times, with feelings of the strongest emotion; and I sent the boy who cleans the boots and shoes, to the office for fifteen copies. No reduction was made on taking that quantity.

It is scarcely necessary for me to say, that our child had been expected. In fact, it had been expected, with comparative confidence, for some months. Mrs. Meek's mother, who resides with us—of the name of Bigby—had made every preparation for its admission to our circle.

I hope and believe I am a quiet man. I will go farther. I know I am a quiet man. My constitution is tremulous, my voice was never loud, and, in point of stature, I have been from infancy, small. I have the greatest respect for Maria Jane's Mama. She is a most remarkable woman. I honour Maria Jane's Mama. In my opinion she would storm a town, single-handed, with a hearth-broom, and carry it. I have never known her to yield any point whatever, to mortal man. She is calculated to terrify the stoutest heart.

Still—but I will not anticipate.

The first intimation I had, of any preparations being in progress, on the part of Maria Jane's Mama, was one afternoon, several months ago. I came home earlier than usual from the office, and, proceeding into the dining-room, found an obstruction behind the door, which prevented it from opening freely. It was an obstruction of a soft nature. On looking in, I found it to be a female.

The female in question stood in the corner behind the door, consuming Sherry Wine. From the nutty smell of that beverage pervading the apartment, I have no doubt she was consuming a second glassful. She wore a black bonnet of large dimensions, and was copious in figure. The expression of her countenance was severe and discontented. The words to which she gave utterance on seeing me, were these, "Oh, git along with you, Sir, if you please; me and Mrs. Bigby don't want no male parties here!"

That female was Mrs. Prodgit.

I immediately withdrew, of course. I was rather hurt, but I made no remark. Whether it was that I showed a lowness of spirits after dinner, in consequence of feeling that I seemed to intrude, I cannot say. But, Maria Jane's Mama said to me on her retiring for the night: in a low distinct voice, and with a look of reproach that completely subdued me: "George Meek, Mrs. Prodgit is your wife's nurse!"

I bear no ill-will towards Mrs. Prodgit. Is it likely that I, writing this with tears in my eyes, should be capable of deliberate animosity towards a female, so essential to the welfare of Maria Jane? I am willing to admit that Fate may have been to blame, and not Mrs. Prodgit; but, it is undeniably true, that the latter female brought desolation and devastation into my lowly dwelling.

We were happy after her first appearance; we were sometimes exceedingly so. But, whenever the parlour door was opened, and 'Mrs. Prodgit!' announced (and she was very often announced), misery ensued. I could not bear Mrs. Prodgit's look. I felt that I was far from wanted, and had no business to exist in Mrs. Prodgit's presence. Between Maria Jane's Mama, and Mrs. Prodgit, there was a dreadful, secret, understanding—a dark mystery and conspiracy, pointing me out as a being to be shunned. I appeared to have done something that was evil. Whenever Mrs. Prodgit called, after dinner, I retired to my dressing-room—where the temperature is very low indeed, in the wintry time of the year—and sat looking at my frosty breath as it rose before me, and at my rack of boots; a serviceable article of furniture, but never, in my opinion, an exhilarating object. The length of the councils that were held with Mrs. Prodgit, under these circumstances, I will not attempt to describe. I will merely remark, that Mrs. Prodgit always consumed Sherry Wine while the deliberations were in progress; that they always ended in Maria Jane's being in wretched spirits on the sofa; and that Maria Jane's Mama always received me, when I was recalled, with a look of desolate triumph that too plainly said, 'Now, George Meek! You see my child, Maria Jane, a ruin, and I hope you are satisfied!'

I pass, generally, over the period that intervened between the day when Mrs. Prodgit entered her protest against male parties, and the ever-memorable midnight when I brought her to my unobtrusive home in a cab, with an extremely large box on the roof, and a bundle, a bandbox, and a basket, between the driver's legs. I have no objection to Mrs. Prodgit (aided and abetted by Mrs. Bigby, who I never can forget is the parent of Maria Jane) taking entire possession of my unassuming establishment. In the recesses of my own breast, the thought may linger that a man in possession cannot be so dreadful as a woman, and that woman Mrs. Prodgit; but, I ought to bear a good deal, and I hope I can, and do. Huffing and snubbing, prey upon my feelings; but, I can bear them without complaint. They may tell in the long run; I may be hustled about, from post to pillar, beyond my strength; nevertheless, I wish to avoid giving rise to words in the family.

The voice of Nature, however, cries aloud in behalf of Augustus George, my infant son. It is for him that I wish to utter a few plaintive household words. I am not at all angry; I am mild—but miserable.

I wish to know why, when my child, Augustus George, was

expected in our circle, a provision of pins was made, as if the little stranger were a criminal who was to be put to the torture immediately, on his arrival, instead of a holy babe? I wish to know why haste was made to stick those pins all over his innocent form, in every direction? I wish to be informed why light and air are excluded from Augustus George, like poisons? Why, I ask, is my unoffending infant so hedged into a basket-bedstead, with dimity and calico, with miniature sheets and blankets, that I can only hear him snuffle (and no wonder!) deep down under the pink hood of a little bathing-machine, and can never peruse even so much of his lineaments as his nose?

Was I expected to be the father of a French Roll, that the brushes of All Nations were laid in, to rasp Augustus George? Am I to be told that his sensitive skin was ever intended by Nature to have rashes brought out upon it, by the premature and incessant use of those formidable little instruments?

Is my son a Nutmeg, that he is to be grated on the stiff edges of sharp frills? Am I the parent of a Muslin boy, that his yielding surface is to be crimped and small plaited? Or is my child composed of Paper or of Linen, that impressions of the finer getting-up art, practised by the laundress, are to be printed off, all over his soft arms and legs, as I constantly observe them? The starch enters his soul; who can wonder that he cries?

Was Augustus George intended to have limbs, or to be born a Torso? I presume that limbs were the intention, as they are the usual practice. Then, why are my poor child's limbs fettered and tied up? Am I to be told that there is any analogy between Augustus George Meek and Jack Sheppard?

Analyse Castor Oil at any Institution of Chemistry that may be agreed upon, and inform me what resemblance, in taste, it bears to that natural provision which it is at once the pride and duty of Maria Jane to administer to Augustus George! Yet, I charge Mrs. Prodgit (aided and abetted by Mrs. Bigby) with systematically forcing Castor Oil on my innocent son, from the first hour of his birth. When that medicine, in its efficient action, causes internal disturbance to Augustus George, I charge Mrs. Prodgit (aided and abetted by Mrs.

Bigby) with insanely and inconsistently administering opium to allay the storm she has raised! What is the meaning of this?

If the days of Egyptian Mummies are past, how dare Mrs. Prodgit require, for the use of my son, an amount of flannel and linen that would carpet my humble roof? Do I wonder that she requires it? No! This morning, within an hour, I beheld this agonising sight. I beheld my son—Augustus George—in Mrs. Prodgit's hands, and on Mrs. Prodgit's knee, being dressed. He was at the moment, comparatively speaking, in a state of nature; having nothing on, but an extremely short shirt, remarkably disproportionate to the length of his usual outer garments. Trailing from Mrs. Prodgit's lap, on the floor, was a long narrow roller or bandage—I should say of several yards in extent. In this, I SAW Mrs. Prodgit tightly roll the body of my unoffending infant, turning him over and over, now presenting his unconscious face upwards, now the back of his bald head, until the unnatural feat was accomplished, and the bandage secured by a pin, which I have every reason to believe entered the body of my only child. In this tourniquet, he passes the present phase of his existence. Can I know it, and smile!

I fear I have been betrayed into expressing myself warmly, but I feel deeply. Not for myself; for Augustus George. I dare not interfere. Will any one? Will any publication? Any doctor? Any parent? Any body? I do not complain that Mrs. Prodgit (aided and abetted by Mrs. Bigby) entirely alienates Maria Jane's affections from me, and interposes an impassable barrier between us. I do not complain of being made of no account. I do not want to be of any account. But, Augustus George is a production of Nature (I cannot think otherwise), and I claim that he should be treated with some remote reference to Nature. In my opinion, Mrs. Prodgit is, from first to last, a convention and a superstition. Are all the faculty afraid of Mrs. Prodgit? If not, why don't they take her in hand and improve her?

P.S. Maria Jane's Mama boasts of her own knowledge of the subject, and says she brought up seven children besides Maria Jane. But how do *I* know that she might not have brought them up much better? Maria Jane herself is far from strong, and is subject to headaches, and nervous indigestion. Besides which, I learn from the statistical tables that one child in five dies within the first year of its life; and one child in three, within the fifth. That don't look as if we could never improve in these particulars, I think!

P.P.S. Augustus George is in convulsions.

18

Prince Bull: A Fairy Tale

Once upon a time, and of course it was in the Golden Age, and I hope you may know when that was, for I am sure I don't, though I have tried hard to find out, there lived in a rich and fertile country, a powerful Prince whose name was Bull. He had gone through a great deal of fighting, in his time, about all sorts of things, including nothing; but, had gradually settled down to be a steady, peaceable, good-natured, corpulent, rather sleepy Prince.

This Puissant Prince was married to a lovely Princess whose name was Fair Freedom. She had brought him a large fortune, and had borne him an immense number of children, and had set them to spinning, and farming, and engineering, and soldiering, and sailoring, and doctoring, and lawyering, and preaching, and all kinds of trades. The coffers of Prince Bull were full of treasure, his cellars were crammed with delicious wines from all parts of the world, the richest gold and silver plate that ever was seen adorned his sideboards, his sons were strong, his daughters were handsome, and in short you might have supposed that if there ever lived upon earth a fortunate and happy Prince, the name of that Prince, take him for all in all, was assuredly Prince Bull.

But, appearances, as we all know, are not always to be trusted—far from it; and if they had led you to this conclusion respecting

Prince Bull, they would have led you wrong as they often have led me.

For, this good Prince had two sharp thorns in his pillow, two hard knobs in his crown, two heavy loads on his mind, two unbridled nightmares in his sleep, two rocks ahead in his course. He could not by any means get servants to suit him, and he had a tyrannical old godmother, whose name was Tape.

She was a Fairy, this Tape, and was a bright red all over. She was disgustingly prim and formal, and could never bend herself a hair's breadth this way or that way, out of her naturally crooked shape. But, she was very potent in her wicked art. She could stop the fastest thing in the world, change the strongest thing into the weakest, and the most useful into the most useless. To do this she had only to put her cold hand upon it, and repeat her own name, Tape. Then it withered away.

At the Court of Prince Bull—at least I don't mean literally at his court, because he was a very genteel Prince, and readily yielded to his godmother when she always reserved that for his hereditary Lords and Ladies—in the dominions of Prince Bull, among the great mass of the community who were called in the language of that polite country the Mobs and the Snobs, were a number of very ingenious men, who were always busy with some invention or other, for promoting the prosperity of the Prince's subjects, and augmenting the Prince's power. But, whenever they submitted their models for the Prince's approval, his godmother stepped forward, laid her hand upon them, and said 'Tape.' Hence it came to pass, that when any particularly good discovery was made, the discoverer usually carried it off to some other Prince, in foreign parts, who had no old godmother who said Tape. This was not on the whole an advantageous state of things for Prince Bull, to the best of my understanding.

The worst of it was, that Prince Bull had in course of years lapsed into such a state of subjection to this unlucky godmother, that he never made any serious effort to rid himself of her tyranny. I have said this was the worst of it, but there I was wrong, because there is a worse consequence still, behind. The Prince's numerous family became so downright sick and tired of Tape, that when they should have helped the Prince out of the difficulties into which that evil creature led him, they fell into a dangerous habit of moodily keeping away from him in an impassive and indifferent manner, as though they had quite forgotten that no harm could happen to the Prince their father, without its inevitably affecting themselves.

Such was the aspect of affairs at the court of Prince Bull, when this great Prince found it necessary to go to war with Prince Bear. He had been for some time very doubtful of his servants, who, besides being indolent and addicted to enriching their families at his expense, domineered over him dreadfully; threatening to discharge themselves if they were found the least fault with, pretending that they had done a wonderful amount of work when they had done nothing, making the most unmeaning speeches that ever were heard in the Prince's name, and uniformly showing themselves to be very inefficient indeed. Though, that some of them had excellent characters from previous situations is not to be denied. Well; Prince Bull called his servants together, and said to them one and all, 'Send out my army against Prince Bear. Clothe it, arm it, feed it, provide it with all necessaries and contingencies, and I will pay the piper! Do your duty by my brave troops,' said the Prince, 'and do it well, and I will pour my treasure out like water, to defray the cost. Who ever heard me complain of money well laid out!' Which indeed he had reason for saying, inasmuch as he was well known to be a truly generous and munificent Prince.

When the servants heard those words, they sent out the army against Prince Bear, and they set the army tailors to work, and the army provision merchants, and the makers of guns both great and small, and the gunpowder makers, and the makers of ball, shell, and shot; and they bought up all manner of stores and ships, without troubling their heads about the price, and appeared to be so busy that the good Prince rubbed his hands, and (using a favourite expression of his), said, 'It's all right!' But, while they were thus employed, the Prince's godmother, who was a great favourite with those servants, looked in upon them continually all day long, and whenever she popped in her head at the door said, How do you do, my children? What are you doing here?' 'Official business, godmother.' 'Oho!' says this wicked Fairy. '—Tape!' And then the business all went wrong, whatever it was, and the servants' heads became so addled and muddled that they thought they were doing wonders.

Now, this was very bad conduct on the part of the vicious old nuisance, and she ought to have been strangled, even if she had stopped here; but, she didn't stop here, as you shall learn. For, a number of the Prince's subjects, being very fond of the Prince's army who were the bravest of men, assembled together and provided all manner of eatables and drinkables, and books to read, and clothes to wear, and tobacco to smoke, and candles to burn, and nailed them up in great packing-cases, and put them aboard a great many ships, to be carried out to that brave army in the cold and inclement country where they were fighting Prince Bear. Then, up comes this wicked Fairy as the ships were weighing anchor, and says, 'How do you do, my children? What are you doing here?'— 'We are going with all these comforts to the army, godmother.'— 'Oho!' says she. 'A pleasant voyage, my darlings.—Tape!' And from that time forth, those enchanting ships went sailing, against wind and tide and rhyme and reason, round and round the world, and whenever they touched at any port were ordered off immediately, and could never deliver their cargoes anywhere.

This, again, was very bad conduct on the part of the vicious old nuisance, and she ought to have been strangled for it if she had done nothing worse; but, she did something worse still, as you shall learn. For, she got astride of an official broomstick, and muttered as a spell these two sentences, 'On Her Majesty's service,' and 'I have the honour to be, sir, your most obedient servant,' and presently alighted in the cold and inclement country where the army of Prince Bull were encamped to fight the army of Prince Bear. On the sea-shore of that country, she found piled together, a number of houses for the army to live in, and a quantity of provisions for the army to live upon, and a quantity of clothes for the army to wear: while, sitting in the mud gazing at them, were a group of officers as red to look at as the wicked old woman herself. So, she said to one of them, 'Who are *you*, my darling, and how do *you* do?'—'I am the Quartermaster General's Department, godmother, and *I* am pretty well.' Then she said to another, 'Who are you, my darling, and how do you do?'—'I am the Commissariat Department, godmother, and I am pretty well! Then she said to another, 'Who are you, my darling, and how do you do?'—'I am the Head of the Medical Department, godmother, and *I* am pretty well.' Then, she said to some gentlemen scented with lavender, who kept themselves at a great distance from the rest, 'And who are *you*, my pretty pets, and how do *you* do?' And they answered, 'We-aw-are-the-aw-Staff-aw-Department, godmother, and we are very well indeed.'—'I am delighted to see you all, my beauties,' says this wicked old Fairy, '—Tape!' Upon that, the houses, clothes, and provisions, all mouldered away; and the soldiers who were sound, fell sick; and the soldiers who were sick, died miserably: and the noble army of Prince Bull perished.

When the dismal news of his great loss was carried to the Prince, he suspected his godmother very much indeed; but, he knew that his servants must have kept company with the malicious beldame, and must have given way to her, and therefore he resolved to turn those servants out of their places. So, he called to him a Roebuck who had the gift of speech, and he said, 'Good Roebuck, tell them they must go.' So, the good Roebuck delivered his message, so like a man that you might have supposed him to be nothing but a man, and they were turned out—but, not without warning, for that they had had a long time.

And now comes the most extraordinary part of the history of this Prince. When he had turned out those servants, of course he wanted others. What was his astonishment to find that in all his dominions, which contained no less than twenty-seven millions of people, there were not above five-and-twenty servants altogether! They were so lofty about it, too, that instead of discussing whether they should hire themselves as servants to Prince Bull, they turned things topsy-turvy, and considered whether as a favour they should hire Prince Bull to be their master! While they were arguing this point among themselves quite at their leisure, the wicked old red

Fairy was incessantly going up and down, knocking at the doors of twelve of the oldest of the five-and-twenty, who were the oldest inhabitants in all that country, and whose united ages amounted to one thousand, saying, 'Will you hire Prince Bull for your master?—Will you hire Prince Bull for your master?' To which one answered, 'I will if next door will;' and another, 'I won't if over the way does;' and another, 'I can't if he, she, or they, might, could, would, or should.' And all this time Prince Bull's affairs were going to rack and ruin.

At last, Prince Bull in the height of his perplexity assumed a thoughtful face, as if he were struck by an entirely new idea. The wicked old Fairy, seeing this, was at his elbow directly, and said, 'How do you do, my Prince, and what are you thinking of?'—'I am thinking, godmother,' says he, 'that among all the seven-and-twenty millions of my subjects who have never been in service, there are men of intellect and business who have made me very famous both among my friends and enemies.'—'Aye, truly?' says the Fairy.—'Aye, truly,' says the Prince.—'And what then?' says the Fairy.—'Why, then,' says he, 'since the regular old class of servants do so ill, are so hard to get, and carry it with so high a hand, perhaps I might try to make good servants of some of these.' The words had no sooner passed his lips than she returned, chuckling, 'You think so, do you? Indeed, my Prince?—Tape!' Thereupon he directly forgot what he was thinking of, and cried out lamentably to the old servants, 'O, do come and hire your poor old master! Pray do! On any terms!'

And this, for the present, finishes the story of Prince Bull. I wish I could wind it up by saying that he lived happy ever afterwards, but I cannot in my conscience do so; for, with Tape at his elbow, and his estranged children fatally repelled by her from coming near him, I do not, to tell you the plain truth, believe in the possibility of such an end to it.

Confucius

(551 BC—479 BC)

19

A Story from Confucius

Confucius once heard two of his pupils quarreling. One was of a gentle nature and was called by all the students a peaceful man. The other had a good brain and a kind heart, but was given to great anger. If he wished to do a thing, he did it, and no man could prevent; if any one tried to hinder him, he would show sudden and terrible rage.

One day, after one of these fits of temper, the blood came from his mouth, and, in great fear, he went to Confucius. "What shall I do with my body?" he asked, "I fear I shall not live long. It may be better that I no longer study and work. I am your pupil and you love me as a father. Tell me what to do for my body."

Confucius answered, "Tsze-Lu, you have a wrong idea about your body. It is not the study, not the work in school, but your great anger that causes the trouble.

"I will help you to see this. You remember when you and Nou-Wui quarreled. He was at peace and happy again in a little time, but you were very long in overcoming your anger. You can not expect to live long if you do that way. Every time one of the pupils says a thing you do not like, you are greatly enraged. There are a thousand in this school. If each offends you only once, you will have a fit of temper a thousand times this year. And you will surely die, if you do not use more self-control. I want to ask you some questions:—

"How many teeth have you?"

"I have thirty-two, teacher."

"How many tongues?"

"Just one."

"How many teeth have you lost?"

"I lost one when I was nine years old, and four when I was about twenty-six years old."

"And your tongue—is it still perfect?"

"Oh, yes."

"You know Mun-Gun, who is quite old?"

"Yes, I know him well."

"How many teeth do you think he had at your age?"

"I do not know."

"How many has he now?"

"Two, I think. But his tongue is perfect, though he is very old."

"You see the teeth are lost because they are strong, and determined to have everything they desire. They are hard and hurt the tongue many times, but the tongue never hurts the teeth. Yet, it endures until the end, while the teeth are the first of man to decay. The tongue is peaceful and gentle with the teeth. It never grows angry and fights them, even when they are in the wrong. It always helps them do their work, in preparing man's food for him, although the teeth never help the tongue, and they always resist everything.

"And so it is with man. The strongest to resist, is the first to decay; and you, Tsze-Lu, will be even so if you learn not the great lesson of self-control."

Edgar Allan Poe

(1809-1849)

20

The Tell-Tale Heart

TRUE!—nervous—very, very dreadfully nervous I had been and am; but why will you say that I am mad? The disease had sharpened my senses—not destroyed—not dulled them. Above all was the sense of hearing acute. I heard all things in the heaven and in the earth. I heard many things in hell. How, then, am I mad? Hearken! and observe how healthily—how calmly I can tell you the whole story.

It is impossible to say how first the idea entered my brain; but once conceived, it haunted me day and night. Object there was none. Passion there was none. I loved the old man. He had never wronged me. He had never given me insult. For his gold I had no desire. I think it was his eye! yes, it was this! He had the eye of a vulture—a pale blue eye, with a film over it. Whenever it fell upon me, my blood ran cold; and so by degrees—very gradually—I made up my mind to take the life of the old man, and thus rid myself of the eye forever.

Now this is the point. You fancy me mad. Madmen know nothing. But you should have seen me. You should have seen how wisely I proceeded—with what caution—with what foresight—with what dissimulation I went to work! I was never kinder to the old man than during the whole week before I killed him. And every night, about midnight, I turned the latch of his door and opened it—oh so gently! And then, when I had made an opening sufficient for my head, I put in a dark lantern, all closed, closed, that no light shone out, and then I thrust in my head. Oh, you would have laughed to see how cunningly I thrust it in! I moved it slowly— very, very slowly, so that I might not disturb the old man's sleep. It took me an hour to place my whole head within the opening so far that I could see him as he lay upon his bed. Ha! would a madman have been so wise as this, And then, when my head was well in the room, I undid the lantern cautiously-oh, so cautiously—cautiously (for the hinges creaked)—I undid it just so much that a single thin ray fell upon the vulture eye. And this I did for seven long nights— every night just at midnight—but I found the eye always closed; and so it was impossible to do the work; for it was not the old man who vexed me, but his Evil Eye. And every morning, when the day broke, I went boldly into the chamber, and spoke courageously to him, calling him by name in a hearty tone, and inquiring how he has passed the night. So you see he would have been a very profound old man, indeed, to suspect that every night, just at twelve, I looked in upon him while he slept.

Upon the eighth night I was more than usually cautious in opening the door. A watch's minute hand moves more quickly than did mine. Never before that night had I felt the extent of my own powers—of my sagacity. I could scarcely contain my feelings of triumph. To think that there I was, opening the door, little by little, and he not even to dream of my secret deeds or thoughts. I fairly chuckled at the idea; and perhaps he heard me; for he moved on the bed suddenly, as if startled. Now you may think that I drew back— but no. His room was as black as pitch with the thick darkness, (for the shutters were close fastened, through fear of robbers,) and so I knew that he could not see the opening of the door, and I kept pushing it on steadily, steadily.

I had my head in, and was about to open the lantern, when my thumb slipped upon the tin fastening, and the old man sprang up in bed, crying out—"Who's there?"

I kept quite still and said nothing. For a whole hour I did not move a muscle, and in the meantime I did not hear him lie down. He was still sitting up in the bed listening; —just as I have done, night after night, hearkening to the death watches in the wall.

Presently I heard a slight groan, and I knew it was the groan of mortal terror. It was not a groan of pain or of grief—oh, no!—it was the low stifled sound that arises from the bottom of the soul when overcharged with awe. I knew the sound well. Many a night, just at midnight, when all the world slept, it has welled up from my own bosom, deepening, with its dreadful echo, the terrors that distracted me. I say I knew it well. I knew what the old man felt, and pitied him, although I chuckled at heart. I knew that he had been lying awake ever since the first slight noise, when he had turned in the bed. His fears had been ever since growing upon him. He had been trying to fancy them causeless, but could not. He had been saying to himself—"It is nothing but the wind in the chimney— it is only a mouse crossing the floor," or "It is merely a cricket which has made a single chirp." Yes, he had been trying to comfort himself with these suppositions: but he had found all in vain. All in vain; because Death, in approaching him had stalked with his black shadow before him, and enveloped the victim. And it was the mournful influence of the unperceived shadow that caused him to feel—although he neither saw nor heard—to feel the presence of my head within the room.

When I had waited a long time, very patiently, without hearing him lie down, I resolved to open a little—a very, very little crevice in the lantern. So I opened it—you cannot imagine how stealthily, stealthily—until, at length a simple dim ray, like the thread of the spider, shot from out the crevice and fell full upon the vulture eye.

It was open—wide, wide open—and I grew furious as I gazed upon it. I saw it with perfect distinctness—all a dull blue, with a hideous veil over it that chilled the very marrow in my bones; but I could see nothing else of the old man's face or person: for I had directed the ray as if by instinct, precisely upon the damned spot.

And have I not told you that what you mistake for madness is but over-acuteness of the sense? —now, I say, there came to my ears a low, dull, quick sound, such as a watch makes when enveloped in cotton. I knew that sound well, too. It was the beating of the old man's heart. It increased my fury, as the beating of a drum stimulates the soldier into courage.

But even yet I refrained and kept still. I scarcely breathed. I held the lantern motionless. I tried how steadily I could maintain the ray upon the eve. Meantime the hellish tattoo of the heart increased. It grew quicker and quicker, and louder and louder every instant. The old man's terror must have been extreme! It grew louder, I say, louder every moment! —do you mark me well I have told you that I am nervous: so I am. And now at the dead hour of the night, amid the dreadful silence of that old house, so strange a noise as this excited me to uncontrollable terror. Yet, for some minutes longer I refrained and stood still. But the beating grew louder, louder! I thought the heart must burst. And now a new anxiety seized me— the sound would be heard by a neighbour! The old man's hour had come! With a loud yell, I threw open the lantern and leaped into the room. He shrieked once—once only. In an instant I dragged him to the floor, and pulled the heavy bed over him. I then smiled gaily, to find the deed so far done. But, for many minutes, the heart beat on with a muffled sound. This, however, did not vex me; it would not be heard through the wall. At length it ceased. The old man was dead. I removed the bed and examined the corpse. Yes, he was stone, stone dead. I placed my hand upon the heart and held it there many minutes. There was no pulsation. He was stone dead. His eve would trouble me no more.

If still you think me mad, you will think so no longer when I describe the wise precautions I took for the concealment of the body. The night waned, and I worked hastily, but in silence. First of all I dismembered the corpse. I cut off the head and the arms and the legs.

I then took up three planks from the flooring of the chamber, and deposited all between the scantlings. I then replaced the boards so cleverly, so cunningly, that no human eye—not even his—could have detected any thing wrong. There was nothing to wash out— no stain of any kind—no blood-spot whatever. I had been too wary for that. A tub had caught all—ha! ha!

When I had made an end of these labors, it was four o'clock—still dark as midnight. As the bell sounded the hour, there came a knocking at the street door. I went down to open it with a light heart, —for what had I now to fear? There entered three men, who introduced themselves, with perfect suavity, as officers of the police. A shriek had been heard by a neighbour during the night; suspicion of foul play had been aroused; information had been lodged at the police office, and they (the officers) had been deputed to search the premises.

I smiled, —for what had I to fear? I bade the gentlemen welcome. The shriek, I said, was my own in a dream. The old man, I mentioned, was absent in the country. I took my visitors all over the house. I bade them search—search well. I led them, at length, to his chamber. I showed them his treasures, secure, undisturbed. In the enthusiasm of my confidence, I brought chairs into the room, and desired them here to rest from their fatigues, while I myself, in the wild audacity of my perfect triumph, placed my own seat upon the very spot beneath which reposed the corpse of the victim.

The officers were satisfied. My manner had convinced them. I was singularly at ease. They sat, and while I answered cheerily, they chatted of familiar things. But, ere long, I felt myself getting pale and wished them gone. My head ached, and I fancied a ringing in my ears: but still they sat and still chatted. The ringing became more distinct:—It continued and became more distinct: I talked more freely to get rid of the feeling: but it continued and gained definiteness—until, at length, I found that the noise was not within my ears.

No doubt I now grew very pale; —but I talked more fluently, and with a heightened voice. Yet the sound increased—and what could I do? It was a low, dull, quick sound—much such a sound as a watch makes when enveloped in cotton. I gasped for breath—and yet the officers heard it not. I talked more quickly—more vehemently; but the noise steadily increased. I arose and argued about trifles, in a high key and with violent gesticulations; but the noise steadily increased. Why would they not be gone? I paced the floor to and fro with heavy strides, as if excited to fury by the observations of the men—but the noise steadily increased. Oh God! what could I do? I foamed—I raved—I swore! I swung the chair upon which I had been sitting, and grated it upon the boards, but the noise arose over all and continually increased. It grew louder—louder—louder! And still the men chatted pleasantly, and smiled. Was it possible they heard not? Almighty God! —no, no! They heard! —they suspected! —they knew! —they were making a mockery of my horror! This I thought, and this I think. But anything was better than this agony! Anything was more tolerable than this derision! I could bear those hypocritical smiles no longer! I felt that I must scream or die! and now—again! —hark! louder! louder! louder! louder!

"Villains!" I shrieked, "dissemble no more! I admit the deed! —tear up the planks! here, here! —It is the beating of his hideous heart!"

21

Von Kempelen and His Discovery

After the very minute and elaborate paper by Arago, to say nothing of the summary in 'Silliman's Journal,' with the detailed statement just published by Lieutenant Maury, it will not be supposed, of course, that in offering a few hurried remarks in reference to Von Kempelen's discovery, I have any design to look at the subject in a scientific point of view. My object is simply, in the first place, to say a few words of Von Kempelen himself (with whom, some years ago, I had the honor of a slight personal acquaintance), since every thing which concerns him must necessarily, at this moment, be of interest; and, in the second place, to look in a general way, and speculatively, at the results of the discovery.

It may be as well, however, to premise the cursory observations which I have to offer, by denying, very decidedly, what seems to be a general impression (gleaned, as usual in a case of this kind, from the newspapers), viz.: that this discovery, astounding as it unquestionably is, is unanticipated.

By reference to the 'Diary of Sir Humphrey Davy' (Cottle and Munroe, London, pp. 150), it will be seen at pp. 53 and 82, that this illustrious chemist had not only conceived the idea now in question, but had actually made no inconsiderable progress, experimentally, in the very identical analysis now so triumphantly brought to an issue by Von Kempelen, who although he makes not the slightest allusion to it, is, without doubt (I say it unhesitatingly, and can prove it, if required), indebted to the 'Diary' for at least the first hint of his own undertaking.

The paragraph from the 'Courier and Enquirer,' which is now going the rounds of the press, and which purports to claim the invention for a Mr. Kissam, of Brunswick, Maine, appears to me, I confess, a little apocryphal, for several reasons; although there is nothing either impossible or very improbable in the statement made. I need not go into details. My opinion of the paragraph is founded principally upon its manner. It does not look true. Persons who are narrating facts, are seldom so particular as Mr. Kissam seems to be, about day and date and precise location. Besides, if Mr. Kissam actually did come upon the discovery he says he did, at the period designated—nearly eight years ago—how happens it that he took no steps, on the instant, to reap the immense benefits which the merest bumpkin must have known would have resulted to him individually, if not to the world at large, from the discovery? It seems to me quite incredible that any man of common understanding could have discovered what Mr. Kissam says he did, and yet have subsequently acted so like a baby—so like an owl—as Mr. Kissam admits that he did. By-the-way, who is Mr. Kissam? and is not the whole paragraph in the 'Courier and Enquirer' a fabrication got up to 'make a talk'? It must be confessed that it has an amazingly moon-hoaxy-air. Very little dependence is to be placed upon it, in my humble opinion; and if I were not well aware, from experience, how very easily men of science are mystified, on points out of their usual range of inquiry, I should be profoundly astonished at finding so eminent a chemist as Professor Draper, discussing Mr. Kissam's (or is it Mr. Quizzem's?) pretensions to the discovery, in so serious a tone.

But to return to the 'Diary' of Sir Humphrey Davy. This pamphlet was not designed for the public eye, even upon the decease of the writer, as any person at all conversant with authorship may satisfy himself at once by the slightest inspection of the style. At page 13, for example, near the middle, we read, in reference to his researches about the protoxide of azote: 'In less than half a minute the respiration being continued, diminished gradually and were succeeded by analogous to gentle pressure on all the muscles.' That the respiration was not 'diminished,' is not only clear by the subsequent context, but by the use of the plural, 'were.' The sentence, no doubt, was thus intended: 'In less than half a minute, the respiration (being continued, these feelings) diminished gradually, and were succeeded by (a sensation) analogous to gentle pressure on all the muscles.' A hundred similar instances go to show that the MS. so inconsiderately published, was merely a rough note-book, meant only for the writer's own eye, but an inspection of the pamphlet will convince almost any thinking person of the truth of my suggestion. The fact is, Sir Humphrey Davy was about the last man in the world to commit himself on scientific topics. Not only had he a more than ordinary dislike to quackery, but he was morbidly afraid of appearing empirical; so that, however fully he might have been convinced that he was on the right track in the matter now in question, he would never have spoken out, until he had every thing ready for the most practical demonstration. I verily believe that his last moments would have been rendered wretched, could he have suspected that his wishes in regard to burning this 'Diary' (full of crude speculations) would have been unattended to; as, it seems, they were. I say 'his wishes,' for that he meant to include this note-book among the miscellaneous papers directed 'to be burnt,' I think there can be no manner of doubt. Whether it escaped the flames by good fortune or by bad, yet remains to be seen. That the passages quoted above, with the other similar ones referred to, gave Von Kempelen the hint, I do not in the slightest degree question; but I repeat, it yet remains to be seen whether this momentous discovery itself (momentous under any circumstances) will be of service or disservice to mankind at large. That Von Kempelen and his immediate friends will reap a rich harvest, it would be folly to doubt for a moment. They will scarcely be so weak as not to 'realize,' in time, by large purchases of houses and land, with other property of intrinsic value.

In the brief account of Von Kempelen which appeared in the 'Home Journal,' and has since been extensively copied, several misapprehensions of the German original seem to have been made by the translator, who professes to have taken the passage from a late number of the Presburg 'Schnellpost.' 'Viele' has evidently been misconceived (as it often is), and what the translator renders by 'sorrows,' is probably 'lieden,' which, in its true version, 'sufferings,' would give a totally different complexion to the whole account; but, of course, much of this is merely guess, on my part.

Von Kempelen, however, is by no means 'a misanthrope,' in appearance, at least, whatever he may be in fact. My acquaintance with him was casual altogether; and I am scarcely warranted in saying that I know him at all; but to have seen and conversed with a man of so prodigious a notoriety as he has attained, or will attain in a few days, is not a small matter, as times go.

'The Literary World' speaks of him, confidently, as a native of Presburg (misled, perhaps, by the account in 'The Home Journal') but I am pleased in being able to state positively, since I have it from his own lips, that he was born in Utica, in the State of New York, although both his parents, I believe, are of Presburg descent. The family is connected, in some way, with Maelzel, of Automaton-chess-player memory. In person, he is short and stout, with large, fat, blue eyes, sandy hair and whiskers, a wide but pleasing mouth, fine teeth, and I think a Roman nose. There is some defect in one of his feet. His address is frank, and his whole manner noticeable for bonhomie. Altogether, he looks, speaks, and acts as little like 'a misanthrope' as any man I ever saw. We were fellow-sojourners for a week about six years ago, at Earl's Hotel, in Providence, Rhode Island; and I presume that I conversed with him, at various times, for some three or four hours altogether. His principal topics were those of the day, and nothing that fell from him led me to suspect his scientific attainments. He left the hotel before me, intending to go to New York, and thence to Bremen; it was in the latter city that his great discovery was first made public; or, rather, it was there that he was first suspected of having made it. This is about all that I personally know of the now immortal Von Kempelen; but

I have thought that even these few details would have interest for the public.

There can be little question that most of the marvellous rumors afloat about this affair are pure inventions, entitled to about as much credit as the story of Aladdin's lamp; and yet, in a case of this kind, as in the case of the discoveries in California, it is clear that the truth may be stranger than fiction. The following anecdote, at least, is so well authenticated, that we may receive it implicitly.

Von Kempelen had never been even tolerably well off during his residence at Bremen; and often, it was well known, he had been put to extreme shifts in order to raise trifling sums. When the great excitement occurred about the forgery on the house of Gutsmuth & Co., suspicion was directed toward Von Kempelen, on account of his having purchased a considerable property in Gasperitch Lane, and his refusing, when questioned, to explain how he became possessed of the purchase money. He was at length arrested, but nothing decisive appearing against him, was in the end set at liberty. The police, however, kept a strict watch upon his movements, and thus discovered that he left home frequently, taking always the same road, and invariably giving his watchers the slip in the neighborhood of that labyrinth of narrow and crooked passages known by the flash name of the 'Dondergat.' Finally, by dint of great perseverance, they traced him to a garret in an old house of seven stories, in an alley called Flatzplatz,—and, coming upon him suddenly, found him, as they imagined, in the midst of his counterfeiting operations. His agitation is represented as so excessive that the officers had not the slightest doubt of his guilt. After hand-cuffing him, they searched his room, or rather rooms, for it appears he occupied all the mansarde.

Opening into the garret where they caught him, was a closet, ten feet by eight, fitted up with some chemical apparatus, of which the object has not yet been ascertained. In one corner of the closet was a very small furnace, with a glowing fire in it, and on the fire a kind of duplicate crucible—two crucibles connected by a tube. One of these crucibles was nearly full of lead in a state of fusion, but not reaching up to the aperture of the tube, which was close to the brim. The other crucible had some liquid in it, which, as the officers entered, seemed to be furiously dissipating in vapor. They relate that, on finding himself taken, Kempelen seized the crucibles with both hands (which were encased in gloves that afterwards turned out to be asbestic), and threw the contents on the tiled floor. It was now that they hand-cuffed him; and before proceeding to ransack the premises they searched his person, but nothing unusual was found about him, excepting a paper parcel, in his coat-pocket, containing what was afterward ascertained to be a mixture of antimony and some unknown substance, in nearly, but not quite, equal proportions. All attempts at analyzing the unknown substance have, so far, failed, but that it will ultimately be analyzed, is not to be doubted.

Passing out of the closet with their prisoner, the officers went through a sort of ante-chamber, in which nothing material was found, to the chemist's sleeping-room. They here rummaged some drawers and boxes, but discovered only a few papers, of no importance, and some good coin, silver and gold. At length, looking under the bed, they saw a large, common hair trunk, without hinges, hasp, or lock, and with the top lying carelessly across the bottom portion. Upon attempting to draw this trunk out from under the bed, they found that, with their united strength (there were three of them, all powerful men), they 'could not stir it one inch.' Much astonished at this, one of them crawled under the bed, and looking into the trunk, said:

"No wonder we couldn't move it—why it's full to the brim of old bits of brass!"

Putting his feet, now, against the wall so as to get a good purchase, and pushing with all his force, while his companions pulled with all theirs, the trunk, with much difficulty, was slid out from under the bed, and its contents examined. The supposed brass with which it was filled was all in small, smooth pieces, varying from the size of a pea to that of a dollar; but the pieces were irregular in shape, although more or less flat-looking, upon the whole, 'very much as lead looks when thrown upon the ground in a molten state, and there suffered to grow cool.' Now, not one of these officers for a moment suspected this metal to be any thing but brass. The idea of its being gold never entered their brains, of course; how could such a wild fancy have entered it? And their astonishment may be well conceived, when the next day it became known, all over Bremen, that the 'lot of brass' which they had carted so contemptuously to the police office, without putting themselves to the trouble of pocketing the smallest scrap, was not only gold—real gold—but gold far finer than any employed in coinage-gold, in fact, absolutely pure, virgin, without the slightest appreciable alloy.

I need not go over the details of Von Kempelen's confession (as far as it went) and release, for these are familiar to the public. That he has actually realized, in spirit and in effect, if not to the letter, the old chimaera of the philosopher's stone, no sane person is at liberty to doubt. The opinions of Arago are, of course, entitled to the greatest consideration; but he is by no means infallible; and what he says of bismuth, in his report to the Academy, must be taken cum grano salis. The simple truth is, that up to this period all analysis has failed; and until Von Kempelen chooses to let us have the key to his own published enigma, it is more than probable that the matter will remain, for years, in statu quo. All that as yet can fairly be said to be known is, that "Pure gold can be made at will, and very readily from lead in connection with certain other substances, in kind and in proportions, unknown."

Speculation, of course, is busy as to the immediate and ultimate results of this discovery—a discovery which few thinking persons will hesitate in referring to an increased interest in the matter of gold generally, by the late developments in California; and this reflection brings us inevitably to another—the exceeding inopportuneness of Von Kempelen's analysis. If many were prevented from adventuring to California, by the mere apprehension that gold would so materially diminish in value, on account of its plentifulness in the mines there, as to render the speculation of going so far in search of it a doubtful one—what impression will be wrought now, upon the minds of those about to emigrate, and especially upon the minds of those actually in the mineral region, by the announcement of this astounding discovery of Von Kempelen? A discovery which declares, in so many words, that beyond its intrinsic worth for manufacturing purposes (whatever that worth may be), gold now is, or at least soon will be (for it cannot be supposed that Von Kempelen can long retain his secret), of no greater value than lead, and of far inferior value to silver. It is, indeed, exceedingly difficult to speculate prospectively upon the consequences of the discovery, but one thing may be positively maintained—that the announcement of the discovery six months ago would have had material influence in regard to the settlement of California.

In Europe, as yet, the most noticeable results have been a rise of two hundred per cent in the price of lead, and nearly twenty-five per cent that of silver.

22

Silence—A Fable

*ALCMAN. The mountain pinnacles slumber; valleys,
crags and caves are silent.*

"Listen to me," said the Demon as he placed his hand upon my head. "The region of which I speak is a dreary region in Libya, by the borders of the river Zaire. And there is no quiet there, nor silence.

"The waters of the river have a saffron and sickly hue; and they flow not onwards to the sea, but palpitate forever and forever beneath the red eye of the sun with a tumultuous and convulsive motion. For many miles on either side of the river's oozy bed is a pale desert of gigantic water-lilies. They sigh one unto the other in that solitude, and stretch towards the heaven their long and ghastly necks, and nod to and fro their everlasting heads. And there is an indistinct murmur which cometh out from among them like the rushing of subterrene water. And they sigh one unto the other.

"But there is a boundary to their realm—the boundary of the dark, horrible, lofty forest. There, like the waves about the Hebrides, the low underwood is agitated continually. But there is no wind throughout the heaven. And the tall primeval trees rock eternally hither and thither with a crashing and mighty sound. And from their high summits, one by one, drop everlasting dews. And at the roots strange poisonous flowers lie writhing in perturbed slumber. And overhead, with a rustling and loud noise, the gray clouds rush westwardly forever, until they roll, a cataract, over the fiery wall of the horizon. But there is no wind throughout the heaven. And by the shores of the river Zaire there is neither quiet nor silence.

"It was night, and the rain fell; and falling, it was rain, but, having fallen, it was blood. And I stood in the morass among the tall and the rain fell upon my head—and the lilies sighed one unto the other in the solemnity of their desolation.

"And, all at once, the moon arose through the thin ghastly mist, and was crimson in color. And mine eyes fell upon a huge gray rock which stood by the shore of the river, and was lighted by the light of the moon. And the rock was gray, and ghastly, and tall, —and the rock was gray. Upon its front were characters engraven in the stone; and I walked through the morass of water-lilies, until I came close unto the shore, that I might read the characters upon the stone. But I could not decypher them. And I was going back into the morass, when the moon shone with a fuller red, and I turned and looked again upon the rock, and upon the characters; —and the characters were DESOLATION.

"And I looked upwards, and there stood a man upon the summit of the rock; and I hid myself among the water-lilies that I might discover the actions of the man. And the man was tall and stately in form, and was wrapped up from his shoulders to his feet in the toga of old Rome. And the outlines of his figure were indistinct—but his features were the features of a deity; for the mantle of the night, and of the mist, and of the moon, and of the dew, had left uncovered the features of his face. And his brow was lofty with thought, and his eye wild with care; and, in the few furrows upon his cheek I read the fables of sorrow, and weariness, and disgust with mankind, and a longing after solitude.

"And the man sat upon the rock, and leaned his head upon his hand, and looked out upon the desolation. He looked down into the low unquiet shrubbery, and up into the tall primeval trees, and up higher at the rustling heaven, and into the crimson moon. And I lay close within shelter of the lilies, and observed the actions of the man. And the man trembled in the solitude; —but the night waned, and he sat upon the rock.

"And the man turned his attention from the heaven, and looked out upon the dreary river Zaire, and upon the yellow ghastly waters, and upon the pale legions of the water-lilies. And the man listened to the sighs of the water-lilies, and to the murmur that came up from among them. And I lay close within my covert and observed the actions of the man. And the man trembled in the solitude; —but the night waned and he sat upon the rock.

"Then I went down into the recesses of the morass, and waded afar in among the wilderness of the lilies, and called unto the hippopotami which dwelt among the fens in the recesses of the morass. And the hippopotami heard my call, and came, with the behemoth, unto the foot of the rock, and roared loudly and fearfully beneath the moon. And I lay close within my covert and observed the actions of the man. And the man trembled in the solitude; —but the night waned and he sat upon the rock.

"Then I cursed the elements with the curse of tumult; and a frightful tempest gathered in the heaven where, before, there had been no wind. And the heaven became livid with the violence of the tempest—and the rain beat upon the head of the man—and the floods of the river came down—and the river was tormented into foam—and the water-lilies shrieked within their beds—and the forest crumbled before the wind—and the thunder rolled— and the lightning fell—and the rock rocked to its foundation. And I lay close within my covert and observed the actions of the man. And the man trembled in the solitude; —but the night waned and he sat upon the rock.

"Then I grew angry and cursed, with the curse of silence, the river, and the lilies, and the wind, and the forest, and the heaven, and the thunder, and the sighs of the water-lilies. And they became accursed, and were still. And the moon ceased to totter up its pathway to heaven—and the thunder died away—and the lightning did not flash—and the clouds hung motionless—and the waters sunk to their level and remained—and the trees ceased to rock—

115

and the water-lilies sighed no more—and the murmur was heard no longer from among them, nor any shadow of sound throughout the vast illimitable desert. And I looked upon the characters of the rock, and they were changed; —and the characters were SILENCE.

"And mine eyes fell upon the countenance of the man, and his countenance was wan with terror. And, hurriedly, he raised his head from his hand, and stood forth upon the rock and listened. But there was no voice throughout the vast illimitable desert, and the characters upon the rock were SILENCE. And the man shuddered, and turned his face away, and fled afar off, in haste, so that I beheld him no more."

Now there are fine tales in the volumes of the Magi—in the iron-bound, melancholy volumes of the Magi. Therein, I say, are glorious histories of the Heaven, and of the Earth, and of the mighty sea—and of the Genii that over-ruled the sea, and the earth, and the lofty heaven. There was much lore too in the sayings which were said by the Sybils; and holy, holy things were heard of old by the dim leaves that trembled around Dodona—but, as Allah liveth, that fable which the Demon told me as he sat by my side in the shadow of the tomb, I hold to be the most wonderful of all! And as the Demon made an end of his story, he fell back within the cavity of the tomb and laughed. And I could not laugh with the Demon, and he cursed me because I could not laugh. And the lynx which dwelleth forever in the tomb, came out therefrom, and lay down at the feet of the Demon, and looked at him steadily in the face.

23

The Masque of the Red Death

The 'Red Death' had long devastated the country. No pestilence had ever been so fatal, or so hideous. Blood was its Avatar and its seal—the redness and the horror of blood. There were sharp pains, and sudden dizziness, and then profuse bleeding at the pores, with dissolution. The scarlet stains upon the body and especially upon the face of the victim, were the pest ban which shut him out from the aid and from the sympathy of his fellow-men. And the whole seizure, progress and termination of the disease, were the incidents of half an hour.

But the Prince Prospero was happy and dauntless and sagacious. When his dominions were half depopulated, he summoned to his presence a thousand hale and light-hearted friends from among the knights and dames of his court, and with these retired to the deep seclusion of one of his castellated abbeys. This was an extensive and magnificent structure, the creation of the prince's own eccentric yet august taste. A strong and lofty wall girdled it in. This wall had gates of iron. The courtiers, having entered, brought furnaces and massy hammers and welded the bolts. They resolved to leave means neither of ingress or egress to the sudden impulses of despair or of frenzy from within. The abbey was amply provisioned. With such precautions the courtiers might bid defiance to contagion. The external world could take care of itself. In the meantime it was folly to grieve, or to think. The prince had provided all the appliances of pleasure. There were buffoons, there were improvisatori, there were ballet-dancers, there were musicians, there was Beauty, there was wine. All these and security were within. Without was the 'Red Death.'

It was toward the close of the fifth or sixth month of his seclusion, and while the pestilence raged most furiously abroad, that the Prince Prospero entertained his thousand friends at a masked ball of the most unusual magnificence.

It was a voluptuous scene, that masquerade. But first let me tell of the rooms in which it was held. There were seven—an imperial suite. In many palaces, however, such suites form a long and straight vista, while the folding doors slide back nearly to the walls on either hand, so that the view of the whole extent is scarcely impeded. Here the case was very different; as might have been expected from the duke's love of the bizarre. The apartments were so irregularly disposed that the vision embraced but little more than one at a time. There was a sharp turn at every twenty or thirty yards, and at each turn a novel effect. To the right and left, in the middle of each wall, a tall and narrow Gothic window looked out upon a closed corridor which pursued the windings of the suite. These windows were of stained glass whose color varied in accordance with the prevailing hue of the decorations of the chamber into which it opened. That at the eastern extremity was hung, for example, in blue—and vividly blue were its windows. The second chamber was purple in its ornaments and tapestries, and here the panes were purple. The third was green throughout, and so were the casements. The fourth was furnished and lighted with orange—the fifth with white—the sixth with violet. The seventh apartment was closely shrouded in black velvet tapestries that hung all over the ceiling and down the walls, falling in heavy folds upon a carpet of the same material and hue. But in this chamber only, the color of the windows failed to correspond with the decorations. The panes here were scarlet—a deep blood color. Now in no one of the seven apartments was there any lamp or candelabrum, amid the profusion of golden ornaments that lay scattered to and fro or depended from the roof. There was no light of any kind emanating from lamp or candle within the suite of chambers. But in the corridors that followed the suite, there stood, opposite to each window, a heavy tripod, bearing a brazier of fire that projected its rays through the tinted glass and so glaringly illumined the room. And thus were produced a multitude of gaudy and fantastic appearances. But in the western or black chamber the effect of the fire-light that streamed upon the dark hangings through the blood-tinted panes, was ghastly in the extreme, and produced so wild a look upon the countenances of those who entered, that there were few of the company bold enough to set foot within its precincts at all.

It was in this apartment, also, that there stood against the western wall, a gigantic clock of ebony. Its pendulum swung to and fro with a dull, heavy, monotonous clang; and when the minute-hand made the circuit of the face, and the hour was to be stricken, there came from the brazen lungs of the clock a sound which was clear and loud and deep and exceedingly musical, but of so peculiar a note and emphasis that, at each lapse of an hour, the musicians of the orchestra were constrained to pause, momentarily, in their performance, to hearken to the sound; and thus the waltzers perforce ceased their evolutions; and there was a brief disconcert of the whole gay company; and, while the chimes of the clock yet rang, it was observed that the giddiest grew pale, and the more aged and sedate passed their hands over their brows as if in confused reverie or meditation. But when the echoes had fully ceased, a light laughter at once pervaded the assembly; the musicians looked at each other and smiled as if at their own nervousness and folly, and made whispering vows, each to the other, that the next chiming of the clock should produce in them no similar emotion; and then, after the lapse of sixty minutes, (which embrace three thousand and six hundred seconds of the Time that flies,) there came yet another chiming of the clock, and then were the same disconcert and tremulousness and meditation as before.

But, in spite of these things, it was a gay and magnificent revel. The tastes of the duke were peculiar. He had a fine eye for colors and effects. He disregarded the decora of mere fashion. His plans were bold and fiery, and his conceptions glowed with barbaric lustre. There are some who would have thought him mad. His followers felt that he was not. It was necessary to hear and see and touch him to be sure that he was not.

He had directed, in great part, the moveable embellishments of the seven chambers, upon occasion of this great fete; and it was his own guiding taste which had given character to the masqueraders. Be sure they were grotesque. There were much glare and glitter and piquancy and phantasm—much of what has been since seen in 'Hernani.' There were arabesque figures with unsuited limbs and appointments. There were delirious fancies such as the madman fashions. There was much of the beautiful, much of the wanton, much of the bizarre, something of the terrible, and not a little of that which might have excited disgust. To and fro in the seven chambers there stalked, in fact, a multitude of dreams. And these— the dreams—writhed in and about, taking hue from the rooms, and causing the wild music of the orchestra to seem as the echo of their steps. And, anon, there strikes the ebony clock which stands in the hall of the velvet. And then, for a moment, all is still, and all is silent save the voice of the clock. The dreams are stiff-frozen as they stand. But the echoes of the chime die away—they have endured but an instant—and a light, half-subdued laughter floats after them as they depart. And now again the music swells, and the dreams live, and writhe to and fro more merrily than ever, taking hue from the many-tinted windows through which stream the rays from the tripods. But to the chamber which lies most westwardly of the seven, there are now none of the maskers who venture; for the night is waning away; and there flows a ruddier light through the blood-colored panes; and the blackness of the sable drapery appals; and to him whose foot falls upon the sable carpet, there comes from the near clock of ebony a muffled peal more solemnly emphatic than any which reaches their ears who indulge in the more remote gaieties of the other apartments.

But these other apartments were densely crowded, and in them beat feverishly the heart of life. And the revel went whirlingly on, until at length there commenced the sounding of midnight upon the clock. And then the music ceased, as I have told; and the evolutions of the waltzers were quieted; and there was an uneasy cessation of all things as before. But now there were twelve strokes to be sounded by the bell of the clock; and thus it happened, perhaps, that more of thought crept, with more of time, into the meditations of the thoughtful among those who revelled. And thus, too, it happened, perhaps, that before the last echoes of the last chime had utterly sunk into silence, there were many individuals in the crowd who had found leisure to become aware of the presence of a masked figure which had arrested the attention of no single individual before. And the rumor of this new presence having spread itself whisperingly around, there arose at length from the whole company a buzz, or murmur, expressive of disapprobation and surprise—then, finally, of terror, of horror, and of disgust.

In an assembly of phantasms such as I have painted, it may well be supposed that no ordinary appearance could have excited such sensation. In truth the masquerade license of the night was nearly unlimited; but the figure in question had out-Heroded Herod, and gone beyond the bounds of even the prince's indefinite decorum. There are chords in the hearts of the most reckless which cannot be touched without emotion. Even with the utterly lost, to whom life and death are equally jests, there are matters of which no jest can be made. The whole company, indeed, seemed now deeply to feel that in the costume and bearing of the stranger neither wit nor propriety existed. The figure was tall and gaunt, and shrouded from head to foot in the habiliments of the grave. The mask which concealed the visage was made so nearly to resemble the countenance of a stiffened corpse that the closest scrutiny must have had difficulty in detecting the cheat. And yet all this might have been endured, if not approved, by the mad revellers around. But the mummer had gone so far as to assume the type of the Red Death. His vesture was dabbled in blood—and his broad brow, with all the features of the face, was besprinkled with the scarlet horror.

When the eyes of Prince Prospero fell upon this spectral image (which with a slow and solemn movement, as if more fully to sustain its role, stalked to and fro among the waltzers) he was seen to be convulsed, in the first moment with a strong shudder either of terror or distaste; but, in the next, his brow reddened with rage.

"Who dares?" he demanded hoarsely of the courtiers who stood near him—"who dares insult us with this blasphemous mockery? Seize him and unmask him—that we may know whom we have to hang at sunrise, from the battlements!"

It was in the eastern or blue chamber in which stood the Prince Prospero as he uttered these words. They rang throughout the seven rooms loudly and clearly—for the prince was a bold and robust man, and the music had become hushed at the waving of his hand.

It was in the blue room where stood the prince, with a group of pale courtiers by his side. At first, as he spoke, there was a slight rushing movement of this group in the direction of the intruder, who at the moment was also near at hand, and now, with deliberate and stately step, made closer approach to the speaker. But from a certain nameless awe with which the mad assumptions of the mummer had inspired the whole party, there were found none who put forth hand to seize him; so that, unimpeded, he passed within a yard of the prince's person; and, while the vast assembly, as if with one impulse, shrank from the centres of the rooms to the walls, he made his way uninterruptedly, but with the same solemn and measured step which had distinguished him from the first, through the blue chamber to the purple—through the purple to the green—through the green to the orange—through this again to the white—and even thence to the violet, ere a decided movement had been made to arrest him. It was then, however, that the Prince Prospero, maddening with rage and the shame of his own momentary cowardice, rushed hurriedly through the six chambers, while none followed him on account of a deadly terror that had seized upon all. He bore aloft a drawn dagger, and had approached, in rapid impetuosity, to within three or four feet of the retreating figure, when the latter, having attained the extremity of the velvet apartment, turned suddenly and confronted his pursuer. There was a sharp cry—and the dagger dropped gleaming upon the sable carpet, upon which, instantly afterwards, fell prostrate in death the Prince Prospero. Then, summoning the wild courage of despair, a throng of the revellers at once threw themselves into the black apartment, and, seizing the mummer, whose tall figure stood erect and motionless within the shadow of the ebony clock, gasped in unutterable horror at finding the grave-cerements and corpse-like mask which they handled with so violent a rudeness, untenanted by any tangible form.

And now was acknowledged the presence of the Red Death. He had come like a thief in the night. And one by one dropped the revellers in the blood-bedewed halls of their revel, and died each in the despairing posture of his fall. And the life of the ebony clock went out with that of the last of the gay. And the flames of the tripods expired. And Darkness and Decay and the Red Death held illimitable dominion over all.

24

The Imp of the Perverse

In the consideration of the faculties and impulses—of the prima mobilia of the human soul, the phrenologists have failed to make room for a propensity which, although obviously existing as a radical, primitive, irreducible sentiment, has been equally overlooked by all the moralists who have preceded them. In the pure arrogance of the reason, we have all overlooked it. We have suffered its existence to escape our senses, solely through want of belief—of faith; —whether it be faith in Revelation, or faith in the Kabbala. The idea of it has never occurred to us, simply because of its supererogation. We saw no need of the impulse— for the propensity. We could not perceive its necessity. We could not understand, that is to say, we could not have understood, had the notion of this primum mobile ever obtruded itself; —we could not have understood in what manner it might be made to further the objects of humanity, either temporal or eternal. It cannot be denied that phrenology and, in great measure, all metaphysicianism have been concocted a priori. The intellectual or logical man, rather than the understanding or observant man, set himself to imagine designs—to dictate purposes to God. Having thus fathomed, to his satisfaction, the intentions of Jehovah, out of these intentions he built his innumerable systems of mind. In the matter of phrenology, for example, we first determined, naturally enough, that it was the design of the Deity that man should eat. We then assigned to man an organ of alimentiveness, and this organ is the scourge with which the Deity compels man, will-I nill-I, into eating. Secondly, having settled it to be God's will that man should continue his species, we discovered an organ of amativeness, forthwith. And so with combativeness, with ideality, with causality, with constructiveness, —so, in short, with every organ, whether representing a propensity, a moral sentiment, or a faculty of the pure intellect. And in these arrangements of the Principia of human action, the Spurzheimites, whether right or wrong, in part, or upon the whole, have but followed, in principle, the footsteps of their predecessors: deducing and establishing every thing from the preconceived destiny of man, and upon the ground of the objects of his Creator.

It would have been wiser, it would have been safer, to classify (if classify we must) upon the basis of what man usually or occasionally did, and was always occasionally doing, rather than upon the basis of what we took it for granted the Deity intended him to do. If we cannot comprehend God in his visible works, how then in his inconceivable thoughts, that call the works into being? If we cannot understand him in his objective creatures, how then in his substantive moods and phases of creation?

Induction, a posteriori, would have brought phrenology to admit, as an innate and primitive principle of human action, a paradoxical something, which we may call perverseness, for want of a more characteristic term. In the sense I intend, it is, in fact, a mobile without motive, a motive not motivirt. Through its promptings we act without comprehensible object; or, if this shall be understood as a contradiction in terms, we may so far modify the proposition as to say, that through its promptings we act, for the reason that we should not. In theory, no reason can be more unreasonable, but, in fact, there is none more strong. With certain minds, under certain conditions, it becomes absolutely irresistible. I am not more certain that I breathe, than that the assurance of the wrong or error of any action is often the one unconquerable force which impels us, and alone impels us to its prosecution. Nor will this overwhelming tendency to do wrong for the wrong's sake, admit of analysis, or resolution into ulterior elements. It is a radical, a primitive impulse-elementary. It will be said, I am aware, that when we persist in acts because we feel we should not persist in them, our conduct is but a modification of that which ordinarily springs from the combativeness of phrenology. But a glance will show the fallacy of this idea. The phrenological combativeness has for its essence, the necessity of self-defence. It is our safeguard against injury. Its principle regards our well-being; and thus the desire to be well is excited simultaneously with its development. It follows, that the desire to be well must be excited simultaneously with any principle which shall be merely a modification of combativeness, but in the case of that something which I term perverseness, the desire to be well is not only not aroused, but a strongly antagonistical sentiment exists.

An appeal to one's own heart is, after all, the best reply to the sophistry just noticed. No one who trustingly consults and thoroughly questions his own soul, will be disposed to deny the entire radicalness of the propensity in question. It is not more incomprehensible than distinctive. There lives no man who at some period has not been tormented, for example, by an earnest desire to tantalize a listener by circumlocution. The speaker is aware that he displeases; he has every intention to please, he is usually curt, precise, and clear, the most laconic and luminous language is struggling for utterance upon his tongue, it is only with difficulty that he restrains himself from giving it flow; he dreads and deprecates the anger of him whom he addresses; yet, the thought strikes him, that by certain involutions and parentheses this anger may be engendered. That single thought is enough. The impulse increases to a wish, the wish to a desire, the desire to an uncontrollable longing, and the longing (to the deep regret and mortification of the speaker, and in defiance of all consequences) is indulged.

We have a task before us which must be speedily performed. We know that it will be ruinous to make delay. The most important crisis of our life calls, trumpet-tongued, for immediate energy and action. We glow, we are consumed with eagerness to commence the work, with the anticipation of whose glorious result our whole souls are on fire. It must, it shall be undertaken to-day, and yet we put it off until to-morrow, and why? There is no answer, except that we feel perverse, using the word with no comprehension of the principle. To-morrow arrives, and with it a more impatient anxiety to do our duty, but with this very increase of anxiety arrives, also, a nameless, a positively fearful, because unfathomable, craving for delay. This craving gathers strength as the moments fly. The last hour for action is at hand. We tremble with the violence of the conflict within us, —of the definite with the indefinite—of the substance with the shadow. But, if the contest have proceeded thus far, it is the shadow which prevails, —we struggle in vain. The clock strikes, and is the knell of our welfare. At the same time, it is the chanticleer—note to the ghost that has so long overawed us. It flies—it disappears—we are free. The old energy returns. We will labor now. Alas, it is too late!

We stand upon the brink of a precipice. We peer into the abyss—we grow sick and dizzy. Our first impulse is to shrink from the danger. Unaccountably we remain. By slow degrees our sickness and dizziness and horror become merged in a cloud of unnamable feeling. By gradations, still more imperceptible, this cloud assumes shape, as did the vapor from the bottle out of which arose the genius in the Arabian Nights. But out of this our cloud upon the precipice's edge, there grows into palpability, a shape, far more terrible than any genius or any demon of a tale, and yet it is but a thought, although a fearful one, and one which chills the very marrow of our bones with the fierceness of the delight of its horror. It is merely the idea of what would be our sensations during the sweeping precipitancy of a fall from such a height. And this fall—this rushing annihilation—for the very reason that it involves that one most ghastly and loathsome of all the most ghastly and loathsome images of death and suffering which have ever presented themselves to our imagination—for this very cause do we now the most vividly desire it. And because our reason violently deters us from the brink, therefore do we the most impetuously approach it. There is no passion in nature so demoniacally impatient, as that of him who, shuddering upon the edge of a precipice, thus meditates a Plunge. To indulge, for a moment, in any attempt at thought, is to be inevitably lost; for reflection but urges us to forbear, and therefore it is, I say, that we cannot. If there be no friendly arm to check us, or if we fail in a sudden effort to prostrate ourselves backward from the abyss, we plunge, and are destroyed.

Examine these similar actions as we will, we shall find them resulting solely from the spirit of the Perverse. We perpetrate them because we feel that we should not. Beyond or behind this there is no intelligible principle; and we might, indeed, deem this perverseness a direct instigation of the Arch-Fiend, were it not occasionally known to operate in furtherance of good.

I have said thus much, that in some measure I may answer your question, that I may explain to you why I am here, that I may assign to you something that shall have at least the faint aspect of a cause for my wearing these fetters, and for my tenanting this cell of the condemned. Had I not been thus prolix, you might either have misunderstood me altogether, or, with the rabble, have fancied me mad. As it is, you will easily perceive that I am one of the many uncounted victims of the Imp of the Perverse.

It is impossible that any deed could have been wrought with a more thorough deliberation. For weeks, for months, I pondered upon the means of the murder. I rejected a thousand schemes, because their accomplishment involved a chance of detection. At length, in reading some French Memoirs, I found an account of a nearly fatal illness that occurred to Madame Pilau, through the agency of a candle accidentally poisoned. The idea struck my fancy at once. I knew my victim's habit of reading in bed. I knew, too, that his apartment was narrow and ill-ventilated. But I need not vex you with impertinent details. I need not describe the easy artifices by which I substituted, in his bed-room candle-stand, a wax-light of my own making for the one which I there found. The next morning he was discovered dead in his bed, and the Coroner's verdict was— "Death by the visitation of God."

Having inherited his estate, all went well with me for years. The idea of detection never once entered my brain. Of the remains of the fatal taper I had myself carefully disposed. I had left no shadow of a clew by which it would be possible to convict, or even to suspect me of the crime. It is inconceivable how rich a sentiment of satisfaction arose in my bosom as I reflected upon my absolute security. For a very long period of time I was accustomed to revel in this sentiment. It afforded me more real delight than all the mere worldly advantages accruing from my sin. But there arrived at length an epoch, from which the pleasurable feeling grew, by scarcely perceptible gradations, into a haunting and harassing thought. It harassed because it haunted. I could scarcely get rid of it for an instant. It is quite a common thing to be thus annoyed with the ringing in our ears, or rather in our memories, of the burthen of some ordinary song, or some unimpressive snatches from an opera. Nor will we be the less tormented if the song in itself be good, or the opera air meritorious. In this manner, at last, I would perpetually catch myself pondering upon my security, and repeating, in a low undertone, the phrase, "I am safe."

One day, whilst sauntering along the streets, I arrested myself in the act of murmuring, half aloud, these customary syllables. In a fit of petulance, I remodelled them thus; "I am safe—I am safe—yes—if I be not fool enough to make open confession!"

No sooner had I spoken these words, than I felt an icy chill creep to my heart. I had had some experience in these fits of perversity, (whose nature I have been at some trouble to explain), and I remembered well that in no instance I had successfully resisted their attacks. And now my own casual self-suggestion that I might possibly be fool enough to confess the murder of which I had been guilty, confronted me, as if the very ghost of him whom I had murdered—and beckoned me on to death.

At first, I made an effort to shake off this nightmare of the soul. I walked vigorously—faster—still faster—at length I ran. I felt a maddening desire to shriek aloud. Every succeeding wave of thought overwhelmed me with new terror, for, alas! I well, too well understood that to think, in my situation, was to be lost. I still quickened my pace. I bounded like a madman through the crowded thoroughfares. At length, the populace took the alarm, and pursued me. I felt then the consummation of my fate. Could I have torn out my tongue, I would have done it, but a rough voice resounded in my ears—a rougher grasp seized me by the shoulder. I turned—I gasped for breath. For a moment I experienced all the pangs of suffocation; I became blind, and deaf, and giddy; and then some invisible fiend, I thought, struck me with his broad palm upon the back. The long imprisoned secret burst forth from my soul.

They say that I spoke with a distinct enunciation, but with marked emphasis and passionate hurry, as if in dread of interruption before concluding the brief, but pregnant sentences that consigned me to the hangman and to hell.

Having related all that was necessary for the fullest judicial conviction, I fell prostrate in a swoon.

But why shall I say more? To-day I wear these chains, and am here! To-morrow I shall be fetterless!—but where?

25

The Island of the Fay

Nullus enim locus sine genio est.—Servius.

"LA MUSIQUE," says Marmontel, in those 'Contes Moraux' which in all our translations, we have insisted upon calling 'Moral Tales', as if in mockery of their spirit—"la musique est le seul des talents qui jouissent de lui-meme; tous les autres veulent des temoins." He here confounds the pleasure derivable from sweet sounds with the capacity for creating them. No more than any other talent, is that for music susceptible of complete enjoyment, where there is no second party to appreciate its exercise. And it is only in common with other talents that it produces effects which may be fully enjoyed in solitude. The idea which the raconteur has either failed to entertain clearly, or has sacrificed in its expression to his national love of point, is, doubtless, the very tenable one that the higher order of music is the most thoroughly estimated when we are exclusively alone. The proposition, in this form, will be admitted at once by those who love the lyre for its own sake, and for its spiritual uses. But there is one pleasure still within the reach of fallen mortality and perhaps only one—which owes even more than does music to the accessory sentiment of seclusion. I mean the happiness experienced in the contemplation of natural

131

scenery. In truth, the man who would behold aright the glory of God upon earth must in solitude behold that glory. To me, at least, the presence—not of human life only, but of life in any other form than that of the green things which grow upon the soil and are voiceless—is a stain upon the landscape—is at war with the genius of the scene. I love, indeed, to regard the dark valleys, and the gray rocks, and the waters that silently smile, and the forests that sigh in uneasy slumbers, and the proud watchful mountains that look down upon all, —I love to regard these as themselves but the colossal members of one vast animate and sentient whole—a whole whose form (that of the sphere) is the most perfect and most inclusive of all; whose path is among associate planets; whose meek handmaiden is the moon, whose mediate sovereign is the sun; whose life is eternity, whose thought is that of a God; whose enjoyment is knowledge; whose destinies are lost in immensity, whose cognizance of ourselves is akin with our own cognizance of the animalculae which infest the brain—a being which we, in consequence, regard as purely inanimate and material much in the same manner as these animalculae must thus regard us.

Our telescopes and our mathematical investigations assure us on every hand—notwithstanding the cant of the more ignorant of the priesthood—that space, and therefore that bulk, is an important consideration in the eyes of the Almighty. The cycles in which the stars move are those best adapted for the evolution, without collision, of the greatest possible number of bodies. The forms of those bodies are accurately such as, within a given surface, to include the greatest possible amount of matter; —while the surfaces themselves are so disposed as to accommodate a denser population than could be accommodated on the same surfaces otherwise arranged. Nor is it any argument against bulk being an object with God, that space itself is infinite; for there may be an infinity of matter to fill it. And since we see clearly that the endowment of matter with vitality is a principle—indeed, as far as our judgments extend, the leading principle in the operations of Deity, —it is scarcely logical to imagine it confined to the regions of the minute, where we daily trace it, and not extending to those of the august. As we find cycle within cycle without end, —yet all revolving around one far-distant centre which is the God-head, may we not analogically suppose in the same manner, life within life, the less within the greater, and all within the Spirit Divine? In short, we are madly erring, through self-esteem, in believing man, in either his temporal or future destinies, to be of more moment in the universe than that vast 'clod of the valley' which he tills and contemns, and to which he denies a soul for no more profound reason than that he does not behold it in operation.

These fancies, and such as these, have always given to my meditations among the mountains and the forests, by the rivers and the ocean, a tinge of what the everyday world would not fail to term fantastic. My wanderings amid such scenes have been many, and far-searching, and often solitary; and the interest with which I have strayed through many a dim, deep valley, or gazed into the reflected Heaven of many a bright lake, has been an interest greatly deepened by the thought that I have strayed and gazed alone. What flippant Frenchman was it who said in allusion to the well-known work of Zimmerman, that, "la solitude est une belle chose; mais il faut quelqu'un pour vous dire que la solitude est une belle chose?" The epigram cannot be gainsayed; but the necessity is a thing that does not exist.

It was during one of my lonely journeyings, amid a far distant region of mountain locked within mountain, and sad rivers and melancholy tarn writhing or sleeping within all—that I chanced upon a certain rivulet and island. I came upon them suddenly in the leafy June, and threw myself upon the turf, beneath the branches of an unknown odorous shrub, that I might doze as I contemplated the scene. I felt that thus only should I look upon it—such was the character of phantasm which it wore.

On all sides—save to the west, where the sun was about sinking—arose the verdant walls of the forest. The little river which turned sharply in its course, and was thus immediately lost to sight, seemed to have no exit from its prison, but to be absorbed by the deep green foliage of the trees to the east—while in the opposite quarter (so it appeared to me as I lay at length and glanced upward) there poured down noiselessly and continuously into the valley, a rich golden and crimson waterfall from the sunset fountains of the sky.

About midway in the short vista which my dreamy vision took in, one small circular island, profusely verdured, reposed upon the bosom of the stream.

So blended bank and shadow there

That each seemed pendulous in air—so mirror-like was the glassy water, that it was scarcely possible to say at what point upon the slope of the emerald turf its crystal dominion began.

My position enabled me to include in a single view both the eastern and western extremities of the islet; and I observed a singularly-marked difference in their aspects. The latter was all one radiant harem of garden beauties. It glowed and blushed beneath the eyes of the slant sunlight, and fairly laughed with flowers. The grass was short, springy, sweet-scented, and Asphodel-interspersed. The trees were lithe, mirthful, erect—bright, slender, and graceful, —of eastern figure and foliage, with bark smooth, glossy, and parti-colored. There seemed a deep sense of life and joy about all; and although no airs blew from out the heavens, yet every thing had motion through the gentle sweepings to and fro of innumerable butterflies, that might have been mistaken for tulips with wings.

The other or eastern end of the isle was whelmed in the blackest shade. A sombre, yet beautiful and peaceful gloom here pervaded all things. The trees were dark in color, and mournful in form and attitude, wreathing themselves into sad, solemn, and spectral shapes that conveyed ideas of mortal sorrow and untimely death. The grass wore the deep tint of the cypress, and the heads of its blades hung droopingly, and hither and thither among it were many small unsightly hillocks, low and narrow, and not very long, that had the aspect of graves, but were not; although over and all about them the rue and the rosemary clambered. The shade of the trees fell heavily upon the water, and seemed to bury itself therein, impregnating the depths of the element with darkness. I fancied that each shadow, as the sun descended lower and lower, separated itself sullenly from the trunk that gave it birth, and thus became absorbed by the stream; while other shadows issued momently from the trees, taking the place of their predecessors thus entombed.

This idea, having once seized upon my fancy, greatly excited it, and I lost myself forthwith in revery. "If ever island were enchanted," said I to myself, "this is it. This is the haunt of the few gentle Fays who remain from the wreck of the race. Are these green tombs theirs? —or do they yield up their sweet lives as mankind yield up their own? In dying, do they not rather waste away mournfully, rendering unto God, little by little, their existence, as these trees render up shadow after shadow, exhausting their substance unto dissolution? What the wasting tree is to the water that imbibes its shade, growing thus blacker by what it preys upon, may not the life of the Fay be to the death which engulfs it?"

As I thus mused, with half-shut eyes, while the sun sank rapidly to rest, and eddying currents careered round and round the island, bearing upon their bosom large, dazzling, white flakes of the bark of the sycamore-flakes which, in their multiform positions upon the water, a quick imagination might have converted into any thing it pleased, while I thus mused, it appeared to me that the form of one of those very Fays about whom I had been pondering made its way slowly into the darkness from out the light at the western end of the island. She stood erect in a singularly fragile canoe, and urged it with the mere phantom of an oar. While within the influence of the lingering sunbeams, her attitude seemed indicative of joy— but sorrow deformed it as she passed within the shade. Slowly she glided along, and at length rounded the islet and re-entered the region of light. "The revolution which has just been made by the Fay," continued I, musingly, "is the cycle of the brief year of her life. She has floated through her winter and through her summer. She is a year nearer unto Death; for I did not fail to see that, as she came into the shade, her shadow fell from her, and was swallowed up in the dark water, making its blackness more black."

And again the boat appeared and the Fay, but about the attitude of the latter there was more of care and uncertainty and less of elastic joy. She floated again from out the light and into the gloom (which deepened momently) and again her shadow fell from her into the ebony water, and became absorbed into its blackness. And again and again she made the circuit of the island, (while the sun rushed down to his slumbers), and at each issuing into the light there was more sorrow about her person, while it grew feebler and far fainter and more indistinct, and at each passage into the gloom there fell from her a darker shade, which became whelmed in a shadow more black. But at length when the sun had utterly departed, the Fay, now the mere ghost of her former self, went disconsolately with her boat into the region of the ebony flood, and that she issued thence at all I cannot say, for darkness fell over all things and I beheld her magical figure no more.

Frank Stockton

(1834-1902)

26

The Lady or the Tiger

In the very olden time there lived a semi-barbaric king, whose ideas, though somewhat polished and sharpened by the progressiveness of distant Latin neighbors, were still large, florid, and untrammeled, as became the half of him which was barbaric. He was a man of exuberant fancy, and, withal, of an authority so irresistible that, at his will, he turned his varied fancies into facts. He was greatly given to self-communing, and, when he and himself agreed upon anything, the thing was done. When every member of his domestic and political systems moved smoothly in its appointed course, his nature was bland and genial; but, whenever there was a little hitch, and some of his orbs got out of their orbits, he was blander and more genial still, for nothing pleased him so much as to make the crooked straight and crush down uneven places.

Among the borrowed notions by which his barbarism had become semified was that of the public arena, in which, by exhibitions of manly and beastly valor, the minds of his subjects were refined and cultured.

But even here the exuberant and barbaric fancy asserted itself. The arena of the king was built, not to give the people an opportunity of hearing the rhapsodies of dying gladiators, nor to enable them to view the inevitable conclusion of a conflict between religious opinions and hungry jaws, but for purposes far better adapted to widen and develop the mental energies of the people. This vast amphitheater, with its encircling galleries, its mysterious vaults, and its unseen passages, was an agent of poetic justice, in which crime was punished, or virtue rewarded, by the decrees of an impartial and incorruptible chance.

When a subject was accused of a crime of sufficient importance to interest the king, public notice was given that on an appointed day the fate of the accused person would be decided in the king's arena, a structure which well deserved its name, for, although its form and plan were borrowed from afar, its purpose emanated solely from the brain of this man, who, every barleycorn a king, knew no tradition to which he owed more allegiance than pleased his fancy, and who ingrafted on every adopted form of human thought and action the rich growth of his barbaric idealism.

When all the people had assembled in the galleries, and the king, surrounded by his court, sat high up on his throne of royal state on one side of the arena, he gave a signal, a door beneath him opened, and the accused subject stepped out into the amphitheater. Directly opposite him, on the other side of the enclosed space, were two doors, exactly alike and side by side. It was the duty and the privilege of the person on trial to walk directly to these doors and open one of them. He could open either door he pleased; he was subject to no guidance or influence but that of the aforementioned impartial and incorruptible chance. If he opened the one, there came out of it a hungry tiger, the fiercest and most cruel that could be procured, which immediately sprang upon him and tore him to pieces as a punishment for his guilt. The moment that the case of the criminal was thus decided, doleful iron bells were clanged, great wails went up from the hired mourners posted on the outer rim of the arena, and the vast audience, with bowed heads and downcast hearts, wended slowly their homeward way, mourning greatly that one so young and fair, or so old and respected, should have merited so dire a fate.

But, if the accused person opened the other door, there came forth from it a lady, the most suitable to his years and station that his majesty could select among his fair subjects, and to this lady he was immediately married, as a reward of his innocence. It mattered not that he might already possess a wife and family, or that his affections might be engaged upon an object of his own selection; the king allowed no such subordinate arrangements to interfere with his great scheme of retribution and reward. The exercises, as in the other instance, took place immediately, and in the arena. Another door opened beneath the king, and a priest, followed by a band of choristers, and dancing maidens blowing joyous airs on golden horns and treading an epithalamic measure, advanced to where the pair stood, side by side, and the wedding was promptly and cheerily solemnized. Then the gay brass bells rang forth their merry peals, the people shouted glad hurrahs, and the innocent man, preceded by children strewing flowers on his path, led his bride to his home.

This was the king's semi-barbaric method of administering justice. Its perfect fairness is obvious. The criminal could not know out of which door would come the lady; he opened either he pleased, without having the slightest idea whether, in the next instant, he was to be devoured or married. On some occasions the tiger came out of one door, and on some out of the other. The decisions of this tribunal were not only fair, they were positively determinate: the accused person was instantly punished if he found himself guilty, and, if innocent, he was rewarded on the spot, whether he liked it or not. There was no escape from the judgments of the king's arena.

The institution was a very popular one. When the people gathered together on one of the great trial days, they never knew whether they were to witness a bloody slaughter or a hilarious wedding. This element of uncertainty lent an interest to the occasion which it could not otherwise have attained. Thus, the masses were entertained and pleased, and the thinking part of the community could bring no charge of unfairness against this plan, for did not the accused person have the whole matter in his own hands?

This semi-barbaric king had a daughter as blooming as his most florid fancies, and with a soul as fervent and imperious as his own. As is usual in such cases, she was the apple of his eye, and was loved by him above all humanity. Among his courtiers was a young man of that fineness of blood and lowness of station common to the conventional heroes of romance who love royal maidens. This royal maiden was well satisfied with her lover, for he was handsome and brave to a degree unsurpassed in all this kingdom, and she loved him with an ardor that had enough of barbarism in it to make it exceedingly warm and strong. This love affair moved on happily for many months, until one day the king happened to discover its existence. He did not hesitate nor waver in regard to his duty in the premises. The youth was immediately cast into prison, and a day was appointed for his trial in the king's arena. This, of course, was an especially important occasion, and his majesty, as well as all the people, was greatly interested in the workings and development of this trial. Never before had such a case occurred; never before had a subject dared to love the daughter of the king. In after years such things became commonplace enough, but then they were in no slight degree novel and startling.

The tiger-cages of the kingdom were searched for the most savage and relentless beasts, from which the fiercest monster might be selected for the arena; and the ranks of maiden youth and beauty throughout the land were carefully surveyed by competent judges in order that the young man might have a fitting bride in case fate did not determine for him a different destiny. Of course, everybody knew that the deed with which the accused was charged had been done. He had loved the princess, and neither he, she, nor any one else, thought of denying the fact; but the king would not think of allowing any fact of this kind to interfere with the workings of the tribunal, in which he took such great delight and satisfaction. No matter how the affair turned out, the youth would be disposed of, and the king would take an aesthetic pleasure in watching the course of events, which would determine whether or not the young man had done wrong in allowing himself to love the princess.

The appointed day arrived. From far and near the people gathered, and thronged the great galleries of the arena, and crowds, unable to gain admittance, massed themselves against its outside walls. The king and his court were in their places, opposite the twin doors, those fateful portals, so terrible in their similarity.

All was ready. The signal was given. A door beneath the royal party opened, and the lover of the princess walked into the arena. Tall, beautiful, fair, his appearance was greeted with a low hum of admiration and anxiety. Half the audience had not known so grand a youth had lived among them. No wonder the princess loved him! What a terrible thing for him to be there!

As the youth advanced into the arena he turned, as the custom was, to bow to the king, but he did not think at all of that royal personage. His eyes were fixed upon the princess, who sat to the right of her father. Had it not been for the moiety of barbarism in her nature it is probable that lady would not have been there, but her intense and fervid soul would not allow her to be absent on an occasion in which she was so terribly interested. From the moment that the decree had gone forth that her lover should decide his fate in the king's arena, she had thought of nothing, night or day, but this great event and the various subjects connected with it. Possessed of more power, influence, and force of character than any one who had ever before been interested in such a case, she had done what no other person had done—she had possessed herself of the secret of the doors. She knew in which of the two rooms, that lay behind those doors, stood the cage of the tiger, with its open front, and in which waited the lady. Through these thick doors, heavily curtained with skins on the inside, it was impossible that any noise or suggestion should come from within to the person who should approach to raise the latch of one of them. But gold, and the power of a woman's will, had brought the secret to the princess.

And not only did she know in which room stood the lady ready to emerge, all blushing and radiant, should her door be opened, but she knew who the lady was. It was one of the fairest and loveliest of the damsels of the court who had been selected as the reward of the accused youth, should he be proved innocent of the crime of aspiring to one so far above him; and the princess hated her. Often had she seen, or imagined that she had seen, this fair creature throwing glances of admiration upon the person of her lover, and sometimes she thought these glances were perceived, and even returned. Now and then she had seen them talking together; it was but for a moment or two, but much can be said in a brief space; it may have been on most unimportant topics, but how could she know that? The girl was lovely, but she had dared to raise her eyes to the loved one of the princess; and, with all the intensity of the savage blood transmitted to her through long lines of wholly barbaric ancestors, she hated the woman who blushed and trembled behind that silent door.

When her lover turned and looked at her, and his eye met hers as she sat there, paler and whiter than any one in the vast ocean of anxious faces about her, he saw, by that power of quick perception which is given to those whose souls are one, that she knew behind which door crouched the tiger, and behind which stood the lady. He had expected her to know it. He understood her nature, and his soul was assured that she would never rest until she had made plain to herself this thing, hidden to all other lookers-on, even to the king. The only hope for the youth in which there was any element of certainty was based upon the success of the princess in discovering this mystery; and the moment he looked upon her, he saw she had succeeded, as in his soul he knew she would succeed.

Then it was that his quick and anxious glance asked the question: "Which?" It was as plain to her as if he shouted it from where he stood. There was not an instant to be lost. The question was asked in a flash; it must be answered in another.

Her right arm lay on the cushioned parapet before her. She raised her hand, and made a slight, quick movement toward the right. No one but her lover saw her. Every eye but his was fixed on the man in the arena.

He turned, and with a firm and rapid step he walked across the empty space. Every heart stopped beating, every breath was held, every eye was fixed immovably upon that man. Without the slightest hesitation, he went to the door on the right, and opened it.

Now, the point of the story is this: Did the tiger come out of that door, or did the lady?

The more we reflect upon this question, the harder it is to answer.

144

It involves a study of the human heart which leads us through devious mazes of passion, out of which it is difficult to find our way. Think of it, fair reader, not as if the decision of the question depended upon yourself, but upon that hot-blooded, semi-barbaric princess, her soul at a white heat beneath the combined fires of despair and jealousy. She had lost him, but who should have him?

How often, in her waking hours and in her dreams, had she started in wild horror, and covered her face with her hands as she thought of her lover opening the door on the other side of which waited the cruel fangs of the tiger!

But how much oftener had she seen him at the other door! How in her grievous reveries had she gnashed her teeth, and torn her hair, when she saw his start of rapturous delight as he opened the door of the lady! How her soul had burned in agony when she had seen him rush to meet that woman, with her flushing cheek and sparkling eye of triumph; when she had seen him lead her forth, his whole frame kindled with the joy of recovered life; when she had heard the glad shouts from the multitude, and the wild ringing of the happy bells; when she had seen the priest, with his joyous followers, advance to the couple, and make them man and wife before her very eyes; and when she had seen them walk away together upon their path of flowers, followed by the tremendous shouts of the hilarious multitude, in which her one despairing shriek was lost and drowned!

Would it not be better for him to die at once, and go to wait for her in the blessed regions of semi-barbaric futurity?

And yet, that awful tiger, those shrieks, that blood!

Her decision had been indicated in an instant, but it had been made after days and nights of anguished deliberation. She had known she would be asked, she had decided what she would answer, and, without the slightest hesitation, she had moved her hand to the right.

The question of her decision is one not to be lightly considered, and it is not for me to presume to set myself up as the one person able to answer it. And so I leave it with all of you: Which came out of the opened door—the lady, or the tiger?

Fyodor Dostoevsky

(1821-1881)

27

The Heavenly Christmas Tree

I am a novelist, and I suppose I have made up this story. I write 'I suppose,' though I know for a fact that I have made it up, but yet I keep fancying that it must have happened somewhere at some time, that it must have happened on Christmas Eve in some great town in a time of terrible frost.

I have a vision of a boy, a little boy, six years old or even younger. This boy woke up that morning in a cold damp cellar. He was dressed in a sort of little dressing-gown and was shivering with cold. There was a cloud of white steam from his breath, and sitting on a box in the corner, he blew the steam out of his mouth and amused himself in his dullness watching it float away. But he was terribly hungry. Several times that morning he went up to the plank bed where his sick mother was lying on a mattress as thin as a pancake, with some sort of bundle under her head for a pillow. How had she come here? She must have come with her boy from some other town and suddenly fallen ill. The landlady who let the 'corners' had been taken two days before to the police station, the lodgers were out and about as the holiday was so near, and the only one left had been lying for the last twenty-four hours dead drunk, not having waited for Christmas. In another corner of the room a wretched old woman of eighty, who had once been a children's nurse but was now left to die friendless, was moaning and groaning with rheumatism, scolding and grumbling at the boy so that he was afraid to go near her corner. He had got a drink of water in the outer room, but could not find a crust anywhere, and had been on the point of waking his mother a dozen times. He felt frightened at last in the darkness: it had long been dusk, but no light was kindled. Touching his mother's face, he was surprised that she did not move at all, and that she was as cold as the wall. 'It is very cold here,' he thought. He stood a little, unconsciously letting his hands rest on the dead woman's shoulders, then he breathed on his fingers to warm them, and then quietly fumbling for his cap on the bed, he went out of the cellar. He would have gone earlier, but was afraid of the big dog which had been howling all day at the neighbour's door at the top of the stairs. But the dog was not there now, and he went out into the street.

Mercy on us, what a town! He had never seen anything like it before. In the town from which he had come, it was always such black darkness at night. There was one lamp for the whole street, the little, low-pitched, wooden houses were closed up with shutters, there was no one to be seen in the street after dusk, all the people shut themselves up in their houses, and there was nothing but the howling of packs of dogs, hundreds and thousands of them barking and howling all night. But there it was so warm and he was given food, while here—oh, dear, if he only had something to eat! And what a noise and rattle here, what light and what people, horses and carriages, and what a frost! The frozen steam hung in clouds over the horses, over their warmly breathing mouths; their hoofs clanged against the stones through the powdery snow, and every one pushed so, and—oh, dear, how he longed for some morsel to eat, and how wretched he suddenly felt. A policeman walked by and turned away to avoid seeing the boy.

Here was another street—oh, what a wide one, here he would be run over for certain; how everyone was shouting, racing and driving along, and the light, the light! And what was this? A huge glass window, and through the window a tree reaching up to the ceiling; it was a fir tree, and on it were ever so many lights, gold papers and apples and little dolls and horses; and there were children clean and dressed in their best running about the room, laughing and playing and eating and drinking something. And then a little girl began dancing with one of the boys, what a pretty little girl! And he could hear the music through the window. The boy looked and wondered and laughed, though his toes were aching with the cold and his fingers were red and stiff so that it hurt him to move them. And all at once the boy remembered how his toes and fingers hurt him, and began crying, and ran on; and again through another window-pane he saw another Christmas tree, and on a table cakes of all sorts—almond cakes, red cakes and yellow cakes, and three grand young ladies were sitting there, and they gave the cakes to any one who went up to them, and the door kept opening, lots of gentlemen and ladies went in from the street. The boy crept up, suddenly opened the door and went in. Oh, how they shouted at him and waved him back! One lady went up to him hurriedly and slipped a kopeck into his hand, and with her own hands opened the door into the street for him! How frightened he was. And the kopeck rolled away and clinked upon the steps; he could not bend his red fingers to hold it tight. The boy ran away and went on, where he did not know. He was ready to cry again but he was afraid, and ran on and on and blew his fingers. And he was miserable because he felt suddenly so lonely and terrified, and all at once, mercy on us! What was this again? People were standing in a crowd admiring. Behind a glass window there were three little dolls, dressed in red and green dresses, and exactly, exactly as though they were alive. One was a little old man sitting and playing a big violin, the two others were standing close by and playing little violins and nodding in time, and looking at one another, and their lips moved, they were speaking, actually speaking, only one couldn't hear through the glass. And at first the boy thought they were alive, and when he grasped that they were dolls he laughed. He had never seen such dolls before, and had no idea there were such dolls! And he wanted to cry, but he felt amused, amused by the dolls. All at once he fancied that some one caught at his smock behind: a wicked big boy was standing beside him and suddenly hit him on the head, snatched off his cap and

149

tripped him up. The boy fell down on the ground, at once there was a shout, he was numb with fright, he jumped up and ran away. He ran, and not knowing where he was going, ran in at the gate of some one's courtyard, and sat down behind a stack of wood: "They won't find me here, besides it's dark!"

He sat huddled up and was breathless from fright, and all at once, quite suddenly, he felt so happy: his hands and feet suddenly left off aching and grew so warm, as warm as though he were on a stove; then he shivered all over, then he gave a start, why, he must have been asleep. How nice to have a sleep here! "I'll sit here a little and go and look at the dolls again," said the boy, and smiled thinking of them. "Just as though they were alive! . . ." And suddenly he heard his mother singing over him. "Mammy, I am asleep; how nice it is to sleep here!"

"Come to my Christmas tree, little one," a soft voice suddenly whispered over his head.

He thought that this was still his mother, but no, it was not she. Who it was calling him, he could not see, but some one bent over and embraced him in the darkness; and he stretched out his hands to him, and . . . and all at once—oh, what a bright light! Oh, what a Christmas tree! And yet it was not a fir tree, he had never seen a tree like that! Where was he now? Everything was bright and shining, and all round him were dolls; but no, they were not dolls, they were little boys and girls, only so bright and shining. They all came flying round him, they all kissed him, took him and carried him along with them, and he was flying himself, and he saw that his mother was looking at him and laughing joyfully. "Mammy, Mammy; oh, how nice it is here, Mammy!" And again he kissed the children and wanted to tell them at once of those dolls in the shop window. "Who are you, boys? Who are you, girls?" he asked, laughing and admiring them.

"This is Christ's Christmas tree," they answered. "Christ always has a Christmas tree on this day, for the little children who have no tree of their own . . ." And he found out that all these little boys and girls were children just like himself; that some had been frozen in the baskets in which they had as babies been laid on the doorsteps of well-to-do Petersburg people, others had been boarded out with Finnish women by the Foundling and had been suffocated, others had died at their starved mother's breasts (in the Samara famine), others had died in the third-class railway carriages from the foul air; and yet they were all here, they were all like angels about Christ, and He was in the midst of them and held out His hands to them and blessed them and their sinful mothers . . . And the mothers of these children stood on one side weeping; each one knew her boy or girl, and the children flew up to them and kissed them and wiped away their tears with their little hands, and begged them not to weep because they were so happy.

And down below in the morning the porter found the little dead body of the frozen child on the woodstack; they sought out his mother too . . . She had died before him. They met before the Lord God in heaven.

Why have I made up such a story, so out of keeping with an ordinary diary, and a writer's above all? And I promised two stories dealing with real events! But that is just it, I keep fancying that all this may have happened really—that is, what took place in the cellar and on the woodstack; but as for Christ's Christmas tree, I cannot tell you whether that could have happened or not.

28

The Peasant Marey

It was the second day in Easter week. The air was warm, the sky was blue, the sun was high, warm, bright, but my soul was very gloomy. I sauntered behind the prison barracks. I stared at the palings of the stout prison fence, counting the movers; but I had no inclination to count them, though it was my habit to do so. This was the second day of the 'holidays' in the prison; the convicts were not taken out to work, there were numbers of men drunk, loud abuse and quarrelling was springing up continually in every corner. There were hideous, disgusting songs and card-parties installed beside the platform-beds. Several of the convicts who had been sentenced by their comrades, for special violence, to be beaten till they were half dead, were lying on the platform-bed, covered with sheepskins till they should recover and come to themselves again; knives had already been drawn several times. For these two days of holiday all this had been torturing me till it made me ill. And indeed I could never endure without repulsion the noise and disorder of drunken people, and especially in this place. On these days even the prison officials did not look into the prison, made no searches, did not look for vodka, understanding that they must allow even these outcasts to enjoy themselves once a year, and that things would be even worse if they did not. At last a sudden fury flamed up in my heart.

A political prisoner called M. met me; he looked at me gloomily, his eyes flashed and his lips quivered. *"Je haïs ces brigands!"* he hissed to me through his teeth, and walked on. I returned to the prison ward, though only a quarter of an hour before I had rushed out of it, as though I were crazy, when six stalwart fellows had all together flung themselves upon the drunken Tatar Gazin to suppress him and had begun beating him; they beat him stupidly, a camel might have been killed by such blows, but they knew that this Hercules was not easy to kill, and so they beat him without uneasiness. Now on returning I noticed on the bed in the furthest corner of the room Gazin lying unconscious, almost without sign of life. He lay covered with a sheepskin, and every one walked round him, without speaking; though they confidently hoped that he would come to himself next morning, yet if luck was against him, maybe from a beating like that, the man would die. I made my way to my own place opposite the window with the iron grating, and lay on my back with my hands behind my head and my eyes shut. I liked to lie like that; a sleeping man is not molested, and meanwhile one can dream and think. But I could not dream, my heart was beating uneasily, and M.'s words, *"Je haïs ces brigands!"* were echoing in my ears. But why describe my impressions; I sometimes dream even now of those times at night, and I have no dreams more agonising. Perhaps it will be noticed that even to this day I have scarcely once spoken in print of my life in prison. *The House of the Dead* I wrote fifteen years ago in the character of an imaginary person, a criminal who had killed his wife. I may add by the way that since then, very many persons have supposed, and even now maintain, that I was sent to penal servitude for the murder of my wife.

Gradually I sank into forgetfulness and by degrees was lost in memories. During the whole course of my four years in prison I was continually recalling all my past, and seemed to live over again the whole of my life in recollection. These memories rose up of themselves, it was not often that of my own will I summoned them. It would begin from some point, some little thing, at times unnoticed, and then by degrees there would rise up a complete picture, some vivid and complete impression. I used to analyse these impressions, give new features to what had happened long ago, and best of all, I used to correct it, correct it continually, that was my great amusement. On this occasion, I suddenly for some reason remembered an unnoticed moment in my early childhood when I was only nine years old—a moment which I should have thought I had utterly forgotten; but at that time I was particularly fond of memories of my early childhood. I remembered the month of August in our country house: a dry bright day but rather cold and windy; summer was waning and soon we should have to go to Moscow to be bored all the winter over French lessons, and I was so sorry to leave the country. I walked past the threshing-floor and, going down the ravine, I went up to the dense thicket of bushes that covered the further side of the ravine as far as the copse. And I plunged right into the midst of the bushes, and heard a peasant ploughing alone on the clearing about thirty paces away. I knew that he was ploughing up the steep hill and the horse was moving with effort, and from time to time the peasant's call "come up!" floated upwards to me. I knew almost all our peasants, but I did not know which it was ploughing now, and I did not care who it was, I was absorbed in my own affairs. I was busy, too; I was breaking off switches from the nut trees to whip the frogs with. Nut sticks make such fine whips, but they do not last; while birch twigs are just the opposite. I was interested, too, in beetles and other insects; I used to collect them, some were very ornamental. I was very fond, too, of the little nimble red and yellow lizards with black spots on them, but I was afraid of snakes. Snakes, however, were much more rare than lizards. There were not many mushrooms there. To get mushrooms one had to go to the birch wood, and I was about to set off there. And there was nothing in the world that I loved so much as the wood with its mushrooms and wild berries, with its beetles and its birds, its hedgehogs and squirrels, with its damp smell of dead leaves which I loved so much, and even as I write I smell the fragrance of our birch wood: these impressions will remain for my whole life. Suddenly in the midst of the profound stillness I heard a clear and distinct shout, "Wolf!" I shrieked and, beside myself with terror, calling out at the top of my voice, ran out into the clearing and straight to the peasant who was ploughing.

It was our peasant Marey. I don't know if there is such a name, but every one called him Marey—a thick-set, rather well-grown peasant of fifty, with a good many grey hairs in his dark brown, spreading beard. I knew him, but had scarcely ever happened to speak to him till then. He stopped his horse on hearing my cry, and when, breathless, I caught with one hand at his plough and with the other at his sleeve, he saw how frightened I was.

"There is a wolf!" I cried, panting.

He flung up his head, and could not help looking round for an instant, almost believing me.

"Where is the wolf?"

"A shout . . . some one shouted: 'wolf' . . ." I faltered out.

"Nonsense, nonsense! A wolf? Why, it was your fancy! How could there be a wolf?" he muttered, reassuring me. But I was trembling all over, and still kept tight hold of his smock frock, and I must have been quite pale. He looked at me with an uneasy smile, evidently anxious and troubled over me.

"Why, you have had a fright, *aïe, aïe!*" He shook his head. "There, dear . . . Come, little one, *aïe!*"

He stretched out his hand, and all at once stroked my cheek.

"Come, come, there; Christ be with you! Cross yourself!"

But I did not cross myself. The corners of my mouth were twitching, and I think that struck him particularly. He put out his thick, black-nailed, earth-stained finger and softly touched my twitching lips.

"*Aïe*, there, there," he said to me with a slow, almost motherly smile. "Dear, dear, what is the matter? There; come, come!"

I grasped at last that there was no wolf, and that the shout that I had heard was my fancy. Yet that shout had been so clear and distinct, but such shouts (not only about wolves) I had imagined once or twice before, and I was aware of that. (These hallucinations passed away later as I grew older.)

"Well, I will go then," I said, looking at him timidly and inquiringly.

"Well, do, and I'll keep watch on you as you go. I won't let the wolf get at you," he added, still smiling at me with the same motherly expression. "Well, Christ be with you! Come, run along then," and he made the sign of the cross over me and then over himself. I walked away, looking back almost at every tenth step. Marey stood still with his mare as I walked away, and looked after me and nodded to me every time I looked round. I must own I felt a little ashamed at having let him see me so frightened, but I was still very much afraid of the wolf as I walked away, until I reached the first barn half-way up the slope of the ravine; there my fright vanished completely, and all at once our yard-dog Voltchok flew to meet me. With Voltchok I felt quite safe, and I turned round to Marey for the last time; I could not see his face distinctly, but I felt that he was still nodding and smiling affectionately to me. I waved to him; he waved back to me and started his little mare. "Come up!" I heard his call in the distance again, and the little mare pulled at the plough again.

All this I recalled all at once, I don't know why, but with extraordinary minuteness of detail. I suddenly roused myself and sat up on the platform-bed, and, I remember, found myself still smiling quietly at my memories. I brooded over them for another minute.

When I got home that day I told no one of my 'adventure' with Marey. And indeed it was hardly an adventure. And in fact I soon forgot Marey. When I met him now and then afterwards, I never even spoke to him about the wolf or anything else; and all at once now, twenty years afterwards in Siberia, I remembered this meeting with such distinctness to the smallest detail. So it must have lain hidden in my soul, though I knew nothing of it, and rose suddenly to my memory when it was wanted; I remembered the soft motherly smile of the poor serf, the way he signed me with the cross and shook his head. "There, there, you have had a fright, little one!" And I remembered particularly the thick earth-stained finger with which he softly and with timid tenderness touched my quivering lips. Of course any one would have reassured a child, but something quite different seemed to have happened in that solitary meeting; and if I had been his own son, he could not have looked at me with eyes shining with greater love. And what made him like that? He was our serf and I was his little master, after all. No one would know that he had been kind to me and reward him for it. Was he, perhaps, very fond of little children? Some people are. It was a solitary meeting in the deserted fields, and only God, perhaps, may have seen from above with what deep and humane civilised feeling, and with what delicate, almost feminine tenderness, the heart of a coarse, brutally ignorant Russian serf, who had as yet no expectation, no idea even of his freedom, may be filled. Was not this, perhaps, what Konstantin Aksakov meant when he spoke of the high degree of culture of our peasantry?

And when I got down off the bed and looked around me, I remember I suddenly felt that I could look at these unhappy creatures with quite different eyes, and that suddenly by some miracle all hatred and anger had vanished utterly from my heart. I walked about, looking into the faces that I met. That shaven peasant, branded on his face as a criminal, bawling his hoarse, drunken song, may be that very Marey; I cannot look into his heart.

I met M. again that evening. Poor fellow! he could have no memories of Russian peasants, and no other view of these people but: "*Je haïs ces brigands!*" Yes, the Polish prisoners had more to bear than I.

George Ade
(1866-1944)

29

The Fable of the Preacher Who Flew His Kite, But Not Because He Wished to Do So

A certain Preacher became wise to the Fact that he was not making a Hit with his Congregation. The Parishioners did not seem inclined to seek him out after Services and tell him he was a Pansy. He suspected that they were Rapping him on the Quiet. The Preacher knew there must be something wrong with his Talk. He had been trying to Expound in a clear and straightforward Manner, omitting Foreign Quotations, setting up for illustration of his Points such Historical Characters as were familiar to his Hearers, putting the stubby Old English words ahead of the Latin, and rather flying low along the Intellectual Plane of the Aggregation that chipped in to pay his Salary. But the Pew-Holders were not tickled. They could Understand everything he said, and they began to think he was Common.

So he studied the Situation and decided that if he wanted to Win them and make everybody believe he was a Nobby and Boss Minister he would have to hand out a little Guff. He fixed it up Good and Plenty.

On the following Sunday Morning he got up in the Lookout and read a Text that didn't mean anything, read from either Direction, and then he sized up his Flock with a Dreamy Eye and said: "We can not more adequately voice the Poetry and Mysticism of our Text than in those familiar Lines of the great Icelandic Poet, Ikon Navrojk:

"To hold is not to have—
Under the seared Firmament,
Where Chaos sweeps, and Vast Futurity
Sneers at these puny Aspirations—
There is the full Reprisal."

When the Preacher concluded this Extract from the Well-Known Icelandic Poet he paused and looked downward, breathing heavily through his Nose, like Camille in the Third Act.

A Stout Woman in the Front Row put on her Eye-Glasses and leaned forward so as not to miss Anything. A Venerable Harness Dealer over at the Right nodded his Head solemnly. He seemed to recognize the Quotation. Members of the Congregation glanced at one another as if to say: "This is certainly Hot Stuff!"

The Preacher wiped his Brow and said he had no Doubt that every one within the Sound of his Voice remembered what Quarolius had said, following the same Line of Thought. It was Quarolius who disputed the Contention of the great Persian Theologian Ramtazuk, that the Soul in its reaching out after the Unknowable was guided by the Spiritual Genesis of Motive rather than by mere Impulse of Mentality. The Preacher didn't know what all This meant, and he didn't care, but you can rest easy that the Pew-Holders were On in a minute. He talked it off in just the Way that Cyrano talks when he gets Roxane so Dizzy that she nearly falls off the Piazza.

The Parishioners bit their Lower Lips and hungered for more First-Class Language. They had paid their Money for Tall Talk and were prepared to solve any and all styles of Delivery. They held on to the Cushions and seemed to be having a Nice Time.

The Preacher quoted copiously from the Great Poet Amebius. He recited eighteen lines of Greek and then said: "How true this is!" And not a Parishioner batted an Eye.

It was Amebius whose Immortal Lines he recited in order to prove the Extreme Error of the Position assumed in the Controversy by the Famous Italian, Polenta.

He had them Going, and there wasn't a Thing to it. When he would get tired of faking Philosophy he would quote from a Celebrated Poet of Ecuador or Tasmania or some other Seaport Town. Compared with this Verse, all of which was of the same School as the Icelandic Masterpiece, the most obscure and clouded Passage in Robert Browning was like a Plate-Glass Front in a State Street Candy Store just after the Colored Boy gets through using the Chamois.

After that he became Eloquent, and began to get rid of long Boston Words that hadn't been used before that Season. He grabbed a rhetorical Roman Candle in each Hand and you couldn't see him for the Sparks.

After which he sank his Voice to a Whisper and talked about the Birds and the Flowers. Then, although there was no Cue for him to Weep, he shed a few real Tears. And there wasn't a dry Glove in the church.

After he sat down he could tell by the Scared Look of the People in Front that he had made a Ten-Strike.

Did they give him the Joyous Palm that Day? Sure!

The Stout Lady could not control her Feelings when she told how much the Sermon had helped her. The venerable Harness Dealer said he wished to indorse the Able and Scholarly Criticism of Polenta.

In fact, every one said the Sermon was Superfine and Dandy. The only thing that worried the Congregation was the Fear that if it wished to retain such a Whale it might have to boost his Salary.

In the Meantime the Preacher waited for some one to come and ask about Polenta, Amebius, Ramtazuk, Quarolius and the great Icelandic Poet, Navrojk. But no one had the Face to step up and confess his Ignorance of these Celebrities. The Pew-Holders didn't even admit among themselves that the Preacher had rung in some New Ones. They stood Pat, and merely said it was an Elegant Sermon.

Perceiving that they would stand for Anything, the Preacher knew what to do after that.

MORAL: Give the People what they Think they want.

Grace James

(1864-1930)

30

The Star Lovers

All you that are true lovers, I beseech you pray the gods for fair weather upon the seventh night of the seventh moon.

For patience's sake and for dear love's sake, pray, and be pitiful that upon that night there may be neither rain, nor hail, nor cloud, nor thunder, nor creeping mist.

Hear the sad tale of the Star Lovers and give them your prayers.

The Weaving Maiden was the daughter of a Deity of Light. Her dwelling was upon the shore of the Milky Way, which is the Bright River of Heaven. All the day long she sat at her loom and plied her shuttle, weaving the gay garments of the gods. Warp and woof, hour by hour the coloured web grew till it lay fold on fold piled at her feet. Still she never ceased her labour, for she was afraid. She had heard a saying:

"Sorrow, age-long sorrow, shall come upon the Weaving Maiden when she leaves her loom."

So she laboured, and the gods had garments to spare. But she herself, poor maiden, was ill-clad; she recked nothing of her attire or of the jewels that her father gave her. She went barefoot, and let her hair hang down unconfined. Ever and anon a long lock fell upon the loom, and back she flung it over her shoulder. She did not play with the children of Heaven, or take her pleasure with celestial

163

youths and maidens. She did not love or weep. She was neither glad nor sorry. She sat weaving, weaving . . . and wove her being into the many-coloured web.

Now her father, the Deity of Light, grew angry. He said, "Daughter, you weave too much."

"It is my duty," she said.

"At your age to talk of duty!" said her father. "Out upon you!"

"Wherefore are you displeased with me, my father?" she said, and her fingers plied the shuttle.

"Are you a stock or a stone, or a pale flower by the wayside?"

"Nay," she said, "I am none of these."

"Then leave your loom, my child, and live; take your pleasure, be as others are."

"And wherefore should I be as others are?" she said.

"Never dare to question me. Come, will you leave your loom?"

She said, "Sorrow, age-long sorrow, shall come upon the Weaving Maiden when she leaves her loom."

"A foolish saying," cried her father, "not worthy of credence. What do we know of age-long sorrow? Are we not gods?" With that he took her shuttle from her hand gently, and covered the loom with a cloth. And he caused her to be very richly attired, and they put jewels upon her and garlanded her head with flowers of Paradise. And her father gave her for spouse the Herd Boy of Heaven, who tended his flocks upon the banks of the Bright River.

Now the Maiden was changed indeed. Her eyes were stars and her lips were ruddy. She went dancing and singing all the day. Long hours she played with the children of Heaven, and she took her pleasure with the celestial youths and maidens. Lightly she went; her feet were shod with silver. Her lover, the Herd Boy, held her by the hand. She laughed so that the very gods laughed with her, and High Heaven re-echoed with sounds of mirth. She was careless; little did she think of duty or of the garments of the gods. As for her loom, she never went near it from one moon's end to another.

"I have my life to live," she said; "I'll weave it into a web no more."

And the Herd Boy, her lover, clasped her in his arms. Her face was all tears and smiles, and she hid it on his breast. So she lived her life. But her father, the Deity of Light, was angry.

"It is too much," he said. "Is the girl mad? She will become the laughing-stock of Heaven. Besides, who is to weave the new spring garments of the gods?"

Three times he warned his daughter.

Three times she laughed softly and shook her head.

"Your hand opened the door, my father," she said, "but of a surety no hand either of god or of mortal can shut it."

He said, "You shall find it otherwise to your cost." And he banished the Herd Boy for ever and ever to the farther side of the Bright River. The magpies flew together, from far and near, and they spread their wings for a frail bridge across the river, and the Herd Boy went over by the frail bridge. And immediately the magpies flew away to the ends of the earth and the Weaving Maiden could not follow. She was the saddest thing in Heaven. Long, long she stood upon the shore, and held out her arms to the Herd Boy, who tended his oxen desolate and in tears. Long, long she lay and wept upon the sand. Long, long she brooded, looking on the ground.

She arose and went to her loom. She cast aside the cloth that covered it. She took her shuttle in her hand.

"Age-long sorrow," she said, "age-long sorrow!" Presently she dropped the shuttle. "Ah," she moaned, "the pain of it," and she leaned her head against the loom.

But in a little while she said, "Yet I would not be as once I was. I did not love or weep, I was neither glad nor sorry. Now I love and I weep—I am glad, and I am sorry."

Her tears fell like rain, but she took up the shuttle and laboured diligently, weaving the garments of the gods. Sometimes the web was grey with grief, sometimes it was rosy with dreams. The gods were fain to go strangely clad. The Maiden's father, the Deity of Light, for once was well pleased.

"That is my good, diligent child," he said. "Now you are quiet and happy."

"The quiet of dark despair," she said. "Happy! I am the saddest thing in Heaven."

"I am sorry," said the Deity of Light; "what shall I do?"

"Give me back my lover."

"Nay, child, that I cannot do. He is banished for ever and ever by the decree of a Deity, that cannot be broken."

"I knew it," she said.

"Yet something I can do. Listen. On the seventh day of the seventh moon, I will summon the magpies together from the ends of the earth, and they shall be a bridge over the Bright River of Heaven, so that the Weaving Maiden shall lightly cross to the waiting Herd Boy on the farther shore."

So it was. On the seventh day of the seventh moon came the magpies from far and near. And they spread their wings for a frail bridge. And the Weaving Maiden went over by the frail bridge. Her eyes were like stars, and her heart like a bird in her bosom. And the Herd Boy was there to meet her upon the farther shore.

And so it is still, oh, true lovers—upon the seventh day of the seventh moon these two keep their tryst. Only if the rain falls with thunder and cloud and hail, and the Bright River of Heaven is swollen and swift, the magpies cannot make a bridge for the Weaving Maiden. Alack, the dreary time!

Therefore, true lovers, pray the gods for fair weather.

Guy de Maupassant

(1850-1893)

31

An Uncomfortable Bed

One autumn I went to spend the hunting season with some friends in a chateau in Picardy.

My friends were fond of practical jokes. I do not care to know people who are not.

When I arrived, they gave me a princely reception, which at once awakened suspicion in my mind. They fired off rifles, embraced me, made much of me, as if they expected to have great fun at my expense.

I said to myself:

"Look out, old ferret! They have something in store for you."

During the dinner the mirth was excessive, exaggerated, in fact. I thought: "Here are people who have more than their share of amusement, and apparently without reason. They must have planned some good joke. Assuredly I am to be the victim of the joke. Attention!"

During the entire evening every one laughed in an exaggerated fashion. I scented a practical joke in the air, as a dog scents game. But what was it? I was watchful, restless. I did not let a word, or a meaning, or a gesture escape me. Every one seemed to me an object of suspicion, and I even looked distrustfully at the faces of the servants.

The hour struck for retiring; and the whole household came to escort me to my room. Why?

They called to me: "Good-night." I entered the apartment, shut the door, and remained standing, without moving a single step, holding the wax candle in my hand.

I heard laughter and whispering in the corridor. Without doubt they were spying on me. I cast a glance round the walls, the furniture, the ceiling, the hangings, the floor. I saw nothing to justify suspicion. I heard persons moving about outside my door. I had no doubt they were looking through the keyhole.

An idea came into my head: "My candle may suddenly go out and leave me in darkness."

Then I went across to the mantelpiece and lighted all the wax candles that were on it. After that I cast another glance around me without discovering anything. I advanced with short steps, carefully examining the apartment. Nothing. I inspected every article, one after the other. Still nothing. I went over to the window. The shutters, large wooden shutters, were open. I shut them with great care, and then drew the curtains, enormous velvet curtains, and placed a chair in front of them, so as to have nothing to fear from outside.

Then I cautiously sat down. The armchair was solid. I did not venture to get into the bed. However, the night was advancing; and I ended by coming to the conclusion that I was foolish. If they were spying on me, as I supposed, they must, while waiting for the success of the joke they had been preparing for me, have been laughing immoderately at my terror. So I made up my mind to go to bed. But the bed was particularly suspicious-looking. I pulled at the curtains. They seemed to be secure.

All the same, there was danger. I was going perhaps to receive a cold shower both from overhead, or perhaps, the moment I stretched myself out, to find myself sinking to the floor with my mattress. I searched in my memory for all the practical jokes of which I ever had experience. And I did not want to be caught. Ah! certainly not! certainly not! Then I suddenly bethought myself of a precaution which I considered insured safety. I caught hold of the side of the mattress gingerly, and very slowly drew it toward me. It came away, followed by the sheet and the rest of the bedclothes. I dragged all these objects into the very middle of the room, facing the entrance door. I made my bed over again as best I could at some distance from the suspected bedstead and the corner which had filled me with such anxiety. Then I extinguished all the candles, and, groping my way, I slipped under the bed clothes.

For at least another hour I remained awake, starting at the slightest sound. Everything seemed quiet in the chateau. I fell asleep.

I must have been in a deep sleep for a long time, but all of a sudden I was awakened with a start by the fall of a heavy body tumbling right on top of my own, and, at the same time, I received on my face, on my neck, and on my chest a burning liquid which made me utter a howl of pain. And a dreadful noise, as if a sideboard laden with plates and dishes had fallen down, almost deafened me.

I was smothering beneath the weight that was crushing me and preventing me from moving. I stretched out my hand to find out what was the nature of this object. I felt a face, a nose, and whiskers. Then, with all my strength, I launched out a blow at this face. But I immediately received a hail of cuffings which made me jump straight out of the soaked sheets, and rush in my nightshirt into the corridor, the door of which I found open.

Oh, heavens! it was broad daylight. The noise brought my friends hurrying into my apartment, and we found, sprawling over my improvised bed, the dismayed valet, who, while bringing me my morning cup of tea, had tripped over this obstacle in the middle of the floor and fallen on his stomach, spilling my breakfast over my face in spite of himself.

The precautions I had taken in closing the shutters and going to sleep in the middle of the room had only brought about the practical joke I had been trying to avoid.

Oh, how they all laughed that day!

32

Two Friends

Besieged Paris was in the throes of famine. Even the sparrows on the roofs and the rats in the sewers were growing scarce. People were eating anything they could get.

As Monsieur Morissot, watchmaker by profession and idler for the nonce, was strolling along the boulevard one bright January morning, his hands in his trousers pockets and stomach empty, he suddenly came face to face with an acquaintance—Monsieur Sauvage, a fishing chum.

Before the war broke out Morissot had been in the habit, every Sunday morning, of setting forth with a bamboo rod in his hand and a tin box on his back. He took the Argenteuil train, got out at Colombes, and walked thence to the Ile Marante. The moment he arrived at this place of his dreams he began fishing, and fished till nightfall.

Every Sunday he met in this very spot Monsieur Sauvage, a stout, jolly, little man, a draper in the Rue Notre Dame de Lorette, and also an ardent fisherman. They often spent half the day side by side, rod in hand and feet dangling over the water, and a warm friendship had sprung up between the two.

Some days they did not speak; at other times they chatted; but they understood each other perfectly without the aid of words, having similar tastes and feelings.

In the spring, about ten o'clock in the morning, when the early sun caused a light mist to float on the water and gently warmed the backs of the two enthusiastic anglers, Morissot would occasionally remark to his neighbor:

"My, but it's pleasant here."

To which the other would reply:

"I can't imagine anything better!"

And these few words sufficed to make them understand and appreciate each other.

In the autumn, toward the close of day, when the setting sun shed a blood-red glow over the western sky, and the reflection of the crimson clouds tinged the whole river with red, brought a glow to the faces of the two friends, and gilded the trees, whose leaves were already turning at the first chill touch of winter, Monsieur Sauvage would sometimes smile at Morissot, and say:

"What a glorious spectacle!"

And Morissot would answer, without taking his eyes from his float:

"This is much better than the boulevard, isn't it?"

As soon as they recognized each other they shook hands cordially, affected at the thought of meeting under such changed circumstances.

Monsieur Sauvage, with a sigh, murmured:

"These are sad times!"

Morissot shook his head mournfully.

"And such weather! This is the first fine day of the year."

The sky was, in fact, of a bright, cloudless blue.

They walked along, side by side, reflective and sad.

"And to think of the fishing!" said Morissot. "What good times we used to have!"

"When shall we be able to fish again?" asked Monsieur Sauvage.

They entered a small cafe and took an absinthe together, then resumed their walk along the pavement.

Morissot stopped suddenly.

"Shall we have another absinthe?" he said.

"If you like," agreed Monsieur Sauvage.

Guy de Maupassant

And they entered another wine shop.

They were quite unsteady when they came out, owing to the effect of the alcohol on their empty stomachs. It was a fine, mild day, and a gentle breeze fanned their faces.

The fresh air completed the effect of the alcohol on Monsieur Sauvage. He stopped suddenly, saying:

"Suppose we go there?"

"Where?"

"Fishing."

"But where?"

"Why, to the old place. The French outposts are close to Colombes. I know Colonel Dumoulin, and we shall easily get leave to pass."

Morissot trembled with desire.

"Very well. I agree."

And they separated, to fetch their rods and lines.

An hour later they were walking side by side on the highroad. Presently they reached the villa occupied by the colonel. He smiled at their request, and granted it. They resumed their walk, furnished with a password.

Soon they left the outposts behind them, made their way through deserted Colombes, and found themselves on the outskirts of the small vineyards which border the Seine. It was about eleven o'clock.

Before them lay the village of Argenteuil, apparently lifeless. The heights of Orgement and Sannois dominated the landscape. The great plain, extending as far as Nanterre, was empty, quite empty-a waste of dun-colored soil and bare cherry trees.

Monsieur Sauvage, pointing to the heights, murmured:

"The Prussians are up yonder!"

And the sight of the deserted country filled the two friends with vague misgivings.

The Prussians! They had never seen them as yet, but they had felt their presence in the neighborhood of Paris for months past— ruining France, pillaging, massacring, starving them. And a kind of superstitious terror mingled with the hatred they already felt toward this unknown, victorious nation.

"Suppose we were to meet any of them?" said Morissot.

"We'd offer them some fish," replied Monsieur Sauvage, with that Parisian light-heartedness which nothing can wholly quench.

Still, they hesitated to show themselves in the open country, overawed by the utter silence which reigned around them.

At last Monsieur Sauvage said boldly:

"Come, we'll make a start; only let us be careful!"

And they made their way through one of the vineyards, bent double, creeping along beneath the cover afforded by the vines, with eye and ear alert.

A strip of bare ground remained to be crossed before they could gain the river bank. They ran across this, and, as soon as they were at the water's edge, concealed themselves among the dry reeds.

Morissot placed his ear to the ground, to ascertain, if possible, whether footsteps were coming their way. He heard nothing. They seemed to be utterly alone.

Their confidence was restored, and they began to fish.

Before them the deserted Ile Marante hid them from the farther shore. The little restaurant was closed, and looked as if it had been deserted for years.

Monsieur Sauvage caught the first gudgeon, Monsieur Morissot the second, and almost every moment one or other raised his line with a little, glittering, silvery fish wriggling at the end; they were having excellent sport.

They slipped their catch gently into a close-meshed bag lying at their feet; they were filled with joy—the joy of once more indulging in a pastime of which they had long been deprived.

The sun poured its rays on their backs; they no longer heard anything or thought of anything. They ignored the rest of the world; they were fishing.

But suddenly a rumbling sound, which seemed to come from the bowels of the earth, shook the ground beneath them: the cannon were resuming their thunder.

Morissot turned his head and could see toward the left, beyond the banks of the river, the formidable outline of Mont-Valerien, from whose summit arose a white puff of smoke.

The next instant a second puff followed the first, and in a few moments a fresh detonation made the earth tremble.

Others followed, and minute by minute the mountain gave forth its deadly breath and a white puff of smoke, which rose slowly into the peaceful heaven and floated above the summit of the cliff.

Monsieur Sauvage shrugged his shoulders.

"They are at it again!" he said.

Morissot, who was anxiously watching his float bobbing up and down, was suddenly seized with the angry impatience of a peaceful man toward the madmen who were firing thus, and remarked indignantly:

"What fools they are to kill one another like that!"

"They're worse than animals," replied Monsieur Sauvage.

And Morissot, who had just caught a bleak, declared:

"And to think that it will be just the same so long as there are governments!"

"The Republic would not have declared war," interposed Monsieur Sauvage.

Morissot interrupted him:

"Under a king we have foreign wars; under a republic we have civil war."

And the two began placidly discussing political problems with the sound common sense of peaceful, matter-of-fact citizens—agreeing on one point: that they would never be free. And Mont-Valerien thundered ceaselessly, demolishing the houses of the French with its cannon balls, grinding lives of men to powder, destroying many a dream, many a cherished hope, many a prospective happiness; ruthlessly causing endless woe and suffering in the hearts of wives, of daughters, of mothers, in other lands.

"Such is life!" declared Monsieur Sauvage.

"Say, rather, such is death!" replied Morissot, laughing.

But they suddenly trembled with alarm at the sound of footsteps behind them, and, turning round, they perceived close at hand four tall, bearded men, dressed after the manner of livery servants and wearing flat caps on their heads. They were covering the two anglers with their rifles.

The rods slipped from their owners' grasp and floated away down the river.

In the space of a few seconds they were seized, bound, thrown into a boat, and taken across to the Ile Marante.

And behind the house they had thought deserted were about a score of German soldiers.

A shaggy-looking giant, who was bestriding a chair and smoking a long clay pipe, addressed them in excellent French with the words:

"Well, gentlemen, have you had good luck with your fishing?"

Then a soldier deposited at the officer's feet the bag full of fish, which he had taken care to bring away. The Prussian smiled.

"Not bad, I see. But we have something else to talk about. Listen to me, and don't be alarmed:

"You must know that, in my eyes, you are two spies sent to reconnoitre me and my movements. Naturally, I capture you and I shoot you. You pretended to be fishing, the better to disguise your real errand. You have fallen into my hands, and must take the consequences. Such is war.

"But as you came here through the outposts you must have a password for your return. Tell me that password and I will let you go."

The two friends, pale as death, stood silently side by side, a slight fluttering of the hands alone betraying their emotion.

"No one will ever know," continued the officer. "You will return peacefully to your homes, and the secret will disappear with you. If you refuse, it means death-instant death. Choose!"

They stood motionless, and did not open their lips.

The Prussian, perfectly calm, went on, with hand outstretched toward the river:

"Just think that in five minutes you will be at the bottom of that water. In five minutes! You have relations, I presume?"

Mont-Valerien still thundered.

The two fishermen remained silent. The German turned and gave an order in his own language. Then he moved his chair a little way off, that he might not be so near the prisoners, and a dozen men stepped forward, rifle in hand, and took up a position, twenty paces off.

"I give you one minute," said the officer; "not a second longer."

Then he rose quickly, went over to the two Frenchmen, took Morissot by the arm, led him a short distance off, and said in a low voice:

"Quick! the password! Your friend will know nothing. I will pretend to relent."

Morissot answered not a word.

Then the Prussian took Monsieur Sauvage aside in like manner, and made him the same proposal.

Monsieur Sauvage made no reply.

Again they stood side by side.

The officer issued his orders; the soldiers raised their rifles.

Then by chance Morissot's eyes fell on the bag full of gudgeon lying in the grass a few feet from him.

A ray of sunlight made the still quivering fish glisten like silver. And Morissot's heart sank. Despite his efforts at self-control his eyes filled with tears.

"Good-by, Monsieur Sauvage," he faltered.

"Good-by, Monsieur Morissot," replied Sauvage.

They shook hands, trembling from head to foot with a dread beyond their mastery.

The officer cried:

"Fire!"

The twelve shots were as one.

Monsieur Sauvage fell forward instantaneously. Morissot, being the taller, swayed slightly and fell across his friend with face turned skyward and blood oozing from a rent in the breast of his coat.

The German issued fresh orders.

His men dispersed, and presently returned with ropes and large stones, which they attached to the feet of the two friends; then they carried them to the river bank.

Mont-Valerien, its summit now enshrouded in smoke, still continued to thunder.

Two soldiers took Morissot by the head and the feet; two others did the same with Sauvage. The bodies, swung lustily by strong hands, were cast to a distance, and, describing a curve, fell feet foremost into the stream.

The water splashed high, foamed, eddied, then grew calm; tiny waves lapped the shore.

A few streaks of blood flecked the surface of the river.

The officer, calm throughout, remarked, with grim humor:

"It's the fishes' turn now!"

Then he retraced his way to the house.

Suddenly he caught sight of the net full of gudgeons, lying forgotten in the grass. He picked it up, examined it, smiled, and called:

"Wilhelm!"

A white-aproned soldier responded to the summons, and the Prussian, tossing him the catch of the two murdered men, said:

"Have these fish fried for me at once, while they are still alive; they'll make a tasty dish."

Then he resumed his pipe.

33

Two Little Soldiers

Every Sunday, as soon as they were free, the little soldiers would go for a walk. They turned to the right on leaving the barracks, crossed Courbevoie with rapid strides, as though on a forced march; then, as the houses grew scarcer, they slowed down and followed the dusty road which leads to Bezons.

They were small and thin, lost in their ill-fitting capes, too large and too long, whose sleeves covered their hands; their ample red trousers fell in folds around their ankles. Under the high, stiff shako one could just barely perceive two thin, hollow-cheeked Breton faces, with their calm, naive blue eyes. They never spoke during their journey, going straight before them, the same idea in each one's mind taking the place of conversation. For at the entrance of the little forest of Champioux they had found a spot which reminded them of home, and they did not feel happy anywhere else.

At the crossing of the Colombes and Chatou roads, when they arrived under the trees, they would take off their heavy, oppressive headgear and wipe their foreheads.

They always stopped for a while on the bridge at Bezons, and looked at the Seine. They stood there several minutes, bending over the railing, watching the white sails, which perhaps reminded them of their home, and of the fishing smacks leaving for the open.

As soon as they had crossed the Seine, they would purchase provisions at the delicatessen, the baker's, and the wine merchant's. A piece of bologna, four cents' worth of bread, and a quart of wine, made up the luncheon which they carried away, wrapped up in their handkerchiefs. But as soon as they were out of the village their gait would slacken and they would begin to talk.

Before them was a plain with a few clumps of trees, which led to the woods, a little forest which seemed to remind them of that other forest at Kermarivan. The wheat and oat fields bordered on the narrow path, and Jean Kerderen said each time to Luc Le Ganidec:

"It's just like home, just like Plounivon."

"Yes, it's just like home."

And they went on, side by side, their minds full of dim memories of home. They saw the fields, the hedges, the forests, and beaches.

Each time they stopped near a large stone on the edge of the private estate, because it reminded them of the dolmen of Locneuven.

As soon as they reached the first clump of trees, Luc Le Ganidec would cut off a small stick, and, whittling it slowly, would walk on, thinking of the folks at home.

Jean Kerderen carried the provisions.

From time to time Luc would mention a name, or allude to some boyish prank which would give them food for plenty of thought. And the home country, so dear and so distant, would little by little gain possession of their minds, sending them back through space, to the well-known forms and noises, to the familiar scenery, with the fragrance of its green fields and sea air. They no longer noticed the smells of the city. And in their dreams they saw their friends leaving, perhaps forever, for the dangerous fishing grounds.

They were walking slowly, Luc Le Ganidec and Jean Kerderen, contented and sad, haunted by a sweet sorrow, the slow and penetrating sorrow of a captive animal which remembers the days of its freedom.

And when Luc had finished whittling his stick, they came to a little nook, where every Sunday they took their meal. They found the two bricks, which they had hidden in a hedge, and they made a little fire of dry branches and roasted their sausages on the ends of their knives.

When their last crumb of bread had been eaten and the last drop of wine had been drunk, they stretched themselves out on the grass side by side, without speaking, their half-closed eyes looking away in the distance, their hands clasped as in prayer, their red-trousered legs mingling with the bright colors of the wild flowers.

Towards noon they glanced, from time to time, towards the village of Bezons, for the dairy maid would soon be coming. Every Sunday she would pass in front of them on the way to milk her cow, the only cow in the neighborhood which was sent out to pasture.

Soon they would see the girl, coming through the fields, and it pleased them to watch the sparkling sunbeams reflected from her shining pail. They never spoke of her. They were just glad to see her, without understanding why.

She was a tall, strapping girl, freckled and tanned by the open air—a girl typical of the Parisian suburbs.

Once, on noticing that they were always sitting in the same place, she said to them:

"Do you always come here?"

Luc Le Ganidec, more daring than his friend, stammered:

"Yes, we come here for our rest."

That was all. But the following Sunday, on seeing them, she smiled with the kindly smile of a woman who understood their shyness, and she asked:

"What are you doing here? Are you watching the grass grow?"

Luc, cheered up, smiled: "P'raps."

She continued: "It's not growing fast, is it?"

He answered, still laughing: "Not exactly."

She went on. But when she came back with her pail full of milk, she stopped before them and said:

"Want some? It will remind you of home."

She had, perhaps instinctively, guessed and touched the right spot.

Both were moved. Then not without difficulty, she poured some milk into the bottle in which they had brought their wine. Luc started to drink, carefully watching lest he should take more than his share. Then he passed the bottle to Jean. She stood before them, her hands on her hips, her pail at her feet, enjoying the pleasure that she was giving them. Then she went on, saying: "Well, bye-bye until next Sunday!"

For a long time they watched her tall form as it receded in the distance, blending with the background, and finally disappeared.

The following week as they left the barracks, Jean said to Luc: "Don't you think we ought to buy her something good?"

They were sorely perplexed by the problem of choosing something to bring to the dairy maid. Luc was in favor of bringing her some chitterlings; but Jean, who had a sweet tooth, thought that candy would be the best thing. He won, and so they went to a grocery to buy two sous' worth, of red and white candies.

This time they ate more quickly than usual, excited by anticipation.

Jean was the first one to notice her. "There she is," he said; and Luc answered: "Yes, there she is."

She smiled when she saw them, and cried:

"Well, how are you to-day?"

They both answered together:

"All right! How's everything with you?"

Then she started to talk of simple things which might interest them; of the weather, of the crops, of her masters.

They didn't dare to offer their candies, which were slowly melting in Jean's pocket. Finally Luc, growing bolder, murmured:

"We have brought you something."

She asked: "Let's see it."

Then Jean, blushing to the tips of his ears, reached in his pocket, and drawing out the little paper bag, handed it to her.

She began to eat the little sweet dainties. The two soldiers sat in front of her, moved and delighted.

At last she went to do her milking, and when she came back she again gave them some milk.

They thought of her all through the week and often spoke of her: The following Sunday she sat beside them for a longer time.

The three of them sat there, side by side, their eyes looking far away in the distance, their hands clasped over their knees, and they told each other little incidents and little details of the villages where they were born, while the cow, waiting to be milked, stretched her heavy head toward the girl and mooed.

Soon the girl consented to eat with them and to take a sip of wine. Often she brought them plums pocket for plums were now ripe. Her presence enlivened the little Breton soldiers, who chattered away like two birds.

One Tuesday something unusual happened to Luc Le Ganidec; he asked for leave and did not return until ten o'clock at night.

Jean, worried and racked his brain to account for his friend's having obtained leave.

The following Friday, Luc borrowed ten sons from one of his friends, and once more asked and obtained leave for several hours.

When he started out with Jean on Sunday he seemed queer, disturbed, changed. Kerderen did not understand; he vaguely suspected something, but he could not guess what it might be.

They went straight to the usual place, and lunched slowly. Neither was hungry.

Soon the girl appeared. They watched her approach as they always did. When she was near, Luc arose and went towards her. She placed her pail on the ground and kissed him. She kissed him passionately, throwing her arms around his neck, without paying attention to Jean, without even noticing that he was there.

Poor Jean was dazed, so dazed that he could not understand. His mind was upset and his heart broken, without his even realizing why.

Then the girl sat down beside Luc, and they started to chat.

Jean was not looking at them. He understood now why his friend had gone out twice during the week. He felt the pain and the sting which treachery and deceit leave in their wake.

Luc and the girl went together to attend to the cow.

Jean followed them with his eyes. He saw them disappear side by side, the red trousers of his friend making a scarlet spot against the white road. It was Luc who sank the stake to which the cow was tethered. The girl stooped down to milk the cow, while he absent-mindedly stroked the animal's glossy neck. Then they left the pail in the grass and disappeared in the woods.

Jean could no longer see anything but the wall of leaves through which they had passed. He was unmanned so that he did not have strength to stand. He stayed there, motionless, bewildered and grieving-simple, passionate grief. He wanted to weep, to run away, to hide somewhere, never to see anyone again.

Then he saw them coming back again. They were walking slowly, hand in hand, as village lovers do. Luc was carrying the pail.

After kissing him again, the girl went on, nodding carelessly to Jean. She did not offer him any milk that day.

The two little soldiers sat side by side, motionless as always, silent and quiet, their calm faces in no way betraying the trouble in their hearts. The sun shone down on them. From time to time they could hear the plaintive lowing of the cow. At the usual time they arose to return.

Luc was whittling a stick. Jean carried the empty bottle. He left it at the wine merchant's in Bezons. Then they stopped on the bridge, as they did every Sunday, and watched the water flowing by.

Jean leaned over the railing, farther and farther, as though he had seen something in the stream which hypnotized him. Luc said to him:

"What's the matter? Do you want a drink?"

He had hardly said the last word when Jean's head carried away the rest of his body, and the little blue and red soldier fell like a shot and disappeared in the water.

Luc, paralyzed with horror, tried vainly to shout for help. In the distance he saw something move; then his friend's head bobbed up out of the water only to disappear again.

Farther down he again noticed a hand, just one hand, which appeared and again went out of sight. That was all.

The boatmen who had rushed to the scene found the body that day.

Luc ran back to the barracks, crazed, and with eyes and voice full of tears, he related the accident: "He leaned—he—he was leaning —so far over—that his head carried him away—and—he—fell —he fell——"

Emotion choked him so that he could say no more. If he had only known.

34

Father Milon

For a month the hot sun has been parching the fields. Nature is expanding beneath its rays; the fields are green as far as the eye can see. The big azure dome of the sky is unclouded. The farms of Normandy, scattered over the plains and surrounded by a belt of tall beeches, look, from a distance, like little woods. On closer view, after lowering the worm-eaten wooden bars, you imagine yourself in an immense garden, for all the ancient apple-trees, as gnarled as the peasants themselves, are in bloom. The sweet scent of their blossoms mingles with the heavy smell of the earth and the penetrating odor of the stables. It is noon. The family is eating under the shade of a pear tree planted in front of the door; father, mother, the four children, and the help—two women and three men are all there. All are silent. The soup is eaten and then a dish of potatoes fried with bacon is brought on.

From time to time one of the women gets up and takes a pitcher down to the cellar to fetch more cider.

The man, a big fellow about forty years old, is watching a grape vine, still bare, which is winding and twisting like a snake along the side of the house.

At last he says: "Father's vine is budding early this year. Perhaps we may get something from it."

The woman then turns round and looks, without saying a word.

This vine is planted on the spot where their father had been shot.

It was during the war of 1870. The Prussians were occupying the whole country. General Faidherbe, with the Northern Division of the army, was opposing them.

The Prussians had established their headquarters at this farm. The old farmer to whom it belonged, Father Pierre Milon, had received and quartered them to the best of his ability.

For a month the German vanguard had been in this village. The French remained motionless, ten leagues away; and yet, every night, some of the Uhlans disappeared.

Of all the isolated scouts, of all those who were sent to the outposts, in groups of not more than three, not one ever returned.

They were picked up the next morning in a field or in a ditch. Even their horses were found along the roads with their throats cut.

These murders seemed to be done by the same men, who could never be found.

The country was terrorized. Farmers were shot on suspicion, women were imprisoned; children were frightened in order to try and obtain information. Nothing could be ascertained.

But, one morning, Father Milon was found stretched out in the barn, with a sword gash across his face.

Two Uhlans were found dead about a mile and a half from the farm. One of them was still holding his bloody sword in his hand. He had fought, tried to defend himself. A court-martial was immediately held in the open air, in front of the farm. The old man was brought before it.

He was sixty-eight years old, small, thin, bent, with two big hands resembling the claws of a crab. His colorless hair was sparse and thin, like the down of a young duck, allowing patches of his scalp to be seen. The brown and wrinkled skin of his neck showed big veins which disappeared behind his jaws and came out again at the temples. He had the reputation of being miserly and hard to deal with.

They stood him up between four soldiers, in front of the kitchen table, which had been dragged outside. Five officers and the colonel seated themselves opposite him.

The colonel spoke in French:

"Father Milon, since we have been here we have only had praise for you. You have always been obliging and even attentive to us. But to-day a terrible accusation is hanging over you, and you must clear the matter up. How did you receive that wound on your face?"

The peasant answered nothing.

The colonel continued:

"Your silence accuses you, Father Milon. But I want you to answer me! Do you understand? Do you know who killed the two Uhlans who were found this morning near Calvaire?"

The old man answered clearly

"I did."

The colonel, surprised, was silent for a minute, looking straight at the prisoner. Father Milon stood impassive, with the stupid look of the peasant, his eyes lowered as though he were talking to the priest. Just one thing betrayed an uneasy mind; he was continually swallowing his saliva, with a visible effort, as though his throat were terribly contracted.

The man's family, his son Jean, his daughter-in-law and his two grandchildren were standing a few feet behind him, bewildered and affrighted.

The colonel went on:

"Do you also know who killed all the scouts who have been found dead, for a month, throughout the country, every morning?"

The old man answered with the same stupid look:

"I did."

"You killed them all?"

"Uh huh! I did."

"You alone? All alone?"

"Uh huh!"

"Tell me how you did it."

This time the man seemed moved; the necessity for talking any length of time annoyed him visibly. He stammered:

"I dunno! I simply did it."

The colonel continued:

"I warn you that you will have to tell me everything. You might as well make up your mind right away. How did you begin?"

The man cast a troubled look toward his family, standing close behind him. He hesitated a minute longer, and then suddenly made up his mind to obey the order.

"I was coming home one night at about ten o'clock, the night after you got here. You and your soldiers had taken more than fifty ecus worth of forage from me, as well as a cow and two sheep. I said to myself: 'As much as they take from you; just so much will you make them pay back.' And then I had other things on my mind which I will tell you. Just then I noticed one of your soldiers who was smoking his pipe by the ditch behind the barn. I went and got my scythe and crept up slowly behind him, so that he couldn't hear me. And I cut his head off with one single blow, just as I would a blade of grass, before he could say 'Booh!' If you should look at the bottom of the pond, you will find him tied up in a potato-sack, with a stone fastened to it.

"I got an idea. I took all his clothes, from his boots to his cap, and hid them away in the little wood behind the yard."

The old man stopped. The officers remained speechless, looking at each other. The questioning began again, and this is what they learned.

Once this murder committed, the man had lived with this one thought: "Kill the Prussians!" He hated them with the blind, fierce hate of the greedy yet patriotic peasant. He had his idea, as he said. He waited several days.

He was allowed to go and come as he pleased, because he had shown himself so humble, submissive and obliging to the invaders. Each night he saw the outposts leave. One night he followed them, having heard the name of the village to which the men were going, and having learned the few words of German which he needed for his plan through associating with the soldiers.

He left through the back yard, slipped into the woods, found the dead man's clothes and put them on. Then he began to crawl through the fields, following along the hedges in order to keep out of sight, listening to the slightest noises, as wary as a poacher.

As soon as he thought the time ripe, he approached the road and hid behind a bush. He waited for a while. Finally, toward midnight, he heard the sound of a galloping horse. The man put his ear to the ground in order to make sure that only one horseman was approaching, then he got ready.

An Uhlan came galloping along, carrying dispatches. As he went, he was all eyes and ears. When he was only a few feet away, Father Milon dragged himself across the road, moaning: "Hilfe! Hilfe!" (Help! Help!) The horseman stopped, and recognizing a German, he thought he was wounded and dismounted, coming nearer without any suspicion, and just as he was leaning over the unknown man, he received, in the pit of his stomach, a heavy thrust from the long curved blade of the sabre. He dropped without suffering pain, quivering only in the final throes. Then the farmer, radiant with the silent joy of an old peasant, got up again, and, for his own pleasure, cut the dead man's throat. He then dragged the body to the ditch and threw it in.

The horse quietly awaited its master. Father Milon mounted him and started galloping across the plains.

About an hour later he noticed two more Uhlans who were returning home, side by side. He rode straight for them, once more crying "Hilfe! Hilfe!"

The Prussians, recognizing the uniform, let him approach without distrust. The old man passed between them like a cannon-ball, felling them both, one with his sabre and the other with a revolver.

Then he killed the horses, German horses! After that he quickly returned to the woods and hid one of the horses. He left his uniform there and again put on his old clothes; then going back into bed, he slept until morning.

For four days he did not go out, waiting for the inquest to be terminated; but on the fifth day he went out again and killed two more soldiers by the same stratagem. From that time on he did not stop. Each night he wandered about in search of adventure, killing

Prussians, sometimes here and sometimes there, galloping through deserted fields, in the moonlight, a lost Uhlan, a hunter of men. Then, his task accomplished, leaving behind him the bodies lying along the roads, the old farmer would return and hide his horse and uniform.

He went, toward noon, to carry oats and water quietly to his mount, and he fed it well as he required from it a great amount of work.

But one of those whom he had attacked the night before, in defending himself slashed the old peasant across the face with his sabre.

However, he had killed them both. He had come back and hidden the horse and put on his ordinary clothes again; but as he reached home he began to feel faint, and had dragged himself as far as the stable, being unable to reach the house.

They had found him there, bleeding, on the straw.

When he had finished his tale, he suddenly lifted up his head and looked proudly at the Prussian officers.

The colonel, who was gnawing at his mustache, asked:

"You have nothing else to say?"

"Nothing more; I have finished my task; I killed sixteen, not one more or less."

"Do you know that you are going to die?"

"I haven't asked for mercy."

"Have you been a soldier?"

"Yes, I served my time. And then, you had killed my father, who was a soldier of the first Emperor. And last month you killed my youngest son, Francois, near Evreux. I owed you one for that; I paid. We are quits."

The officers were looking at each other.

The old man continued:

"Eight for my father, eight for the boy—we are quits. I did not seek any quarrel with you. I don't know you. I don't even know where you come from. And here you are, ordering me about in my home as though it were your own. I took my revenge upon the others. I'm not sorry."

And, straightening up his bent back, the old man folded his arms in the attitude of a modest hero.

The Prussians talked in a low tone for a long time. One of them, a captain, who had also lost his son the previous month, was defending the poor wretch. Then the colonel arose and, approaching Father Milon, said in a low voice:

"Listen, old man, there is perhaps a way of saving your life, it is to—"

But the man was not listening, and, his eyes fixed on the hated officer, while the wind played with the downy hair on his head, he distorted his slashed face, giving it a truly terrible expression, and, swelling out his chest, he spat, as hard as he could, right in the Prussian's face.

The colonel, furious, raised his hand, and for the second time the man spat in his face.

All the officers had jumped up and were shrieking orders at the same time.

In less than a minute the old man, still impassive, was pushed up against the wall and shot, looking smilingly the while toward Jean, his eldest son, his daughter-in-law and his two grandchildren, who witnessed this scene in dumb terror.

35

Lieutenant Lare's Marriage

Since the beginning of the campaign Lieutenant Lare had taken two cannon from the Prussians. His general had said: "Thank you, lieutenant," and had given him the cross of honor.

As he was as cautious as he was brave, wary, inventive, wily and resourceful, he was entrusted with a hundred soldiers and he organized a company of scouts who saved the army on several occasions during a retreat.

But the invading army entered by every frontier like a surging sea. Great waves of men arrived one after the other, scattering all around them a scum of freebooters. General Carrel's brigade, separated from its division, retreated continually, fighting each day, but remaining almost intact, thanks to the vigilance and agility of Lieutenant Lare, who seemed to be everywhere at the same moment, baffling all the enemy's cunning, frustrating their plans, misleading their Uhlans and killing their vanguards.

One morning the general sent for him.

"Lieutenant," said he, "here is a dispatch from General de Lacere, who will be destroyed if we do not go to his aid by sunrise to-morrow. He is at Blainville, eight leagues from here. You will start at nightfall with three hundred men, whom you will echelon along the road. I will follow you two hours later. Study the road carefully; I fear we may meet a division of the enemy."

It had been freezing hard for a week. At two o'clock it began to snow, and by night the ground was covered and heavy white swirls concealed objects hard by.

At six o'clock the detachment set out.

Two men walked alone as scouts about three yards ahead. Then came a platoon of ten men commanded by the lieutenant himself. The rest followed them in two long columns. To the right and left of the little band, at a distance of about three hundred feet on either side, some soldiers marched in pairs.

The snow, which was still falling, covered them with a white powder in the darkness, and as it did not melt on their uniforms, they were hardly distinguishable in the night amid the dead whiteness of the landscape.

From time to time they halted. One heard nothing but that indescribable, nameless flutter of falling snow—a sensation rather than a sound, a vague, ominous murmur. A command was given in a low tone and when the troop resumed its march it left in its wake a sort of white phantom standing in the snow. It gradually grew fainter and finally disappeared. It was the echelons who were to lead the army.

The scouts slackened their pace. Something was ahead of them.

"Turn to the right," said the lieutenant; "it is the Ronfi wood; the chateau is more to the left."

Presently the command "Halt" was passed along. The detachment stopped and waited for the lieutenant, who, accompanied by only ten men, had undertaken a reconnoitering expedition to the chateau.

They advanced, creeping under the trees. Suddenly they all remained motionless. Around them was a dead silence. Then, quite near them, a little clear, musical young voice was heard amid the stillness of the wood.

"Father, we shall get lost in the snow. We shall never reach Blainville."

A deeper voice replied:

"Never fear, little daughter; I know the country as well as I know my pocket."

The lieutenant said a few words and four men moved away silently, like shadows.

All at once a woman's shrill cry was heard through the darkness. Two prisoners were brought back, an old man and a young girl. The lieutenant questioned them, still in a low tone:

"Your name?"

"Pierre Bernard."

"Your profession?"

"Butler to Comte de Ronfi."

"Is this your daughter?"

"Yes!"

"What does she do?"

"She is laundress at the chateau."

"Where are you going?"

"We are making our escape."

"Why?"

"Twelve Uhlans passed by this evening. They shot three keepers and hanged the gardener. I was alarmed on account of the little one."

"Whither are you bound?"

"To Blainville."

"Why?"

"Because there is a French army there."

"Do you know the way?"

"Perfectly."

"Well then, follow us."

They rejoined the column and resumed their march across country. The old man walked in silence beside the lieutenant, his daughter walking at his side. All at once she stopped.

"Father," she said, "I am so tired I cannot go any farther."

And she sat down. She was shaking with cold and seemed about to lose consciousness. Her father wanted to carry her, but he was too old and too weak.

"Lieutenant," said he, sobbing, "we shall only impede your march. France before all. Leave us here."

The officer had given a command. Some men had started off. They came back with branches they had cut, and in a minute a litter was ready. The whole detachment had joined them by this time.

"Here is a woman dying of cold," said the lieutenant. "Who will give his cape to cover her?"

Two hundred capes were taken off. The young girl was wrapped up in these warm soldiers' capes, gently laid in the litter, and then four' hardy shoulders lifted her up, and like an Eastern queen borne by her slaves she was placed in the center of the detachment of soldiers, who resumed their march with more energy, more courage, more cheerfulness, animated by the presence of a woman, that sovereign inspiration that has stirred the old French blood to so many deeds of valor.

At the end of an hour they halted again and every one lay down in the snow. Over yonder on the level country a big, dark shadow was moving. It looked like some weird monster stretching itself out like a serpent, then suddenly coiling itself into a mass, darting forth again, then back, and then forward again without ceasing. Some whispered orders were passed around among the soldiers, and an occasional little, dry, metallic click was heard. The moving object suddenly came nearer, and twelve Uhlans were seen approaching at a gallop, one behind the other, having lost their way in the darkness. A brilliant flash suddenly revealed to them two hundred men lying on the ground before them. A rapid fire was heard, which died away in the snowy silence, and all the twelve fell to the ground, their horses with them.

After a long rest the march was resumed. The old man whom they had captured acted as guide.

Presently a voice far off in the distance cried out: "Who goes there?"

Another voice nearer by gave the countersign.

They made another halt; some conferences took place. It had stopped snowing. A cold wind was driving the clouds, and innumerable stars were sparkling in the sky behind them, gradually paling in the rosy light of dawn.

A staff officer came forward to receive the detachment. But when he asked who was being carried in the litter, the form stirred; two little hands moved aside the big blue army capes and, rosy as the dawn, with two eyes that were brighter than the stars that had just faded from sight, and a smile as radiant as the morn, a dainty face appeared.

"It is I, monsieur."

The soldiers, wild with delight, clapped their hands and bore the young girl in triumph into the midst of the camp, that was just getting to arms. Presently General Carrel arrived on the scene. At nine o'clock the Prussians made an attack. They beat a retreat at noon.

That evening, as Lieutenant Lare, overcome by fatigue, was sleeping on a bundle of straw, he was sent for by the general. He found the commanding officer in his tent, chatting with the old man whom they had come across during the night. As soon as he entered the tent the general took his hand, and addressing the stranger, said:

"My dear comte, this is the young man of whom you were telling me just now; he is one of my best officers."

He smiled, lowered his tone, and added:

"The best."

Then, turning to the astonished lieutenant, he presented "Comte de Ronfi-Quedissac."

The old man took both his hands, saying:

"My dear lieutenant, you have saved my daughter's life. I have only one way of thanking you. You may come in a few months to tell me—if you like her."

One year later, on the very same day, Captain Lare and Miss Louise-Hortense-Genevieve de Ronfi-Quedissac were married in the church of St. Thomas Aquinas.

She brought a dowry of six thousand francs, and was said to be the prettiest bride that had been seen that year.

Hans Christian Andersen

(1805-1875)

36

The Wicked Prince

There lived once upon a time a wicked prince whose heart and mind were set upon conquering all the countries of the world, and on frightening the people; he devastated their countries with fire and sword, and his soldiers trod down the crops in the fields and destroyed the peasants' huts by fire, so that the flames licked the green leaves off the branches, and the fruit hung dried up on the singed black trees. Many a poor mother fled, her naked baby in her arms, behind the still smoking walls of her cottage; but also there the soldiers followed her, and when they found her, she served as new nourishment to their diabolical enjoyments; demons could not possibly have done worse things than these soldiers! The prince was of opinion that all this was right, and that it was only the natural course which things ought to take. His power increased day by day, his name was feared by all, and fortune favoured his deeds.

He brought enormous wealth home from the conquered towns, and gradually accumulated in his residence riches which could nowhere be equalled. He erected magnificent palaces, churches, and halls, and all who saw these splendid buildings and great treasures exclaimed admiringly: "What a mighty prince!" But they did not know what endless misery he had brought upon other countries, nor did they hear the sighs and lamentations which rose up from the debris of the destroyed cities.

The prince often looked with delight upon his gold and his magnificent edifices, and thought, like the crowd: "What a mighty prince! But I must have more—much more. No power on earth must equal mine, far less exceed it."

He made war with all his neighbours, and defeated them. The conquered kings were chained up with golden fetters to his chariot when he drove through the streets of his city. These kings had to kneel at his and his courtiers' feet when they sat at table, and live on the morsels which they left. At last the prince had his own statue erected on the public places and fixed on the royal palaces; nay, he even wished it to be placed in the churches, on the altars, but in this the priests opposed him, saying: "Prince, you are mighty indeed, but God's power is much greater than yours; we dare not obey your orders."

"Well," said the prince. "Then I will conquer God too." And in his haughtiness and foolish presumption he ordered a magnificent ship to be constructed, with which he could sail through the air; it was gorgeously fitted out and of many colours; like the tail of a peacock, it was covered with thousands of eyes, but each eye was the barrel of a gun. The prince sat in the centre of the ship, and had only to touch a spring in order to make thousands of bullets fly out in all directions, while the guns were at once loaded again. Hundreds of eagles were attached to this ship, and it rose with the swiftness of an arrow up towards the sun. The earth was soon left far below, and looked, with its mountains and woods, like a cornfield where the plough had made furrows which separated green meadows; soon it looked only like a map with indistinct lines upon it; and at last it entirely disappeared in mist and clouds. Higher and higher rose the eagles up into the air; then God sent one of his numberless angels against the ship. The wicked prince showered thousands of bullets upon him, but they rebounded from his shining wings and fell down like ordinary hailstones. One drop of blood, one single drop, came out of the white feathers of the angel's wings and fell upon the ship in which the prince sat, burnt into it, and weighed upon it like thousands of hundredweights, dragging it rapidly down to the earth again; the strong wings of the eagles gave way, the wind roared round the prince's head, and the clouds around—were they formed by the smoke rising up from the burnt cities?—took strange shapes, like crabs many, many miles long, which stretched their claws out after him, and rose up like enormous rocks, from which rolling masses dashed down, and became fire-spitting dragons.

The prince was lying half-dead in his ship, when it sank at last with a terrible shock into the branches of a large tree in the wood.

"I will conquer God!" said the prince. "I have sworn it: my will must be done!"

And he spent seven years in the construction of wonderful ships to sail through the air, and had darts cast from the hardest steel to break the walls of heaven with. He gathered warriors from all countries, so many that when they were placed side by side they covered the space of several miles. They entered the ships and the prince was approaching his own, when God sent a swarm of gnats—one swarm of little gnats. They buzzed round the prince and stung his face and hands; angrily he drew his sword and brandished it, but he only touched the air and did not hit the gnats. Then he ordered his servants to bring costly coverings and wrap him in them, that the gnats might no longer be able to reach him. The servants carried out his orders, but one single gnat had placed itself inside one of the coverings, crept into the prince's ear and stung him. The place burnt like fire, and the poison entered into his blood. Mad with pain, he tore off the coverings and his clothes too, flinging them far away, and danced about before the eyes of his ferocious soldiers, who now mocked at him, the mad prince, who wished to make war with God, and was overcome by a single little gnat.

37

The Little Match Girl

Most terribly cold it was; it snowed, and was nearly quite dark, and evening—the last evening of the year. In this cold and darkness there went along the street a poor little girl, bareheaded, and with naked feet. When she left home she had slippers on, it is true; but what was the good of that? They were very large slippers, which her mother had hitherto worn; so large were they; and the poor little thing lost them as she scuffled away across the street, because of two carriages that rolled by dreadfully fast.

One slipper was nowhere to be found; the other had been laid hold of by an urchin, and off he ran with it; he thought it would do capitally for a cradle when he some day or other should have children himself. So the little maiden walked on with her tiny naked feet, that were quite red and blue from cold. She carried a quantity of matches in an old apron, and she held a bundle of them in her hand. Nobody had bought anything of her the whole livelong day; no one had given her a single farthing.

She crept along trembling with cold and hunger—a very picture of sorrow, the poor little thing!

The flakes of snow covered her long fair hair, which fell in beautiful curls around her neck; but of that, of course, she never once now thought. From all the windows the candles were gleaming, and it smelt so deliciously of roast goose, for you know it was New Year's Eve; yes, of that she thought.

In a corner formed by two houses, of which one advanced more than the other, she seated herself down and cowered together. Her little feet she had drawn close up to her, but she grew colder and colder, and to go home she did not venture, for she had not sold any matches and could not bring a farthing of money: from her father she would certainly get blows, and at home it was cold too, for above her she had only the roof, through which the wind whistled, even though the largest cracks were stopped up with straw and rags.

Her little hands were almost numbed with cold. Oh! a match might afford her a world of comfort, if she only dared take a single one out of the bundle, draw it against the wall, and warm her fingers by it. She drew one out. "Rischt!" how it blazed, how it burnt! It was a warm, bright flame, like a candle, as she held her hands over it: it was a wonderful light. It seemed really to the little maiden as though she were sitting before a large iron stove, with burnished brass feet and a brass ornament at top. The fire burned with such blessed influence; it warmed so delightfully. The little girl had already stretched out her feet to warm them too; but—the small flame went out, the stove vanished: she had only the remains of the burnt-out match in her hand.

She rubbed another against the wall: it burned brightly, and where the light fell on the wall, there the wall became transparent like a veil, so that she could see into the room. On the table was spread a snow-white tablecloth; upon it was a splendid porcelain service, and the roast goose was steaming famously with its stuffing of apple and dried plums. And what was still more capital to behold was, the goose hopped down from the dish, reeled about on the floor with knife and fork in its breast, till it came up to the poor little girl; when—the match went out and nothing but the thick, cold, damp wall was left behind. She lighted another match. Now there she was sitting under the most magnificent Christmas tree: it was still larger, and more decorated than the one which she had seen through the glass door in the rich merchant's house.

Thousands of lights were burning on the green branches, and gaily-colored pictures, such as she had seen in the shop-windows, looked down upon her. The little maiden stretched out her hands towards them when—the match went out. The lights of the Christmas tree rose higher and higher, she saw them now as stars in heaven; one fell down and formed a long trail of fire.

"Someone is just dead!" said the little girl; for her old grandmother, the only person who had loved her, and who was now no more, had told her, that when a star falls, a soul ascends to God.

She drew another match against the wall: it was again light, and in the lustre there stood the old grandmother, so bright and radiant, so mild, and with such an expression of love.

"Grandmother!" cried the little one. "Oh, take me with you! You go away when the match burns out; you vanish like the warm stove, like the delicious roast goose, and like the magnificent Christmas tree!" And she rubbed the whole bundle of matches quickly against the wall, for she wanted to be quite sure of keeping her grandmother near her. And the matches gave such a brilliant light that it was brighter than at noon-day: never formerly had the grandmother been so beautiful and so tall. She took the little maiden, on her arm, and both flew in brightness and in joy so high, so very high, and then above was neither cold, nor hunger, nor anxiety—they were with God.

But in the corner, at the cold hour of dawn, sat the poor girl, with rosy cheeks and with a smiling mouth, leaning against the wall—frozen to death on the last evening of the old year. Stiff and stark sat the child there with her matches, of which one bundle had been burnt. "She wanted to warm herself," people said. No one had the slightest suspicion of what beautiful things she had seen; no one even dreamed of the splendor in which, with her grandmother she had entered on the joys of a new year.

38

Red Shoes

BY HANS CHRISTIAN ANDERSEN

Once upon a time there was little girl, pretty and dainty. But in summer time she was obliged to go barefooted because she was poor, and in winter she had to wear large wooden shoes, so that her little instep grew quite red.

In the middle of the village lived an old shoemaker's wife; she sat down and made, as well as she could, a pair of little shoes out of some old pieces of red cloth. They were clumsy, but she meant well, for they were intended for the little girl, whose name was Karen.

Karen received the shoes and wore them for the first time on the day of her mother's funeral. They were certainly not suitable for mourning; but she had no others, and so she put her bare feet into them and walked behind the humble coffin.

Just then a large old carriage came by, and in it sat an old lady; she looked at the little girl, and taking pity on her, said to the clergyman, "Look here, if you will give me the little girl, I will take care of her."

Karen believed that this was all on account of the red shoes, but the old lady thought them hideous, and so they were burnt.

Karen herself was dressed very neatly and cleanly; she was taught to read and to sew, and people said that she was pretty. But the mirror told her, "You are more than pretty—you are beautiful."

One day the Queen was travelling through that part of the country, and had her little daughter, who was a princess, with her. All the people, amongst them Karen too, streamed towards the castle, where the little princess, in fine white clothes, stood before the window and allowed herself to be stared at. She wore neither a train nor a golden crown, but beautiful red morocco shoes; they were indeed much finer than those which the shoemaker's wife had sewn for little Karen. There is really nothing in the world that can be compared to red shoes!

Karen was now old enough to be confirmed; she received some new clothes, and she was also to have some new shoes. The rich shoemaker in the town took the measure of her little foot in his own room, in which there stood great glass cases full of pretty shoes and white slippers. It all looked very lovely, but the old lady could not see very well, and therefore did not get much pleasure out of it. Amongst the shoes stood a pair of red ones, like those which the princess had worn. How beautiful they were! and the shoemaker said that they had been made for a count's daughter, but that they had not fitted her.

"I suppose they are of shiny leather?" asked the old lady. "They shine so."

"Yes, they do shine," said Karen. They fitted her, and were bought. But the old lady knew nothing of their being red, for she would never have allowed Karen to be confirmed in red shoes, as she was now to be.

Everybody looked at her feet, and the whole of the way from the church door to the choir it seemed to her as if even the ancient figures on the monuments, in their stiff collars and long black robes, had their eyes fixed on her red shoes. It was only of these that she thought when the clergyman laid his hand upon her head and spoke of the holy baptism, of the covenant with God, and told her that she was now to be a grown-up Christian. The organ pealed forth solemnly, and the sweet children's voices mingled with that of their old leader; but Karen thought only of her red shoes. In the afternoon the old lady heard from everybody that Karen had worn red shoes. She said that it was a shocking thing to do, that it was very improper, and that Karen was always to go to church in future in black shoes, even if they were old.

On the following Sunday there was Communion. Karen looked first at the black shoes, then at the red ones—looked at the red ones again, and put them on.

The sun was shining gloriously, so Karen and the old lady went along the footpath through the corn, where it was rather dusty.

At the church door stood an old crippled soldier leaning on a crutch; he had a wonderfully long beard, more red than white, and he bowed down to the ground and asked the old lady whether he might wipe her shoes. Then Karen put out her little foot too. "Dear me, what pretty dancing-shoes!" said the soldier. "Sit fast, when you dance," said he, addressing the shoes, and slapping the soles with his hand.

The old lady gave the soldier some money and then went with Karen into the church.

And all the people inside looked at Karen's red shoes, and all the figures gazed at them; when Karen knelt before the altar and put the golden goblet to her mouth, she thought only of the red shoes. It seemed to her as though they were swimming about in the goblet, and she forgot to sing the psalm, forgot to say the "Lord's Prayer."

Now every one came out of church, and the old lady stepped into her carriage. But just as Karen was lifting up her foot to get in too, the old soldier said: "Dear me, what pretty dancing shoes!" and Karen could not help it, she was obliged to dance a few steps; and when she had once begun, her legs continued to dance. It seemed as if the shoes had got power over them. She danced round the church corner, for she could not stop; the coachman had to run after her and seize her. He lifted her into the carriage, but her feet continued to dance, so that she kicked the good old lady violently. At last they took off her shoes, and her legs were at rest.

At home the shoes were put into the cupboard, but Karen could not help looking at them.

Now the old lady fell ill, and it was said that she would not rise from her bed again. She had to be nursed and waited upon, and this was no one's duty more than Karen's. But there was a grand ball in the town, and Karen was invited. She looked at the red shoes, saying to herself that there was no sin in doing that; she put the red shoes on, thinking there was no harm in that either; and then she went to the ball; and commenced to dance.

But when she wanted to go to the right, the shoes danced to the left, and when she wanted to dance up the room, the shoes danced down the room, down the stairs through the street, and out through the gates of the town. She danced, and was obliged to dance, far out into the dark wood. Suddenly something shone up among the trees, and she believed it was the moon, for it was a face. But it was the old soldier with the red beard; he sat there nodding his head and said: "Dear me, what pretty dancing shoes!"

She was frightened, and wanted to throw the red shoes away; but they stuck fast. She tore off her stockings, but the shoes had grown fast to her feet. She danced and was obliged to go on dancing over field and meadow, in rain and sunshine, by night and by day— but by night it was most horrible.

She danced out into the open churchyard; but the dead there did not dance. They had something better to do than that. She wanted to sit down on the pauper's grave where the bitter fern grows; but for her there was neither peace nor rest. And as she danced past the open church door she saw an angel there in long white robes, with wings reaching from his shoulders down to the earth; his face was stern and grave, and in his hand he held a broad shining sword.

"Dance you shall," said he, "dance in your red shoes till you are pale and cold, till your skin shrivels up and you are a skeleton! Dance you shall, from door to door, and where proud and wicked children live you shall knock, so that they may hear you and fear you! Dance you shall, dance—!"

"Mercy!" cried Karen. But she did not hear what the angel answered, for the shoes carried her through the gate into the fields, along highways and byways, and unceasingly she had to dance.

One morning she danced past a door that she knew well; they were singing a psalm inside, and a coffin was being carried out covered with flowers. Then she knew that she was forsaken by every one and damned by the angel of God.

She danced, and was obliged to go on dancing through the dark night. The shoes bore her away over thorns and stumps till she was all torn and bleeding; she danced away over the heath to a lonely little house. Here, she knew, lived the executioner; and she tapped with her finger at the window and said:

"Come out, come out! I cannot come in, for I must dance."

And the executioner said: "I don't suppose you know who I am. I strike off the heads of the wicked, and I notice that my axe is tingling to do so."

"Don't cut off my head!" said Karen, "for then I could not repent of my sin. But cut off my feet with the red shoes."

And then she confessed all her sin, and the executioner struck off her feet with the red shoes; but the shoes danced away with the little feet across the field into the deep forest.

And he carved her a pair of wooden feet and some crutches, and taught her a psalm which is always sung by sinners; she kissed the hand that guided the axe, and went away over the heath.

"Now, I have suffered enough for the red shoes," she said; "I will go to church, so that people can see me." And she went quickly up to the church-door; but when she came there, the red shoes were dancing before her, and she was frightened, and turned back.

During the whole week she was sad and wept many bitter tears, but when Sunday came again she said: "Now I have suffered and striven enough. I believe I am quite as good as many of those who sit in church and give themselves airs." And so she went boldly on; but she had not got farther than the churchyard gate when she saw the red shoes dancing along before her. Then she became terrified, and turned back and repented right heartily of her sin.

She went to the parsonage, and begged that she might be taken into service there. She would be industrious, she said, and do everything that she could; she did not mind about the wages as long as she had a roof over her, and was with good people. The pastor's wife had pity on her, and took her into service. And she was industrious and thoughtful. She sat quiet and listened when the pastor read aloud from the Bible in the evening. All the children liked her very much, but when they spoke about dress and grandeur and beauty she would shake her head.

On the following Sunday they all went to church, and she was asked whether she wished to go too; but, with tears in her eyes, she looked sadly at her crutches. And then the others went to hear God's Word, but she went alone into her little room; this was only large enough to hold the bed and a chair. Here she sat down with her hymn-book, and as she was reading it with a pious mind, the wind carried the notes of the organ over to her from the church, and in tears she lifted up her face and said: "O God! help me!"

Then the sun shone so brightly, and right before her stood an angel of God in white robes; it was the same one whom she had seen that night at the church-door. He no longer carried the sharp sword, but a beautiful green branch, full of roses; with this he touched the ceiling, which rose up very high, and where he had touched it there shone a golden star. He touched the walls, which opened wide apart, and she saw the organ which was pealing forth; she saw the pictures of the old pastors and their wives, and the congregation sitting in the polished chairs and singing from their hymn-books. The church itself had come to the poor girl in her narrow room, or the room had gone to the church. She sat in the pew with the rest of the pastor's household, and when they had finished the hymn and looked up, they nodded and said, "It was right of you to come, Karen."

"It was mercy," said she.

The organ played and the children's voices in the choir sounded soft and lovely. The bright warm sunshine streamed through the window into the pew where Karen sat, and her heart became so filled with it, so filled with peace and joy, that it broke. Her soul flew on the sunbeams to Heaven, and no one was there who asked after the Red Shoes.

♄ G Wells
(1866-1946)

39

The Red Room

"I can assure you," said I, "that it will take a very tangible ghost to frighten me." And I stood up before the fire with my glass in my hand.

"It is your own choosing," said the man with the withered arm, and glanced at me askance.

"Eight-and-twenty years," said I, "I have lived, and never a ghost have I seen as yet."

The old woman sat staring hard into the fire, her pale eyes wide open. "Ay," she broke in; "and eight-and-twenty years you have lived and never seen the likes of this house, I reckon. There's a many things to see, when one's still but eight-and-twenty." She swayed her head slowly from side to side. "A many things to see and sorrow for."

I half suspected the old people were trying to enhance the spiritual terrors of their house by their droning insistence. I put down my empty glass on the table and looked about the room, and caught a glimpse of myself, abbreviated and broadened to an impossible sturdiness, in the queer old mirror at the end of the room. "Well," I said, "if I see anything to-night, I shall be so much the wiser. For I come to the business with an open mind."

"It's your own choosing," said the man with the withered arm once more.

I heard the faint sound of a stick and a shambling step on the flags in the passage outside. The door creaked on its hinges as a second old man entered, more bent, more wrinkled, more aged even than the first. He supported himself by the help of a crutch, his eyes were covered by a shade, and his lower lip, half averted, hung pale and pink from his decaying yellow teeth. He made straight for an armchair on the opposite side of the table, sat down clumsily, and began to cough. The man with the withered hand gave the newcomer a short glance of positive dislike; the old woman took no notice of his arrival, but remained with her eyes fixed steadily on the fire.

"I said—it's your own choosing," said the man with the withered hand, when the coughing had ceased for a while.

"It's my own choosing," I answered.

The man with the shade became aware of my presence for the first time, and threw his head back for a moment, and sidewise, to see me. I caught a momentary glimpse of his eyes, small and bright and inflamed. Then he began to cough and splutter again.

"Why don't you drink?" said the man with the withered arm, pushing the beer toward him. The man with the shade poured out a glassful with a shaking hand, that splashed half as much again on the deal table. A monstrous shadow of him crouched upon the wall, and mocked his action as he poured and drank. I must confess I had scarcely expected these grotesque custodians. There is, to my mind, something inhuman in senility, something crouching and atavistic; the human qualities seem to drop from old people insensibly day by day. The three of them made me feel uncomfortable with their gaunt silences, their bent carriage, their evident unfriendliness to me and to one another. And that night, perhaps, I was in the mood for uncomfortable impressions. I resolved to get away from their vague fore-shadowings of the evil things upstairs.

"If," said I, "you will show me to this haunted room of yours, I will make myself comfortable there."

The old man with the cough jerked his head back so suddenly

that it startled me, and shot another glance of his red eyes at me from out of the darkness under the shade, but no one answered me. I waited a minute, glancing from one to the other. The old woman stared like a dead body, glaring into the fire with lack-lustre eyes.

"If," I said, a little louder, "if you will show me to this haunted room of yours, I will relieve you from the task of entertaining me."

"There's a candle on the slab outside the door," said the man with the withered hand, looking at my feet as he addressed me. "But if you go to the Red Room to-night—"

"This night of all nights!" said the old woman, softly.

"—You go alone."

"Very well," I answered, shortly, "and which way do I go?"

"You go along the passage for a bit," said he, nodding his head on his shoulder at the door, "until you come to a spiral staircase; and on the second landing is a door covered with green baize. Go through that, and down the long corridor to the end, and the Red Room is on your left up the steps."

"Have I got that right?" I said, and repeated his directions.

He corrected me in one particular.

"And you are really going?" said the man with the shade, looking at me again for the third time with that queer, unnatural tilting of the face.

"This night of all nights!" whispered the old woman.

"It is what I came for," I said, and moved toward the door. As I did so, the old man with the shade rose and staggered round the table, so as to be closer to the others and to the fire. At the door I turned and looked at them, and saw they were all close together, dark against the firelight, staring at me over their shoulders, with an intent expression on their ancient faces.

"Good-night," I said, setting the door open. "It's your own choosing," said the man with the withered arm.

I left the door wide open until the candle was well alight, and then I shut them in, and walked down the chilly, echoing passage.

I must confess that the oddness of these three old pensioners in whose charge her ladyship had left the castle, and the deep-toned, old-fashioned furniture of the housekeeper's room, in which they foregathered, had affected me curiously in spite of my effort to keep myself at a matter-of-fact phase. They seemed to belong to another age, an older age, an age when things spiritual were indeed to be feared, when common sense was uncommon, an age when omens and witches were credible, and ghosts beyond denying. Their very existence, thought I, is spectral; the cut of their clothing, fashions born in dead brains; the ornaments and conveniences in the room about them even are ghostly—the thoughts of vanished men, which still haunt rather than participate in the world of today. And the passage I was in, long and shadowy, with a film of moisture glistening on the wall, was as gaunt and cold as a thing that is dead and rigid. But with an effort I sent such thoughts to the right-about. The long, drafty subterranean passage was chilly and dusty, and my candle flared and made the shadows cower and quiver. The echoes rang up and down the spiral staircase, and a shadow came sweeping up after me, and another fled before me into the darkness overhead. I came to the wide landing and stopped there for a moment listening to a rustling that I fancied I heard creeping behind me, and then, satisfied of the absolute silence, pushed open the unwilling baize-covered door and stood in the silent corridor.

The effect was scarcely what I expected, for the moonlight, coming in by the great window on the grand staircase, picked out everything in vivid black shadow or reticulated silvery illumination. Everything seemed in its proper position; the house might have been deserted on the yesterday instead of twelve months ago. There were candles in the sockets of the sconces, and whatever dust had gathered on the carpets or upon the polished flooring was distributed so evenly as to be invisible in my candlelight. A waiting stillness was over everything. I was about to advance, and stopped abruptly. A bronze group stood upon the landing hidden from me by a corner of the wall; but its shadow fell with marvelous distinctness upon the white paneling, and gave me the impression of some one crouching to waylay me. The thing jumped upon my attention suddenly. I stood rigid for half a moment, perhaps. Then, with my hand in the pocket that held the revolver, I advanced, only to discover a Ganymede and Eagle, glistening in the moonlight. That incident for a time restored my nerve, and a dim porcelain Chinaman on a buhl table, whose head rocked as I passed, scarcely startled me.

The door of the Red Room and the steps up to it were in a shadowy corner. I moved my candle from side to side in order to see clearly the nature of the recess in which I stood, before opening the door. Here it was, thought I, that my predecessor was found, and the memory of that story gave me a sudden twinge of apprehension. I glanced over my shoulder at the black Ganymede in the moonlight, and opened the door of the Red Room rather hastily, with my face half turned to the pallid silence of the corridor.

I entered, closed the door behind me at once, turned the key I found in the lock within, and stood with the candle held aloft surveying the scene of my vigil, the great Red Room of Lorraine Castle, in which the young Duke had died; or rather in which he had begun his dying, for he had opened the door and fallen headlong down the steps I had just ascended. That had been the end of his vigil, of his gallant attempt to conquer the ghostly tradition of the place, and never, I thought, had apoplexy better served the ends of superstition. There were other and older stories that clung to the room, back to the half-incredible beginning of it all, the tale of a timid wife and the tragic end that came to her husband's jest of frightening her. And looking round that huge shadowy room with its black window bays, its recesses and alcoves, its dusty brown-red hangings and dark gigantic furniture, one could well understand the legends that had sprouted in its black corners, its germinating darknesses. My candle was a little tongue of light in the vastness of the chamber; its rays failed to pierce to the opposite end of the room, and left an ocean of dull red mystery and suggestion, sentinel shadows and watching darknesses beyond its island of light. And the stillness of desolation brooded over it all.

I must confess some impalpable quality of that ancient room disturbed me. I tried to fight the feeling down. I resolved to make a systematic examination of the place, and so, by leaving nothing to the imagination, dispel the fanciful suggestions of the obscurity before they obtained a hold upon me. After satisfying myself of the fastening of the door, I began to walk round the room, peering round each article of furniture, tucking up the valances of the bed and opening its curtains wide. In one place there was a distinct echo to my footsteps, the noises I made seemed so little that they enhanced rather than broke the silence of the place. I pulled up the blinds and examined the fastenings of the several windows. Attracted by the fall of a particle of dust, I leaned forward and looked up the blackness of the wide chimney. Then, trying to preserve my scientific attitude of mind, I walked round and began tapping the oak paneling for any secret opening, but I desisted before reaching the alcove. I saw my face in a mirror—white.

There were two big mirrors in the room, each with a pair of sconces bearing candles, and on the mantelshelf, too, were candles in china candle-sticks. All these I lit one after the other. The fire was laid—an unexpected consideration from the old housekeeper— and I lit it, to keep down any disposition to shiver, and when it was burning well I stood round with my back to it and regarded the room again. I had pulled up a chintz-covered armchair and a table to form a kind of barricade before me. On this lay my revolver, ready to hand. My precise examination had done me a little good, but I still found the remoter darkness of the place and its perfect stillness too stimulating for the imagination. The echoing of the stir and crackling of the fire was no sort of comfort to me. The shadow in the alcove at the end of the room began to display that undefinable quality of a presence, that odd suggestion of a lurking living thing that comes so easily in silence and solitude. And to reassure myself, I walked with a candle into it and satisfied myself that there was nothing tangible there. I stood that candle upon the floor of the alcove and left it in that position.

By this time I was in a state of considerable nervous tension, although to my reason there was no adequate cause for my condition. My mind, however, was perfectly clear. I postulated quite unreservedly that nothing supernatural could happen, and to pass the time I began stringing some rhymes together, Ingoldsby fashion, concerning the original legend of the place. A few I spoke aloud, but the echoes were not pleasant. For the same reason I also abandoned, after a time, a conversation with myself upon the impossibility of ghosts and haunting. My mind reverted to the three old and distorted people downstairs, and I tried to keep it upon that topic.

The sombre reds and grays of the room troubled me; even with its seven candles the place was merely dim. The light in the alcove flaring in a draft, and the fire flickering, kept the shadows and penumbra perpetually shifting and stirring in a noiseless flighty dance. Casting about for a remedy, I recalled the wax candles I had seen in the corridor, and, with a slight effort, carrying a candle and leaving the door open, I walked out into the moonlight, and presently returned with as many as ten. These I put in the various knick-knacks of china with which the room was sparsely adorned, and lit and placed them where the shadows had lain deepest, some on the floor, some in the window recesses, arranging and rearranging them until at last my seventeen candles were so placed that not an inch of the room but had the direct light of at least one of them. It occurred to me that when the ghost came I could warn him not to trip over them. The room was now quite brightly illuminated. There was something very cheering and reassuring in these little silent streaming flames, and to notice their steady diminution of length offered me an occupation and gave me a reassuring sense of the passage of time.

Even with that, however, the brooding expectation of the vigil weighed heavily enough upon me. I stood watching the minute hand of my watch creep towards midnight.

Then something happened in the alcove. I did not see the candle go out, I simply turned and saw that the darkness was there, as one might start and see the unexpected presence of a stranger. The black shadow had sprung back to its place. "By Jove," said I aloud, recovering from my surprise, "that draft's a strong one;" and taking the matchbox from the table, I walked across the room in a leisurely manner to relight the corner again. My first match would not strike, and as I succeeded with the second, something seemed

221

to blink on the wall before me. I turned my head involuntarily and saw that the two candles on the little table by the fireplace were extinguished. I rose at once to my feet.

"Odd," I said. "Did I do that myself in a flash of absent-mindedness?"

I walked back, relit one, and as I did so I saw the candle in the right sconce of one of the mirrors wink and go right out, and almost immediately its companion followed it. The flames vanished as if the wick had been suddenly nipped between a finger and thumb, leaving the wick neither glowing nor smoking, but black. While I stood gaping the candle at the foot of the bed went out, and the shadows seemed to take another step toward me.

"This won't do!" said I, and first one and then another candle on the mantelshelf followed.

"What's up?" I cried, with a queer high note getting into my voice somehow. At that the candle on the corner of the wardrobe went out, and the one I had relit in the alcove followed.

"Steady on!" I said, "those candles are wanted," speaking with a half-hysterical facetiousness, and scratching away at a match the while, "for the mantel candlesticks." My hands trembled so much that twice I missed the rough paper of the matchbox. As the mantel emerged from darkness again, two candles in the remoter end of the room were eclipsed. But with the same match I also relit the larger mirror candles, and those on the floor near the doorway, so that for the moment I seemed to gain on the extinctions. But then in a noiseless volley there vanished four lights at once in different corners of the room, and I struck another match in quivering haste, and stood hesitating whither to take it.

As I stood undecided, an invisible hand seemed to sweep out the two candles on the table. With a cry of terror I dashed at the alcove, then into the corner and then into the window, relighting three as two more vanished by the fireplace, and then, perceiving a better way, I dropped matches on the iron-bound deedbox in the corner, and caught up the bedroom candlestick. With this I avoided the delay of striking matches, but for all that the steady process of extinction went on, and the shadows I feared and fought against returned, and crept in upon me, first a step gained on this side of me, then on that. I was now almost frantic with the horror of the coming darkness, and my self-possession deserted me. I leaped panting from candle to candle in a vain struggle against that remorseless advance.

I bruised myself in the thigh against the table, I sent a chair headlong, I stumbled and fell and whisked the cloth from the table in my fall. My candle rolled away from me and I snatched another as I rose. Abruptly this was blown out as I swung it off the table by the wind of my sudden movement, and immediately the two remaining candles followed. But there was light still in the room, a red light, that streamed across the ceiling and staved off the shadows from me. The fire! Of course I could still thrust my candle between the bars and relight it.

I turned to where the flames were still dancing between the glowing coals and splashing red reflections upon the furniture; made two steps toward the grate, and incontinently the flames dwindled and vanished, the glow vanished, the reflections rushed together and disappeared, and as I thrust the candle between the bars darkness closed upon me like the shutting of an eye, wrapped about me in a stifling embrace, sealed my vision, and crushed the last vestiges of self-possession from my brain. And it was not only palpable darkness, but intolerable terror. The candle fell from my hands. I flung out my arms in a vain effort to thrust that ponderous blackness away from me, and lifting up my voice, screamed with all my might, once, twice, thrice. Then I think I must have staggered to my feet. I know I thought suddenly of the moonlit corridor, and with my head bowed and my arms over my face, made a stumbling run for the door.

But I had forgotten the exact position of the door, and I struck myself heavily against the corner of the bed. I staggered back, turned, and was either struck or struck myself against some other bulky furnishing. I have a vague memory of battering myself thus to and fro in the darkness, of a heavy blow at last upon my forehead, of a horrible sensation of falling that lasted an age, of my last frantic effort to keep my footing, and then I remember no more.

I opened my eyes in daylight. My head was roughly bandaged, and the man with the withered hand was watching my face. I looked about me trying to remember what had happened, and for a space I could not recollect. I rolled my eyes into the corner and saw the old woman, no longer abstracted, no longer terrible, pouring out some drops of medicine from a little blue phial into a glass. "Where am I?" I said. "I seem to remember you, and yet I can not remember who you are."

They told me then, and I heard of the haunted Red Room as one who hears a tale. "We found you at dawn," said he, "and there was blood on your forehead and lips."

I wondered that I had ever disliked him. The three of them in the daylight seemed commonplace old folk enough. The man with the green shade had his head bent as one who sleeps.

It was very slowly I recovered the memory of my experience. "You believe now," said the old man with the withered hand, "that the room is haunted?" He spoke no longer as one who greets an intruder, but as one who condoles with a friend.

"Yes," said I, "the room is haunted."

"And you have seen it. And we who have been here all our lives have never set eyes upon it. Because we have never dared. Tell us, is it truly the old earl who—"

"No," said I, "it is not."

"I told you so," said the old lady, with the glass in her hand. "It is his poor young countess who was frightened—"

"It is not," I said. "There is neither ghost of earl nor ghost of countess in that room; there is no ghost there at all, but worse, far worse, something impalpable—"

"Well?" they said.

"The worst of all the things that haunt poor mortal men," said I; "and that is, in all its nakedness—'Fear!' Fear that will not have light nor sound, that will not bear with reason, that deafens and darkens and overwhelms. It followed me through the corridor, it fought against me in the room—"

I stopped abruptly. There was an interval of silence. My hand went up to my bandages. "The candles went out one after another, and I fled—"

Then the man with the shade lifted his face sideways to see me and spoke.

"That is it," said he. "I knew that was it. A Power of Darkness. To put such a curse upon a home! It lurks there always. You can feel it even in the daytime, even of a bright summer's day, in the hangings, in the curtains, keeping behind you however you face about. In the dusk it creeps in the corridor and follows you, so that you dare not turn. It is even as you say. Fear itself is in that room. Black Fear . . . And there it will be . . . so long as this house of sin endures."

♄ H Munro (Saki)
(1870-1916)

40

The Open Window

"My aunt will come down very soon, Mr. Nuttel," said a very calm young lady of fifteen years of age; "meanwhile you must try to bear my company."

Framton Nuttel tried to say something which would please the niece now present, without annoying the aunt that was about to come. He was supposed to be going through a cure for his nerves; but he doubted whether these polite visits to a number of total strangers would help much.

I know how it will be, "his sister had said when he was preparing to go away into the country; "you will lose yourself down there and not speak to a living soul, and your nerves will be worse than ever through loneliness. I shall just give you letters of introduction to all the people I know there. Some of them, as far as I can remember, were quite nice."

Framton wondered whether Mrs. Sappleton, the lady to whom he was bringing one of the letters of introduction, was one of the nice ones.

"Do you know many of the people round here?" asked the niece, when she thought that they had sat long enough in silence.

"Hardly one," said Framton. "My sister was staying here, you know, about four years ago, and she gave me letters of introduction to some of the people here."

He made the last statement in a sad voice.

"Then you know almost nothing about my aunt?" continued the calm young lady.

"Only her name and address," Framton admitted. He was wondering whether Mrs. Sappleton was married; perhaps she had been married and her husband was dead. But there was something of a man in the room.

"Her great sorrow came just three years ago," said the child. "That would be after your sister's time."

"Her sorrow?" asked Framton. Somehow, in this restful country place, sorrows seemed far away.

"You may wonder why we keep that window wide open on an October afternoon," said the niece, pointing to a long window that opened like a door on to the grass outside.

"It is quite warm for the time of the year," said Framton; "but has that window got anything to do with your aunt's sorrow?"

"Out through that window, exactly three years ago, her husband and her two young brothers went off for their day's shooting. They never came back. In crossing the country to the shooting-ground, they were all three swallowed in a bog. It had been that terrible wet summer, you know, and places that were safe in other years became suddenly dangerous. Their bodies were never found. That was the worst part of it." Here the child's voice lost its calm sound and became almost human. "Poor aunt always thinks that they will come back some day, they and the little brown dog that was lost with them, and walk in at that window just as they used to do. That is why the window is kept open every evening till it is quite dark. Poor dear aunt, she has often told me how they went out, her husband with his white coat over his arm, and Ronnie, her youngest brother, singing a song, as he always did to annoy her, because she said it affected her nerves. Do you know, sometimes on quiet evenings like this, I almost get a strange feeling that they will all walk in through the window——"

She stopped and trembled. It was a relief to Framton when the aunt came busily into the room and apologized for being late.

"I hope Vera has been amusing you?" she said.

"She has been very interesting," said Framton.

"I hope you don't mind the open window," said Mrs. Sappleton brightly; "my husband and brothers will be home soon from shooting, and they always come in this way. They've been shooting birds to-day near the bog, so they'll make my poor carpets dirty. All you men do that sort of thing, don't you?"

She talked on cheerfully about the shooting and the scarcity of birds, and the hopes of shooting in the winter. To Framton it was all quite terrible. He made a great effort, which was only partly successful, to turn the talk on to a more cheerful subject. He was conscious that his hostess was giving him only a part of her attention, and her eyes were frequently looking past him to the open window and the grass beyond. It was certainly unfortunate that he should have paid his visit on this sorrowful day.

"The doctors agree in ordering me complete rest, no excitement and no bodily exercise," said Framton, who had the common idea that total strangers want to know the least detail of one's illnesses, their cause and cure. "On the matter of food, they are not so much in agreement," he continued.

"No?" said Mrs. Sappleton in a tired voice. Then she suddenly brightened into attention—but not to what Framton was saying.

"Here they are at last!" she cried. "Just in time for tea, and don't they look as if they were muddy up to the eyes!"

Framton trembled slightly and turned towards the niece with a look intended to show sympathetic understanding.

The child was looking out through the open window with fear in her eyes. With a shock Framton turned round in his seat and looked in the same direction.

In the increasing darkness three figures were walking across the grass towards the window; they all carried guns under their arms, and one of them had also a white coat hung over his shoulders. A tired brown dog kept close at their heels. Noiselessly they drew near to the house, and then a young voice started to sing in the darkness.

Framton wildly seized his hat and stick; he ran out through the front door and through the gate. He nearly ran into a man on a bicycle.

"Here we are, my dear," said the bearer of the white coat, coming in through the window; "fairly muddy, but most of it's dry. Who was that who ran out as we came up?"

"A most extraordinary man, a Mr. Nuttel," said Mrs. Sappleton; "he could only talk about his illnesses, and ran off without a word of good-bye or apology when you arrived. One would think he had seen a ghost."

"I expect it was the dog," said the niece calmly; "he told me he had a terrible fear of dogs. He was once hunted into a graveyard somewhere in India by a lot of wild dogs, and had to spend the night in a newly-dug grave with the creatures just above him. Enough to make anyone lose their nerve."

She was very clever at making up stories quickly.

41

Clovis on Parental Responsibilities

Marion Eggelby sat talking to Clovis on the only subject that she ever willingly talked about—her offspring and their varied perfections and accomplishments. Clovis was not in what could be called a receptive mood; the younger generation of Eggelby, depicted in the glowing improbable colours of parent impressionism, aroused in him no enthusiasm. Mrs. Eggelby, on the other hand, was furnished with enthusiasm enough for two.

"You would like Eric," she said, argumentatively rather than hopefully. Clovis had intimated very unmistakably that he was unlikely to care extravagantly for either Amy or Willie. "Yes, I feel sure you would like Eric. Every one takes to him at once. You know, he always reminds me of that famous picture of the youthful David—I forget who it's by, but it's very well known."

"That would be sufficient to set me against him, if I saw much of him," said Clovis. "Just imagine at auction bridge, for instance, when one was trying to concentrate one's mind on what one's partner's original declaration had been, and to remember what suits one's opponents had originally discarded, what it would be like to have some one persistently reminding one of a picture of the youthful David. It would be simply maddening. If Eric did that I should detest him."

"Eric doesn't play bridge," said Mrs. Eggelby with dignity.

"Doesn't he?" asked Clovis; "why not?"

"None of my children have been brought up to play card games," said Mrs. Eggelby; "draughts and halma and those sorts of games I encourage. Eric is considered quite a wonderful draughts-player."

"You are strewing dreadful risks in the path of your family," said Clovis; "a friend of mine who is a prison chaplain told me that among the worst criminal cases that have come under his notice, men condemned to death or to long periods of penal servitude, there was not a single bridge-player. On the other hand, he knew at least two expert draughts-players among them."

"I really don't see what my boys have got to do with the criminal classes," said Mrs. Eggelby resentfully. "They have been most carefully brought up, I can assure you that."

"That shows that you were nervous as to how they would turn out," said Clovis. "Now, my mother never bothered about bringing me up. She just saw to it that I got whacked at decent intervals and was taught the difference between right and wrong; there is some difference, you know, but I've forgotten what it is."

"Forgotten the difference between right and wrong!" exclaimed Mrs. Eggelby.

"Well, you see, I took up natural history and a whole lot of other subjects at the same time, and one can't remember everything, can one? I used to know the difference between the Sardinian dormouse and the ordinary kind, and whether the wry-neck arrives at our shores earlier than the cuckoo, or the other way round, and how long the walrus takes in growing to maturity; I daresay you knew all those sorts of things once, but I bet you've forgotten them."

"Those things are not important," said Mrs. Eggelby, "but—"

"The fact that we've both forgotten them proves that they are important," said Clovis; "you must have noticed that it's always the important things that one forgets, while the trivial, unnecessary facts of life stick in one's memory. There's my cousin, Editha Clubberley, for instance; I can never forget that her birthday is on the 12th of October. It's a matter of utter indifference to me on what date her birthday falls, or whether she was born at all; either fact seems to me absolutely trivial, or unnecessary - I've heaps of other cousins to go on with. On the other hand, when I'm staying with Hildegarde Shrubley I can never remember the important circumstance whether her first husband got his unenviable reputation on the Turf or the Stock Exchange, and that uncertainty rules Sport and Finance out of the conversation at once. One can never mention travel, either, because her second husband had to live permanently abroad."

"Mrs. Shrubley and I move in very different circles," said Mrs. Eggelby stiffly.

"No one who knows Hildegarde could possibly accuse her of moving in a circle," said Clovis; "her view of life seems to be a non-stop run with an inexhaustible supply of petrol. If she can get some one else to pay for the petrol so much the better. I don't mind confessing to you that she has taught me more than any other woman I can think of."

"What kind of knowledge?" demanded Mrs. Eggelby, with the air a jury might collectively wear when finding a verdict without leaving the box.

"Well, among other things, she's introduced me to at least four different ways of cooking lobster," said Clovis gratefully. "That, of course, wouldn't appeal to you; people who abstain from the pleasures of the card- table never really appreciate the finer possibilities of the dining-table. I suppose their powers of enlightened enjoyment get atrophied from disuse."

"An aunt of mine was very ill after eating a lobster," said Mrs. Eggelby.

"I daresay, if we knew more of her history, we should find out that she'd often been ill before eating the lobster. Aren't you concealing the fact that she'd had measles and influenza and nervous headache and hysteria, and other things that aunts do have, long before she ate the lobster? Aunts that have never known a day's illness are very rare; in fact, I don't personally know of any. Of course if she ate it as a child of two weeks old it might have been her first illness—and her last. But if that was the case I think you should have said so."

"I must be going," said Mrs. Eggelby, in a tone which had been thoroughly sterilised of even perfunctory regret.

Clovis rose with an air of graceful reluctance.

"I have so enjoyed our little talk about Eric," he said; "I quite look forward to meeting him some day."

"Good-bye," said Mrs. Eggelby frostily; the supplementary remark which she made at the back of her throat was—

"I'll take care that you never shall!"

42

Mrs. Packletide's Tiger

It was Mrs. Packletide's pleasure and intention that she should shoot a tiger. Not that the lust to kill had suddenly descended on her, or that she felt that she would leave India safer and more wholesome than she had found it, with one fraction less of wild beast per million of inhabitants. The compelling motive for her sudden deviation towards the footsteps of Nimrod was the fact that Loona Bimberton had recently been carried eleven miles in an aeroplane by an Algerian aviator, and talked of nothing else; only a personally procured tiger-skin and a heavy harvest of Press photographs could successfully counter that sort of thing. Mrs. Packletide had already arranged in her mind the lunch she would give at her house in Curzon Street, ostensibly in Loona Bimberton's honour, with a tiger-skin rug occupying most of the foreground and all of the conversation. She had also already designed in her mind the tiger-claw broach that she was going to give Loona Bimberton on her next birthday. In a world that is supposed to be chiefly swayed by hunger and by love Mrs. Packletide was an exception; her movements and motives were largely governed by dislike of Loona Bimberton.

Circumstances proved propitious. Mrs. Packletide had offered a thousand rupees for the opportunity of shooting a tiger without over-much risk or exertion, and it so happened that a neighbouring village could boast of being the favoured rendezvous of an animal of respectable antecedents, which had been driven by the increasing infirmities of age to abandon game-killing and confine its appetite to the smaller domestic animals. The prospect of earning the thousand rupees had stimulated the sporting and commercial instinct of the villagers; children were posted night and day on the outskirts of the local jungle to head the tiger back in the unlikely event of his attempting to roam away to fresh hunting-grounds, and the cheaper kinds of goats were left about with elaborate carelessness to keep him satisfied with his present quarters. The one great anxiety was lest he should die of old age before the date appointed for the memsahib's shoot. Mothers carrying their babies home through the jungle after the day's work in the fields hushed their singing lest they might curtail the restful sleep of the venerable herd-robber.

The great night duly arrived, moonlit and cloudless. A platform had been constructed in a comfortable and conveniently placed tree, and thereon crouched Mrs. Packletide and her paid companion, Miss Mebbin. A goat, gifted with a particularly persistent bleat, such as even a partially deaf tiger might be reasonably expected to hear on a still night, was tethered at the correct distance. With an accurately sighted rifle and a thumb-nail pack of patience cards the sportswoman awaited the coming of the quarry.

"I suppose we are in some danger?" said Miss Mebbin.

She was not actually nervous about the wild beast, but she had a morbid dread of performing an atom more service than she had been paid for.

"Nonsense," said Mrs. Packletide; "it's a very old tiger. It couldn't spring up here even if it wanted to."

"If it's an old tiger I think you ought to get it cheaper. A thousand rupees is a lot of money."

Louisa Mebbin adopted a protective elder-sister attitude towards money in general, irrespective of nationality or denomination. Her energetic intervention had saved many a rouble from dissipating itself in tips in some Moscow hotel, and francs and centimes clung to her instinctively under circumstances which would have driven them headlong from less sympathetic hands. Her speculations as to the market depreciation of tiger remnants were cut short by the appearance on the scene of the animal itself. As soon as it caught sight of the tethered goat it lay flat on the earth, seemingly less from a desire to take advantage of all available cover than for the purpose of snatching a short rest before commencing the grand attack.

"I believe it's ill," said Louisa Mebbin, loudly in Hindustani, for the benefit of the village headman, who was in ambush in a neighbouring tree.

"Hush!" said Mrs. Packletide, and at that moment the tiger commenced ambling towards his victim.

"Now, now!" urged Miss Mebbin with some excitement; "if he doesn't touch the goat we needn't pay for it." (The bait was an extra.)

The rifle flashed out with a loud report, and the great tawny beast sprang to one side and then rolled over in the stillness of death. In a moment a crowd of excited natives had swarmed on to the scene, and their shouting speedily carried the glad news to the village, where a thumping of tom-toms took up the chorus of triumph. And their triumph and rejoicing found a ready echo in the heart of Mrs. Packletide; already that luncheon-party in Curzon Street seemed immeasurably nearer.

It was Louisa Mebbin who drew attention to the fact that the goat was in death-throes from a mortal bullet-wound, while no trace of the rifle's deadly work could be found on the tiger. Evidently the wrong animal had been hit, and the beast of prey had succumbed to heart-failure, caused by the sudden report of the rifle, accelerated by senile decay. Mrs. Packletide was pardonably annoyed at the discovery; but, at any rate, she was the possessor of a dead tiger, and the villagers, anxious for their thousand rupees, gladly connived at the fiction that she had shot the beast. And Miss Mebbin was a paid companion. Therefore did Mrs. Packletide face the cameras with a light heart, and her pictured fame reached from the pages of the Texas Weekly Snapshot to the illustrated Monday supplement of the Novoe Vremya. As for Loona Bimberton, she refused to look at an illustrated paper for weeks, and her letter of thanks for the gift of a tiger-claw brooch was a model of repressed emotions. The luncheon-party she declined; there are limits beyond which repressed emotions become dangerous.

From Curzon Street the tiger-skin rug travelled down to the Manor House, and was duly inspected and admired by the county, and it seemed a fitting and appropriate thing when Mrs. Packletide went to the County Costume Ball in the character of Diana. She refused to fall in, however, with Clovis's tempting suggestion of a primeval dance party, at which every one should wear the skins of beasts they had recently slain. "I should be in rather a Baby Bunting condition," confessed Clovis, "with a miserable rabbit-skin or two to wrap up in, but then," he added, with a rather malicious glance at Diana's proportions, "my figure is quite as good as that Russian dancing boy's."

"How amused every one would be if they knew what really happened," said Louisa Mebbin a few days after the ball.

"What do you mean?" asked Mrs. Packletide quickly.

"How you shot the goat and frightened the tiger to death," said Miss Mebbin, with her disagreeably pleasant laugh.

"No one would believe it," said Mrs. Packletide, her face changing colour as rapidly as though it were going through a book of patterns before post-time.

"Loona Bimberton would," said Miss Mebbin. Mrs. Packletide's face settled on an unbecoming shade of greenish white.

"You surely wouldn't give me away?" she asked.

"I've seen a week-end cottage near Darking that I should rather like to buy," said Miss Mebbin with seeming irrelevance. "Six hundred and eighty, freehold. Quite a bargain, only I don't happen to have the money."

***

Louisa Mebbin's pretty week-end cottage, christened by her "Les Fauves," and gay in summer-time with its garden borders of tiger-lilies, is the wonder and admiration of her friends.

"It is a marvel how Louisa manages to do it," is the general verdict.

Mrs. Packletide indulges in no more big-game shooting.

"The incidental expenses are so heavy," she confides to inquiring friends.

43

The Music on the Hill

Sylvia Seltoun ate her breakfast in the morning-room at Yessney with a pleasant sense of ultimate victory, such as a fervent Ironside might have permitted himself on the morrow of Worcester fight. She was scarcely pugnacious by temperament, but belonged to that more successful class of fighters who are pugnacious by circumstance. Fate had willed that her life should be occupied with a series of small struggles, usually with the odds slightly against her, and usually she had just managed to come through winning. And now she felt that she had brought her hardest and certainly her most important struggle to a successful issue. To have married Mortimer Seltoun, 'Dead Mortimer' as his more intimate enemies called him, in the teeth of the cold hostility of his family, and in spite of his unaffected indifference to women, was indeed an achievement that had needed some determination and adroitness to carry through; yesterday she had brought her victory to its concluding stage by wrenching her husband away from Town and its group of satellite watering-places and 'settling him down,' in the vocabulary of her kind, in this remote wood-girt manor farm which was his country house.

"You will never get Mortimer to go," his mother had said carpingly, "but if he once goes he'll stay; Yessney throws almost as much a spell over him as Town does. One can understand what holds him to Town, but Yessney—" and the dowager had shrugged her shoulders.

There was a sombre almost savage wildness about Yessney that was certainly not likely to appeal to town-bred tastes, and Sylvia, notwithstanding her name, was accustomed to nothing much more sylvan than 'leafy Kensington'. She looked on the country as something excellent and wholesome in its way, which was apt to become troublesome if you encouraged it overmuch. Distrust of town-life had been a new thing with her, born of her marriage with Mortimer, and she had watched with satisfaction the gradual fading of what she called 'the Jermyn-street-look' in his eyes as the woods and heather of Yessney had closed in on them yesternight. Her will-power and strategy had prevailed; Mortimer would stay.

Outside the morning-room windows was a triangular slope of turf, which the indulgent might call a lawn, and beyond its low hedge of neglected fuchsia bushes a steeper slope of heather and bracken dropped down into cavernous combes overgrown with oak and yew. In its wild open savagery there seemed a stealthy linking of the joy of life with the terror of unseen things. Sylvia smiled complacently as she gazed with a School-of-Art appreciation at the landscape, and then of a sudden she almost shuddered.

"It is very wild," she said to Mortimer, who had joined her; "one could almost think that in such a place the worship of Pan had never quite died out."

"The worship of Pan never has died out," said Mortimer. "Other newer gods have drawn aside his votaries from time to time, but he is the Nature-God to whom all must come back at last. He has been called the Father of all the Gods, but most of his children have been stillborn."

Sylvia was religious in an honest vaguely devotional kind of way, and did not like to hear her beliefs spoken of as mere aftergrowths, but it was at least something new and hopeful to hear Dead Mortimer speak with such energy and conviction on any subject.

"You don't really believe in Pan?" she asked incredulously.

"I've been a fool in most things," said Mortimer quietly, "but I'm not such a fool as not to believe in Pan when I'm down here. And if you're wise you won't disbelieve in him too boastfully while you're in his country."

It was not till a week later, when Sylvia had exhausted the attractions of the woodland walks round Yessney, that she ventured on a tour of inspection of the farm buildings. A farmyard suggested in her mind a scene of cheerful bustle, with churns and flails and smiling dairymaids, and teams of horses drinking knee-deep in duck-crowded ponds. As she wandered among the gaunt grey buildings of Yessney manor farm her first impression was one of crushing stillness and desolation, as though she had happened on some lone deserted homestead long given over to owls and cobwebs; then came a sense of furtive watchful hostility, the same shadow of unseen things that seemed to lurk in the wooded combes and coppices. From behind heavy doors and shuttered windows came the restless stamp of hoof or rasp of chain halter, and at times a muffled bellow from some stalled beast. From a distant corner a shaggy dog watched her with intent unfriendly eyes; as she drew near it slipped quietly into its kennel, and slipped out again as noiselessly when she had passed by. A few hens, questing for food under a rick, stole away under a gate at her approach. Sylvia felt that if she had come across any human beings in this wilderness of barn and byre they would have fled wraith-like from her gaze. At last, turning a corner quickly, she came upon a living thing that did not fly from her. Astretch in a pool of mud was an enormous sow, gigantic beyond the town-woman's wildest computation of swine-flesh, and speedily alert to resent and if necessary repel the unwonted intrusion. It was Sylvia's turn to make an unobtrusive retreat. As she threaded her way past rickyards and cowsheds and long blank walls, she started suddenly at a strange sound—the echo of a boy's laughter, golden and equivocal. Jan, the only boy employed on the farm, a tow-headed, wizen-faced yokel, was visibly at work on a potato clearing half-way up the nearest hillside, and Mortimer, when questioned, knew of no other probable or possible begetter of the hidden mockery that had ambushed

Sylvia's retreat. The memory of that untraceable echo was added to her other impressions of a furtive sinister "something" that hung around Yessney.

Of Mortimer she saw very little; farm and woods and trout-streams seemed to swallow him up from dawn till dusk. Once, following the direction she had seen him take in the morning, she came to an open space in a nut copse, further shut in by huge yew trees, in the centre of which stood a stone pedestal surmounted by a small bronze figure of a youthful Pan. It was a beautiful piece of workmanship, but her attention was chiefly held by the fact that a newly cut bunch of grapes had been placed as an offering at its feet. Grapes were none too plentiful at the manor house, and Sylvia snatched the bunch angrily from the pedestal. Contemptuous annoyance dominated her thoughts as she strolled slowly homeward, and then gave way to a sharp feeling of something that was very near fright; across a thick tangle of undergrowth a boy's face was scowling at her, brown and beautiful, with unutterably evil eyes. It was a lonely pathway, all pathways round Yessney were lonely for the matter of that, and she sped forward without waiting to give a closer scrutiny to this sudden apparition. It was not till she had reached the house that she discovered that she had dropped the bunch of grapes in her flight.

"I saw a youth in the wood to-day," she told Mortimer that evening, "brown-faced and rather handsome, but a scoundrel to look at. A gipsy lad, I suppose."

"A reasonable theory," said Mortimer, "only there aren't any gipsies in these parts at present."

"Then who was he?" asked Sylvia, and as Mortimer appeared to have no theory of his own, she passed on to recount her finding of the votive offering.

"I suppose it was your doing," she observed; "it's a harmless piece of lunacy, but people would think you dreadfully silly if they knew of it."

"Did you meddle with it in any way?" asked Mortimer.

"I—I threw the grapes away. It seemed so silly," said Sylvia, watching Mortimer's impassive face for a sign of annoyance.

"I don't think you were wise to do that," he said reflectively. "I've heard it said that the Wood Gods are rather horrible to those who molest them."

"Horrible perhaps to those that believe in them, but you see I don't," retorted Sylvia.

"All the same," said Mortimer in his even, dispassionate tone, "I should avoid the woods and orchards if I were you, and give a wide berth to the horned beasts on the farm."

It was all nonsense, of course, but in that lonely wood-girt spot nonsense seemed able to rear a bastard brood of uneasiness.

"Mortimer," said Sylvia suddenly, "I think we will go back to Town some time soon."

Her victory had not been so complete as she had supposed; it had carried her on to ground that she was already anxious to quit.

"I don't think you will ever go back to Town," said Mortimer. He seemed to be paraphrasing his mother's prediction as to himself.

Sylvia noted with dissatisfaction and some self-contempt that the course of her next afternoon's ramble took her instinctively clear of the network of woods. As to the horned cattle, Mortimer's warning was scarcely needed, for she had always regarded them as of doubtful neutrality at the best: her imagination unsexed the most matronly dairy cows and turned them into bulls liable to "see red" at any moment. The ram who fed in the narrow paddock below the orchards she had adjudged, after ample and cautious probation, to be of docile temper; to-day, however, she decided to leave his docility untested, for the usually tranquil beast was roaming with every sign of restlessness from corner to corner of his meadow. A low, fitful piping, as of some reedy flute, was coming from the depth of a neighbouring copse, and there seemed to be some subtle connection between the animal's restless pacing and the wild music from the wood. Sylvia turned her steps in an upward direction and climbed the heather-clad slopes that stretched in rolling shoulders high above Yessney. She had left the piping notes behind her, but across the wooded combes at her feet the wind brought her another kind of music, the straining bay of hounds in full chase. Yessney was just on the outskirts of the Devon-and-Somerset country, and the hunted deer sometimes came that way. Sylvia could presently see a dark body, breasting hill after hill, and sinking again and again out of sight as he crossed the combes, while behind him steadily swelled that relentless chorus, and she grew tense with the excited sympathy that one feels for any hunted thing in whose capture one is not directly interested. And at last he broke through the outermost line of oak scrub and fern and stood panting in the open, a fat September stag carrying a well-furnished head. His obvious course was to drop down to the brown pools of Undercombe, and thence make his way towards the red deer's favoured sanctuary, the sea. To Sylvia's surprise, however, he turned his head to the upland slope and came lumbering resolutely onward over the heather. "It will be dreadful," she thought, "the hounds will pull him down under my very eyes." But the music of the pack seemed to have died away for a moment, and in its place she heard again that wild piping, which rose now on this side, now on that, as though urging the failing stag to a final effort. Sylvia stood well aside from his path, half hidden in a thick growth of whortle bushes, and watched him swing stiffly upward, his flanks dark with sweat, the coarse hair on his neck showing light by contrast. The pipe music shrilled suddenly around her, seeming to come from the bushes at her very feet, and at the same moment the great beast slewed round and bore directly down upon her. In an instant her pity for the hunted animal was changed to wild terror at her own danger; the thick heather roots mocked her scrambling efforts at flight, and she looked frantically downward for a glimpse of oncoming hounds. The huge antler spikes were within a few yards of her, and in a flash of numbing fear she remembered Mortimer's warning, to beware of horned beasts on the farm. And then with a quick throb of joy she saw that she was not alone; a human figure stood a few paces aside, knee-deep in the whortle bushes.

"Drive it off!" she shrieked. But the figure made no answering movement.

The antlers drove straight at her breast, the acrid smell of the hunted animal was in her nostrils, but her eyes were filled with the horror of something she saw other than her oncoming death. And in her ears rang the echo of a boy's laughter, golden and equivocal.

44

Down Pens

"Have you written to thank the Froplinsons for what they sent us?" asked Egbert.

"No," said Janetta, with a note of tired defiance in her voice; "I've written eleven letters to-day expressing surprise and gratitude for sundry unmerited gifts, but I haven't written to the Froplinsons."

"Some one will have to write to them," said Egbert.

"I don't dispute the necessity, but I don't think the some one should be me," said Janetta. "I wouldn't mind writing a letter of angry recrimination or heartless satire to some suitable recipient; in fact, I should rather enjoy it, but I've come to the end of my capacity for expressing servile amiability. Eleven letters to-day and nine yesterday, all couched in the same strain of ecstatic thankfulness: really, you can't expect me to sit down to another. There is such a thing as writing oneself out."

"I've written nearly as many," said Egbert, "and I've had my usual business correspondence to get through, too. Besides, I don't know what it was that the Froplinsons sent us."

"A William the Conqueror calendar," said Janetta, "with a quotation of one of his great thoughts for every day in the year."

"Impossible," said Egbert; "he didn't have three hundred and sixty-five thoughts in the whole of his life, or, if he did, he kept them to himself. He was a man of action, not of introspection."

"Well, it was William Wordsworth, then," said Janetta; "I know William came into it somewhere."

"That sounds more probable," said Egbert; "well, let's collaborate on this letter of thanks and get it done. I'll dictate, and you can scribble it down. 'Dear Mrs. Froplinson—thank you and your husband so much for the very pretty calendar you sent us. It was very good of you to think of us.'"

"You can't possibly say that," said Janetta, laying down her pen.

"It's what I always do say, and what every one says to me," protested Egbert.

"We sent them something on the twenty-second," said Janetta, "so they simply had to think of us. There was no getting away from it."

"What did we send them?" asked Egbert gloomily.

"Bridge-markers," said Janetta, "in a cardboard case, with some inanity about 'digging for fortune with a royal spade' emblazoned on the cover. The moment I saw it in the shop I said to myself 'Froplinsons' and to the attendant 'How much?' When he said 'Ninepence,' I gave him their address, jabbed our card in, paid tenpence or elevenpence to cover the postage, and thanked heaven. With less sincerity and infinitely more trouble they eventually thanked me."

"The Froplinsons don't play bridge," said Egbert.

"One is not supposed to notice social deformities of that sort," said Janetta; "it wouldn't be polite. Besides, what trouble did they take to find out whether we read Wordsworth with gladness? For all they knew or cared we might be frantically embedded in the belief that all poetry begins and ends with John Masefield, and it might infuriate or depress us to have a daily sample of Wordsworthian products flung at us."

"Well, let's get on with the letter of thanks," said Egbert.

"Proceed," said Janetta.

"How clever of you to guess that Wordsworth is our favourite poet," dictated Egbert.

Again Janetta laid down her pen.

"Do you realise what that means?" she asked; "a Wordsworth booklet next Christmas, and another calendar the Christmas after, with the same problem of having to write suitable letters of thankfulness. No, the best thing to do is to drop all further allusion to the calendar and switch off on to some other topic."

"But what other topic?"

"Oh, something like this: 'What do you think of the New Year Honours List? A friend of ours made such a clever remark when he read it.' Then you can stick in any remark that comes into your head; it needn't be clever. The Froplinsons won't know whether it is or isn't."

"We don't even know on which side they are in politics," objected Egbert; "and anyhow you can't suddenly dismiss the subject of the calendar. Surely there must be some intelligent remark that can be made about it."

"Well, we can't think of one," said Janetta wearily; "the fact is, we've both written ourselves out. Heavens! I've just remembered Mrs. Stephen Ludberry. I haven't thanked her for what she sent."

"What did she send?"

"I forget; I think it was a calendar."

There was a long silence, the forlorn silence of those who are bereft of hope and have almost ceased to care.

Presently Egbert started from his seat with an air of resolution. The light of battle was in his eyes.

"Let me come to the writing-table," he exclaimed.

"Gladly," said Janetta. "Are you going to write to Mrs. Ludberry or the Froplinsons?"

"To neither," said Egbert, drawing a stack of notepaper towards him; "I'm going to write to the editor of every enlightened and influential newspaper in the Kingdom, I'm going to suggest that there should be a sort of epistolary Truce of God during the festivities of Christmas and New Year. From the twenty-fourth of December to the third or fourth of January it shall be considered an offence against good sense and good feeling to write or expect any letter or communication that does not deal with the necessary events of the moment. Answers to invitations, arrangements about trains, renewal of club subscriptions, and, of course, all the ordinary everyday affairs of business, sickness, engaging new cooks, and so forth, these will be dealt with in the usual manner as something inevitable, a legitimate part of our daily life. But all the devastating accretions of correspondence, incident to the festive season, these should be swept away to give the season a chance of being really festive, a time of untroubled, unpunctuated peace and good will."

"But you would have to make some acknowledgment of presents received," objected Janetta; "otherwise people would never know whether they had arrived safely."

"Of course, I have thought of that," said Egbert; "every present that was sent off would be accompanied by a ticket bearing the date of dispatch and the signature of the sender, and some conventional hieroglyphic to show that it was intended to be a Christmas or New Year gift; there would be a counterfoil with space for the recipient's name and the date of arrival, and all you would have to do would be to sign and date the counterfoil, add a conventional hieroglyphic indicating heartfelt thanks and gratified surprise, put the thing into an envelope and post it."

"It sounds delightfully simple," said Janetta wistfully, "but people would consider it too cut-and-dried, too perfunctory."

"It is not a bit more perfunctory than the present system," said Egbert; "I have only the same conventional language of gratitude at my disposal with which to thank dear old Colonel Chuttle for his perfectly delicious Stilton, which we shall devour to the last morsel, and the Froplinsons for their calendar, which we shall never look at. Colonel Chuttle knows that we are grateful for the Stilton, without having to be told so, and the Froplinsons know that we are bored with their calendar, whatever we may say to the contrary, just as we know that they are bored with the bridge-markers in spite of their written assurance that they thanked us for our charming little gift. What is more, the Colonel knows that even if we had taken a sudden aversion to Stilton or been forbidden it by the doctor, we should still have written a letter of hearty thanks around it. So you see the present system of acknowledgment is just as perfunctory and conventional as the counterfoil business would be, only ten times more tiresome and brain-racking."

"Your plan would certainly bring the ideal of a Happy Christmas a step nearer realisation," said Janetta.

"There are exceptions, of course," said Egbert, "people who really try to infuse a breath of reality into their letters of acknowledgment. Aunt Susan, for instance, who writes: 'Thank you very much for the ham; not such a good flavour as the one you sent last year, which itself was not a particularly good one. Hams are not what they used to be.' It would be a pity to be deprived of her Christmas comments, but that loss would be swallowed up in the general gain."

"Meanwhile," said Janetta, "what am I to say to the Froplinsons?"

45

The Phantom Luncheon

"The Smithly-Dubbs are in Town," said Sir James. "I wish you would show them some attention. Ask them to lunch with you at the Ritz or somewhere."

"From the little I've seen of the Smithly-Dubbs I don't think I want to cultivate their acquaintance," said Lady Drakmanton.

"They always work for us at election times," said her husband; "I don't suppose they influence very many votes, but they have an uncle who is on one of my ward committees, and another uncle speaks sometimes at some of our less important meetings. Those sort of people expect some return in the shape of hospitality."

"Expect it!" exclaimed Lady Drakmanton; "the Misses Smithly-Dubb do more than that; they almost demand it. They belong to my club, and hang about the lobby just about lunch-time, all three of them, with their tongues hanging out of their mouths and the six-course look in their eyes. If I were to breathe the word 'lunch' they would hustle me into a taxi and scream 'Ritz' or 'Dieudonne's' to the driver before I knew what was happening."

"All the same, I think you ought to ask them to a meal of some sort," persisted Sir James.

"I consider that showing hospitality to the Smithly-Dubbs is carrying Free Food principles to a regrettable extreme," said Lady

Drakmanton; "I've entertained the Joneses and the Browns and the Snapheimers and the Lubrikoffs, and heaps of others whose names I forget, but I don't see why I should inflict the society of the Misses Smithly-Dubb on myself for a solid hour. Imagine it, sixty minutes, more or less, of unrelenting gobble and gabble. Why can't you take them on, Milly?" she asked, turning hopefully to her sister.

"I don't know them," said Milly hastily.

"All the better; you can pass yourself off as me. People say that we are so alike that they can hardly tell us apart, and I've only spoken to these tiresome young women about twice in my life, at committee-rooms, and bowed to them in the club. Any of the club page-boys will point them out to you; they're always to be found lolling about the hall just before lunch-time."

"My dear Betty, don't be absurd," protested Milly; "I've got some people lunching with me at the Carlton to-morrow, and I'm leaving Town the day afterwards."

"What time is your lunch to-morrow?" asked Lady Drakmanton reflectively.

"Two o'clock," said Milly.

"Good," said her sister; "the Smithly-Dubbs shall lunch with me tomorrow. It shall be rather an amusing lunch-party. At least, I shall be amused."

The last two remarks she made to herself. Other people did not always appreciate her ideas of humour. Sir James never did.

The next day Lady Drakmanton made some marked variations in her usual toilet effects. She dressed her hair in an unaccustomed manner, and put on a hat that added to the transformation of her appearance. When she had made one or two minor alterations she was sufficiently unlike her usual smart self to produce some hesitation in the greeting which the Misses Smithly-Dubb bestowed on her in the club-lobby. She responded, however, with a readiness which set their doubts at rest.

"What is the Carlton like for lunching in?" she asked breezily.

The restaurant received an enthusiastic recommendation from the three sisters.

"Let's go and lunch there, shall we?" she suggested, and in a few minutes' time the Smithly-Dubb mind was contemplating at close quarters a happy vista of baked meats and approved vintage.

"Are you going to start with caviare? I am," confided Lady Drakmanton, and the Smithly-Dubbs started with caviare. The subsequent dishes were chosen in the same ambitious spirit, and by the time they had arrived at the wild duck course it was beginning to be a rather expensive lunch.

The conversation hardly kept pace with the brilliancy of the menu. Repeated references on the part of the guests to the local political conditions and prospects in Sir James's constituency were met with vague 'ahs' and 'indeeds' from Lady Drakmanton, who might have been expected to be specially interested.

"I think when the Insurance Act is a little better understood it will lose some of its present unpopularity," hazarded Cecilia Smithly-Dubb.

"Will it? I dare say. I'm afraid politics don't interest me very much," said Lady Drakmanton.

The three Miss Smithly-Dubbs put down their cups of Turkish coffee and stared. Then they broke into protesting giggles.

"Of course, you're joking," they said.

"Not me," was the disconcerting answer; "I can't make head or tail of these bothering old politics. Never could, and never want to. I've quite enough to do to manage my own affairs, and that's a fact."

"But," exclaimed Amanda Smithly-Dubb, with a squeal of bewilderment breaking into her voice, "I was told you spoke so informingly about the Insurance Act at one of our social evenings."

It was Lady Drakmanton who stared now. "Do you know," she said, with a scared look around her, "rather a dreadful thing is happening. I'm suffering from a complete loss of memory. I can't even think who I am. I remember meeting you somewhere, and I remember you asking me to come and lunch with you here, and that I accepted your kind invitation. Beyond that my mind is a positive blank."

The scared look was transferred with intensified poignancy to the faces of her companions.

"You asked us to lunch," they exclaimed hurriedly. That seemed a more immediately important point to clear up than the question of identity.

"Oh, no," said the vanishing hostess, "That I do remember about. You insisted on my coming here because the feeding was so good, and I must say it comes up to all you said about it. A very nice lunch it's been. What I'm worrying about is who on earth am I? I haven't the faintest notion?"

"You are Lady Drakmanton," exclaimed the three sisters in chorus.

"Now, don't make fun of me," she replied, crossly, "I happen to know her quite well by sight, and she isn't a bit like me. And it's an odd thing you should have mentioned her, for it so happens she's just come into the room. That lady in black, with the yellow plume in her hat, there over by the door."

The Smithly-Dubbs looked in the indicated direction, and the uneasiness in their eyes deepened into horror. In outward appearance the lady who had just entered the room certainly came rather nearer to their recollection of their Member's wife than the individual who was sitting at table with them.

"Who are you, then, if that is Lady Drakmanton?" they asked in panic-stricken bewilderment.

"That is just what I don't know," was the answer; "and you don't seem to know much better than I do."

"You came up to us in the club—"

"In what club?"

"The New Didactic, in Calais Street."

"The New Didactic!" exclaimed Lady Drakmanton with an air of returning illumination; "thank you so much. Of course, I remember now who I am. I'm Ellen Niggle, of the Ladies' Brasspolishing Guild. The Club employs me to come now and then and see to the polishing of the brass fittings. That's how I came to know Lady Drakmanton by sight; she's very often in the Club. And you are the ladies who so kindly asked me out to lunch. Funny

254

how it should all have slipped my memory, all of a sudden. The unaccustomed good food and wine must have been too much for me; for the moment I really couldn't call to mind who I was. Good gracious," she broke off suddenly, "it's ten past two; I should be at a polishing job in Whitehall. I must scuttle off like a giddy rabbit. Thanking you ever so."

She left the room with a scuttle sufficiently suggestive of the animal she had mentioned, but the giddiness was all on the side of her involuntary hostesses. The restaurant seemed to be spinning round them; and the bill when it appeared did nothing to restore their composure. They were as nearly in tears as it is permissible to be during the luncheon hour in a really good restaurant. Financially speaking, they were well able to afford the luxury of an elaborate lunch, but their ideas on the subject of entertaining differed very sharply, according to the circumstances of whether they were dispensing or receiving hospitality. To have fed themselves liberally at their own expense was, perhaps, an extravagance to be deplored, but, at any rate, they had had something for their money; to have drawn an unknown and socially unremunerative Ellen Niggle into the net of their hospitality was a catastrophe that they could not contemplate with any degree of calmness.

The Smithly-Dubbs never quite recovered from their unnerving experience. They have given up politics and taken to doing good.

ℌenry Van Dyke

(1852-1933)

46

A Handful of Clay

There was a handful of clay in the bank of a river. It was only common clay, coarse and heavy; but it had high thoughts of its own value, and wonderful dreams of the great place which it was to fill in the world when the time came for its virtues to be discovered.

Overhead, in the spring sunshine, the trees whispered together of the glory which descended upon them when the delicate blossoms and leaves began to expand, and the forest glowed with fair, clear colours, as if the dust of thousands of rubies and emeralds were hanging, in soft clouds, above the earth.

The flowers, surprised with the joy of beauty, bent their heads to one another, as the wind caressed them, and said: "Sisters, how lovely you have become. You make the day bright."

The river, glad of new strength and rejoicing in the unison of all its waters, murmured to the shores in music, telling of its release from icy fetters, its swift flight from the snow-clad mountains, and the mighty work to which it was hurrying—the wheels of many mills to be turned, and great ships to be floated to the sea.

Waiting blindly in its bed, the clay comforted itself with lofty hopes. "My time will come," it said. "I was not made to be hidden forever. Glory and beauty and honour are coming to me in due season."

One day the clay felt itself taken from the place where it had waited so long. A flat blade of iron passed beneath it, and lifted it, and tossed it into a cart with other lumps of clay, and it was carried far away, as it seemed, over a rough and stony road. But it was not afraid, nor discouraged, for it said to itself: "This is necessary. The path to glory is always rugged. Now I am on my way to play a great part in the world."

But the hard journey was nothing compared with the tribulation and distress that came after it. The clay was put into a trough and mixed and beaten and stirred and trampled. It seemed almost unbearable. But there was consolation in the thought that something very fine and noble was certainly coming out of all this trouble. The clay felt sure that, if it could only wait long enough, a wonderful reward was in store for it.

Then it was put upon a swiftly turning wheel, and whirled around until it seemed as if it must fly into a thousand pieces. A strange power pressed it and moulded it, as it revolved, and through all the dizziness and pain it felt that it was taking a new form.

Then an unknown hand put it into an oven, and fires were kindled about it—fierce and penetrating—hotter than all the heats of summer that had ever brooded upon the bank of the river. But through all, the clay held itself together and endured its trials, in the confidence of a great future. "Surely," it thought, "I am intended for something very splendid, since such pains are taken with me. Perhaps I am fashioned for the ornament of a temple, or a precious vase for the table of a king."

At last the baking was finished. The clay was taken from the furnace and set down upon a board, in the cool air, under the blue sky. The tribulation was passed. The reward was at hand.

Close beside the board there was a pool of water, not very deep, nor very clear, but calm enough to reflect, with impartial truth, every image that fell upon it. There, for the first time, as it was lifted from the board, the clay saw its new shape, the reward of all its patience and pain, the consummation of its hopes—a common flower-pot, straight and stiff, red and ugly. And then it felt that it was not destined for a king's house, nor for a palace of art, because it was made without glory or beauty or honour; and it murmured against the unknown maker, saying, "Why hast thou made me thus?"

Many days it passed in sullen discontent. Then it was filled with earth, and something—it knew not what—but something rough and brown and dead-looking, was thrust into the middle of the earth and covered over. The clay rebelled at this new disgrace. "This is the worst of all that has happened to me, to be filled with dirt and rubbish. Surely I am a failure."

But presently it was set in a greenhouse, where the sunlight fell warm upon it, and water was sprinkled over it, and day by day as it waited, a change began to come to it. Something was stirring within it—a new hope. Still it was ignorant, and knew not what the new hope meant.

One day the clay was lifted again from its place, and carried into a great church. Its dream was coming true after all. It had a fine part to play in the world. Glorious music flowed over it. It was surrounded with flowers. Still it could not understand. So it whispered to another vessel of clay, like itself, close beside it, "Why have they set me here? Why do all the people look toward us?" And the other vessel answered, "Do you not know? You are carrying a royal sceptre of lilies. Their petals are white as snow, and the heart of them is like pure gold. The people look this way because the flower is the most wonderful in the world. And the root of it is in your heart."

Then the clay was content, and silently thanked its maker, because, though an earthen vessel, it held so great a treasure.

ħ P Lovecraft

(1890-1937)

47

Ex Oblivione

When the last days were upon me, and the ugly trifles of existence began to drive me to madness like the small drops of water that torturers let fall ceaselessly upon one spot of their victims body, I loved the irradiate refuge of sleep. In my dreams I found a little of the beauty I had vainly sought in life, and wandered through old gardens and enchanted woods.

Once when the wind was soft and scented I heard the south calling, and sailed endlessly and languorously under strange stars.

Once when the gentle rain fell I glided in a barge down a sunless stream under the earth till I reached another world of purple twilight, iridescent arbours, and undying roses.

And once I walked through a golden valley that led to shadowy groves and ruins, and ended in a mighty wall green with antique vines, and pierced by a little gate of bronze.

Many times I walked through that valley, and longer and longer would I pause in the spectral half-light where the giant trees squirmed and twisted grotesquely, and the grey ground stretched damply from trunk to trunk, some times disclosing the mould-stained stones of buried temples. And always the goal of my fancies was the mighty vine-grown wall with the little gate of bronze therein.

After a while, as the days of waking became less and less bearable from their greyness and sameness, I would often drift in opiate peace through the valley and the shadowy groves, and wonder how I might seize them for my eternal dwelling-place, so that I need no more crawl back to a dull world stript of interest and new colours. And as I looked upon the little gate in the mighty wall, I felt that beyond it lay a dream-country from which, once it was entered, there would be no return.

So each night in sleep I strove to find the hidden latch of the gate in the ivied antique wall, though it was exceedingly well hidden. And I would tell myself that the realm beyond the wall was not more lasting merely, but more lovely and radiant as well.

Then one night in the dream-city of Zakarion I found a yellowed papyrus filled with the thoughts of dream-sages who dwelt of old in that city, and who were too wise ever to be born in the waking world. Therein were written many things concerning the world of dream, and among them was lore of a golden valley and a sacred grove with temples, and a high wall pierced by a little bronze gate. When I saw this lore, I knew that it touched on the scenes I had haunted, and I therefore read long in the yellowed papyrus.

Some of the dream-sages wrote gorgeously of the wonders beyond the irrepassable gate, but others told of horror and disappointment. I knew not which to believe, yet longed more and more to cross for ever into the unknown land; for doubt and secrecy are the lure of lures, and no new horror can be more terrible than the daily torture of the commonplace. So when I learned of the drug which would unlock the gate and drive me through, I resolved to take it when next I awaked.

Last night I swallowed the drug and floated dreamily into the golden valley and the shadowy groves; and when I came this time to the antique wall, I saw that the small gate of bronze was ajar. From beyond came a glow that weirdly lit the giant twisted trees and the tops of the buried temples, and I drifted on songfully, expectant of the glories of the land from whence I should never return.

But as the gate swung wider and the sorcery of the drug and the dream pushed me through, I knew that all sights and glories were at an end; for in that new realm was neither land nor sea, but only the white void of unpeopled and illimitable space. So, happier than I had ever dared hope to be, I dissolved again into that native infinity of crystal oblivion from which the daemon Life had called me for one brief and desolate hour.

Jacob Grimm
(1785-1863)

Wilhelm Grimm
(1786-1859)

48

The Children of Hameln

In the year 1284 a mysterious man appeared in Hameln. He was wearing a coat of many colored, bright cloth, for which reason he was called the Pied Piper. He claimed to be a ratcatcher, and he promised that for a certain sum that he would rid the city of all mice and rats. The citizens struck a deal, promising him a certain price. The ratcatcher then took a small fife from his pocket and began to blow on it. Rats and mice immediately came from every house and gathered around him. We he thought that he had them all he led them to the River Weser where he pulled up his clothes and walked into the water. The animals all followed him, fell in, and drowned.

Now that the citizens had been freed of their plague, they regretted having promised so much money, and, using all kinds of excuses, they refused to pay him. Finally he went away, bitter and angry. He returned on June 26, Saint John's and Saint Paul's Day, early in the morning at seven o'clock (others say it was at noon), now dressed in a hunter's costume, with a dreadful look on his face and wearing a strange red hat. He sounded his fife in the streets, but this time it wasn't rats and mice that came to him, but rather children: a great number of boys and girls from their fourth year on. Among them was the mayor's grown daughter. The swarm followed him, and he led them to a mountain, where he disappeared with them.

All this was seen by a babysitter who, carrying a child in her arms, had followed them from a distance, but had then turned around and carried the news back to the town. The anxious parents ran in droves to the town gates seeking their children. The mothers cried out and sobbed pitifully. Within the hour messengers were sent everywhere by water and by land inquiring if the children—or any of them—had been seen, but it was all for naught.

In total, one hundred thirty were lost. Two, as some say, had lagged behind and came back. One of them was blind and the other mute. The blind one was not able to point out the place, but was able to tell how they had followed the piper. The mute one was able to point out the place, although he (or she) had heard nothing. One little boy in shirtsleeves had gone along with the others, but had turned back to fetch his jacket and thus escaped the tragedy, for when he returned, the others had already disappeared into a cave within a hill. This cave is still shown.

Until the middle of the eighteenth century, and probably still today, the street through which the children were led out to the town gate was called the *bungelose* (drumless, soundless, quiet) street, because no dancing or music was allowed there. Indeed, when a bridal procession on its way to church crossed this street, the musicians would have to stop playing. The mountain near Hamelin where the children disappeared is called Poppenberg. Two stone monuments in the form of crosses have been erected there, one on the left side, and one on the right. Some say that the children were led into a cave, and that they came out again in Transylvania.

The citizens of Hamelin recorded this event in their town register, and they came to date all their proclamations according to the years and days since the loss of their children.

According to Seyfried the 22nd rather than the 26th of June was entered into the town register.

The following lines were described on the town hall:

In the year 1284 after the birth of Christ
From Hamelin were led away
One hundred thirty children, born at this place
Led away by a piper into a mountain.

And on the new gate was inscribed: Centum ter denos cum magus ab urbe puellos duxerat ante annos CCLXXII condita porta fuit. (This gate was built 272 years after the magician led one hundred thirty children from the city)

In the year 1572 the mayor had the story portrayed in the church windows. The accompanying inscription has become largely illegible. In addition, a coin was minted in memory of the event.

James Joyce
(1882-1941)

49

After the Race

The cars came scudding in towards Dublin, running evenly like pellets in the groove of the Naas Road. At the crest of the hill at Inchicore sightseers had gathered in clumps to watch the cars careering homeward and through this channel of poverty and inaction the Continent sped its wealth and industry. Now and again the clumps of people raised the cheer of the gratefully oppressed. Their sympathy, however, was for the blue cars—the cars of their friends, the French.

The French, moreover, were virtual victors. Their team had finished solidly; they had been placed second and third and the driver of the winning German car was reported a Belgian. Each blue car, therefore, received a double measure of welcome as it topped the crest of the hill and each cheer of welcome was acknowledged with smiles and nods by those in the car. In one of these trimly built cars was a party of four young men whose spirits seemed to be at present well above the level of successful Gallicism: in fact, these four young men were almost hilarious. They were Charles Ségouin, the owner of the car; André Rivière, a young electrician of Canadian birth; a huge Hungarian named Villona and a neatly groomed young man named Doyle. Ségouin was in good humour because he had unexpectedly received some orders in advance (he was about to start a motor establishment in Paris) and Rivière was in good humour because he was to be appointed manager of the establishment; these two young men (who were cousins) were also in good humour because of the success of the French cars. Villona was in good humour because he had had a very satisfactory luncheon; and besides he was an optimist by nature. The fourth member of the party, however, was too excited to be genuinely happy.

He was about twenty-six years of age, with a soft, light brown moustache and rather innocent-looking grey eyes. His father, who had begun life as an advanced Nationalist, had modified his views early. He had made his money as a butcher in Kingstown and by opening shops in Dublin and in the suburbs he had made his money many times over. He had also been fortunate enough to secure some of the police contracts and in the end he had become rich enough to be alluded to in the Dublin newspapers as a merchant prince. He had sent his son to England to be educated in a big Catholic college and had afterwards sent him to Dublin University to study law. Jimmy did not study very earnestly and took to bad courses for a while. He had money and he was popular; and he divided his time curiously between musical and motoring circles. Then he had been sent for a term to Cambridge to see a little life. His father, remonstrative, but covertly proud of the excess, had paid his bills and brought him home. It was at Cambridge that he had met Ségouin. They were not much more than acquaintances as yet but Jimmy found great pleasure in the society of one who had seen so much of the world and was reputed to own some of the biggest hotels in France. Such a person (as his father agreed) was well worth knowing, even if he had not been the charming companion he was. Villona was entertaining also—a brilliant pianist—but, unfortunately, very poor.

The car ran on merrily with its cargo of hilarious youth. The two cousins sat on the front seat; Jimmy and his Hungarian friend sat behind. Decidedly Villona was in excellent spirits; he kept up a deep bass hum of melody for miles of the road. The Frenchmen flung their laughter and light words over their shoulders and often

Jimmy had to strain forward to catch the quick phrase. This was not altogether pleasant for him, as he had nearly always to make a deft guess at the meaning and shout back a suitable answer in the face of a high wind. Besides Villona's humming would confuse anybody; the noise of the car, too.

Rapid motion through space elates one; so does notoriety; so does the possession of money. These were three good reasons for Jimmy's excitement. He had been seen by many of his friends that day in the company of these Continentals. At the control Ségouin had presented him to one of the French competitors and, in answer to his confused murmur of compliment, the swarthy face of the driver had disclosed a line of shining white teeth. It was pleasant after that honour to return to the profane world of spectators amid nudges and significant looks. Then as to money—he really had a great sum under his control. Ségouin, perhaps, would not think it a great sum but Jimmy who, in spite of temporary errors, was at heart the inheritor of solid instincts knew well with what difficulty it had been got together. This knowledge had previously kept his bills within the limits of reasonable recklessness and, if he had been so conscious of the labour latent in money when there had been question merely of some freak of the higher intelligence, how much more so now when he was about to stake the greater part of his substance! It was a serious thing for him.

Of course, the investment was a good one and Ségouin had managed to give the impression that it was by a favour of friendship the mite of Irish money was to be included in the capital of the concern. Jimmy had a respect for his father's shrewdness in business matters and in this case it had been his father who had first suggested the investment; money to be made in the motor business, pots of money. Moreover Ségouin had the unmistakable air of wealth. Jimmy set out to translate into days' work that lordly car in which he sat. How smoothly it ran. In what style they had come careering along the country roads! The journey laid a magical finger on the genuine pulse of life and gallantly the machinery of human nerves strove to answer the bounding courses of the swift blue animal.

They drove down Dame Street. The street was busy with unusual traffic, loud with the horns of motorists and the gongs of impatient tram-drivers. Near the Bank Ségouin drew up and Jimmy and his friend alighted. A little knot of people collected on the footpath to pay homage to the snorting motor. The party was to dine together that evening in Ségouin's hotel and, meanwhile, Jimmy and his friend, who was staying with him, were to go home to dress. The car steered out slowly for Grafton Street while the two young men pushed their way through the knot of gazers. They walked northward with a curious feeling of disappointment in the exercise, while the city hung its pale globes of light above them in a haze of summer evening.

In Jimmy's house this dinner had been pronounced an occasion. A certain pride mingled with his parents' trepidation, a certain eagerness, also, to play fast and loose for the names of great foreign cities have at least this virtue. Jimmy, too, looked very well when he was dressed and, as he stood in the hall giving a last equation to the bows of his dress tie, his father may have felt even commercially satisfied at having secured for his son qualities often unpurchaseable. His father, therefore, was unusually friendly with Villona and his manner expressed a real respect for foreign accomplishments; but this subtlety of his host was probably lost upon the Hungarian, who was beginning to have a sharp desire for his dinner.

The dinner was excellent, exquisite. Ségouin, Jimmy decided, had a very refined taste. The party was increased by a young Englishman named Routh whom Jimmy had seen with Ségouin at Cambridge. The young men supped in a snug room lit by electric candle-lamps. They talked volubly and with little reserve. Jimmy, whose imagination was kindling, conceived the lively youth of the Frenchmen twined elegantly upon the firm framework of the Englishman's manner. A graceful image of his, he thought, and a just one. He admired the dexterity with which their host directed the conversation. The five young men had various tastes and their tongues had been loosened. Villona, with immense respect, began to discover to the mildly surprised Englishman the beauties of the English madrigal, deploring the loss of old instruments.

Rivière, not wholly ingenuously, undertook to explain to Jimmy the triumph of the French mechanicians. The resonant voice of the Hungarian was about to prevail in ridicule of the spurious lutes of the romantic painters when Ségouin shepherded his party into politics. Here was congenial ground for all. Jimmy, under generous influences, felt the buried zeal of his father wake to life within him: he aroused the torpid Routh at last. The room grew doubly hot and Ségouin's task grew harder each moment: there was even danger of personal spite. The alert host at an opportunity lifted his glass to Humanity and, when the toast had been drunk, he threw open a window significantly.

That night the city wore the mask of a capital. The five young men strolled along Stephen's Green in a faint cloud of aromatic smoke. They talked loudly and gaily and their cloaks dangled from their shoulders. The people made way for them. At the corner of Grafton Street a short fat man was putting two handsome ladies on a car in charge of another fat man. The car drove off and the short fat man caught sight of the party.

"André."

"It's Farley!"

A torrent of talk followed. Farley was an American. No one knew very well what the talk was about. Villona and Rivière were the noisiest, but all the men were excited. They got up on a car, squeezing themselves together amid much laughter. They drove by the crowd, blended now into soft colours, to a music of merry bells. They took the train at Westland Row and in a few seconds, as it seemed to Jimmy, they were walking out of Kingstown Station. The ticket-collector saluted Jimmy; he was an old man:

"Fine night, sir!"

It was a serene summer night; the harbour lay like a darkened mirror at their feet. They proceeded towards it with linked arms, singing Cadet Roussel in chorus, stamping their feet at every:

"Ho! Ho! Hohé, vraiment!"

They got into a rowboat at the slip and made out for the American's yacht. There was to be supper, music, cards. Villona said with conviction:

"It is delightful!"

There was a yacht piano in the cabin. Villona played a waltz for Farley and Rivière, Farley acting as cavalier and Rivière as lady. Then an impromptu square dance, the men devising original figures. What merriment! Jimmy took his part with a will; this was seeing life, at least. Then Farley got out of breath and cried "Stop!" A man brought in a light supper, and the young men sat down to it for form's sake. They drank, however: it was Bohemian. They drank Ireland, England, France, Hungary, the United States of America. Jimmy made a speech, a long speech, Villona saying: "Hear! hear!" whenever there was a pause. There was a great clapping of hands when he sat down. It must have been a good speech. Farley clapped him on the back and laughed loudly. What jovial fellows! What good company they were!

Cards! cards! The table was cleared. Villona returned quietly to his piano and played voluntaries for them. The other men played game after game, flinging themselves boldly into the adventure. They drank the health of the Queen of Hearts and of the Queen of Diamonds. Jimmy felt obscurely the lack of an audience: the wit was flashing. Play ran very high and paper began to pass. Jimmy did not know exactly who was winning but he knew that he was losing. But it was his own fault for he frequently mistook his cards and the other men had to calculate his I.O.U.'s for him. They were devils of fellows but he wished they would stop: it was getting late. Someone gave the toast of the yacht The Belle of Newport and then someone proposed one great game for a finish.

The piano had stopped; Villona must have gone up on deck. It was a terrible game. They stopped just before the end of it to drink for luck. Jimmy understood that the game lay between Routh and Ségouin. What excitement! Jimmy was excited too; he would lose, of course. How much had he written away? The men rose to their feet to play the last tricks, talking and gesticulating. Routh won. The cabin shook with the young men's cheering and the cards were bundled together. They began then to gather in what they had won. Farley and Jimmy were the heaviest losers.

He knew that he would regret in the morning but at present he was glad of the rest, glad of the dark stupor that would cover up his folly. He leaned his elbows on the table and rested his head between his hands, counting the beats of his temples. The cabin door opened and he saw the Hungarian standing in a shaft of grey light:

"Daybreak, gentlemen!"

50

Araby

North Richmond Street being blind, was a quiet street except at the hour when the Christian Brothers' School set the boys free. An uninhabited house of two storeys stood at the blind end, detached from its neighbours in a square ground. The other houses of the street, conscious of decent lives within them, gazed at one another with brown imperturbable faces.

The former tenant of our house, a priest, had died in the back drawing-room. Air, musty from having been long enclosed, hung in all the rooms, and the waste room behind the kitchen was littered with old useless papers. Among these I found a few paper-covered books, the pages of which were curled and damp: The Abbot, by Walter Scott, The Devout Communnicant and The Memoirs of Vidocq. I liked the last best because its leaves were yellow. The wild garden behind the house contained a central apple-tree and a few straggling bushes under one of which I found the late tenant's rusty bicycle-pump. He had been a very charitable priest; in his will he had left all his money to institutions and the furniture of his house to his sister.

When the short days of winter came dusk fell before we had well eaten our dinners. When we met in the street the houses had grown sombre. The space of sky above us was the colour of ever-changing violet and towards it the lamps of the street lifted their feeble lanterns. The cold air stung us and we played till our bodies glowed. Our shouts echoed in the silent street. The career of our play brought us through the dark muddy lanes behind the houses where we ran the gauntlet of the rough tribes from the cottages, to the back doors of the dark dripping gardens where odours arose from the ashpits, to the dark odorous stables where a coachman smoothed and combed the horse or shook music from the buckled harness. When we returned to the street light from the kitchen windows had filled the areas. If my uncle was seen turning the corner we hid in the shadow until we had seen him safely housed. Or if Mangan's sister came out on the doorstep to call her brother in to his tea we watched her from our shadow peer up and down the street. We waited to see whether she would remain or go in and, if she remained, we left our shadow and walked up to Mangan's steps resignedly. She was waiting for us, her figure defined by the light from the half-opened door. Her brother always teased her before he obeyed and I stood by the railings looking at her. Her dress swung as she moved her body and the soft rope of her hair tossed from side to side.

Every morning I lay on the floor in the front parlour watching her door. The blind was pulled down to within an inch of the sash so that I could not be seen. When she came out on the doorstep my heart leaped. I ran to the hall, seized my books and followed her. I kept her brown figure always in my eye and, when we came near the point at which our ways diverged, I quickened my pace and passed her. This happened morning after morning. I had never spoken to her, except for a few casual words, and yet her name was like a summons to all my foolish blood.

Her image accompanied me even in places the most hostile to romance. On Saturday evenings when my aunt went marketing I had to go to carry some of the parcels. We walked through the flaring streets, jostled by drunken men and bargaining women, amid the curses of labourers, the shrill litanies of shop-boys who stood on guard by the barrels of pigs' cheeks, the nasal chanting of street-singers, who sang a come-all-you about O'Donovan Rossa, or a ballad about the troubles in our native land. These noises converged in a single sensation of life for me: I imagined that I bore my chalice safely through a throng of foes. Her name sprang to my lips at moments in strange prayers and praises which I myself did not understand. My eyes were often full of tears (I could not tell why) and at times a flood from my heart seemed to pour itself out into my bosom. I thought little of the future. I did not know whether I would ever speak to her or not or, if I spoke to her, how I could tell her of my confused adoration. But my body was like a harp and her words and gestures were like fingers running upon the wires.

One evening I went into the back drawing-room in which the priest had died. It was a dark rainy evening and there was no sound in the house. Through one of the broken panes I heard the rain impinge upon the earth, the fine incessant needles of water playing in the sodden beds. Some distant lamp or lighted window gleamed below me. I was thankful that I could see so little. All my senses seemed to desire to veil themselves and, feeling that I was about to slip from them, I pressed the palms of my hands together until they trembled, murmuring: "O love! O love!" many times.

At last she spoke to me. When she addressed the first words to me I was so confused that I did not know what to answer. She asked me was I going to Araby. I forgot whether I answered yes or no. It would be a splendid bazaar, she said she would love to go.

"And why can't you?" I asked.

While she spoke she turned a silver bracelet round and round her wrist. She could not go, she said, because there would be a retreat that week in her convent. Her brother and two other boys were fighting for their caps and I was alone at the railings. She held one of the spikes, bowing her head towards me. The light from the lamp opposite our door caught the white curve of her neck, lit up her hair that rested there and, falling, lit up the hand upon the railing. It fell over one side of her dress and caught the white border of a petticoat, just visible as she stood at ease.

"It's well for you," she said.

"If I go," I said, "I will bring you something."

What innumerable follies laid waste my waking and sleeping thoughts after that evening! I wished to annihilate the tedious intervening days. I chafed against the work of school. At night in my bedroom and by day in the classroom her image came between me and the page I strove to read. The syllables of the word Araby were called to me through the silence in which my soul luxuriated and cast an Eastern enchantment over me. I asked for leave to go to the bazaar on Saturday night. My aunt was surprised and hoped it was not some Freemason affair. I answered few questions in class. I watched my master's face pass from amiability to sternness; he hoped I was not beginning to idle. I could not call my wandering thoughts together. I had hardly any patience with the serious work of life which, now that it stood between me and my desire, seemed to me child's play, ugly monotonous child's play.

On Saturday morning I reminded my uncle that I wished to go to the bazaar in the evening. He was fussing at the hallstand, looking for the hat-brush, and answered me curtly:

"Yes, boy, I know."

As he was in the hall I could not go into the front parlour and lie at the window. I left the house in bad humour and walked slowly towards the school. The air was pitilessly raw and already my heart misgave me.

When I came home to dinner my uncle had not yet been home. Still it was early. I sat staring at the clock for some time and. when its ticking began to irritate me, I left the room. I mounted the staircase and gained the upper part of the house. The high cold empty gloomy rooms liberated me and I went from room to room singing. From the front window I saw my companions playing below in the street. Their cries reached me weakened and indistinct and, leaning my forehead against the cool glass, I looked over at the dark house where she lived. I may have stood there for an hour, seeing nothing but the brown-clad figure cast by my imagination, touched discreetly by the lamplight at the curved neck, at the hand upon the railings and at the border below the dress.

When I came downstairs again I found Mrs. Mercer sitting at

the fire. She was an old garrulous woman, a pawnbroker's widow, who collected used stamps for some pious purpose. I had to endure the gossip of the tea-table. The meal was prolonged beyond an hour and still my uncle did not come. Mrs. Mercer stood up to go: she was sorry she couldn't wait any longer, but it was after eight o'clock and she did not like to be out late as the night air was bad for her. When she had gone I began to walk up and down the room, clenching my fists. My aunt said:

"I'm afraid you may put off your bazaar for this night of Our Lord."

At nine o'clock I heard my uncle's latchkey in the halldoor. I heard him talking to himself and heard the hallstand rocking when it had received the weight of his overcoat. I could interpret these signs. When he was midway through his dinner I asked him to give me the money to go to the bazaar. He had forgotten.

"The people are in bed and after their first sleep now," he said.

I did not smile. My aunt said to him energetically:

"Can't you give him the money and let him go? You've kept him late enough as it is."

My uncle said he was very sorry he had forgotten. He said he believed in the old saying: "All work and no play makes Jack a dull boy." He asked me where I was going and, when I had told him a second time he asked me did I know The Arab's Farewell to his Steed. When I left the kitchen he was about to recite the opening lines of the piece to my aunt.

I held a florin tightly in my hand as I strode down Buckingham Street towards the station. The sight of the streets thronged with buyers and glaring with gas recalled to me the purpose of my journey. I took my seat in a third-class carriage of a deserted train. After an intolerable delay the train moved out of the station slowly. It crept onward among ruinous house and over the twinkling river. At Westland Row Station a crowd of people pressed to the carriage doors; but the porters moved them back, saying that it was a special train for the bazaar. I remained alone in the bare carriage. In a few minutes the train drew up beside an improvised wooden platform. I passed out on to the road and saw by the lighted dial of a clock that it was ten minutes to ten. In front of me was a large building which displayed the magical name.

I could not find any sixpenny entrance and, fearing that the bazaar would be closed, I passed in quickly through a turnstile, handing a shilling to a weary-looking man. I found myself in a big hall girdled at half its height by a gallery. Nearly all the stalls were closed and the greater part of the hall was in darkness. I recognised a silence like that which pervades a church after a service. I walked into the centre of the bazaar timidly. A few people were gathered about the stalls which were still open. Before a curtain, over which the words Cafe Chantant were written in coloured lamps, two men were counting money on a salver. I listened to the fall of the coins.

Remembering with difficulty why I had come I went over to one of the stalls and examined porcelain vases and flowered tea sets. At the door of the stall a young lady was talking and laughing with two young gentlemen. I remarked their English accents and listened vaguely to their conversation.

"O, I never said such a thing!"

"O, but you did!"

"O, but I didn't!"

"Didn't she say that?"

"Yes. I heard her."

"O, there's a . . . fib!"

Observing me the young lady came over and asked me did I wish to buy anything. The tone of her voice was not encouraging; she seemed to have spoken to me out of a sense of duty. I looked humbly at the great jars that stood like eastern guards at either side of the dark entrance to the stall and murmured:

"No, thank you."

The young lady changed the position of one of the vases and went back to the two young men. They began to talk of the same subject. Once or twice the young lady glanced at me over her shoulder.

I lingered before her stall, though I knew my stay was useless, to make my interest in her wares seem the more real. Then I turned away slowly and walked down the middle of the bazaar. I allowed the two pennies to fall against the sixpence in my pocket. I heard a voice call from one end of the gallery that the light was out. The upper part of the hall was now completely dark.

Gazing up into the darkness I saw myself as a creature driven and derided by vanity; and my eyes burned with anguish and anger.

Kate Chopin
(1850-1904)

51

The Story of an Hour

Knowing that Mrs. Mallard was afflicted with a heart trouble, great care was taken to break to her as gently as possible the news of her husband's death.

It was her sister Josephine who told her, in broken sentences; veiled hints that revealed in half concealing. Her husband's friend Richards was there, too, near her. It was he who had been in the newspaper office when intelligence of the railroad disaster was received, with Brently Mallard's name leading the list of 'killed'. He had only taken the time to assure himself of its truth by a second telegram, and had hastened to forestall any less careful, less tender friend in bearing the sad message.

She did not hear the story as many women have heard the same, with a paralyzed inability to accept its significance. She wept at once, with sudden, wild abandonment, in her sister's arms. When the storm of grief had spent itself she went away to her room alone. She would have no one follow her.

There stood, facing the open window, a comfortable, roomy armchair. Into this she sank, pressed down by a physical exhaustion that haunted her body and seemed to reach into her soul.

She could see in the open square before her house the tops of trees that were all aquiver with the new spring life. The delicious breath of rain was in the air. In the street below a peddler was crying his wares. The notes of a distant song which some one was singing reached her faintly, and countless sparrows were twittering in the eaves.

There were patches of blue sky showing here and there through the clouds that had met and piled one above the other in the west facing her window.

She sat with her head thrown back upon the cushion of the chair, quite motionless, except when a sob came up into her throat and shook her, as a child who has cried itself to sleep continues to sob in its dreams.

She was young, with a fair, calm face, whose lines bespoke repression and even a certain strength. But now there was a dull stare in her eyes, whose gaze was fixed away off yonder on one of those patches of blue sky. It was not a glance of reflection, but rather indicated a suspension of intelligent thought.

There was something coming to her and she was waiting for it, fearfully. What was it? She did not know; it was too subtle and elusive to name. But she felt it, creeping out of the sky, reaching toward her through the sounds, the scents, the color that filled the air.

Now her bosom rose and fell tumultuously. She was beginning to recognize this thing that was approaching to possess her, and she was striving to beat it back with her will—as powerless as her two white slender hands would have been. When she abandoned herself a little whispered word escaped her slightly parted lips. She said it over and over under her breath: "free, free, free!" The vacant stare and the look of terror that had followed it went from her eyes. They stayed keen and bright. Her pulses beat fast, and the coursing blood warmed and relaxed every inch of her body.

She did not stop to ask if it were or were not a monstrous joy that held her. A clear and exalted perception enabled her to dismiss the suggestion as trivial. She knew that she would weep again when she saw the kind, tender hands folded in death; the face that had never looked save with love upon her, fixed and gray and dead. But she saw beyond that bitter moment a long procession of years to come that would belong to her absolutely. And she opened and spread her arms out to them in welcome.

There would be no one to live for during those coming years; she would live for herself. There would be no powerful will bending hers in that blind persistence with which men and women believe they have a right to impose a private will upon a fellow-creature. A kind intention or a cruel intention made the act seem no less a crime as she looked upon it in that brief moment of illumination.

And yet she had loved him—sometimes. Often she had not. What did it matter! What could love, the unsolved mystery, count for in the face of this possession of self-assertion which she suddenly recognized as the strongest impulse of her being!

"Free! Body and soul free!" she kept whispering.

Josephine was kneeling before the closed door with her lips to the keyhole, imploring for admission. "Louise, open the door! I beg; open the door—you will make yourself ill. What are you doing, Louise? For heaven's sake open the door."

"Go away. I am not making myself ill." No; she was drinking in a very elixir of life through that open window.

Her fancy was running riot along those days ahead of her. Spring days, and summer days, and all sorts of days that would be her own. She breathed a quick prayer that life might be long. It was only yesterday she had thought with a shudder that life might be long.

She arose at length and opened the door to her sister's importunities. There was a feverish triumph in her eyes, and she carried herself unwittingly like a goddess of Victory. She clasped her sister's waist, and together they descended the stairs. Richards stood waiting for them at the bottom.

Some one was opening the front door with a latchkey. It was Brently Mallard who entered, a little travel-stained, composedly carrying his grip-sack and umbrella. He had been far from the scene of the accident, and did not even know there had been one. He stood amazed at Josephine's piercing cry; at Richards' quick motion to screen him from the view of his wife.

When the doctors came they said she had died of heart disease—of the joy that kills.

52

The Night Came Slowly

I am losing my interest in human beings; in the significance of their lives and their actions. Some one has said it is better to study one man than ten books. I want neither books nor men; they make me suffer. Can one of them talk to me like the night—the Summer night? Like the stars or the caressing wind?

The night came slowly, softly, as I lay out there under the maple tree. It came creeping, creeping stealthily out of the valley, thinking I did not notice. And the outlines of trees and foliage nearby blended in one black mass and the night came stealing out from them, too, and from the east and west, until the only light was in the sky, filtering through the maple leaves and a star looking down through every cranny.

The night is solemn and it means mystery.

Human shapes flitted by like intangible things. Some stole up like little mice to peep at me. I did not mind. My whole being was abandoned to the soothing and penetrating charm of the night.

The katydids began their slumber song: they are at it yet. How wise they are. They do not chatter like people. They tell me only: "sleep, sleep, sleep." The wind rippled the maple leaves like little warm love thrills.

Why do fools cumber the Earth! It was a man's voice that broke the necromancer's spell. A man came to-day with his 'Bible Class'. He is detestable with his red cheeks and bold eyes and coarse manner and speech. What does he know of Christ? Shall I ask a young fool who was born yesterday and will die tomorrow to tell me things of Christ? I would rather ask the stars: they have seen him.

53

An Idle Fellow

I am tired. At the end of these years I am very tired. I have been studying in books the languages of the living and those we call dead. Early in the fresh morning I have studied in books, and throughout the day when the sun was shining; and at night when there were stars, I have lighted my oil-lamp and studied in books. Now my brain is weary and I want rest.

I shall sit here on the door-step beside my friend Paul. He is an idle fellow with folded hands. He laughs when I upbraid him, and bids me, with a motion, hold my peace. He is listening to a thrush's song that comes from the blur of yonder apple-tree. He tells me the thrush is singing a complaint. She wants her mate that was with her last blossom-time and builded a nest with her. She will have no other mate. She will call for him till she hears the notes of her beloved-one's song coming swiftly towards her across forest and field.

Paul is a strange fellow. He gazed idly at a billowy white cloud that rolls lazily over and over along the edge of the blue sky.

He turns away from me and the words with which I would instruct him, to drink deep the scent of the clover-field and the thick perfume from the rose-hedge.

We rise from the door-step and walk together down the gentle slope of the hill; past the apple-tree, and the rose-hedge; and along the border of the field where wheat is growing. We walk down to the foot of the gentle slope where women and men and children are living.

Paul is a strange fellow. He looks into the faces of people who pass us by. He tells me that in their eyes he reads the story of their souls. He knows men and women and the little children, and why they look this way and that way. He knows the reasons that turn them to and fro and cause them to go and come. I think I shall walk a space through the world with my friend Paul. He is very wise, he knows the language of God which I have not learned.

54

The Kiss

It was still quite light out of doors, but inside with the curtains drawn and the smouldering fire sending out a dim, uncertain glow, the room was full of deep shadows.

Brantain sat in one of these shadows; it had overtaken him and he did not mind. The obscurity lent him courage to keep his eyes fastened as ardently as he liked upon the girl who sat in the firelight.

She was very handsome, with a certain fine, rich coloring that belongs to the healthy brune type. She was quite composed, as she idly stroked the satiny coat of the cat that lay curled in her lap, and she occasionally sent a slow glance into the shadow where her companion sat. They were talking low, of indifferent things which plainly were not the things that occupied their thoughts. She knew that he loved her—a frank, blustering fellow without guile enough to conceal his feelings, and no desire to do so. For two weeks past he had sought her society eagerly and persistently. She was confidently waiting for him to declare himself and she meant to accept him. The rather insignificant and unattractive Brantain was enormously rich; and she liked and required the entourage which wealth could give her.

During one of the pauses between their talk of the last tea and the next reception the door opened and a young man entered whom Brantain knew quite well. The girl turned her face toward him. A stride or two brought him to her side, and bending over her chair—before she could suspect his intention, for she did not realize that he had not seen her visitor—he pressed an ardent, lingering kiss upon her lips.

Brantain slowly arose; so did the girl arise, but quickly, and the newcomer stood between them, a little amusement and some defiance struggling with the confusion in his face.

"I believe," stammered Brantain, "I see that I have stayed too long. I—I had no idea—that is, I must wish you good-by." He was clutching his hat with both hands, and probably did not perceive that she was extending her hand to him, her presence of mind had not completely deserted her; but she could not have trusted herself to speak.

"Hang me if I saw him sitting there, Nattie! I know it's deuced awkward for you. But I hope you'll forgive me this once—this very first break. Why, what's the matter?"

"Don't touch me; don't come near me," she returned angrily. "What do you mean by entering the house without ringing?"

"I came in with your brother, as I often do," he answered coldly, in self-justification. "We came in the side way. He went upstairs and I came in here hoping to find you. The explanation is simple enough and ought to satisfy you that the misadventure was unavoidable. But do say that you forgive me, Nathalie," he entreated, softening.

"Forgive you! You don't know what you are talking about. Let me pass. It depends upon—a good deal whether I ever forgive you."

At that next reception which she and Brantain had been talking about she approached the young man with a delicious frankness of manner when she saw him there.

"Will you let me speak to you a moment or two, Mr. Brantain?" she asked with an engaging but perturbed smile. He seemed extremely unhappy; but when she took his arm and walked away with him, seeking a retired corner, a ray of hope mingled with the almost comical misery of his expression. She was apparently very outspoken.

"Perhaps I should not have sought this interview, Mr. Brantain; but—but, oh, I have been very uncomfortable, almost miserable since that little encounter the other afternoon. When I thought how you might have misinterpreted it, and believed things"—hope was plainly gaining the ascendancy over misery in Brantain's round, guileless face—"Of course, I know it is nothing to you, but for my own sake I do want you to understand that Mr. Harvy is an intimate friend of long standing. Why, we have always been like cousins— like brother and sister, I may say. He is my brother's most intimate associate and often fancies that he is entitled to the same privileges as the family. Oh, I know it is absurd, uncalled for, to tell you this; undignified even," she was almost weeping, "but it makes so much difference to me what you think of—of me." Her voice had grown very low and agitated. The misery had all disappeared from Brantain's face.

"Then you do really care what I think, Miss Nathalie? May I call you Miss Nathalie?" They turned into a long, dim corridor that was lined on either side with tall, graceful plants. They walked slowly to the very end of it. When they turned to retrace their steps Brantain's face was radiant and hers was triumphant.

Harvy was among the guests at the wedding; and he sought her out in a rare moment when she stood alone.

"Your husband," he said, smiling, "has sent me over to kiss you."

A quick blush suffused her face and round polished throat. "I suppose it's natural for a man to feel and act generously on an occasion of this kind. He tells me he doesn't want his marriage to interrupt wholly that pleasant intimacy which has existed between you and me. I don't know what you've been telling him," with an insolent smile, "but he has sent me here to kiss you."

She felt like a chess player who, by the clever handling of his pieces, sees the game taking the course intended. Her eyes were bright and tender with a smile as they glanced up into his; and her lips looked hungry for the kiss which they invited.

"But, you know," he went on quietly, "I didn't tell him so, it would have seemed ungrateful, but I can tell you. I've stopped kissing women; it's dangerous."

Well, she had Brantain and his million left. A person can't have everything in this world; and it was a little unreasonable of her to expect it.

55

A Pair of Silk Stockings

Little Mrs. Sommers one day found herself the unexpected possessor of fifteen dollars. It seemed to her a very large amount of money, and the way in which it stuffed and bulged her worn old porte-monnaie gave her a feeling of importance such as she had not enjoyed for years.

The question of investment was one that occupied her greatly. For a day or two she walked about apparently in a dreamy state, but really absorbed in speculation and calculation. She did not wish to act hastily, to do anything she might afterward regret. But it was during the still hours of the night when she lay awake revolving plans in her mind that she seemed to see her way clearly toward a proper and judicious use of the money.

A dollar or two should be added to the price usually paid for Janie's shoes, which would insure their lasting an appreciable time longer than they usually did. She would buy so and so many yards of percale for new shirt waists for the boys and Janie and Mag. She had intended to make the old ones do by skillful patching. Mag should have another gown. She had seen some beautiful patterns, veritable bargains in the shop windows. And still there would be left enough for new stockings–two pairs apiece–and what darning that would save for a while! She would get caps for the boys and sailor-hats for the girls. The vision of her little brood looking fresh and dainty and new for once in their lives excited her and made her restless and wakeful with anticipation.

The neighbors sometimes talked of certain 'better days' that little Mrs. Sommers had known before she had ever thought of being Mrs. Sommers. She herself indulged in no such morbid retrospection. She had no time—no second of time to devote to the past. The needs of the present absorbed her every faculty. A vision of the future like some dim, gaunt monster sometimes appalled her, but luckily to-morrow never comes.

Mrs. Sommers was one who knew the value of bargains; who could stand for hours making her way inch by inch toward the desired object that was selling below cost. She could elbow her way if need be; she had learned to clutch a piece of goods and hold it and stick to it with persistence and determination till her turn came to be served, no matter when it came.

But that day she was a little faint and tired. She had swallowed a light luncheon—no! when she came to think of it, between getting the children fed and the place righted, and preparing herself for the shopping bout, she had actually forgotten to eat any luncheon at all!

She sat herself upon a revolving stool before a counter that was comparatively deserted, trying to gather strength and courage to charge through an eager multitude that was besieging breastworks of shirting and figured lawn. An all-gone limp feeling had come over her and she rested her hand aimlessly upon the counter. She wore no gloves. By degrees she grew aware that her hand had encountered something very soothing, very pleasant to touch. She looked down to see that her hand lay upon a pile of silk stockings. A placard nearby announced that they had been reduced in price from two dollars and fifty cents to one dollar and ninety-eight cents; and a young girl who stood behind the counter asked her if she wished to examine their line of silk hosiery. She smiled, just as if she had been asked to inspect a tiara of diamonds with the ultimate view of purchasing it. But she went on feeling the soft, sheeny luxurious things—with both hands now, holding them up to see them glisten, and to feel them glide serpent-like through her fingers.

Two hectic blotches came suddenly into her pale cheeks. She looked up at the girl.

"Do you think there are any eights-and-a-half among these?"

There were any number of eights-and-a-half. In fact, there were more of that size than any other. Here was a light-blue pair; there were some lavender, some all black and various shades of tan and gray. Mrs. Sommers selected a black pair and looked at them very long and closely. She pretended to be examining their texture, which the clerk assured her was excellent.

"A dollar and ninety-eight cents," she mused aloud. "Well, I'll take this pair." She handed the girl a five-dollar bill and waited for her change and for her parcel. What a very small parcel it was! It seemed lost in the depths of her shabby old shopping-bag.

Mrs. Sommers after that did not move in the direction of the bargain counter. She took the elevator, which carried her to an upper floor into the region of the ladies' waiting-rooms. Here, in a retired corner, she exchanged her cotton stockings for the new silk ones which she had just bought. She was not going through any acute mental process or reasoning with herself, nor was she striving to explain to her satisfaction the motive of her action. She was not thinking at all. She seemed for the time to be taking a rest from that laborious and fatiguing function and to have abandoned herself to some mechanical impulse that directed her actions and freed her of responsibility.

How good was the touch of the raw silk to her flesh! She felt like lying back in the cushioned chair and reveling for a while in the luxury of it. She did for a little while. Then she replaced her shoes, rolled the cotton stockings together and thrust them into her bag. After doing this she crossed straight over to the shoe department and took her seat to be fitted.

She was fastidious. The clerk could not make her out; he could not reconcile her shoes with her stockings, and she was not too easily pleased. She held back her skirts and turned her feet one way and her head another way as she glanced down at the polished, pointed-tipped boots. Her foot and ankle looked very pretty. She could not realize that they belonged to her and were a part of herself. She wanted an excellent and stylish fit, she told the young fellow who served her, and she did not mind the difference of a dollar or two more in the price so long as she got what she desired.

It was a long time since Mrs. Sommers had been fitted with gloves. On rare occasions when she had bought a pair they were always 'bargains', so cheap that it would have been preposterous and unreasonable to have expected them to be fitted to the hand.

Now she rested her elbow on the cushion of the glove counter, and a pretty, pleasant young creature, delicate and deft of touch, drew a long-wristed 'kid' over Mrs. Sommers's hand. She smoothed it down over the wrist and buttoned it neatly, and both lost themselves for a second or two in admiring contemplation of the little symmetrical gloved hand. But there were other places where money might be spent.

There were books and magazines piled up in the window of a stall a few paces down the street. Mrs. Sommers bought two high-priced magazines such as she had been accustomed to read in the days when she had been accustomed to other pleasant things. She carried them without wrapping. As well as she could she lifted her skirts at the crossings. Her stockings and boots and well fitting gloves had worked marvels in her bearing—had given her a feeling of assurance, a sense of belonging to the well-dressed multitude.

She was very hungry. Another time she would have stilled the cravings for food until reaching her own home, where she would have brewed herself a cup of tea and taken a snack of anything that was available. But the impulse that was guiding her would not suffer her to entertain any such thought.

There was a restaurant at the corner. She had never entered its doors; from the outside she had sometimes caught glimpses of spotless damask and shining crystal, and soft-stepping waiters serving people of fashion.

When she entered her appearance created no surprise, no consternation, as she had half feared it might. She seated herself at a small table alone, and an attentive waiter at once approached to take her order. She did not want a profusion; she craved a nice and tasty bite—a half dozen blue-points, a plump chop with cress, a something sweet—a creme-frappee, for instance; a glass of Rhine wine, and after all a small cup of black coffee.

While waiting to be served she removed her gloves very leisurely and laid them beside her. Then she picked up a magazine and glanced through it, cutting the pages with a blunt edge of her knife. It was all very agreeable. The damask was even more spotless than it had seemed through the window, and the crystal more sparkling. There were quiet ladies and gentlemen, who did not notice her, lunching at the small tables like her own. A soft, pleasing strain of music could be heard, and a gentle breeze, was blowing through the window. She tasted a bite, and she read a word or two, and she sipped the amber wine and wiggled her toes in the silk stockings. The price of it made no difference. She counted the money out to the waiter and left an extra coin on his tray, whereupon he bowed before her as before a princess of royal blood.

There was still money in her purse, and her next temptation presented itself in the shape of a matinee poster.

It was a little later when she entered the theatre, the play had begun and the house seemed to her to be packed. But there were vacant seats here and there, and into one of them she was ushered, between brilliantly dressed women who had gone there to kill time and eat candy and display their gaudy attire. There were many others who were there solely for the play and acting. It is safe to say there was no one present who bore quite the attitude which Mrs. Sommers did to her surroundings. She gathered in the whole—stage and players and people in one wide impression, and absorbed it and enjoyed it. She laughed at the comedy and wept—she and the gaudy woman next to her wept over the tragedy. And they talked a little together over it. And the gaudy woman wiped her eyes and sniffled on a tiny square of filmy, perfumed lace and passed little Mrs. Sommers her box of candy.

The play was over, the music ceased, the crowd filed out. It was like a dream ended. People scattered in all directions. Mrs. Sommers went to the corner and waited for the cable car.

A man with keen eyes, who sat opposite to her, seemed to like the study of her small, pale face. It puzzled him to decipher what he saw there. In truth, he saw nothing-unless he were wizard enough to detect a poignant wish, a powerful longing that the cable car would never stop anywhere, but go on and on with her forever.

Katherine Mansfield

(1888-1923)

56

The Fly

"Y'are very snug in here," piped old Mr. Woodifield, and peered out of the great, green-leather armchair by his friend the boss's desk as a baby peers out of its pram. His talk was over; it was time for him to be off. But he did not want to go. Since he had retired, since his . . . stroke, the wife and the girls kept him boxed up in the house every day of the week except Tuesday. On Tuesday he was dressed and brushed and allowed to cut back to the City for the day. Though what he did there the wife and girls couldn't imagine. Made a nuisance of himself to his friends, they supposed . . .Well, perhaps so. All the same, we cling to our last pleasures as the tree clings to its last leaves. So there sat old Woodifield, smoking a cigar and staring almost greedily at the boss, who rolled in his office chair, stout, rosy, five years older than he, and still going strong, still at the helm. It did one good to see him.

Wistfully, admiringly, the old voice added, "It's snug in here, upon my word!"

"Yes, it's comfortable enough," agreed the boss, and he flipped the Financial Times with a paper-knife. As a matter of fact he was proud of his room; he liked to have it admired, especially by old Woodifield. It gave him a feeling of deep, solid satisfaction to be planted there in the midst of it in full view of that frail old figure in the muffler.

"I've had it done up lately," he explained, as he had explained for the past—how many!—weeks. "New carpet," and he pointed to the bright red carpet with a pattern of large white rings. "New furniture," and he nodded towards the massive bookcase and the table with legs like twisted treacle. "Electric heating!" He waved almost exultantly towards the five transparent, pearly sausages glowing so softly in the tilted copper pan.

But he did not draw old Woodifield's attention to the photograph over the table of a grave-looking boy in uniform standing in one of those spectral photographers' parks with photographers' storm-clouds behind him. It was not new. It had been there for over six years.

"There was something I wanted to tell you," said old Woodifield, and his eyes grew dim remembering. "Now what was it? I had it in my mind when I started out this morning." His hands began to tremble, and patches of red showed above his beard.

Poor old chap, he's on his last pins, thought the boss. And, feeling kindly, he winked at the old man, and said jokingly, "I tell you what. I've got a little drop of something here that'll do you good before you go out into the cold again. It's beautiful stuff. It wouldn't hurt a child." He took a key off his watch-chain, unlocked a cupboard below his desk, and drew forth a dark, squat bottle. "That's the medicine," said he. "And the man from whom I got it told me on the strict Q.T. it came from the cellars at Windsor Castle."

Old Woodifield's mouth fell open at the sight. He couldn't have looked more surprised if the boss had produced a rabbit. "It's whisky, ain't it?" he piped feebly.

The boss turned the bottle and lovingly showed him the label. Whisky it was.

"D'you know," said he, peering up at the boss wonderingly, "they won't let me touch it at home." And he looked as though he was going to cry.

"Ah, that's where we know a bit more than the ladies," cried the boss, swooping across for two tumblers that stood on the table with the water-bottle, and pouring a generous finger into each. "Drink it down. It'll do you good. And don't put any water with it. It's sacrilege to tamper with stuff like this. Ah!" He tossed off his, pulled out his handkerchief, hastily wiped his moustaches, and cocked an eye at old Woodifield, who was rolling his in his chaps.

The old man swallowed, was silent a moment, and then said faintly, "It's nutty!"

But it warmed him; it crept into his chill old brain he remembered.

"That was it," he said, heaving himself out of his chair. "I thought you'd like to know. The girls were in Belgium last week having a look at poor Reggie's grave, and they happened to come across your boy's. They're quite near each other, it seems."

Old Woodifield paused, but the boss made no reply. Only a quiver in his eyelids showed that he heard.

"The girls were delighted with the way the place is kept," piped the old voice. "Beautifully looked after. Couldn't be better if they were at home. You've not been across, have yer?"

"No, no!" For various reasons the boss had not been across.

"There's miles of it," quavered old Woodifield, "and it's all as neat as a garden. Flowers growing on all the graves. Nice broad paths." It was plain from his voice how much he liked a nice broad path.

The pause came again. Then the old man brightened wonderfully.

"D'you know what the hotel made the girls pay for a pot of jam?" he piped. "Ten francs! Robbery, I call it. It was a little pot, so Gertrude says, no bigger than a half-crown. And she hadn't taken more than a spoonful when they charged her ten francs. Gertrude brought the pot away with her to teach 'em a lesson. Quite right, too; it's trading on our feelings. They think because we're over there having a look round we're ready to pay anything. That's what it is." And he turned towards the door.

"Quite right, quite right!" cried the boss, though what was quite right he hadn't the least idea. He came round by his desk, followed the shuffling footsteps to the door, and saw the old fellow out. Woodifield was gone.

For a long moment the boss stayed, staring at nothing, while the grey-haired office messenger, watching him, dodged in and out of his cubby-hole like a dog that expects to be taken for a run. Then: "I'll see nobody for half an hour, Macey," said the boss. "Understand! Nobody at all."

"Very good, sir."

The door shut, the firm heavy steps recrossed the bright carpet, the fat body plumped down in the spring chair, and leaning forward, the boss covered his face with his hands. He wanted, he intended, he had arranged to weep . . .

It had been a terrible shock to him when old Woodifield sprang that remark upon him about the boy's grave. It was exactly as though the earth had opened and he had seen the boy lying there with Woodifield's girls staring down at him. For it was strange. Although over six years had passed away, the boss never thought of the boy except as lying unchanged, unblemished in his uniform, asleep for ever. "My son!" groaned the boss. But no tears came yet. In the past, in the first months and even years after the boy's death, he had only to say those words to be overcome by such grief that nothing short of a violent fit of weeping could relieve him. Time, he had declared then, he had told everybody, could make no difference. Other men perhaps might recover, might live their loss down, but not he. How was it possible! His boy was an only son. Ever since his birth the boss had worked at building up this business for him; it had no other meaning if it was not for the boy. Life itself had come to have no other meaning. How on earth could he have slaved, denied himself, kept going all those years without the promise for ever before him of the boy's stepping into his shoes and carrying on where he left off?

And that promise had been so near being fulfilled. The boy had been in the office learning the ropes for a year before the war. Every morning they had started off together; they had come back by the same train. And what congratulations he had received as the boy's father! No wonder; he had taken to it marvellously. As to his popularity with the staff, every man jack of them down to old Macey couldn't make enough of the boy. And he wasn't in the least spoilt. No, he was just his bright natural self, with the right word for everybody, with that boyish look and his habit of saying, "Simply splendid!"

But all that was over and done with as though it never had been. The day had come when Macey had handed him the telegram that brought the whole place crashing about his head. "Deeply regret to inform you . . ." And he had left the office a broken man, with his life in ruins.

Six years ago, six years . . . How quickly time passed! It might have happened yesterday. The boss took his hands from his face; he was puzzled. Something seemed to be wrong with him. He wasn't feeling as he wanted to feel. He decided to get up and have a look at the boy's photograph. But it wasn't a favourite photograph of his; the expression was unnatural. It was cold, even stern-looking. The boy had never looked like that.

At that moment the boss noticed that a fly had fallen into his broad inkpot, and was trying feebly but desperately to clamber out again. Help! Help! said those struggling legs. But the sides of the inkpot were wet and slippery; it fell back again and began to swim. The boss took up a pen, picked the fly out of the ink, and shook it on to a piece of blotting-paper. For a fraction of a second it lay still on the dark patch that oozed round it. Then the front legs waved, took hold, and, pulling its small, sodden body up, it began the immense task of cleaning the ink from its wings. Over and under, over and under, went a leg along a wing as the stone goes over and under the scythe. Then there was a pause, while the fly, seeming to stand on the tips of its toes, tried to expand first one wing and then the other. It succeeded at last, and, sitting down, it began, like a minute cat, to clean its face. Now one could Imagine that the little front legs rubbed against each other lightly, joyfully. The horrible danger was over; it had escaped; it was ready for life again.

But just then the boss had an idea. He plunged his pen back into the ink, leaned his thick wrist on the blotting-paper, and as the fly tried its wings down came a great heavy blot. What would it make of that! What indeed! The little beggar seemed absolutely cowed, stunned, and afraid to move because of what would happen next. But then, as if painfully, it dragged itself forward. The front legs waved, caught hold, and, more slowly this time, the task began from the beginning.

He's a plucky little devil, thought the boss, and he felt a real admiration for the fly's courage. That was the way to tackle things; that was the right spirit. Never say die; it was only a question of . . . But the fly had again finished its laborious task, and the boss had just time to refill his pen, to shake fair and square on the new-cleaned body yet another dark drop. What about it this time? A painful moment of suspense followed. But behold, the front legs were again waving; the boss felt a rush of relief. He leaned over the fly and said to it tenderly, "You artful little b . . ." And he actually had the brilliant notion of breathing on it to help the drying process. All the same, there was something timid and weak about its efforts now, and the boss decided that this time should be the last, as he dipped the pen deep into the inkpot.

It was. The last blot fell on the soaked blotting-paper, and the draggled fly lay in it and did not stir. The back legs were stuck to the body; the front legs were not to be seen.

"Come on," said the boss. "Look sharp!" And he stirred it with his pen in vain. Nothing happened or was likely to happen. The fly was dead.

The boss lifted the corpse on the end of the paper-knife and flung it into the waste-paper basket. But such a grinding feeling of wretchedness seized him that he felt positively frightened. He started forward and pressed the bell for Macey.

"Bring me some fresh blotting-paper," he said sternly, "and look sharp about it." And while the old dog padded away he fell to wondering what it was he had been thinking about before. What was it? It was . . . He took out his handkerchief and passed it inside his collar. For the life of him he could not remember.

57

Mr. and Mrs. Dove

Of course he knew—no man better—that he hadn't a ghost of a chance, he hadn't an earthly. The very idea of such a thing was preposterous. So preposterous that he'd perfectly understand it if her father—well, whatever her father chose to do he'd perfectly understand. In fact, nothing short of desperation, nothing short of the fact that this was positively his last day in England for God knows how long, would have screwed him up to it. And even now . . . He chose a tie out of the chest of drawers, a blue and cream check tie, and sat on the side of his bed. Supposing she replied, "What impertinence!" would he be surprised? Not in the least, he decided, turning up his soft collar and turning it down over the tie. He expected her to say something like that. He didn't see, if he looked at the affair dead soberly, what else she could say.

Here he was! And nervously he tied a bow in front of the mirror, jammed his hair down with both hands, pulled out the flaps of his jacket pockets. Making between £500 and £600 a year on a fruit farm in—of all places—Rhodesia. No capital. Not a penny coming to him. No chance of his income increasing for at least four years. As for looks and all that sort of thing, he was completely out of the running. He couldn't even boast of top-hole health, for the East Africa business had knocked him out so thoroughly that he'd had to take six months' leave. He was still fearfully pale— worse even than usual this afternoon, he thought, bending forward and peering into the mirror. Good heavens! What had happened? His hair looked almost bright green. Dash it all, he hadn't green hair at all events. That was a bit too steep. And then the green light trembled in the glass; it was the shadow from the tree outside. Reggie turned away, took out his cigarette case, but remembering how the mater hated him to smoke in his bedroom, put it back again and drifted over to the chest of drawers. No, he was dashed if he could think of one blessed thing in his favour, while she . . . Ah! . . . He stopped dead, folded his arms, and leaned hard against the chest of drawers.

And in spite of her position, her father's wealth, the fact that she was an only child and far and away the most popular girl in the neighbourhood; in spite of her beauty and her cleverness— cleverness!—it was a great deal more than that, there was really nothing she couldn't do; he fully believed, had it been necessary, she would have been a genius at anything—in spite of the fact that her parents adored her, and she them, and they'd as soon let her go all that way as . . . In spite of every single thing you could think of, so terrific was his love that he couldn't help hoping. Well, was it hope? Or was this queer, timid longing to have the chance of looking after her, of making it his job to see that she had everything she wanted, and that nothing came near her that wasn't perfect— just love? How he loved her! He squeezed hard against the chest of drawers and murmured to it, "I love her, I love her!" And just for the moment he was with her on the way to Umtali. It was night. She sat in a corner asleep. Her soft chin was tucked into her soft collar, her gold-brown lashes lay on her cheeks. He doted on her delicate little nose, her perfect lips, her ear like a baby's, and the gold-brown curl that half covered it. They were passing through the jungle. It was warm and dark and far away. Then she woke up and said, "Have I been asleep?" and he answered, "Yes. Are you all right? Here, let me—" And he leaned forward to . . . He bent over her. This was such bliss that he could dream no further. But it gave him the courage to bound downstairs, to snatch his straw hat from the hall, and to say as he closed the front door, "Well, I can only try my luck, that's all."

But his luck gave him a nasty jar, to say the least, almost immediately. Promenading up and down the garden path with Chinny and Biddy, the ancient Pekes, was the mater. Of course Reginald was fond of the mater and all that. She—she meant well, she had no end of grit, and so on. But there was no denying it, she was rather a grim parent. And there had been moments, many of them, in Reggie's life, before Uncle Alick died and left him the fruit farm, when he was convinced that to be a widow's only son was about the worst punishment a chap could have. And what made it rougher than ever was that she was positively all that he had. She wasn't only a combined parent, as it were, but she had quarrelled with all her own and the governor's relations before Reggie had won his first trouser pockets. So that whenever Reggie was homesick out there, sitting on his dark veranda by starlight, while the gramophone cried, "Dear, what is Life but Love?" his only vision was of the mater, tall and stout, rustling down the garden path, with Chinny and Biddy at her heels . . .

The mater, with her scissors outspread to snap the head of a dead something or other, stopped at the sight of Reggie.

"You are not going out, Reginald?" she asked, seeing that he was.

"I'll be back for tea, mater," said Reggie weakly, plunging his hands into his jacket pockets.

Snip. Off came a head. Reggie almost jumped.

"I should have thought you could have spared your mother your last afternoon," said she.

Silence. The Pekes stared. They understood every word of the mater's. Biddy lay down with her tongue poked out; she was so fat and glossy she looked like a lump of half-melted toffee. But Chinny's porcelain eyes gloomed at Reginald, and he sniffed faintly, as though the whole world were one unpleasant smell. Snip, went the scissors again. Poor little beggars; they were getting it!

"And where are you going, if your mother may ask?" asked the mater.

It was over at last, but Reggie did not slow down until he was out of sight of the house and half-way to Colonel Proctor's. Then only he noticed what a top-hole afternoon it was. It had been raining all the morning, late summer rain, warm, heavy, quick, and now the sky was clear, except for a long tail of little clouds, like duckings, sailing over the forest. There was just enough wind to shake the last drops off the trees; one warm star splashed on his hand. Ping!—another drummed on his hat. The empty road gleamed, the hedges smelled of briar, and how big and bright the hollyhocks glowed in the cottage gardens. And here was Colonel Proctor's—here it was already. His hand was on the gate, his elbow jogged the syringa bushes, and petals and pollen scattered over his coat sleeve. But wait a bit. This was too quick altogether. He'd meant to think the whole thing out again. Here, steady. But he was walking up the path, with the huge rose bushes on either side. It can't be done like this. But his hand had grasped the bell, given it a pull, and started it pealing wildly, as if he'd come to say the house was on fire. The housemaid must have been in the hall, too, for the front door flashed open, and Reggie was shut in the empty drawing-room before that confounded bell had stopped ringing. Strangely enough, when it did, the big room, shadowy, with some one's parasol lying on top of the grand piano, bucked him up—or rather, excited him. It was so quiet, and yet in one moment the door would open, and his fate be decided. The feeling was not unlike that of being at the dentist's; he was almost reckless. But at the same time, to his immense surprise, Reggie heard himself saying, "Lord, Thou knowest, Thou hast not done *much* for me . . ." That pulled him up; that made him realize again how dead serious it was. Too late. The door handle turned. Anne came in, crossed the shadowy space between them, gave him her hand, and said, in her small, soft voice, "I'm so sorry, father is out. And mother is having a day in town, hat-hunting. There's only me to entertain you, Reggie."

Reggie gasped, pressed his own hat to his jacket buttons, and stammered out, "As a matter of fact, I've only come . . . to say good-bye."

"Oh!" cried Anne softly—she stepped back from him and her grey eyes danced—"what a *very* short visit!"

Then, watching him, her chin tilted, she laughed outright, a long, soft peal, and walked away from him over to the piano, and leaned against it, playing with the tassel of the parasol.

"I'm so sorry," she said, "to be laughing like this. I don't know why I do. It's just a bad ha-habit." And suddenly she stamped her grey shoe, and took a pocket-handkerchief out of her white woolly jacket. "I really must conquer it, it's too absurd," said she.

"Good heavens, Anne," cried Reggie, "I love to hear you laughing! I can't imagine anything more—"

But the truth was, and they both knew it, she wasn't always laughing; it wasn't really a habit. Only ever since the day they'd met, ever since that very first moment, for some strange reason that Reggie wished to God he understood, Anne had laughed at him. Why? It didn't matter where they were or what they were talking about. They might begin by being as serious as possible, dead serious—at any rate, as far as he was concerned—but then suddenly, in the middle of a sentence, Anne would glance at him, and a little quick quiver passed over her face. Her lips parted, her eyes danced, and she began laughing.

Another queer thing about it was, Reggie had an idea she didn't herself know why she laughed. He had seen her turn away, frown, suck in her cheeks, press her hands together. But it was no use. The long, soft peal sounded, even while she cried, "I don't know why I'm laughing." It was a mystery . . .

Now she tucked the handkerchief away.

"Do sit down," said she. "And smoke, won't you? There are cigarettes in that little box beside you. I'll have one too." He lighted a match for her, and as she bent forward he saw the tiny flame glow in the pearl ring she wore. "It is to-morrow that you're going, isn't it?" said Anne.

"Yes, to-morrow as ever was," said Reggie, and he blew a little fan of smoke. Why on earth was he so nervous? Nervous wasn't the word for it.

"It's—it's frightfully hard to believe," he added.

"Yes—isn't it?" said Anne softly, and she leaned forward and rolled the point of her cigarette round the green ash-tray. How beautiful she looked like that!—simply beautiful—and she was so small in that immense chair. Reginald's heart swelled with tenderness, but it was her voice, her soft voice, that made him tremble. "I feel you've been here for years," she said.

Reginald took a deep breath of his cigarette. "It's ghastly, this idea of going back," he said.

"*Coo-roo-coo-coo-coo,*" sounded from the quiet.

"But you're fond of being out there, aren't you?" said Anne. She hooked her finger through her pearl necklace. "Father was saying only the other night how lucky he thought you were to have a life of your own." And she looked up at him. Reginald's smile was rather wan. "I don't feel fearfully lucky," he said lightly.

"*Roo-coo-coo-coo,*" came again. And Anne murmured, "You mean it's lonely."

"Oh, it isn't the loneliness I care about," said Reginald, and he stumped his cigarette savagely on the green ash-tray. "I could stand any amount of it, used to like it even. It's the idea of—" Suddenly, to his horror, he felt himself blushing.

"*Roo-coo-coo-coo! Roo-coo-coo-coo!*"

Anne jumped up. "Come and say good-bye to my doves," she said. "They've been moved to the side veranda. You do like doves, don't you, Reggie?"

"Awfully," said Reggie, so fervently that as he opened the French window for her and stood to one side, Anne ran forward and laughed at the doves instead.

To and fro, to and fro over the fine red sand on the floor of the dove house, walked the two doves. One was always in front of the other. One ran forward, uttering a little cry, and the other followed, solemnly bowing and bowing. "You see," explained Anne, "the one in front, she's Mrs. Dove. She looks at Mr. Dove and gives that little laugh and runs forward, and he follows her, bowing and bowing. And that makes her laugh again. Away she runs, and after her," cried Anne, and she sat back on her heels, "comes poor Mr. Dove, bowing and bowing... and that's their whole life. They never do anything else, you know." She got up and took some yellow grains out of a bag on the roof of the dove house. "When you think of them, out in Rhodesia, Reggie, you can be sure that is what they will be doing . . ."

Reggie gave no sign of having seen the doves or of having heard a word. For the moment he was conscious only of the immense effort it took to tear his secret out of himself and offer it to Anne. "Anne, do you think you could ever care for me?" It was done. It was over. And in the little pause that followed Reginald saw the garden open to the light, the blue quivering sky, the flutter of leaves on the veranda poles, and Anne turning over the grains of maize on her palm with one finger. Then slowly she shut her hand, and the new world faded as she murmured slowly, "No, never in that way." But he had scarcely time to feel anything before she walked quickly away, and he followed her down the steps, along the garden path, under the pink rose arches, across the lawn. There, with the gay herbaceous border behind her, Anne faced Reginald. "It isn't that I'm not awfully fond of you," she said. "I am. But"—her eyes widened—"not in the way"—a quiver passed over her face—"one ought to be fond of—" Her lips parted, and she couldn't stop herself. She began laughing. "There, you see, you see," she cried, "it's your check t-tie. Even at this moment, when one would think one really would be solemn, your tie reminds me fearfully of the bow-tie that cats wear in pictures! Oh, please forgive me for being so horrid, please!"

Reggie caught hold of her little warm hand. "There's no question of forgiving you," he said quickly. "How could there be? And I do believe I know why I make you laugh. It's because you're so far above me in every way that I am somehow ridiculous. I see that, Anne. But if I were to—"

"No, no." Anne squeezed his hand hard. "It's not that. That's all wrong. I'm not far above you at all. You're much better than I am. You're marvellously unselfish and . . . and kind and simple.

I'm none of those things. You don't know me. I'm the most awful character," said Anne. "Please don't interrupt. And besides, that's not the point. The point is"—she shook her head—"I couldn't possibly marry a man I laughed at. Surely you see that. The man I marry—" breathed Anne softly. She broke off. She drew her hand away, and looking at Reggie she smiled strangely, dreamily. "The man I marry—"

And it seemed to Reggie that a tall, handsome, brilliant stranger stepped in front of him and took his place—the kind of man that Anne and he had seen often at the theatre, walking on to the stage from nowhere, without a word catching the heroine in his arms, and after one long, tremendous look, carrying her off to anywhere . . .

Reggie bowed to his vision. "Yes, I see," he said huskily.

"Do you?" said Anne. "Oh, I do hope you do. Because I feel so horrid about it. It's so hard to explain. You know I've never—" She stopped. Reggie looked at her. She was smiling. "Isn't it funny?" she said. "I can say anything to you. I always have been able to from the very beginning."

He tried to smile, to say "I'm glad." She went on. "I've never known anyone I like as much as I like you. I've never felt so happy with anyone. But I'm sure it's not what people and what books mean when they talk about love. Do you understand? Oh, if you only knew how horrid I feel. But we'd be like . . . like Mr. and Mrs. Dove."

That did it. That seemed to Reginald final, and so terribly true that he could hardly bear it. "Don't drive it home," he said, and he turned away from Anne and looked across the lawn. There was the gardener's cottage, with the dark ilex-tree beside it. A wet, blue thumb of transparent smoke hung above the chimney. It didn't look real. How his throat ached! Could he speak? He had a shot. "I must be getting along home," he croaked, and he began walking across the lawn. But Anne ran after him. "No, don't. You can't go yet," she said imploringly. "You can't possibly go away feeling like that." And she stared up at him frowning, biting her lip.

"Oh, that's all right," said Reggie, giving himself a shake. "I'll . . . I'll—" And he waved his hand as much to say "get over it."

"But this is awful," said Anne. She clasped her hands and stood in front of him. "Surely you do see how fatal it would be for us to marry, don't you?"

"Oh, quite, quite," said Reggie, looking at her with haggard eyes.

"How wrong, how wicked, feeling as I do. I mean, it's all very well for Mr. and Mrs. Dove. But imagine that in real life—imagine it!"

"Oh, absolutely," said Reggie, and he started to walk on. But again Anne stopped him. She tugged at his sleeve, and to his astonishment, this time, instead of laughing, she looked like a little girl who was going to cry.

"Then why, if you understand, are you so un-unhappy?" she wailed. "Why do you mind so fearfully? Why do you look so aw-awful?"

Reggie gulped, and again he waved something away. "I can't help it," he said, "I've had a blow. If I cut off now, I'll be able to—"

"How can you talk of cutting off now?" said Anne scornfully. She stamped her foot at Reggie; she was crimson. "How can you be so cruel? I can't let you go until I know for certain that you are just as happy as you were before you asked me to marry you. Surely you must see that, it's so simple."

But it did not seem at all simple to Reginald. It seemed impossibly difficult.

"Even if I can't marry you, how can I know that you're all that way away, with only that awful mother to write to, and that you're miserable, and that it's all my fault?"

"It's not your fault. Don't think that. It's just fate." Reggie took her hand off his sleeve and kissed it. "Don't pity me, dear little Anne," he said gently. And this time he nearly ran, under the pink arches, along the garden path.

"*Roo-coo-coo-coo! Roo-coo-coo-coo!*" sounded from the veranda. "Reggie, Reggie," from the garden.

He stopped, he turned. But when she saw his timid, puzzled look, she gave a little laugh.

"Come back, Mr. Dove," said Anne. And Reginald came slowly across the lawn.

58

The Young Girl

In her blue dress, with her cheeks lightly flushed, her blue, blue eyes, and her gold curls pinned up as though for the first time—pinned up to be out of the way for her flight—Mrs. Raddick's daughter might have just dropped from this radiant heaven. Mrs. Raddick's timid, faintly astonished, but deeply admiring glance looked as if she believed it, too; but the daughter didn't appear any too pleased—why should she?—to have alighted on the steps of the Casino. Indeed, she was bored—bored as though Heaven had been full of casinos with snuffy old saints for *croupiers* and crowns to play with.

"You don't mind taking Hennie?" said Mrs. Raddick. "Sure you don't? There's the car, and you'll have tea and we'll be back here on this step—right here—in an hour. You see, I want her to go in. She's not been before, and it's worth seeing. I feel it wouldn't be fair to her."

"Oh, shut up, mother," said she wearily. "Come along. Don't talk so much. And your bag's open; you'll be losing all your money again."

"I'm sorry, darling," said Mrs. Raddick.

"Oh, *do* come in! I want to make money," said the impatient voice. "It's all jolly well for you—but I'm broke!"

"Here—take fifty francs, darling, take a hundred!" I saw Mrs. Raddick pressing notes into her hand as they passed through the swing doors.

Hennie and I stood on the steps a minute, watching the people. He had a very broad, delighted smile.

"I say," he cried, "there's an English bulldog. Are they allowed to take dogs in there?"

"No, they're not."

"He's a ripping chap, isn't he? I wish I had one. They're such fun. They frighten people so, and they're never fierce with their— the people they belong to." Suddenly he squeezed my arm. "I say, *do* look at that old woman. Who is she? Why does she look like that? Is she a gambler?"

The ancient, withered creature, wearing a green satin dress, a black velvet cloak and a white hat with purple feathers, jerked slowly, slowly up the steps as though she were being drawn up on wires. She stared in front of her, she was laughing and nodding and cackling to herself; her claws clutched round what looked like a dirty boot-bag.

But just at that moment there was Mrs. Raddick again with— *her*—and another lady hovering in the background. Mrs. Raddick rushed at me. She was brightly flushed, gay, a different creature. She was like a woman who is saying 'good-bye' to her friends on the station platform, with not a minute to spare before the train starts.

"Oh, you're here, still. Isn't that lucky! You've not gone. Isn't that fine! I've had the most dreadful time with—her," and she waved to her daughter, who stood absolutely still, disdainful, looking down, twiddling her foot on the step, miles away. "They won't let her in. I swore she was twenty-one. But they won't believe me. I showed the man my purse; I didn't dare to do more. But it was no use. He simply scoffed . . . And now I've just met Mrs. MacEwen from New York, and she just won thirteen thousand in the *Salle Privée*—and she wants me to go back with her while the luck lasts. Of course I can't leave—her. But if you'd—"

At that "she" looked up; she simply withered her mother. "Why

319

can't you leave me?" she said furiously. "What utter rot! How dare you make a scene like this? This is the last time I'll come out with you. You really are too awful for words." She looked her mother up and down. "Calm yourself," she said superbly.

Mrs. Raddick was desperate, just desperate. She was "wild" to go back with Mrs. MacEwen, but at the same time . . .

I seized my courage. "Would you—do you care to come to tea with—us?"

"Yes, yes, she'll be delighted. That's just what I wanted, isn't it, darling? Mrs. MacEwen . . . I'll be back here in an hour . . . or less . . . I'll—"

Mrs. R. dashed up the steps. I saw her bag was open again.

So we three were left. But really it wasn't my fault. Hennie looked crushed to the earth, too. When the car was there she wrapped her dark coat round her—to escape contamination. Even her little feet looked as though they scorned to carry her down the steps to us.

"I am so awfully sorry," I murmured as the car started.

"Oh, I don't *mind*," said she. "I don't *want* to look twenty-one. Who would—if they were seventeen! It's"—and she gave a faint shudder—"the stupidity I loathe, and being stared at by old fat men. Beasts!"

Hennie gave her a quick look and then peered out of the window.

We drew up before an immense palace of pink-and-white marble with orange-trees outside the doors in gold-and-black tubs.

"Would you care to go in?" I suggested.

She hesitated, glanced, bit her lip, and resigned herself. "Oh well, there seems nowhere else," said she. "Get out, Hennie."

I went first—to find the table, of course—she followed. But the worst of it was having her little brother, who was only twelve, with us. That was the last, final straw—having that child, trailing at her heels.

There was one table. It had pink carnations and pink plates with little blue tea-napkins for sails.

"Shall we sit here?"

She put her hand wearily on the back of a white wicker chair. "We may as well. Why not?" said she.

Hennie squeezed past her and wriggled on to a stool at the end. He felt awfully out of it. She didn't even take her gloves off. She lowered her eyes and drummed on the table. When a faint violin sounded she winced and bit her lip again. Silence.

The waitress appeared. I hardly dared to ask her. "Tea—coffee? China tea—or iced tea with lemon?"

Really she didn't mind. It was all the same to her. She didn't really want anything. Hennie whispered, "Chocolate!"

But just as the waitress turned away she cried out carelessly, "Oh, you may as well bring me a chocolate, too."

While we waited she took out a little, gold powder-box with a mirror in the lid, shook the poor little puff as though she loathed it, and dabbed her lovely nose.

"Hennie," she said, "take those flowers away." She pointed with her puff to the carnations, and I heard her murmur, "I can't bear flowers on a table." They had evidently been giving her intense pain, for she positively closed her eyes as I moved them away.

The waitress came back with the chocolate and the tea. She put the big, frothing cups before them and pushed across my clear glass. Hennie buried his nose, emerged, with, for one dreadful moment, a little trembling blob of cream on the tip. But he hastily wiped it off like a little gentleman. I wondered if I should dare draw her attention to her cup. She didn't notice it—didn't see it—until suddenly, quite by chance, she took a sip. I watched anxiously; she faintly shuddered.

"Dreadfully sweet!" said she.

A tiny boy with a head like a raisin and a chocolate body came round with a tray of pastries—row upon row of little freaks, little inspirations, little melting dreams. He offered them to her. "Oh, I'm not at all hungry. Take them away."

He offered them to Hennie. Hennie gave me a swift look— it must have been satisfactory—for he took a chocolate cream, a coffee éclair, a meringue stuffed with chestnut and a tiny horn filled with fresh strawberries. She could hardly bear to watch him. But just as the boy swerved away she held up her plate.

"Oh well, give me *one*," said she.

The silver tongs dropped one, two, three—and a cherry tartlet. "I don't know why you're giving me all these," she said, and nearly smiled. "I shan't eat them; I couldn't!"

I felt much more comfortable. I sipped my tea, leaned back, and even asked if I might smoke. At that she paused, the fork in her hand, opened her eyes, and really did smile. "Of course," said she. "I always expect people to."

But at that moment a tragedy happened to Hennie. He speared his pastry horn too hard, and it flew in two, and one half spilled on the table. Ghastly affair! He turned crimson. Even his ears flared, and one ashamed hand crept across the table to take what was left of the body away.

"You *utter* little beast!" said she.

Good heavens! I had to fly to the rescue. I cried hastily, "Will you be abroad long?"

But she had already forgotten Hennie. I was forgotten, too. She was trying to remember something . . . She was miles away.

"I—don't—know," she said slowly, from that far place.

"I suppose you prefer it to London. It's more—more—"

When I didn't go on she came back and looked at me, very puzzled. "More—?"

"*Enfin*—gayer," I cried, waving my cigarette.

But that took a whole cake to consider. Even then, "Oh well, that depends!" was all she could safely say.

Hennie had finished. He was still very warm.

I seized the butterfly list off the table. "I say—what about an ice, Hennie? What about tangerine and ginger? No, something cooler. What about a fresh pineapple cream?"

Hennie strongly approved. The waitress had her eye on us. The order was taken when she looked up from her crumbs.

"Did you say tangerine and ginger? I like ginger. You can bring me one." And then quickly, "I wish that orchestra wouldn't play things from the year One. We were dancing to that all last Christmas. It's too sickening!"

But it was a charming air. Now that I noticed it, it warmed me. "I think this is rather a nice place, don't you, Hennie?" I said.

Hennie said: "Ripping!" He meant to say it very low, but it came out very high in a kind of squeak.

Nice? This place? Nice? For the first time she stared about her, trying to see what there was . . . She blinked; her lovely eyes wondered. A very good-looking elderly man stared back at her through a monocle on a black ribbon. But him she simply couldn't see. There was a hole in the air where he was. She looked through and through him.

Finally the little flat spoons lay still on the glass plates. Hennie looked rather exhausted, but she pulled on her white gloves again. She had some trouble with her diamond wrist-watch; it got in her way. She tugged at it—tried to break the stupid little thing—it wouldn't break. Finally, she had to drag her glove over. I saw, after that, she couldn't stand this place a moment longer, and, indeed, she jumped up and turned away while I went through the vulgar act of paying for the tea.

And then we were outside again. It had grown dusky. The sky was sprinkled with small stars; the big lamps glowed. While we waited for the car to come up she stood on the step, just as before, twiddling her foot, looking down.

Hennie bounded forward to open the door and she got in and sank back with—oh—such a sigh!

"Tell him," she gasped, "to drive as fast as he can."

Hennie grinned at his friend the chauffeur. "*Allie veet!*" said he. Then he composed himself and sat on the small seat facing us.

The gold powder-box came out again. Again the poor little puff was shaken; again there was that swift, deadly-secret glance between her and the mirror.

We tore through the black-and-gold town like a pair of scissors tearing through brocade. Hennie had great difficulty not to look as though he were hanging on to something.

And when we reached the Casino, of course Mrs. Raddick wasn't there. There wasn't a sign of her on the steps—not a sign.

"Will you stay in the car while I go and look?"

But no—she wouldn't do that. Good heavens, no! Hennie could stay. She couldn't bear sitting in a car. She'd wait on the steps.

"But I scarcely like to leave you," I murmured. "I'd very much rather not leave you here."

At that she threw back her coat; she turned and faced me; her lips parted. "Good heavens—why! I—I don't mind it a bit. I—I like waiting." And suddenly her cheeks crimsoned, her eyes grew dark—for a moment I thought she was going to cry. "L—let me, please," she stammered, in a warm, eager voice. "I like it. I love waiting! Really—really I do! I'm always waiting—in all kinds of places . . ."

Her dark coat fell open, and her white throat—all her soft young body in the blue dress—was like a flower that is just emerging from its dark bud.

59

Miss Brill

Although it was so brilliantly fine—the blue sky powdered with gold and great spots of light like white wine splashed over the Jardins Publiques—Miss Brill was glad that she had decided on her fur. The air was motionless, but when you opened your mouth there was just a faint chill, like a chill from a glass of iced water before you sip, and now and again a leaf came drifting—from nowhere, from the sky. Miss Brill put up her hand and touched her fur. Dear little thing! It was nice to feel it again. She had taken it out of its box that afternoon, shaken out the moth-powder, given it a good brush, and rubbed the life back into the dim little eyes. "What has been happening to me?" said the sad little eyes. Oh, how sweet it was to see them snap at her again from the red eiderdown! ... But the nose, which was of some black composition, wasn't at all firm. It must have had a knock, somehow. Never mind—a little dab of black sealing-wax when the time came—when it was absolutely necessary ... Little rogue! Yes, she really felt like that about it. Little rogue biting its tail just by her left ear. She could have taken it off and laid it on her lap and stroked it. She felt a tingling in her hands and arms, but that came from walking, she supposed. And when she breathed, something light and sad—no, not sad, exactly—something gentle seemed to move in her bosom.

There were a number of people out this afternoon, far more than last Sunday. And the band sounded louder and gayer. That was because the Season had begun. For although the band played all the year round on Sundays, out of season it was never the same. It was like some one playing with only the family to listen; it didn't care how it played if there weren't any strangers present. Wasn't the conductor wearing a new coat, too? She was sure it was new. He scraped with his foot and flapped his arms like a rooster about to crow, and the bandsmen sitting in the green rotunda blew out their cheeks and glared at the music. Now there came a little 'flutey' bit—very pretty!—a little chain of bright drops. She was sure it would be repeated. It was; she lifted her head and smiled.

Only two people shared her 'special' seat: a fine old man in a velvet coat, his hands clasped over a huge carved walking-stick, and a big old woman, sitting upright, with a roll of knitting on her embroidered apron. They did not speak. This was disappointing, for Miss Brill always looked forward to the conversation. She had become really quite expert, she thought, at listening as though she didn't listen, at sitting in other people's lives just for a minute while they talked round her.

She glanced, sideways, at the old couple. Perhaps they would go soon. Last Sunday, too, hadn't been as interesting as usual. An Englishman and his wife, he wearing a dreadful Panama hat and she button boots. And she'd gone on the whole time about how she ought to wear spectacles; she knew she needed them; but that it was no good getting any; they'd be sure to break and they'd never keep on. And he'd been so patient. He'd suggested everything—gold rims, the kind that curved round your ears, little pads inside the bridge. No, nothing would please her. "They'll always be sliding down my nose!" Miss Brill had wanted to shake her.

The old people sat on the bench, still as statues. Never mind, there was always the crowd to watch. To and fro, in front of the flower-beds and the band rotunda, the couples and groups paraded, stopped to talk, to greet, to buy a handful of flowers from the old beggar who had his tray fixed to the railings. Little children ran among them, swooping and laughing; little boys with big white silk bows under their chins, little girls, little French dolls, dressed up in velvet and lace. And sometimes a tiny staggerer came suddenly rocking into the open from under the trees, stopped, stared, as suddenly sat down 'flop', until its small high-stepping mother, like a young hen, rushed scolding to its rescue. Other people sat on the benches and green chairs, but they were nearly always the same, Sunday after Sunday, and—Miss Brill had often noticed—there was something funny about nearly all of them. They were odd, silent, nearly all old, and from the way they stared they looked as though they'd just come from dark little rooms or even—even cupboards!

Behind the rotunda the slender trees with yellow leaves down drooping, and through them just a line of sea, and beyond the blue sky with gold-veined clouds.

Tum-tum-tum tiddle-um! tiddle-um! tum tiddley-um tum ta! blew the band.

Two young girls in red came by and two young soldiers in blue met them, and they laughed and paired and went off arm-in-arm. Two peasant women with funny straw hats passed, gravely, leading beautiful smoke-coloured donkeys. A cold, pale nun hurried by. A beautiful woman came along and dropped her bunch of violets, and a little boy ran after to hand them to her, and she took them and threw them away as if they'd been poisoned. Dear me! Miss Brill didn't know whether to admire that or not! And now an ermine toque and a gentleman in grey met just in front of her. He was tall, stiff, dignified, and she was wearing the ermine toque she'd bought when her hair was yellow. Now everything, her hair, her face, even her eyes, was the same colour as the shabby ermine, and her hand, in its cleaned glove, lifted to dab her lips, was a tiny yellowish paw. Oh, she was so pleased to see him—delighted! She rather thought they were going to meet that afternoon. She described where she'd been—everywhere, here, there, along by the sea. The day was so charming—didn't he agree? And wouldn't he, perhaps? . . . But he shook his head, lighted a cigarette, slowly breathed a great deep puff into her face, and even while she was still talking and laughing, flicked the match away and walked on. The ermine toque was alone; she smiled more brightly than ever.

But even the band seemed to know what she was feeling and played more softly, played tenderly, and the drum beat, "The Brute! The Brute!" over and over. What would she do? What was going to happen now? But as Miss Brill wondered, the ermine toque turned, raised her hand as though she'd seen some one else, much nicer, just over there, and pattered away. And the band changed again and played more quickly, more gayly than ever, and the old couple on Miss Brill's seat got up and marched away, and such a funny old man with long whiskers hobbled along in time to the music and was nearly knocked over by four girls walking abreast.

Oh, how fascinating it was! How she enjoyed it! How she loved sitting here, watching it all! It was like a play. It was exactly like a play. Who could believe the sky at the back wasn't painted? But it wasn't till a little brown dog trotted on solemn and then slowly trotted off, like a little 'theatre' dog, a little dog that had been drugged, that Miss Brill discovered what it was that made it so exciting. They were all on the stage. They weren't only the audience, not only looking on; they were acting. Even she had a part and came every Sunday. No doubt somebody would have noticed if she hadn't been there; she was part of the performance after all. How strange she'd never thought of it like that before! And yet it explained why she made such a point of starting from home at just the same time each week—so as not to be late for the performance—and it also explained why she had quite a queer, shy feeling at telling her English pupils how she spent her Sunday afternoons. No wonder! Miss Brill nearly laughed out loud. She was on the stage. She thought of the old invalid gentleman to whom she read the newspaper four afternoons a week while he slept in the garden. She had got quite used to the frail head on the cotton pillow, the hollowed eyes, the open mouth and the high pinched nose. If he'd been dead she mightn't have noticed for weeks; she wouldn't have minded. But suddenly he knew he was having the paper read to him by an actress! "An actress!" The old head lifted; two points of light quivered in the old eyes. "An actress—are ye?" And Miss Brill smoothed the newspaper as though it were the manuscript of her part and said gently; "Yes, I have been an actress for a long time."

The band had been having a rest. Now they started again. And what they played was warm, sunny, yet there was just a faint chill—a something, what was it?—not sadness—no, not sadness—a something that made you want to sing. The tune lifted, lifted, the light shone; and it seemed to Miss Brill that in another moment all of them, all the whole company, would begin singing. The young ones, the laughing ones who were moving together, they would begin, and the men's voices, very resolute and brave, would join them. And then she too, she too, and the others on the benches—they would come in with a kind of accompaniment—something low, that scarcely rose or fell, something so beautiful—moving . . . And Miss Brill's eyes filled with tears and she looked smiling at all the other members of the company. Yes, we understand, we understand, she thought—though what they understood she didn't know.

Just at that moment a boy and girl came and sat down where the old couple had been. They were beautifully dressed; they were in love. The hero and heroine, of course, just arrived from his father's yacht. And still soundlessly singing, still with that trembling smile, Miss Brill prepared to listen.

"No, not now," said the girl. "Not here, I can't."

"But why? Because of that stupid old thing at the end there?" asked the boy. "Why does she come here at all—who wants her? Why doesn't she keep her silly old mug at home?"

"It's her fu-fur which is so funny," giggled the girl. "It's exactly like a fried whiting."

"Ah, be off with you!" said the boy in an angry whisper. Then: "Tell me, ma petite chère—"

"No, not here," said the girl. "Not *yet*."

On her way home she usually bought a slice of honey-cake at the baker's. It was her Sunday treat. Sometimes there was an almond in her slice, sometimes not. It made a great difference. If there was an almond it was like carrying home a tiny present—a surprise—something that might very well not have been there. She hurried on the almond Sundays and struck the match for the kettle in quite a dashing way.

But to-day she passed the baker's by, climbed the stairs, went into the little dark room—her room like a cupboard—and sat down on the red eiderdown. She sat there for a long time. The box that the fur came out of was on the bed. She unclasped the necklet quickly; quickly, without looking, laid it inside. But when she put the lid on she thought she heard something crying.

Lafcadio Hearn

(1850-1904)

60

Yuki-Onna

In a village of Musashi Province, there lived two woodcutters: Mosaku and Minokichi. At the time of which I am speaking, Mosaku was an old man; and Minokichi, his apprentice, was a lad of eighteen years. Every day they went together to a forest situated about five miles from their village. On the way to that forest there is a wide river to cross; and there is a ferry-boat. Several times a bridge was built where the ferry is; but the bridge was each time carried away by a flood. No common bridge can resist the current there when the river rises.

Mosaku and Minokichi were on their way home, one very cold evening, when a great snowstorm overtook them. They reached the ferry; and they found that the boatman had gone away, leaving his boat on the other side of the river. It was no day for swimming; and the woodcutters took shelter in the ferryman's hut, —thinking themselves lucky to find any shelter at all. There was no brazier in the hut, nor any place in which to make a fire: it was only a two-mat hut, with a single door, but no window. Mosaku and Minokichi fastened the door, and lay down to rest, with their straw rain-coats over them. At first they did not feel very cold; and they thought that the storm would soon be over.

The old man almost immediately fell asleep; but the boy, Minokichi, lay awake a long time, listening to the awful wind, and the continual slashing of the snow against the door. The river was roaring; and the hut swayed and creaked like a junk at sea. It was a terrible storm; and the air was every moment becoming colder; and Minokichi shivered under his rain-coat. But at last, in spite of the cold, he too fell asleep.

He was awakened by a showering of snow in his face. The door of the hut had been forced open; and, by the snow-light (yuki-akari), he saw a woman in the room, —a woman all in white. She was bending above Mosaku, and blowing her breath upon him; — and her breath was like a bright white smoke. Almost in the same moment she turned to Minokichi, and stooped over him. He tried to cry out, but found that he could not utter any sound. The white woman bent down over him, lower and lower, until her face almost touched him; and he saw that she was very beautiful, —though her eyes made him afraid. For a little time she continued to look at him; —then she smiled, and she whispered:—"I intended to treat you like the other man. But I cannot help feeling some pity for you, — because you are so young . . . You are a pretty boy, Minokichi; and I will not hurt you now. But, if you ever tell anybody—even your own mother—about what you have seen this night, I shall know it; and then I will kill you . . . Remember what I say!"

With these words, she turned from him, and passed through the doorway. Then he found himself able to move; and he sprang up, and looked out. But the woman was nowhere to be seen; and the snow was driving furiously into the hut. Minokichi closed the door, and secured it by fixing several billets of wood against it. He wondered if the wind had blown it open; —he thought that he might have been only dreaming, and might have mistaken the gleam of the snow-light in the doorway for the figure of a white woman: but he could not be sure. He called to Mosaku, and was frightened because the old man did not answer. He put out his hand in the dark, and touched Mosaku's face, and found that it was ice! Mosaku was stark and dead . . .

By dawn the storm was over; and when the ferryman returned to his station, a little after sunrise, he found Minokichi lying senseless beside the frozen body of Mosaku. Minokichi was promptly cared for, and soon came to himself; but he remained a long time ill from the effects of the cold of that terrible night. He had been greatly frightened also by the old man's death; but he said nothing about the vision of the woman in white. As soon as he got well again, he returned to his calling, —going alone every morning to the forest, and coming back at nightfall with his bundles of wood, which his mother helped him to sell.

One evening, in the winter of the following year, as he was on his way home, he overtook a girl who happened to be traveling by the same road. She was a tall, slim girl, very good-looking; and she answered Minokichi's greeting in a voice as pleasant to the ear as the voice of a song-bird. Then he walked beside her; and they began to talk. The girl said that her name was O-Yuki; that she had lately lost both of her parents; and that she was going to Yedo, where she happened to have some poor relations, who might help her to find a situation as a servant. Minokichi soon felt charmed by this strange girl; and the more that he looked at her, the handsomer she appeared to be. He asked her whether she was yet betrothed; and she answered, laughingly, that she was free. Then, in her turn, she asked Minokichi whether he was married, or pledged to marry; and he told her that, although he had only a widowed mother to support, the question of an 'honorable daughter-in-law' had not yet been considered, as he was very young . . . After these confidences, they walked on for a long while without speaking; but, as the proverb declares, Ki ga areba, me mo kuchi hodo ni mono wo iu: "When the wish is there, the eyes can say as much as the mouth." By the time they reached the village, they had become very much pleased with each other; and then Minokichi asked O-Yuki to rest awhile at his house. After some shy hesitation, she went there with him; and his mother made her welcome, and prepared a warm meal for her. O-Yuki behaved so nicely that Minokichi's mother took a sudden fancy to her, and persuaded her to delay her journey to Yedo. And the natural end of the matter was that Yuki never went to Yedo at all. She remained in the house, as an 'honorable daughter-in-law'.

O-Yuki proved a very good daughter-in-law. When Minokichi's mother came to die, —some five years later, —her last words were words of affection and praise for the wife of her son. And O-Yuki bore Minokichi ten children, boys and girls, —handsome children all of them, and very fair of skin.

The country-folk thought O-Yuki a wonderful person, by nature different from themselves. Most of the peasant-women age early; but O-Yuki, even after having become the mother of ten children, looked as young and fresh as on the day when she had first come to the village.

One night, after the children had gone to sleep, O-Yuki was sewing by the light of a paper lamp; and Minokichi, watching her, said:—

"To see you sewing there, with the light on your face, makes me think of a strange thing that happened when I was a lad of eighteen. I then saw somebody as beautiful and white as you are now—indeed, she was very like you."

Without lifting her eyes from her work, O-Yuki responded:—

"Tell me about her . . . Where did you see her?"

Then Minokichi told her about the terrible night in the ferryman's hut, —and about the White Woman that had stooped above him, smiling and whispering, —and about the silent death of old Mosaku. And he said:—

"Asleep or awake, that was the only time that I saw a being as beautiful as you. Of course, she was not a human being; and I was afraid of her, —very much afraid, —but she was so white! Indeed, I have never been sure whether it was a dream that I saw, or the Woman of the Snow."

O-Yuki flung down her sewing, and arose, and bowed above Minokichi where he sat, and shrieked into his face:—

"It was I—I—I! Yuki it was! And I told you then that I would kill you if you ever said one word about it!... But for those children asleep there, I would kill you this moment! And now you had better take very, very good care of them; for if ever they have reason to complain of you, I will treat you as you deserve!"

Even as she screamed, her voice became thin, like a crying of wind; —then she melted into a bright white mist that spired to the roof-beams, and shuddered away through the smoke-hold . . . Never again was she seen.

L Frank Baum

(1856-1919)

61

The Box of Robbers

No one intended to leave Martha alone that afternoon, but it happened that everyone was called away, for one reason or another. Mrs. McFarland was attending the weekly card party held by the Women's Anti-Gambling League. Sister Nell's young man had called quite unexpectedly to take her for a long drive. Papa was at the office, as usual. It was Mary Ann's day out. As for Emeline, she certainly should have stayed in the house and looked after the little girl; but Emeline had a restless nature.

"Would you mind, miss, if I just crossed the alley to speak a word to Mrs. Carleton's girl?" she asked Martha.

"Course not," replied the child. "You'd better lock the back door, though, and take the key, for I shall be upstairs."

"Oh, I'll do that, of course, miss," said the delighted maid, and ran away to spend the afternoon with her friend, leaving Martha quite alone in the big house, and locked in, into the bargain.

The little girl read a few pages in her new book, sewed a few stitches in her embroidery and started to "play visiting" with her four favorite dolls. Then she remembered that in the attic was a doll's playhouse that hadn't been used for months, so she decided she would dust it and put it in order.

Filled with this idea, the girl climbed the winding stairs to the big room under the roof. It was well lighted by three dormer windows and was warm and pleasant. Around the walls were rows of boxes and trunks, piles of old carpeting, pieces of damaged furniture, bundles of discarded clothing and other odds and ends of more or less value. Every well-regulated house has an attic of this sort, so I need not describe it.

The doll's house had been moved, but after a search Martha found it away over in a corner near the big chimney.

She drew it out and noticed that behind it was a black wooden chest which Uncle Walter had sent over from Italy years and years ago—before Martha was born, in fact. Mamma had told her about it one day; how there was no key to it, because Uncle Walter wished it to remain unopened until he returned home; and how this wandering uncle, who was a mighty hunter, had gone into Africa to hunt elephants and had never been heard from afterwards.

The little girl looked at the chest curiously, now that it had by accident attracted her attention.

It was quite big—bigger even than mamma's traveling trunk—and was studded all over with tarnished brassheaded nails. It was heavy, too, for when Martha tried to lift one end of it she found she could not stir it a bit. But there was a place in the side of the cover for a key. She stooped to examine the lock, and saw that it would take a rather big key to open it.

Then, as you may suspect, the little girl longed to open Uncle Walter's big box and see what was in it. For we are all curious, and little girls are just as curious as the rest of us.

"I don't b'lieve Uncle Walter'll ever come back," she thought. "Papa said once that some elephant must have killed him. If I only had a key—" She stopped and clapped her little hands together gayly as she remembered a big basket of keys on the shelf in the linen closet. They were of all sorts and sizes; perhaps one of them would unlock the mysterious chest!

She flew down the stairs, found the basket and returned with it to the attic. Then she sat down before the brass-studded box and began trying one key after another in the curious old lock.

Some were too large, but most were too small. One would go into the lock but would not turn; another stuck so fast that she feared for a time that she would never get it out again. But at last, when the basket was almost empty, an oddly-shaped, ancient brass key slipped easily into the lock. With a cry of joy Martha turned the key with both hands; then she heard a sharp 'click', and the next moment the heavy lid flew up of its own accord!

The little girl leaned over the edge of the chest an instant, and the sight that met her eyes caused her to start back in amazement.

Slowly and carefully a man unpacked himself from the chest, stepped out upon the floor, stretched his limbs and then took off his hat and bowed politely to the astonished child.

He was tall and thin and his face seemed badly tanned or sunburnt.

Then another man emerged from the chest, yawning and rubbing his eyes like a sleepy schoolboy. He was of middle size and his skin seemed as badly tanned as that of the first.

While Martha stared open-mouthed at the remarkable sight a third man crawled from the chest. He had the same complexion as his fellows, but was short and fat.

All three were dressed in a curious manner. They wore short jackets of red velvet braided with gold, and knee breeches of sky-blue satin with silver buttons. Over their stockings were laced wide ribbons of red and yellow and blue, while their hats had broad brims with high, peaked crowns, from which fluttered yards of bright-colored ribbons.

They had big gold rings in their ears and rows of knives and pistols in their belts. Their eyes were black and glittering and they wore long, fierce mustaches, curling at the ends like a pig's tail.

"My! but you were heavy," exclaimed the fat one, when he had pulled down his velvet jacket and brushed the dust from his sky-blue breeches. "And you squeezed me all out of shape."

"It was unavoidable, Luigi," responded the thin man, lightly; "the lid of the chest pressed me down upon you. Yet I tender you my regrets."

"As for me," said the middle-sized man, carelessly rolling a cigarette and lighting it, "you must acknowledge I have been your nearest friend for years; so do not be disagreeable."

"You mustn't smoke in the attic," said Martha, recovering herself at sight of the cigarette. "You might set the house on fire."

The middle-sized man, who had not noticed her before, at this speech turned to the girl and bowed.

"Since a lady requests it," said he, "I shall abandon my cigarette," and he threw it on the floor and extinguished it with his foot.

"Who are you?" asked Martha, who until now had been too astonished to be frightened.

"Permit us to introduce ourselves," said the thin man, flourishing his hat gracefully. "This is Lugui," the fat man nodded; "and this is Beni," the middle-sized man bowed; "and I am Victor. We are three bandits—Italian bandits."

"Bandits!" cried Martha, with a look of horror.

"Exactly. Perhaps in all the world there are not three other bandits so terrible and fierce as ourselves," said Victor, proudly.

"'Tis so," said the fat man, nodding gravely.

"But it's wicked!" exclaimed Martha.

"Yes, indeed," replied Victor. "We are extremely and tremendously wicked. Perhaps in all the world you could not find three men more wicked than those who now stand before you."

"'Tis so," said the fat man, approvingly.

"But you shouldn't be so wicked," said the girl; "it's—it's—naughty!"

Victor cast down his eyes and blushed.

"Naughty!" gasped Beni, with a horrified look.

"'Tis a hard word," said Luigi, sadly, and buried his face in his hands.

"I little thought," murmured Victor, in a voice broken by emotion, "ever to be so reviled—and by a lady! Yet, perhaps you spoke thoughtlessly. You must consider, miss, that our wickedness has an excuse. For how are we to be bandits, let me ask, unless we are wicked?"

Martha was puzzled and shook her head, thoughtfully. Then she remembered something.

"You can't remain bandits any longer," said she, "because you are now in America."

"America!" cried the three, together.

"Certainly. You are on Prairie avenue, in Chicago. Uncle Walter sent you here from Italy in this chest."

The bandits seemed greatly bewildered by this announcement. Lugui sat down on an old chair with a broken rocker and wiped his forehead with a yellow silk handkerchief. Beni and Victor fell back upon the chest and looked at her with pale faces and staring eyes.

When he had somewhat recovered himself Victor spoke.

"Your Uncle Walter has greatly wronged us," he said, reproachfully. "He has taken us from our beloved Italy, where bandits are highly respected, and brought us to a strange country where we shall not know whom to rob or how much to ask for a ransom."

"'Tis so!" said the fat man, slapping his leg sharply.

"And we had won such fine reputations in Italy!" said Beni, regretfully.

"Perhaps Uncle Walter wanted to reform you," suggested Martha.

"Are there, then, no bandits in Chicago?" asked Victor.

"Well," replied the girl, blushing in her turn, "we do not call them bandits."

"Then what shall we do for a living?" inquired Beni, despairingly.

"A great deal can be done in a big American city," said the child. "My father is a lawyer" (the bandits shuddered), "and my mother's cousin is a police inspector."

"Ah," said Victor, "that is a good employment. The police need to be inspected, especially in Italy."

"Everywhere!" added Beni.

"Then you could do other things," continued Martha, encouragingly. "You could be motor men on trolley cars, or clerks in a department store. Some people even become aldermen to earn a living."

The bandits shook their heads sadly.

"We are not fitted for such work," said Victor. "Our business is to rob."

Martha tried to think.

"It is rather hard to get positions in the gas office," she said, "but you might become politicians."

"No!" cried Beni, with sudden fierceness; "we must not abandon our high calling. Bandits we have always been, and bandits we must remain!"

"'Tis so!" agreed the fat man.

"Even in Chicago there must be people to rob," remarked Victor, with cheerfulness.

Martha was distressed.

"I think they have all been robbed," she objected.

"Then we can rob the robbers, for we have experience and talent beyond the ordinary," said Beni.

"Oh, dear; oh, dear!" moaned the girl; "why did Uncle Walter ever send you here in this chest?"

The bandits became interested.

"That is what we should like to know," declared Victor, eagerly.

"But no one will ever know, for Uncle Walter was lost while hunting elephants in Africa," she continued, with conviction.

"Then we must accept our fate and rob to the best of our ability," said Victor. "So long as we are faithful to our beloved profession we need not be ashamed."

"'Tis so!" cried the fat man.

"Brothers! we will begin now. Let us rob the house we are in."

"Good!" shouted the others and sprang to their feet.

Beni turned threateningly upon the child.

"Remain here!" he commanded. "If you stir one step your blood will be on your own head!" Then he added, in a gentler voice: "Don't be afraid; that's the way all bandits talk to their captives. But of course we wouldn't hurt a young lady under any circumstances."

"Of course not," said Victor.

The fat man drew a big knife from his belt and flourished it about his head.

"S'blood!" he ejaculated, fiercely.

"S'bananas!" cried Beni, in a terrible voice.

"Confusion to our foes!" hissed Victor.

And then the three bent themselves nearly double and crept stealthily down the stairway with cocked pistols in their hands and glittering knives between their teeth, leaving Martha trembling with fear and too horrified to even cry for help.

How long she remained alone in the attic she never knew, but finally she heard the catlike tread of the returning bandits and saw them coming up the stairs in single file.

All bore heavy loads of plunder in their arms, and Lugui was balancing a mince pie on the top of a pile of her mother's best evening dresses. Victor came next with an armful of bric-a-brac, a brass candelabra and the parlor clock. Beni had the family Bible, the basket of silverware from the sideboard, a copper kettle and papa's fur overcoat.

"Oh, joy!" said Victor, putting down his load; "it is pleasant to rob once more."

"Oh, ecstacy!" said Beni; but he let the kettle drop on his toe and immediately began dancing around in anguish, while he muttered queer words in the Italian language.

"We have much wealth," continued Victor, holding the mince pie while Lugui added his spoils to the heap; "and all from one house! This America must be a rich place."

With a dagger he then cut himself a piece of the pie and handed the remainder to his comrades. Whereupon all three sat upon the floor and consumed the pie while Martha looked on sadly.

"We should have a cave," remarked Beni; "for we must store our plunder in a safe place. Can you tell us of a secret cave?" he asked Martha.

"There's a Mammoth cave," she answered, "but it's in Kentucky. You would be obliged to ride on the cars a long time to get there."

The three bandits looked thoughtful and munched their pie silently, but the next moment they were startled by the ringing of the electric doorbell, which was heard plainly even in the remote attic.

"What's that?" demanded Victor, in a hoarse voice, as the three scrambled to their feet with drawn daggers.

Martha ran to the window and saw it was only the postman, who had dropped a letter in the box and gone away again. But the incident gave her an idea of how to get rid of her troublesome bandits, so she began wringing her hands as if in great distress and cried out:

"It's the police!"

The robbers looked at one another with genuine alarm, and Lugui asked, tremblingly:

"Are there many of them?"

"A hundred and twelve!" exclaimed Martha, after pretending to count them.

"Then we are lost!" declared Beni; "for we could never fight so many and live."

"Are they armed?" inquired Victor, who was shivering as if cold.

"Oh, yes," said she. "They have guns and swords and pistols and axes and—and—"

"And what?" demanded Lugui.

"And cannons!"

The three wicked ones groaned aloud and Beni said, in a hollow voice:

"I hope they will kill us quickly and not put us to the torture. I have been told these Americans are painted Indians, who are bloodthirsty and terrible."

"'Tis so!" gasped the fat man, with a shudder.

Suddenly Martha turned from the window.

"You are my friends, are you not?" she asked.

"We are devoted!" answered Victor.

"We adore you!" cried Beni.

"We would die for you!" added Lugui, thinking he was about to die anyway.

"Then I will save you," said the girl.

"How?" asked the three, with one voice.

"Get back into the chest," she said. "I will then close the lid, so they will be unable to find you."

They looked around the room in a dazed and irresolute way, but she exclaimed:

"You must be quick! They will soon be here to arrest you."

Then Lugui sprang into the chest and lay fat upon the bottom. Beni tumbled in next and packed himself in the back side. Victor followed after pausing to kiss her hand to the girl in a graceful manner.

Then Martha ran up to press down the lid, but could not make it catch.

"You must squeeze down," she said to them.

Lugui groaned.

"I am doing my best, miss," said Victor, who was nearest the top; "but although we fitted in very nicely before, the chest now seems rather small for us."

"'Tis so!" came the muffled voice of the fat man from the bottom.

"I know what takes up the room," said Beni.

"What?" inquired Victor, anxiously.

"The pie," returned Beni.

"'Tis so!" came from the bottom, in faint accents.

Then Martha sat upon the lid and pressed it down with all her weight. To her great delight the lock caught, and, springing down, she exerted all her strength and turned the key.

62

The Enchanted Types

One time a knook became tired of his beautiful life and longed for something new to do. The knooks have more wonderful powers than any other immortal folk—except, perhaps, the fairies and ryls. So one would suppose that a knook who might gain anything he desired by a simple wish could not be otherwise than happy and contented. But such was not the case with Popopo, the knook we are speaking of. He had lived thousands of years, and had enjoyed all the wonders he could think of. Yet life had become as tedious to him now as it might be to one who was unable to gratify a single wish.

Finally, by chance, Popopo thought of the earth people who dwell in cities, and so he resolved to visit them and see how they lived. This would surely be fine amusement, and serve to pass away many wearisome hours.

Therefore one morning, after a breakfast so dainty that you could scarcely imagine it, Popopo set out for the earth and at once was in the midst of a big city.

His own dwelling was so quiet and peaceful that the roaring noise of the town startled him. His nerves were so shocked that before he had looked around three minutes he decided to give up the adventure, and instantly returned home.

This satisfied for a time his desire to visit the earth cities, but soon the monotony of his existence again made him restless and gave him another thought. At night the people slept and the cities would be quiet. He would visit them at night.

So at the proper time Popopo transported himself in a jiffy to a great city, where he began wandering about the streets. Everyone was in bed. No wagons rattled along the pavements; no throngs of busy men shouted and halloaed. Even the policemen slumbered slyly and there happened to be no prowling thieves abroad.

His nerves being soothed by the stillness, Popopo began to enjoy himself. He entered many of the houses and examined their rooms with much curiosity. Locks and bolts made no difference to a knook, and he saw as well in darkness as in daylight.

After a time he strolled into the business portion of the city. Stores are unknown among the immortals, who have no need of money or of barter and exchange; so Popopo was greatly interested by the novel sight of so many collections of goods and merchandise.

During his wanderings he entered a millinery shop, and was surprised to see within a large glass case a great number of women's hats, each bearing in one position or another a stuffed bird. Indeed, some of the most elaborate hats had two or three birds upon them.

Now knooks are the especial guardians of birds, and love them dearly. To see so many of his little friends shut up in a glass case annoyed and grieved Popopo, who had no idea they had purposely been placed upon the hats by the milliner. So he slid back one of the doors of the case, gave the little chirruping whistle of the knooks that all birds know well, and called:

"Come, friends; the door is open—fly out!"

Popopo did not know the birds were stuffed; but, stuffed or not, every bird is bound to obey a knook's whistle and a knook's call. So they left the hats, flew out of the case and began fluttering about the room.

"Poor dears!" said the kind-hearted knook, "you long to be in the fields and forests again."

Then he opened the outer door for them and cried: "Off with you! Fly away, my beauties, and be happy again."

The astonished birds at once obeyed, and when they had soared away into the night air the knook closed the door and continued his wandering through the streets.

By dawn he saw many interesting sights, but day broke before he had finished the city, and he resolved to come the next evening a few hours earlier.

As soon as it was dark the following day he came again to the city and on passing the millinery shop noticed a light within. Entering he found two women, one of whom leaned her head upon the table and sobbed bitterly, while the other strove to comfort her.

Of course Popopo was invisible to mortal eyes, so he stood by and listened to their conversation.

"Cheer up, sister," said one. "Even though your pretty birds have all been stolen the hats themselves remain."

"Alas!" cried the other, who was the milliner, "no one will buy my hats partly trimmed, for the fashion is to wear birds upon them. And if I cannot sell my goods I shall be utterly ruined."

Then she renewed her sobbing and the knook stole away, feeling a little ashamed to realized that in his love for the birds he had unconsciously wronged one of the earth people and made her unhappy.

This thought brought him back to the millinery shop later in the night, when the two women had gone home. He wanted, in some way, to replace the birds upon the hats, that the poor woman might be happy again. So he searched until he came upon a nearby cellar full of little gray mice, who lived quite undisturbed and gained a livelihood by gnawing through the walls into neighboring houses and stealing food from the pantries.

"Here are just the creatures," thought Popopo, "to place upon the woman's hats. Their fur is almost as soft as the plumage of the birds, and it strikes me the mice are remarkably pretty and graceful animals. Moreover, they now pass their lives in stealing, and were they obliged to remain always upon women's hats their morals would be much improved."

So he exercised a charm that drew all the mice from the cellar and placed them upon the hats in the glass case, where they occupied the places the birds had vacated and looked very becoming—at least, in the eyes of the unworldly knook. To prevent their running about and leaving the hats Popopo rendered them motionless, and then he was so pleased with his work that he decided to remain in the shop and witness the delight of the milliner when she saw how daintily her hats were now trimmed.

She came in the early morning, accompanied by her sister, and her face wore a sad and resigned expression. After sweeping and dusting the shop and drawing the blinds she opened the glass case and took out a hat.

But when she saw a tiny gray mouse nestling among the ribbons and laces she gave a loud shriek, and, dropping the hat, sprang with one bound to the top of the table. The sister, knowing the shriek to be one of fear, leaped upon a chair and exclaimed:

"What is it? Oh! what is it?"

"A mouse!" gasped the milliner, trembling with terror.

Popopo, seeing this commotion, now realized that mice are especially disagreeable to human beings, and that he had made a grave mistake in placing them upon the hats; so he gave a low whistle of command that was heard only by the mice.

Instantly they all jumped from the hats, dashed out the open door of the glass case and scampered away to their cellar. But this action so frightened the milliner and her sister that after giving several loud screams they fell upon their backs on the floor and fainted away.

Popopo was a kind-hearted knook, but on witnessing all this misery, caused by his own ignorance of the ways of humans, he straightway wished himself at home, and so left the poor women to recover as best they could.

Yet he could not escape a sad feeling of responsibility, and after thinking upon the matter he decided that since he had caused the milliner's unhappiness by freeing the birds, he could set the matter right by restoring them to the glass case. He loved the birds, and disliked to condemn them to slavery again; but that seemed the only way to end the trouble.

So he set off to find the birds. They had flown a long distance, but it was nothing to Popopo to reach them in a second, and he discovered them sitting upon the branches of a big chestnut tree and singing gayly.

When they saw the knook the birds cried:

"Thank you, Popopo. Thank you for setting us free."

"Do not thank me," returned the knook, "for I have come to send you back to the millinery shop."

"Why?" demanded a blue jay, angrily, while the others stopped their songs.

"Because I find the woman considers you her property, and your loss has caused her much unhappiness," answered Popopo.

"But remember how unhappy we were in her glass case," said a robin redbreast, gravely. "And as for being her property, you are a knook, and the natural guardian of all birds; so you know that Nature created us free. To be sure, wicked men shot and stuffed us, and sold us to the milliner; but the idea of our being her property is nonsense!"

Popopo was puzzled.

"If I leave you free," he said, "wicked men will shoot you again, and you will be no better off than before."

"Pooh!" exclaimed the blue jay, "we cannot be shot now, for we are stuffed. Indeed, two men fired several shots at us this morning, but the bullets only ruffled our feathers and buried themselves in our stuffing. We do not fear men now."

"Listen!" said Popopo, sternly, for he felt the birds were getting the best of the argument; "the poor milliner's business will be ruined if I do not return you to her shop. It seems you are necessary to trim the hats properly. It is the fashion for women to wear birds upon their headgear. So the poor milliner's wares, although beautified by lace and ribbons, are worthless unless you are perched upon them."

"Fashions," said a black bird, solemnly, "are made by men. What law is there, among birds or knooks, that requires us to be the slaves of fashion?"

"What have we to do with fashions, anyway?" screamed a linnet.

"If it were the fashion to wear knooks perched upon women's hats would you be contented to stay there? Answer me, Popopo!"

But Popopo was in despair. He could not wrong the birds by sending them back to the milliner, nor did he wish the milliner to suffer by their loss. So he went home to think what could be done.

After much meditation he decided to consult the king of the knooks, and going at once to his majesty he told him the whole story.

The king frowned.

"This should teach you the folly of interfering with earth people," he said. "But since you have caused all this trouble, it is your duty to remedy it. Our birds cannot be enslaved, that is certain; therefore you must have the fashions changed, so it will no longer be stylish for women to wear birds upon their hats."

"How shall I do that?" asked Popopo.

"Easily enough. Fashions often change among the earth people, who tire quickly of any one thing. When they read in their newspapers and magazines that the style is so-and-so, they never question the matter, but at once obey the mandate of fashion. So you must visit the newspapers and magazines and enchant the types."

"Enchant the types!" echoed Popopo, in wonder.

"Just so. Make them read that it is no longer the fashion to wear birds upon hats. That will afford relief to your poor milliner and at the same time set free thousands of our darling birds who have been so cruelly used."

Popopo thanked the wise king and followed his advice.

The office of every newspaper and magazine in the city was visited by the knook, and then he went to other cities, until there was not a publication in the land that had not a "new fashion note" in its pages. Sometimes Popopo enchanted the types, so that whoever read the print would see only what the knook wished them to. Sometimes he called upon the busy editors and befuddled their brains until they wrote exactly what he wanted them to. Mortals seldom know how greatly they are influenced by fairies, knooks and ryls, who often put thoughts into their heads that only the wise little immortals could have conceived.

The following morning when the poor milliner looked over her newspaper she was overjoyed to read that "no woman could now wear a bird upon her hat and be in style, for the newest fashion required only ribbons and laces."

Popopo after this found much enjoyment in visiting every millinery shop he could find and giving new life to the stuffed birds which were carelessly tossed aside as useless. And they flew to the fields and forests with songs of thanks to the good knook who had rescued them.

Sometimes a hunter fires his gun at a bird and then wonders why he did not hit it. But, having read this story, you will understand that the bird must have been a stuffed one from some millinery shop, which cannot, of course, be killed by a gun.

Leo Tolstoy

(1828-1910)

63

Work, Death and Sickness

This is a legend current among the South American Indians.

God, say they, at first made men so that they had no need to work: they needed neither houses, nor clothes, nor food, and they all lived till they were a hundred, and did not know what illness was.

When, after some time, God looked to see how people were living, he saw that instead of being happy in their life, they had quarrelled with one another, and, each caring for himself, had brought matters to such a pass that far from enjoying life, they cursed it.

Then God said to himself: 'This comes of their living separately, each for himself.' And to change this state of things, God so arranged matters that it became impossible for people to live without working. To avoid suffering from cold and hunger, they were now obliged to build dwellings, and to dig the ground, and to grow and gather fruits and grain.

'Work will bring them together,' thought God. 'They cannot make their tools, prepare and transport their timber, build their houses, sow and gather their harvests, spin and weave, and make their clothes, each one alone by himself.'

'It will make them understand that the more heartily they work together, the more they will have and the better they will live; and this will unite them.'

Time passed on, and again God came to see how men were living, and whether they were now happy.

But he found them living worse than before. They worked together (that they could not help doing), but not all together, being broken up into little groups. And each group tried to snatch work from other groups, and they hindered one another, wasting time and strength in their struggles, so that things went ill with them all.

Having seen that this, too, was not well, God decided so as to arrange things that man should not know the time of his death, but might die at any moment; and he announced this to them.

'Knowing that each of them may die at any moment,' thought God, 'they will not, by grasping at gains that may last so short a time, spoil the hours of life allotted to them.'

But it turned out otherwise. When God returned to see how people were living, he saw that their life was as bad as ever.

Those who were strongest, availing themselves of the fact that men might die at any time, subdued those who were weaker, killing some and threatening others with death. And it came about that the strongest and their descendants did no work, and suffered from the weariness of idleness, while those who were weaker had to work beyond their strength, and suffered from lack of rest. Each set of men feared and hated the other. And the life of man became yet more unhappy.

Having seen all this, God, to mend matters, decided to make use of one last means; he sent all kinds of sickness among men. God thought that when all men were exposed to sickness they would understand that those who are well should have pity on those who are sick, and should help them, that when they themselves fall ill those who are well might in turn help them.

And again God went away, but when He came back to see how men lived now that they were subject to sicknesses, he saw that their life was worse even than before. The very sickness that in God's purpose should have united men, had divided them more than ever. Those men who were strong enough to make others work, forced them also to wait on them in times of sickness; but they did not, in their turn, look after others who were ill. And those who were forced to work for others and to look after them when sick, were so worn with work that they had no time to look after their own sick, but left them without attendance. That the sight of sick folk might not disturb the pleasures of the wealthy, houses were arranged in which these poor people suffered and died, far from those whose sympathy might have cheered them, and in the arms of hired people who nursed them without compassion, or even with disgust. Moreover, people considered many of the illnesses infectious, and, fearing to catch them, not only avoided the sick, but even separated themselves from those who attended the sick.

Then God said to Himself: 'If even this means will not bring men to understand wherein their happiness lies, let them be taught by suffering.' And God left men to themselves.

And, left to themselves, men lived long before they understood that they all ought to, and might be, happy. Only in the very latest times have a few of them begun to understand that work ought not to be a bugbear to some and like galley-slavery for others, but should be a common and happy occupation, uniting all men. They have begun to understand that with death constantly threatening each of us, the only reasonable business of every man is to spend the years, months, hours, and minutes, allotted him—in unity and love. They have begun to understand that sickness, far from dividing men, should, on the contrary, give opportunity for loving union with one another.

64

Elias

There dwelt once upon a time in the Ufimsk government a Bashkir named Elias. The father of Elias had left him a poor man. His father had only gotten him a wife a year before, and then died. In those days Elias owned seven mares, two cows, and twice ten sheep. But Elias was now the master, and began to spread himself out; from morn to eve he laboured with his wife, rose up earlier and lay down later than all other men, and grew richer every year. Five-and-thirty years did Elias continue to labour, and won for himself great possessions.

Elias now had two hundred head of horses, a hundred and fifty head of horned cattle, and one thousand two hundred sheep. Many men-servants pastured the *tabuns* and the herds of Elias, and many maid-servants milked the mares and the cows and made kumis, butter and cheese. Elias had much of everything, and everybody round about envied the life of Elias. People said: "Ah, what a lucky fellow that Elias is! He has everything in abundance, he has no need to die." And good people began to know Elias and make his acquaintance. And guests came to him from afar. And Elias welcomed them all, and gave them to eat and to drink. Whosoever came to him found abundance of kumis, and tea, and sherbet, and the flesh of rams. Whenever guests came a ram or

360

two was immediately killed, and if there were many guests they killed a mare.

Elias had three children—two sons and a daughter. Elias had provided his sons with wives, and had given his daughter in marriage. While Elias was poor his sons had worked with him and guarded the herds and the *tabuns* themselves, but when the sons became rich they began to amuse themselves, and one of them took to drink. One of them—the eldest—was presently killed in a brawl, and the younger son fell into the power of a stuck-up wife, and this son no longer listened to his father, and Elias had to give him his portion and get rid of him.

So Elias paid him out and gave him a house and cattle, and the riches of Elias were diminished. And shortly after this a disease fell upon the sheep of Elias, and many of them perished. And then came a year of scarceness—no hay would grow—and many cattle starved in the winter. Then the Kirghiz came and stole the best part of the horses, and the estate of Elias diminished still further. Elias began to fall lower and lower, and his natural forces were less. And when he had reached his seventieth year things came to such a pass that he began to sell his furs, his carpets, his *kibitki* and then he began to sell his cattle, down to the very last one; and so Elias came to nought. And he himself perceived that he had nothing left, and he was obliged in his old age to go with his wife to live among the common people. And the only things which Elias could now call his own were the clothes he had on his body, his fur cloak, his hat, and his shoes; and his wife, Shem Shemagi, was also an old woman. The son whom he had bought off departed into a distant land, and his daughter died. And there was none to help the old folks.

Their neighbour, Muhamedshah, pitied the old folks. He himself was neither rich nor poor, but lived at his ease, and he was a good man. He remembered that he had eaten bread and salt with Elias, and he was filled with compassion and said to Elias:

"Come to me, Elias, and live with me along with thine old woman. In the summer thou shalt work for me according to thy strength in the melon fields, and in the winter thou shalt feed my cattle and let Shem Shemagi milk the cows and make kumis. I will feed and clothe you both, and whatever ye may want tell it me and I will give it you."

Elias thanked his neighbour and dwelt with his wife in the house of Muhamedshah as one of his servants. At first it seemed grievous to them, but soon they grew accustomed to it, and the old people continued to live there and work according to their strength.

It was profitable to the master to have such people, for the old folks had themselves been masters and knew how things should be rightly ordered, and were not idle but worked according to their ability; the only thing which grieved Muhamedshah was to see people who had been so high fall to such a low estate.

And it chanced one day that distant relations came as guests, to Muhamedshah, and a Mullah came also. And Muhamedshah bade Elias take a ram and slay it Elias skinned the ram and cooked it, and set it before the guests. The guests ate the ram's flesh, drank as much tea as they wanted, and then fell a-drinking kumis. The guests sat with their host on down cushions on the floor and drank their kumis out of little cups, and conversed together, and Elias went about his work and passed by the door where they were sitting.

Muhamedshah saw him and said to one of his guests: "Didst thou see that old man who passed by my door?"

"I saw him," said the guest; "is there anything extraordinary about him?"

"There is this much extraordinary about him—that he was once upon a time our richest man—Elias they called him; perchance thou hast heard concerning him?"

"How could I help hearing of him?" replied the guest; "seen it all I have not, but the fame of him was spread far and wide."

"Well, now he hath nought, and he lives with me as a servant, and his old woman lives with him and milks my cows."

The guest was astonished. He clicked with his tongue, shook his head, and said: "Ah! 'tis plain how fortune goes flying round like a wheel. One she raises on high, another she thrusts down below. Tell me," said the guest, "is the heart of the old man sore within him, perchance?"

"Who can tell? He lives peaceably and quietly, and looks well.

"May one converse with him?" said the guest; "I should like to question him concerning his life."

"Certainly, it is possible," replied the host, and he shouted from behind the *kibitka*, "Babad," which signifies grandfather in the Bashkir language, "go and drink kumis and call hither the old man!"

And Elias came to them with his wife. Elias greeted the guests and the host, recited a prayer, and squatted down on his knees at the door, and his wife went behind the curtain and sat down with her mistress.

They gave Elias a cup full of kumis. Elias drank the healths of the guests and the host, did obeisance, drank a little more, and then placed the cup aside.

"Now, tell me, grandfather," said one of the guests, "I suppose it grieves thee looking at us, to call to mind thy former life, and to recollect how fortunate thou wert, and how now thou dwellest in misery?"

And Elias smiled and said: "If I were to speak to thee of good fortune and ill fortune thou wouldst not believe me—far better it would be if thou didst ask my old wife concerning this thing. She is a woman, and therefore what her heart feeleth that her tongue speaketh; she will tell thee the whole truth about this matter."

And the guest spake, turning towards the curtain: "Speak now, old woman! tell me, how judgest thou concerning thy former good fortune and thy present ill fortune?"

And Shem Shemagi answered from behind the curtain: "This is how I judge: I and my old man lived together for fifty years; we sought after happiness and we could not find it, and only now this is the second year in which we have wanted for nothing, and we live as working folks and have found real happiness, and we want nothing else."

The guests were astonished and the host was astonished; he even rose up and threw aside the curtain to behold the old woman. And there the old woman stood with folded arms, and she was smiling, and she looked at her old man, and he smiled also.

And the old woman also said: "I speak the truth, I jest not:

we sought happiness for half a hundred years, and while we were rich we did not find it at all; now that we have nothing left and live among working people we have found such happiness that we need nothing better."

"And in what, then, does your present happiness consist?"

"It consists in this: while we were rich I and my old man had not a single quiet hour together, we had no time to talk, no time to think of our souls, no time to pray to God. So many cares were we saddled with. At one time guests came to see us, and it was a worry what to set before each and with what presents to gratify them lest they should speak scornfully concerning us. Then there was the trouble of seeing to it that the wolves did not rend the lambs or kids or that thieves did not chase away the horses. Even when we lay down it was not to sleep, for we feared that the sheep might overlay the lambs in the night. You might get up and go about at night, and no sooner would your mind be at ease than a fresh worry would arise: how to find hay or pasturage in the winter time—and so it would go on. And all this was nothing to the disagreements between my old man and me. He would say: 'We ought to do this,' and then I would say: 'No! we ought to do that!' and so we began to curse each other, and that was sinful. Thus we lived, and went on from care to care, from sin to sin, and we found no happiness in life."

"Well, but now?"

"Now I and my old man rise up together, we converse lovingly and agree in all things, we have nought to quarrel about and nought to trouble us—our sole care is to serve our master. We labour according as we are able, we labour gladly, so that our master may have no loss and may prosper. We come to the house—there is dinner, there is supper, there is kumis. If it be cold there is the *kizyak* wherewith to warm ourselves, and there are furs. And there is time, when we wish it, to talk together, to think of our souls, and to pray to God. For fifty years we sought happiness, and only now have we found it."

The guests began to laugh.

But Elias said: "Laugh not, brethren! this is no jest, but human life. And at first my old woman and I were fools and wept because we had lost our wealth, but now God hath revealed the truth to us, and now we also reveal it to you, not for our amusement but for your good."

And the Mullah said: "These be wise sayings, and Elias hath spoken the real truth, and all this is written down in the Scriptures."

And the guests ceased to laugh, and they pondered these things in their hearts.

65

Three Questions

It once occurred to a certain king, that if he always knew the right time to begin everything; if he knew who were the right people to listen to, and whom to avoid; and, above all, if he always knew what was the most important thing to do, he would never fail in anything he might undertake.

And this thought having occurred to him, he had it proclaimed throughout his kingdom that he would give a great reward to any one who would teach him what was the right time for every action, and who were the most necessary people, and how he might know what was the most important thing to do.

And learned men came to the King, but they all answered his questions differently.

In reply to the first question, some said that to know the right time for every action, one must draw up in advance, a table of days, months and years, and must live strictly according to it. Only thus, said they, could everything be done at its proper time. Others declared that it was impossible to decide beforehand the right time for every action; but that, not letting oneself be absorbed in idle pastimes, one should always attend to all that was going on, and then do what was most needful. Others, again, said that however attentive the King might be to what was going on, it was impossible for one man to decide correctly the right time for every action, but that he should have a Council of wise men, who would help him to fix the proper time for everything.

But then again others said there were some things which could not wait to be laid before a Council, but about which one had at once to decide whether to undertake them or not. But in order to decide that, one must know beforehand what was going to happen. It is only magicians who know that; and, therefore, in order to know the right time for every action, one must consult magicians.

Equally various were the answers to the second question. Some said, the people the King most needed were his councillors; others, the priests; others, the doctors; while some said the warriors were the most necessary.

To the third question, as to what was the most important occupation: some replied that the most important thing in the world was science. Others said it was skill in warfare; and others, again, that it was religious worship.

All the answers being different, the King agreed with none of them, and gave the reward to none. But still wishing to find the right answers to his questions, he decided to consult a hermit, widely renowned for his wisdom.

The hermit lived in a wood which he never quitted, and he received none but common folk. So the King put on simple clothes, and before reaching the hermit's cell dismounted from his horse, and, leaving his body-guard behind, went on alone.

When the King approached, the hermit was digging the ground in front of his hut. Seeing the King, he greeted him and went on digging. The hermit was frail and weak, and each time he stuck his spade into the ground and turned a little earth, he breathed heavily.

The King went up to him and said: "I have come to you, wise hermit, to ask you to answer three questions: How can I learn to do the right thing at the right time? Who are the people I most need, and to whom should I, therefore, pay more attention than to the rest? And, what affairs are the most important, and need my first attention?"

The hermit listened to the King, but answered nothing. He just spat on his hand and recommenced digging.

"You are tired," said the King, "let me take the spade and work awhile for you."

"Thanks!" said the hermit, and, giving the spade to the King, he sat down on the ground.

When he had dug two beds, the King stopped and repeated his questions. The hermit again gave no answer, but rose, stretched out his hand for the spade, and said:

"Now rest awhile—and let me work a bit."

But the King did not give him the spade, and continued to dig. One hour passed, and another. The sun began to sink behind the trees, and the King at last stuck the spade into the ground, and said:

"I came to you, wise man, for an answer to my questions. If you can give me none, tell me so, and I will return home."

"Here comes some one running," said the hermit, "let us see who it is."

The King turned round, and saw a bearded man come running out of the wood. The man held his hands pressed against his stomach, and blood was flowing from under them. When he reached the King, he fell fainting on the ground moaning feebly. The King and the hermit unfastened the man's clothing. There was a large wound in his stomach. The King washed it as best he could, and bandaged it with his handkerchief and with a towel the hermit had. But the blood would not stop flowing, and the King again and again removed the bandage soaked with warm blood, and washed and rebandaged the wound. When at last the blood ceased flowing, the man revived and asked for something to drink. The King brought fresh water and gave it to him. Meanwhile the sun had set, and it had become cool. So the King, with the hermit's help, carried the wounded man into the hut and laid him on the bed. Lying on the bed the man closed his eyes and was quiet; but the King was so tired with his walk and with the work he had done, that he crouched down on the threshold, and also fell asleep—so soundly that he slept all through the short summer night. When he awoke in the morning, it was long before he could remember where he was, or who was the strange bearded man lying on the bed and gazing intently at him with shining eyes.

"Forgive me!" said the bearded man in a weak voice, when he saw that the King was awake and was looking at him.

"I do not know you, and have nothing to forgive you for," said the King.

"You do not know me, but I know you. I am that enemy of yours who swore to revenge himself on you, because you executed his brother and seized his property. I knew you had gone alone to see the hermit, and I resolved to kill you on your way back. But the day passed and you did not return. So I came out from my ambush to find you, and I came upon your bodyguard, and they recognized me, and wounded me. I escaped from them, but should have bled to death had you not dressed my wound. I wished to kill you, and you have saved my life. Now, if I live, and if you wish it, I will serve you as your most faithful slave, and will bid my sons do the same. Forgive me!"

The King was very glad to have made peace with his enemy so easily, and to have gained him for a friend, and he not only forgave him, but said he would send his servants and his own physician to attend him, and promised to restore his property.

Having taken leave of the wounded man, the King went out into the porch and looked around for the hermit. Before going away he wished once more to beg an answer to the questions he had put. The hermit was outside, on his knees, sowing seeds in the beds that had been dug the day before.

The King approached him, and said:

"For the last time, I pray you to answer my questions, wise man."

"You have already been answered!" said the hermit, still crouching on his thin legs, and looking up at the King, who stood before him.

"How answered? What do you mean?" asked the King.

"Do you not see," replied the hermit. "If you had not pitied my weakness yesterday, and had not dug those beds for me, but had gone your way, that man would have attacked you, and you would have repented of not having stayed with me. So the most important time was when you were digging the beds; and I was the most important man; and to do me good was your most important business. Afterwards when that man ran to us, the most important time was when you were attending to him, for if you had not bound up his wounds he would have died without having made peace with you. So he was the most important man, and what you did for him was your most important business. Remember then: there is only one time that is important—Now! It is the most important time because it is the only time when we have any power. The most necessary man is he with whom you are, for no man knows whether he will ever have dealings with any one else: and the most important affair is, to do him good, because for that purpose alone was man sent into this life!"

Louisa May Alcott

(1832-1888)

66

Cousin Tribulation's Story

Dear Merrys:—As a subject appropriate to the season, I want to tell you about a New Year's breakfast which I had when I was a little girl. What do you think it was? A slice of dry bread and an apple. This is how it happened, and it is a true story, every word.

As we came down to breakfast that morning, with very shiny faces and spandy clean aprons, we found father alone in the dining-room.

"Happy New Year, papa! Where is mother?" we cried.

"A little boy came begging and said they were starving at home, so your mother went to see and—ah, here she is."

As papa spoke, in came mamma, looking very cold, rather sad, and very much excited.

"Children, don't begin till you hear what I have to say," she cried; and we sat staring at her, with the breakfast untouched before us.

"Not far away from here, lies a poor woman with a little new-born baby. Six children are huddled into one bed to keep from freezing, for they have no fire. There is nothing to eat over there; and the oldest boy came here to tell me they were starving this bitter cold day. My little girls, will you give them your breakfast, as a New Year's gift?"

We sat silent a minute, and looked at the nice, hot porridge, creamy milk, and good bread and butter; for we were brought up like English children, and never drank tea or coffee, or ate anything but porridge for our breakfast.

"I wish we'd eaten it up," thought I, for I was rather a selfish child, and very hungry.

"I'm so glad you come before we began," said Nan, cheerfully.

"May I go and help carry it to the poor, little children?" asked Beth, who had the tenderest heart that ever beat under a pinafore.

"I can carry the lassy pot," said little May, proudly giving the thing she loved best.

"And I shall take all the porridge," I burst in, heartily ashamed of my first feeling.

"You shall put on your things and help me, and when we come back, we'll get something to eat," said mother, beginning to pile the bread and butter into a big basket.

We were soon ready, and the procession set out. First, papa, with a basket of wood on one arm and coal on the other; mamma next, with a bundle of warm things and the teapot; Nan and I carried a pail of hot porridge between us, and each a pitcher of milk; Beth brought some cold meat, May the "lassy pot," and her old hood and boots; and Betsey, the girl, brought up the rear with a bag of potatoes and some meal.

Fortunately it was early, and we went along back streets, so few people saw us, and no one laughed at the funny party.

What a poor, bare, miserable place it was, to be sure, —broken windows, no fire, ragged clothes, wailing baby, sick mother, and a pile of pale, hungry children cuddled under one quilt, trying to keep warm. How the big eyes stared and the blue lips smiled as we came in!

"Ah, mein Gott! it is the good angels that come to us!" cried the poor woman, with tears of joy.

"Funny angels, in woollen hoods and red mittens," said I; and they all laughed.

Then we fell to work, and in fifteen minutes, it really did seem as if fairies had been at work there. Papa made a splendid fire in the old fireplace and stopped up the broken window with his own hat and coat. Mamma set the shivering children round the fire, and wrapped the poor woman in warm things. Betsey and the rest of us spread the table, and fed the starving little ones.

"Das ist gute!" "Oh, nice!" "Der angel—Kinder!" cried the poor things as they ate and smiled and basked in the warm blaze. We had never been called "angel-children" before, and we thought it very charming, especially I who had often been told I was "a regular Sancho." What fun it was! Papa, with a towel for an apron, fed the smallest child; mamma dressed the poor little new-born baby as tenderly as if it had been her own. Betsey gave the mother gruel and tea, and comforted her with assurance of better days for all. Nan, Lu, Beth, and May flew about among the seven children, talking and laughing and trying to understand their funny, broken English. It was a very happy breakfast, though we didn't get any of it; and when we came away, leaving them all so comfortable, and promising to bring clothes and food by and by, I think there were not in all the hungry little girls who gave away their breakfast, and contented themselves with a bit of bread and an apple of New Year's day.

Mark Twain

(1835-1910)

67

Wit Inspirations of the Two-Year-Olds

All infants appear to have an impertinent and disagreeable fashion nowadays of saying 'smart' things on most occasions that offer, and especially on occasions when they ought not to be saying anything at all. Judging by the average published specimens of smart sayings, the rising generation of children are little better than idiots. And the parents must surely be but little better than the children, for in most cases they are the publishers of the sunbursts of infantile imbecility which dazzle us from the pages of our periodicals. I may seem to speak with some heat, not to say a suspicion of personal spite; and I do admit that it nettles me to hear about so many gifted infants in these days, and remember that I seldom said anything smart when I was a child. I tried it once or twice, but it was not popular. The family were not expecting brilliant remarks from me, and so they snubbed me sometimes and spanked me the rest. But it makes my flesh creep and my blood run cold to think what might have happened to me if I had dared to utter some of the smart things of this generation's 'four-year-olds' where my father could hear me. To have simply skinned me alive and considered his duty at an end would have seemed to him criminal leniency toward one so sinning. He was a stern, unsmiling man, and hated all forms of precocity. If I had said some of the things I have referred to, and said them in his hearing, he would have destroyed me. He would, indeed. He would, provided the opportunity remained with him. But it would not, for I would have had judgment enough to take some strychnine first and say my smart thing afterward. The fair record of my life has been tarnished by just one pun. My father overheard that, and he hunted me over four or five townships seeking to take my life. If I had been full-grown, of course he would have been right; but, child as I was, I could not know how wicked a thing I had done.

I made one of those remarks ordinarily called 'smart things' before that, but it was not a pun. Still, it came near causing a serious rupture between my father and myself. My father and mother, my uncle Ephraim and his wife, and one or two others were present, and the conversation turned on a name for me. I was lying there trying some India-rubber rings of various patterns, and endeavoring to make a selection, for I was tired of trying to cut my teeth on people's fingers, and wanted to get hold of something that would enable me to hurry the thing through and get something else. Did you ever notice what a nuisance it was cutting your teeth on your nurse's finger, or how back-breaking and tiresome it was trying to cut them on your big toe? And did you never get out of patience and wish your teeth were in Jerico long before you got them half cut? To me it seems as if these things happened yesterday. And they did, to some children. But I digress. I was lying there trying the India-rubber rings. I remember looking at the clock and noticing that in an hour and twenty-five minutes I would be two weeks old, and thinking how little I had done to merit the blessings that were so unsparingly lavished upon me. My father said:

"Abraham is a good name. My grandfather was named Abraham."

My mother said:

"Abraham is a good name. Very well. Let us have Abraham for one of his names."

I said:

"Abraham suits the subscriber."

My father frowned, my mother looked pleased; my aunt said:

"What a little darling it is!"

My father said:

"Isaac is a good name, and Jacob is a good name."

My mother assented, and said:

"No names are better. Let us add Isaac and Jacob to his names."

I said:

"All right. Isaac and Jacob are good enough for yours truly. Pass me that rattle, if you please. I can't chew India-rubber rings all day."

Not a soul made a memorandum of these sayings of mine, for publication. I saw that, and did it myself, else they would have been utterly lost. So far from meeting with a generous encouragement like other children when developing intellectually, I was now furiously scowled upon by my father; my mother looked grieved and anxious, and even my aunt had about her an expression of seeming to think that maybe I had gone too far. I took a vicious bite out of an India-rubber ring, and covertly broke the rattle over the kitten's head, but said nothing. Presently my father said:

"Samuel is a very excellent name."

I saw that trouble was coming. Nothing could prevent it. I laid down my rattle; over the side of the cradle I dropped my uncle's silver watch, the clothes-brush, the toy dog, my tin soldier, the nutmeg-grater, and other matters which I was accustomed to examine, and meditate upon and make pleasant noises with, and bang and batter and break when I needed wholesome entertainment. Then I put on my little frock and my little bonnet, and took my pygmy shoes in one hand and my licorice in the other, and climbed out on the floor. I said to myself, Now, if the worse comes to worst, I am ready. Then I said aloud, in a firm voice:

"Father, I cannot, cannot wear the name of Samuel."

"My son!"

"Father, I mean it. I cannot."

"Why?"

"Father, I have an invincible antipathy to that name."

"My son, this is unreasonable. Many great and good men have been named Samuel."

"Sir, I have yet to hear of the first instance."

"What! There was Samuel the prophet. Was not he great and good?"

"Not so very."

"My son! With His own voice the Lord called him."

"Yes, sir, and had to call him a couple times before he could come!"

And then I sallied forth, and that stern old man sallied forth after me. He overtook me at noon the following day, and when the interview was over I had acquired the name of Samuel, and a thrashing, and other useful information; and by means of this compromise my father's wrath was appeased and a misunderstanding bridged over which might have become a permanent rupture if I had chosen to be unreasonable. But just judging by this episode, what would my father have done to me if I had ever uttered in his hearing one of the flat, sickly things these 'two-years-olds' say in print nowadays? In my opinion there would have been a case of infanticide in our family.

68

The Five Boons of Life

CHAPTER I

In the morning of life came a good fairy with her basket, and said:

"Here are gifts. Take one, leave the others. And be wary, chose wisely; oh, choose wisely! for only one of them is valuable."

The gifts were five: Fame, Love, Riches, Pleasure, Death. The youth said, eagerly:

"There is no need to consider"; and he chose Pleasure.

He went out into the world and sought out the pleasures that youth delights in. But each in its turn was short-lived and disappointing, vain and empty; and each, departing, mocked him. In the end he said: "These years I have wasted. If I could but choose again, I would choose wisely."

CHAPTER II

The fairy appeared, and said:

"Four of the gifts remain. Choose once more; and oh, remember—time is flying, and only one of them is precious."

The man considered long, then chose Love; and did not mark the tears that rose in the fairy's eyes.

381

After many, many years the man sat by a coffin, in an empty home. And he communed with himself, saying: "One by one they have gone away and left me; and now she lies here, the dearest and the last. Desolation after desolation has swept over me; for each hour of happiness the treacherous trader, Love, as sold me I have paid a thousand hours of grief. Out of my heart of hearts I curse him."

CHAPTER III

"Choose again." It was the fairy speaking.

"The years have taught you wisdom—surely it must be so. Three gifts remain. Only one of them has any worth—remember it, and choose warily."

The man reflected long, then chose Fame; and the fairy, sighing, went her way.

Years went by and she came again, and stood behind the man where he sat solitary in the fading day, thinking. And she knew his thought:

"My name filled the world, and its praises were on every tongue, and it seemed well with me for a little while. How little a while it was! Then came envy; then detraction; then calumny; then hate; then persecution. Then derision, which is the beginning of the end. And last of all came pity, which is the funeral of fame. Oh, the bitterness and misery of renown! target for mud in its prime, for contempt and compassion in its decay."

CHAPTER IV

"Chose yet again." It was the fairy's voice.

"Two gifts remain. And do not despair. In the beginning there was but one that was precious, and it is still here."

"Wealth—which is power! How blind I was!" said the man. "Now, at last, life will be worth the living. I will spend, squander, dazzle. These mockers and despisers will crawl in the dirt before me, and I will feed my hungry heart with their envy. I will have all luxuries, all joys, all enchantments of the spirit, all contentments of the body that man holds dear. I will buy, buy, buy! deference, respect, esteem, worship—every pinchbeck grace of life the market of a trivial world can furnish forth. I have lost much time, and chosen badly heretofore, but let that pass; I was ignorant then, and could but take for best what seemed so."

Three short years went by, and a day came when the man sat shivering in a mean garret; and he was gaunt and wan and hollow-eyed, and clothed in rags; and he was gnawing a dry crust and mumbling:

"Curse all the world's gifts, for mockeries and gilded lies! And miscalled, every one. They are not gifts, but merely lendings. Pleasure, Love, Fame, Riches: they are but temporary disguises for lasting realities—Pain, Grief, Shame, Poverty. The fairy said true; in all her store there was but one gift which was precious, only one that was not valueless. How poor and cheap and mean I know those others now to be, compared with that inestimable one, that dear and sweet and kindly one, that steeps in dreamless and enduring sleep the pains that persecute the body, and the shames and griefs that eat the mind and heart. Bring it! I am weary, I would rest."

CHAPTER V

The fairy came, bringing again four of the gifts, but Death was wanting. She said:

"I gave it to a mother's pet, a little child. It was ignorant, but trusted me, asking me to choose for it. You did not ask me to choose."

"Oh, miserable me! What is left for me?"

"What not even you have deserved: the wanton insult of Old Age."

69

A Fable

Once upon a time an artist who had painted a small and very beautiful picture placed it so that he could see it in the mirror. He said, "This doubles the distance and softens it, and it is twice as lovely as it was before."

The animals out in the woods heard of this through the housecat, who was greatly admired by them because he was so learned, and so refined and civilized, and so polite and high-bred, and could tell them so much which they didn't know before, and were not certain about afterward. They were much excited about this new piece of gossip, and they asked questions, so as to get at a full understanding of it. They asked what a picture was, and the cat explained.

"It is a flat thing," he said; "wonderfully flat, marvelously flat, enchantingly flat and elegant. And, oh, so beautiful!"

That excited them almost to a frenzy, and they said they would give the world to see it. Then the bear asked:

"What is it that makes it so beautiful?"

"It is the looks of it," said the cat.

This filled them with admiration and uncertainty, and they were more excited than ever. Then the cow asked:

"What is a mirror?"

"It is a hole in the wall," said the cat. "You look in it, and there you see the picture, and it is so dainty and charming and ethereal and inspiring in its unimaginable beauty that your head turns round and round, and you almost swoon with ecstasy."

The ass had not said anything as yet; he now began to throw doubts. He said there had never been anything as beautiful as this before, and probably wasn't now. He said that when it took a whole basketful of sesquipedalian adjectives to whoop up a thing of beauty, it was time for suspicion.

It was easy to see that these doubts were having an effect upon the animals, so the cat went off offended. The subject was dropped for a couple of days, but in the meantime curiosity was taking a fresh start, and there was a revival of interest perceptible. Then the animals assailed the ass for spoiling what could possibly have been a pleasure to them, on a mere suspicion that the picture was not beautiful, without any evidence that such was the case. The ass was not troubled; he was calm, and said there was one way to find out who was in the right, himself or the cat: he would go and look in that hole, and come back and tell what he found there. The animals felt relieved and grateful, and asked him to go at once—which he did.

But he did not know where he ought to stand; and so, through error, he stood between the picture and the mirror. The result was that the picture had no chance, and didn't show up. He returned home and said:

"The cat lied. There was nothing in that hole but an ass. There wasn't a sign of a flat thing visible. It was a handsome ass, and friendly, but just an ass, and nothing more."

The elephant asked:

"Did you see it good and clear? Were you close to it?"

"I saw it good and clear, O Hathi, King of Beasts. I was so close that I touched noses with it."

"This is very strange," said the elephant; "the cat was always truthful before—as far as we could make out. Let another witness try. Go, Baloo, look in the hole, and come and report."

So the bear went. When he came back, he said:

"Both the cat and the ass have lied; there was nothing in the hole but a bear."

Great was the surprise and puzzlement of the animals. Each was now anxious to make the test himself and get at the straight truth. The elephant sent them one at a time.

First, the cow. She found nothing in the hole but a cow.

The tiger found nothing in it but a tiger.

The lion found nothing in it but a lion.

The leopard found nothing in it but a leopard.

The camel found a camel, and nothing more.

Then Hathi was wroth, and said he would have the truth, if he had to go and fetch it himself. When he returned, he abused his whole subjectry for liars, and was in an unappeasable fury with the moral and mental blindness of the cat. He said that anybody but a near-sighted fool could see that there was nothing in the hole but an elephant.

Moral, by the cat:

You can find in a text whatever you bring, if you will stand between it and the mirror of your imagination. You may not see your ears, but they will be there.

70

A Telephonic Conversation

Consider that a conversation by telephone—when you are simply sitting by and not taking any part in that conversation—is one of the solemnest curiosities of modern life. Yesterday I was writing a deep article on a sublime philosophical subject while such a conversation was going on in the room. I notice that one can always write best when somebody is talking through a telephone close by. Well, the thing began in this way. A member of our household came in and asked me to have our house put into communication with Mr. Bagley's downtown. I have observed, in many cities, that the sex always shrink from calling up the central office themselves. I don't know why, but they do. So I touched the bell, and this talk ensued:

CENTRAL OFFICE. (*gruffly.*) Hello!

I. Is it the Central Office?

C. O. Of course it is. What do you want?

I. Will you switch me on to the Bagleys, please?

C. O. All right. Just keep your ear to the telephone.

Then I heard *k-look, k-look, k-look—klook-klook-klook-look-look*! then a horrible 'gritting' of teeth, and finally a piping female voice: Y-e-s? (*rising inflection.*) Did you wish to speak to me?

Without answering, I handed the telephone to the applicant, and sat down. Then followed that queerest of all the queer things in this world—a conversation with only one end of it. You hear questions asked; you don't hear the answer. You hear invitations given; you hear no thanks in return. You have listening pauses of dead silence, followed by apparently irrelevant and unjustifiable exclamations of glad surprise or sorrow or dismay. You can't make head or tail of the talk, because you never hear anything that the person at the other end of the wire says. Well, I heard the following remarkable series of observations, all from the one tongue, and all shouted—for you can't ever persuade the sex to speak gently into a telephone:

Yes? Why, how did *that* happen?

Pause.

What did you say?

Pause.

Oh no, I don't think it was.

Pause.

No! Oh no, I didn't mean *that.* I meant, put it in while it is still boiling—or just before it *comes* to a boil.

Pause.

What?

Pause.

I turned it over with a backstitch on the selvage edge.

Pause.

Yes, I like that way, too; but I think it's better to baste it on with Valenciennes or bombazine, or something of that sort. It gives it such an air—and attracts so much noise.

Pause.

It's forty-ninth Deuteronomy, sixty-forth to ninety-seventh inclusive. I think we ought all to read it often.

Pause.

Perhaps so; I generally use a hair pin.

Pause.

What did you say? (*aside.*) Children, do be quiet!

Pause

Oh! B *flat!* Dear me, I thought you said it was the cat!

Pause.

Since *when?*

Pause.

Why, *I* never heard of it.

Pause.

You astound me! It seems utterly impossible!

Pause.

Who did?

Pause.

Good-ness gracious!

Pause.

Well, what *is* this world coming to? Was it right in *church?*

Pause.

And was her *mother* there?

Pause.

Why, Mrs. Bagley, I should have died of humiliation! What did they *do?*

Long pause.

I can't be perfectly sure, because I haven't the notes by me; but I think it goes something like this: te-rolly-loll-loll, loll lolly-loll-loll, O tolly-loll-loll-*lee-ly-li*-I-do! And then *repeat*, you know.

Pause.

Yes, I think it *is* very sweet—and very solemn and impressive, if you get the andantino and the pianissimo right.

Pause.

Oh, gum-drops, gum-drops! But I never allow them to eat striped candy. And of course they *can't*, till they get their teeth, anyway.

Pause.

What?

Pause.

Oh, not in the least—go right on. He's here writing—it doesn't bother *him*.

Pause.

Very well, I'll come if I can. (*aside.*) Dear me, how it does tire a person's arm to hold this thing up so long! I wish she'd—

Pause.

Oh no, not at all; I *like* to talk—but I'm afraid I'm keeping you from your affairs.

Pause.

Visitors?

Pause.

No, we never use butter on them.

Pause.

Yes, that is a very good way; but all the cook-books say they are very unhealthy when they are out of season. And *he* doesn't like them, anyway—especially canned.

Pause.

Oh, I think that is too high for them; we have never paid over fifty cents a bunch.

Pause.

Must you go? Well, *good*-by.

Pause.

Yes, I think so. *Good*-by.

Pause.

Four o'clock, then—I'll be ready. *Good*-by.

Pause.

Thank you ever so much. *Good*-by.

Pause.

Oh, not at all!—just as fresh—*which*? Oh, I'm glad to hear you say that. *Good*-by.

(Hangs up the telephone and says, "Oh, it *does* tire a person's arm so!")

A man delivers a single brutal "Good-by," and that is the end of it. Not so with the gentle sex—I say it in their praise; they cannot abide abruptness.

71

Party Cries in Ireland

Belfast is a peculiarly religious community. This may be said of the whole of the North of Ireland. About one-half of the people are Protestants and the other half Catholics. Each party does all it can to make its own doctrines popular and draw the affections of the irreligious toward them. One hears constantly of the most touching instances of this zeal. A week ago a vast concourse of Catholics assembled at Armagh to dedicate a new Cathedral; and when they started home again the roadways were lined with groups of meek and lowly Protestants who stoned them till all the region round about was marked with blood. I thought that only Catholics argued in that way, but it seems to be a mistake.

Every man in the community is a missionary and carries a brick to admonish the erring with. The law has tried to break this up, but not with perfect success. It has decreed that irritating "party cries" shall not be indulged in, and that persons uttering them shall be fined forty shillings and costs. And so, in the police court reports every day, one sees these fines recorded. Last week a girl of twelve years old was fined the usual forty shillings and costs for proclaiming in the public streets that she was "a Protestant." The usual cry is, "To hell with the Pope!" or "To hell with the Protestants!" according to the utterer's system of salvation.

One of Belfast's local jokes was very good. It referred to the uniform and inevitable fine of forty shillings and costs for uttering a party cry—and it is no economical fine for a poor man, either, by the way. They say that a policeman found a drunken man lying on the ground, up a dark alley, entertaining himself with shouting, "To hell with!" "To hell with!" The officer smelt a fine—informers get half.

"What's that you say?"

"To hell with!"

"To hell with who? To hell with what?"

"Ah, bedad, ye can finish it yourself—it's too expansive for me!"

I think the seditious disposition, restrained by the economical instinct, is finely put in that.

72

Concerning the American Language

There was as Englishman in our compartment, and he complimented me on—on what? But you would never guess. He complimented me on my English. He said Americans in general did not speak the English language as correctly as I did. I said I was obliged to him for his compliment, since I knew he meant it for one, but that I was not fairly entitled to it, for I did not speak English at all—I only spoke American.

He laughed, and said it was a distinction without a difference. I said no, the difference was not prodigious, but still it was considerable. We fell into a friendly dispute over the matter. I put my case as well as I could, and said:

"The languages were identical several generations ago, but our changed conditions and the spread of our people far to the south and far to the west have made many alterations in our pronunciation, and have introduced new words among us and changed the meanings of many old ones. English people talk through their noses; we do not. We say know, English people say nao; we say cow, the Briton says kaow; we—"

"Oh, come! that is pure Yankee; everybody knows that."

"Yes, it is pure Yankee; that is true. One cannot hear it in America outside of the little corner called New England, which is Yankee land. The English themselves planted it there, two hundred and fifty years ago, and there it remains; it has never spread. But England talks through her nose yet; the Londoner and the backwoods New-Englander pronounce 'know' and 'cow' alike, and then the Briton unconsciously satirizes himself by making fun of the Yankee's pronunciation."

We argued this point at some length; nobody won; but no matter, the fact remains Englishmen say nao and kaow for 'know' and 'cow', and that is what the rustic inhabitant of a very small section of America does.

"You conferred your 'a' upon New England, too, and there it remains; it has not traveled out of the narrow limits of those six little states in all these two hundred and fifty years. All England uses it, New England's small population—say four millions—use it, but we have forty-five millions who do not use it. You say 'glahs of wawtah,' so does New England; at least, New England says 'glahs.' America at large flattens the 'a', and says 'glass of water.' These sounds are pleasanter than yours; you may think they are not right—well, in English they are not right, but 'American' they are. You say 'flahsk' and 'bahsket,' and 'jackahss'; we say 'flask,' 'basket,' 'jackass'—sounding the 'a' as it is in 'tallow,' 'fallow,' and so on. Up to as late as 1847 Mr. Webster's Dictionary had the impudence to still pronounce 'basket' bahsket, when he knew that outside of his little New England all America shortened the 'a' and paid no attention to his English broadening of it. However, it called itself an English Dictionary, so it was proper enough that it should stick to English forms, perhaps. It still calls itself an English Dictionary today, but it has quietly ceased to pronounce 'basket' as if it were spelt 'bahsket.' In the American language the 'h' is respected; the 'h' is not dropped or added improperly."

"The same is the case in England—I mean among the educated classes, of course."

"Yes, that is true; but a nation's language is a very large matter. It is not simply a manner of speech obtaining among the educated handful; the manner obtaining among the vast uneducated multitude must be considered also. Your uneducated masses speak English, you will not deny that; our uneducated masses speak American it won't be fair for you to deny that, for you can see, yourself, that when your stable-boy says, 'It isn't the 'unting that 'urts the 'orse, but the 'ammer, 'ammer, 'ammer on the 'ard 'ighway,' and our stable-boy makes the same remark without suffocating a single h, these two people are manifestly talking two different languages. But if the signs are to be trusted, even your educated classes used to drop the 'h.' They say humble, now, and heroic, and historic etc., but I judge that they used to drop those 'hs' because your writers still keep up the fashion of patting an before those words instead of a. This is what Mr. Darwin might call a 'rudimentary' sign that as an was justifiable once, and useful when your educated classes used to say 'umble, and 'eroic, and 'istorical. Correct writers of the American language do not put an before three words."

The English gentleman had something to say upon this matter, but never mind what he said—I'm not arguing his case. I have him at a disadvantage, now. I proceeded:

"In England you encourage an orator by exclaiming, 'H'yaah! 'yaah!' We pronounce it heer in some sections, 'h'yer' in others, and so on; but our whites do not say 'h'yaah,' pronouncing the a's like the a in ah. I have heard English ladies say 'don't you'— making two separate and distinct words of it; your Mr. Burnand has satirized it. But we always say 'dontchu.' This is much better. Your ladies say, 'Oh, it's oful nice!' Ours say, 'Oh, it's awful nice!' We say, 'Four hundred,' you say 'For'–as in the word or. Your clergymen speak of 'the Lawd,' ours of 'the Lord'; yours speak of 'the gawds of the heathen,' ours of 'the gods of the heathen.' When you are exhausted, you say you are 'knocked up.' We don't. When you say you will do a thing 'directly,' you mean 'immediately'; in the American language—generally speaking—the word signifies 'after a little.' When you say 'clever,' you mean 'capable'; with us the word used to mean 'accommodating,' but I don't know what it means now. Your word 'stout' means 'fleshy'; our word 'stout' usually means 'strong.' Your words 'gentleman' and 'lady' have a very restricted meaning; with us they include the barmaid, butcher, burglar, harlot, and horse-thief. You say, 'I haven't got any stockings on,' 'I haven't got any memory,' 'I haven't got any money in my purse; we usually say, 'I haven't any stockings on,' 'I haven't any memory!' 'I haven't any money in my purse.' You say 'out of window'; we always put in a 'the'. If one asks 'How old is that man?' the Briton answers, 'He will be about forty'; in the American language we should say, 'He is about forty.' However, I won't tire you, sir; but if I wanted to, I could pile up differences here until I not only convinced you that English and American are separate languages, but that when I speak my native tongue in its utmost purity an Englishman can't understand me at all."

"I don't wish to flatter you, but it is about all I can do to understand you now."

That was a very pretty compliment, and it put us on the pleasantest terms directly—I use the word in the English sense.

(Later—1882. Esthetes in many of our schools are now beginning to teach the pupils to broaden the 'a,' and to say "don't you," in the elegant foreign way.)

Maxim Gorky

(1868-1936)

73

Her Lover

An acquaintance of mine once told me the following story.

When I was a student at Moscow I happened to live alongside one of those ladies whose repute is questionable. She was a Pole, and they called her Teresa. She was a tallish, powerfully-built brunette, with black, bushy eyebrows and a large coarse face as if carved out by a hatchet—the bestial gleam of her dark eyes, her thick bass voice, her cabman-like gait and her immense muscular vigour, worthy of a fishwife, inspired me with horror. I lived on the top flight and her garret was opposite to mine. I never left my door open when I knew her to be at home. But this, after all, was a very rare occurrence. Sometimes I chanced to meet her on the staircase or in the yard, and she would smile upon me with a smile which seemed to me to be sly and cynical. Occasionally, I saw her drunk, with bleary eyes, tousled hair, and a particularly hideous grin. On such occasions she would speak to me.

"How d'ye do, Mr. Student!" and her stupid laugh would still further intensify my loathing of her. I should have liked to have changed my quarters in order to have avoided such encounters and greetings; but my little chamber was a nice one, and there was such a wide view from the window, and it was always so quiet in the street below—so I endured.

And one morning I was sprawling on my couch, trying to find some sort of excuse for not attending my class, when the door opened, and the bass voice of Teresa the loathsome resounded from my threshold:

"Good health to you, Mr. Student!"

"What do you want?" I said. I saw that her face was confused and supplicatory . . . It was a very unusual sort of face for her.

"Sir! I want to beg a favour of you. Will you grant it me?"

I lay there silent, and thought to myself:

"Gracious! . . . Courage, my boy!"

"I want to send a letter home, that's what it is," she said; her voice was beseeching, soft, timid.

"Deuce take you!" I thought; but up I jumped, sat down at my table, took a sheet of paper, and said:

"Come here, sit down, and dictate!"

She came, sat down very gingerly on a chair, and looked at me with a guilty look.

"Well, to whom do you want to write?"

"To Boleslav Kashput, at the town of Svieptziana, on the Warsaw Road . . ."

"Well, fire away!"

"My dear Boles . . . my darling . . . my faithful lover. May the Mother of God protect thee! Thou heart of gold, why hast thou not written for such a long time to thy sorrowing little dove, Teresa?"

I very nearly burst out laughing. "A sorrowing little dove!" more than five feet high, with fists a stone and more in weight, and as black a face as if the little dove had lived all its life in a chimney, and had never once washed itself! Restraining myself somehow, I asked:

"Who is this Bolest?"

"Boles, Mr. Student," she said, as if offended with me for blundering over the name, "he is Boles—my young man."

"Young man!"

"Why are you so surprised, sir? Cannot I, a girl, have a young man?"

She? A girl? Well!

"Oh, why not?" I said. "All things are possible. And has he been your young man long?"

"Six years."

"Oh, ho!" I thought. "Well, let us write your letter . . ."

And I tell you plainly that I would willingly have changed places with this Boles if his fair correspondent had been not Teresa but something less than she.

"I thank you most heartily, sir, for your kind services," said Teresa to me, with a curtsey. "Perhaps I can show you some service, eh?"

"No, I most humbly thank you all the same."

"Perhaps, sir, your shirts or your trousers may want a little mending?"

I felt that this mastodon in petticoats had made me grow quite red with shame, and I told her pretty sharply that I had no need whatever of her services.

She departed.

A week or two passed away. It was evening. I was sitting at my window whistling and thinking of some expedient for enabling me to get away from myself. I was bored; the weather was dirty. I didn't want to go out, and out of sheer ennui I began a course of self-analysis and reflection. This also was dull enough work, but I didn't care about doing anything else. Then the door opened. Heaven be praised! Some one came in.

"Oh, Mr. Student, you have no pressing business, I hope?"

It was Teresa. Humph!

"No. What is it?"

"I was going to ask you, sir, to write me another letter."

"Very well! To Boles, eh?"

"No, this time it is from him."

"Wha-at?"

"Stupid that I am! It is not for me, Mr. Student, I beg your pardon. It is for a friend of mine, that is to say, not a friend but an acquaintance—a man acquaintance. He has a sweetheart just like me here, Teresa. That's how it is. Will you, sir, write a letter to this Teresa?"

I looked at her—her face was troubled, her fingers were trembling. I was a bit fogged at first—and then I guessed how it was.

"Look here, my lady," I said, "there are no Boleses or Teresas at all, and you've been telling me a pack of lies. Don't you come sneaking about me any longer. I have no wish whatever to cultivate your acquaintance. Do you understand?"

And suddenly she grew strangely terrified and distraught; she began to shift from foot to foot without moving from the place, and spluttered comically, as if she wanted to say something and couldn't. I waited to see what would come of all this, and I saw and felt that, apparently, I had made a great mistake in suspecting her of wishing to draw me from the path of righteousness. It was evidently something very different.

"Mr. Student!" she began, and suddenly, waving her hand, she turned abruptly towards the door and went out. I remained with a very unpleasant feeling in my mind. I listened. Her door was flung violently to—plainly the poor wench was very angry . . . I thought it over, and resolved to go to her, and, inviting her to come in here, write everything she wanted.

I entered her apartment. I looked round. She was sitting at the table, leaning on her elbows, with her head in her hands.

"Listen to me," I said.

Now, whenever I come to this point in my story, I always feel horribly awkward and idiotic. Well, well!

"Listen to me," I said.

She leaped from her seat, came towards me with flashing eyes, and laying her hands on my shoulders, began to whisper, or rather to hum in her peculiar bass voice:

"Look you, now! It's like this. There's no Boles at all, and there's no Teresa either. But what's that to you? Is it a hard thing for you to draw your pen over paper? Eh? Ah, and you, too! Still such a little fair-haired boy! There's nobody at all, neither Boles, nor Teresa, only me. There you have it, and much good may it do you!"

"Pardon me!" said I, altogether flabbergasted by such a reception, "what is it all about? There's no Boles, you say?"

"No. So it is."

"And no Teresa either?"

"And no Teresa. I'm Teresa."

I didn't understand it at all. I fixed my eyes upon her, and tried to make out which of us was taking leave of his or her senses. But she went again to the table, searched about for something, came back to me, and said in an offended tone:

"If it was so hard for you to write to Boles, look, there's your letter, take it! Others will write for me."

I looked. In her hand was my letter to Boles. Phew!

"Listen, Teresa! What is the meaning of all this? Why must you get others to write for you when I have already written it, and you haven't sent it?"

"Sent it where?"

"Why, to this—Boles."

"There's no such person."

I absolutely did not understand it. There was nothing for me but to spit and go. Then she explained.

"What is it?" she said, still offended. "There's no such person, I tell you," and she extended her arms as if she herself did not understand why there should be no such person. "But I wanted him to be... Am I then not a human creature like the rest of them? Yes, yes, I know, I know, of course... Yet no harm was done to any one by my writing to him that I can see . . ."

"Pardon me—to whom?"

"To Boles, of course."

"But he doesn't exist."

"Alas! alas! But what if he doesn't? He doesn't exist, but he might! I write to him, and it looks as if he did exist. And Teresa—that's me, and he replies to me, and then I write to him again . . ."

I understood at last. And I felt so sick, so miserable, so ashamed, somehow. Alongside of me, not three yards away, lived a human creature who had nobody in the world to treat her kindly, affectionately, and this human being had invented a friend for herself!

"Look, now! you wrote me a letter to Boles, and I gave it to some one else to read it to me; and when they read it to me I listened and fancied that Boles was there. And I asked you to write me a letter from Boles to Teresa—that is to me. When they write such a letter for me, and read it to me, I feel quite sure that Boles is there. And life grows easier for me in consequence."

"Deuce take you for a blockhead!" said I to myself when I heard this.

And from thenceforth, regularly, twice a week, I wrote a letter to Boles, and an answer from Boles to Teresa. I wrote those answers well . . . She, of course, listened to them, and wept like anything, roared, I should say, with her bass voice. And in return for my thus moving her to tears by real letters from the imaginary Boles, she began to mend the holes I had in my socks, shirts, and other articles of clothing. Subsequently, about three months after this history began, they put her in prison for something or other. No doubt by this time she is dead.

My acquaintance shook the ash from his cigarette, looked pensively up at the sky, and thus concluded:

Well, well, the more a human creature has tasted of bitter things the more it hungers after the sweet things of life. And we, wrapped round in the rags of our virtues, and regarding others through the mist of our self-sufficiency, and persuaded of our universal impeccability, do not understand this.

And the whole thing turns out pretty stupidly—and very cruelly. The fallen classes, we say. And who are the fallen classes, I should like to know? They are, first of all, people with the same bones, flesh, and blood and nerves as ourselves. We have been told this day after day for ages. And we actually listen—and the devil only knows how hideous the whole thing is. Or are we completely depraved by the loud sermonising of humanism? In reality, we also are fallen folks, and, so far as I can see, very deeply fallen into the abyss of self-sufficiency and the conviction of our own superiority. But enough of this. It is all as old as the hills—so old that it is a shame to speak of it. Very old indeed—yes, that's what it is!

Nathaniel Hawthorne

(1804-1864)

74

Mrs. Bullfrog

It makes me melancholy to see how like fools some very sensible people act in the matter of choosing wives. They perplex their judgments by a most undue attention to little niceties of personal appearance, habits, disposition, and other trifles which concern nobody but the lady herself. An unhappy gentleman, resolving to wed nothing short of perfection, keeps his heart and hand till both get so old and withered that no tolerable woman will accept them. Now this is the very height of absurdity. A kind Providence has so skilfully adapted sex to sex and the mass of individuals to each other, that, with certain obvious exceptions, any male and female may be moderately happy in the married state. The true rule is to ascertain that the match is fundamentally a good one, and then to take it for granted that all minor objections, should there be such, will vanish, if you let them alone. Only put yourself beyond hazard as to the real basis of matrimonial bliss, and it is scarcely to be imagined what miracles, in the way of recognizing smaller incongruities, connubial love will effect.

For my own part I freely confess that, in my bachelorship, I was precisely such an over-curious simpleton as I now advise the reader not to be. My early habits had gifted me with a feminine sensibility and too exquisite refinement. I was the accomplished graduate of a dry goods store, where, by dint of ministering to the whims of fine ladies, and suiting silken hose to delicate limbs, and handling satins, ribbons, chintzes calicoes, tapes, gauze, and cambric needles, I grew up a very ladylike sort of a gentleman. It is not assuming too much to affirm that the ladies themselves were hardly so ladylike as Thomas Bullfrog. So painfully acute was my sense of female imperfection, and such varied excellence did I require in the woman whom I could love, that there was an awful risk of my getting no wife at all, or of being driven to perpetrate matrimony with my own image in the looking-glass. Besides the fundamental principle already hinted at, I demanded the fresh bloom of youth, pearly teeth, glossy ringlets, and the whole list of lovely items, with the utmost delicacy of habits and sentiments, a silken texture of mind, and, above all, a virgin heart. In a word, if a young angel just from paradise, yet dressed in earthly fashion, had come and offered me her hand, it is by no means certain that I should have taken it. There was every chance of my becoming a most miserable old bachelor, when, by the best luck in the world, I made a journey into another state, and was smitten by, and smote again, and wooed, won, and married, the present Mrs. Bullfrog, all in the space of a fortnight. Owing to these extempore measures, I not only gave my bride credit for certain perfections which have not as yet come to light, but also overlooked a few trifling defects, which, however, glimmered on my perception long before the close of the honeymoon. Yet, as there was no mistake about the fundamental principle aforesaid, I soon learned, as will be seen, to estimate Mrs. Bullfrog's deficiencies and superfluities at exactly their proper value.

The same morning that Mrs. Bullfrog and I came together as a unit, we took two seats in the stage-coach and began our journey towards my place of business. There being no other passengers, we were as much alone and as free to give vent to our raptures as if I had hired a hack for the matrimonial jaunt. My bride looked charmingly in a green silk calash and riding habit of pelisse cloth; and whenever her red lips parted with a smile, each tooth appeared like an inestimable pearl. Such was my passionate warmth that—

we had rattled out of the village, gentle reader, and were lonely as Adam and Eve in paradise—I plead guilty to no less freedom than a kiss. The gentle eye of Mrs. Bullfrog scarcely rebuked me for the profanation. Emboldened by her indulgence, I threw back the calash from her polished brow, and suffered my fingers, white and delicate as her own, to stray among those dark and glossy curls which realized my daydreams of rich hair.

"My love," said Mrs. Bullfrog tenderly, "you will disarrange my curls."

"Oh, no, my sweet Laura!" replied I, still playing with the glossy ringlet. "Even your fair hand could not manage a curl more delicately than mine. I propose myself the pleasure of doing up your hair in papers every evening at the same time with my own."

"Mr. Bullfrog," repeated she, "you must not disarrange my curls."

This was spoken in a more decided tone than I had happened to hear, until then, from my gentlest of all gentle brides. At the same time she put up her hand and took mine prisoner; but merely drew it away from the forbidden ringlet, and then immediately released it. Now, I am a fidgety little man, and always love to have something in my fingers; so that, being debarred from my wife's curls, I looked about me for any other plaything. On the front seat of the coach there was one of those small baskets in which travelling ladies who are too delicate to appear at a public table generally carry a supply of gingerbread, biscuits and cheese, cold ham, and other light refreshments, merely to sustain nature to the journey's end. Such airy diet will sometimes keep them in pretty good flesh for a week together. Laying hold of this same little basket, I thrust my hand under the newspaper with which it was carefully covered.

"What's this, my dear?" cried I; for the black neck of a bottle had popped out of the basket.

"A bottle of Kalydor, Mr. Bullfrog," said my wife, coolly taking the basket from my hands and replacing it on the front seat.

There was no possibility of doubting my wife's word; but I never knew genuine Kalydor, such as I use for my own complexion, to smell so much like cherry brandy. I was about to express my fears that the lotion would injure her skin, when an accident occurred which threatened more than a skin-deep injury. Our Jehu had carelessly driven over a heap of gravel and fairly capsized the coach, with the wheels in the air and our heels where our heads should have been. What became of my wits I cannot imagine; they have always had a perverse trick of deserting me just when they were most needed; but so it chanced, that in the confusion of our overthrow I quite forgot that there was a Mrs. Bullfrog in the world. Like many men's wives, the good lady served her husband as a steppingstone. I had scrambled out of the coach and was instinctively settling my cravat, when somebody brushed roughly by me, and I heard a smart thwack upon the coachman's ear.

"Take that, you villain!" cried a strange, hoarse voice. "You have ruined me, you blackguard! I shall never be the woman I have been!"

And then came a second thwack, aimed at the driver's other ear; but which missed it, and hit him on the nose, causing a terrible effusion of blood. Now, who or what fearful apparition was inflicting this punishment on the poor fellow remained an impenetrable mystery to me. The blows were given by a person of grisly aspect, with a head almost bald, and sunken cheeks, apparently of the feminine gender, though hardly to be classed in the gentler sex. There being no teeth to modulate the voice, it had a mumbled fierceness, not passionate, but stern, which absolutely made me quiver like calf's-foot jelly. Who could the phantom be? The most awful circumstance of the affair is yet to be told: for this ogre, or whatever it was, had a riding habit like Mrs. Bullfrog's, and also a green silk calash dangling down her back by the strings. In my terror and turmoil of mind I could imagine nothing less than that the Old Nick, at the moment of our overturn, had annihilated my wife and jumped into her petticoats. This idea seemed the most probable, since I could nowhere perceive Mrs. Bullfrog alive, nor, though I looked very sharply about the coach, could I detect any traces of that beloved woman's dead body. There would have been a comfort in giving her Christian burial.

"Come, sir, bestir yourself! Help this rascal to set up the coach," said the hobgoblin to me; then, with a terrific screech at three countrymen at a distance, "Here, you fellows, ain't you ashamed to stand off when a poor woman is in distress?"

The countrymen, instead of fleeing for their lives, came running at full speed, and laid hold of the topsy-turvy coach. I, also, though a small-sized man, went to work like a son of Anak. The coachman, too, with the blood still streaming from his nose, tugged and toiled most manfully, dreading, doubtless, that the next blow might break his head. And yet, bemauled as the poor fellow had been, he seemed to glance at me with an eye of pity, as if my case were more deplorable than his. But I cherished a hope that all would turn out a dream, and seized the opportunity, as we raised the coach, to jam two of my fingers under the wheel, trusting that the pain would awaken me.

"Why, here we are, all to rights again!" exclaimed a sweet voice behind. "Thank you for your assistance, gentlemen. My dear Mr. Bullfrog, how you perspire! Do let me wipe your face. Don't take this little accident too much to heart, good driver. We ought to be thankful that none of our necks are broken."

"We might have spared one neck out of the three," muttered the driver, rubbing his ear and pulling his nose, to ascertain whether he had been cuffed or not. "Why, the woman's a witch!"

I fear that the reader will not believe, yet it is positively a fact, that there stood Mrs. Bullfrog, with her glossy ringlets curling on her brow, and two rows of orient pearls gleaming between her parted lips, which wore a most angelic smile. She had regained her riding habit and calash from the grisly phantom, and was, in all respects, the lovely woman who had been sitting by my side at the instant of our overturn. How she had happened to disappear, and who had supplied her place, and whence she did now return, were problems too knotty for me to solve. There stood my wife. That was the one thing certain among a heap of mysteries. Nothing remained but to help her into the coach, and plod on, through the journey of the day and the journey of life, as comfortably as we could. As the driver closed the door upon us, I heard him whisper to the three countrymen, "How do you suppose a fellow feels shut up in the cage with a she tiger?"

Of course this query could have no reference to my situation. Yet, unreasonable as it may appear, I confess that my feelings were not altogether so ecstatic as when I first called Mrs. Bullfrog mine. True, she was a sweet woman and an angel of a wife; but what if a Gorgon should return, amid the transports of our connubial bliss, and take the angel's place. I recollected the tale of a fairy, who half the time was a beautiful woman and half the time a hideous monster. Had I taken that very fairy to be the wife of my bosom? While such whims and chimeras were flitting across my fancy I began to look askance at Mrs. Bullfrog, almost expecting that the transformation would be wrought before my eyes.

To divert my mind, I took up the newspaper which had covered the little basket of refreshments, and which now lay at the bottom of the coach, blushing with a deep-red stain and emitting a potent spirituous fume from the contents of the broken bottle of Kalydor. The paper was two or three years old, but contained an article of several columns, in which I soon grew wonderfully interested. It was the report of a trial for breach of promise of marriage, giving the testimony in full, with fervid extracts from both the gentleman's and lady's amatory correspondence. The deserted damsel had personally appeared in court, and had borne energetic evidence to her lover's perfidy and the strength of her blighted affections. On the defendant's part there had been an attempt, though insufficiently sustained, to blast the plaintiff's character, and a plea, in mitigation of damages, on account of her unamiable temper. A horrible idea was suggested by the lady's name.

"Madam," said I, holding the newspaper before Mrs. Bullfrog's eyes, —and, though a small, delicate, and thin-visaged man, I feel assured that I looked very terrific,—"madam," repeated I, through my shut teeth, "were you the plaintiff in this cause?"

"Oh, my dear Mr. Bullfrog," replied my wife, sweetly, "I thought all the world knew that!"

"Horror! horror!" exclaimed I, sinking back on the seat.

Covering my face with both hands, I emitted a deep and deathlike groan, as if my tormented soul were rending me asunder—I, the most exquisitely fastidious of men, and whose wife was to have been the most delicate and refined of women, with all the fresh dew-drops glittering on her virgin rosebud of a heart!

I thought of the glossy ringlets and pearly teeth; I thought of the Kalydor; I thought of the coachman's bruised ear and bloody nose; I thought of the tender love secrets which she had whispered to the judge and jury and a thousand tittering auditors, —and gave another groan!

"Mr. Bullfrog," said my wife.

As I made no reply, she gently took my hands within her own, removed them from my face, and fixed her eyes steadfastly on mine.

"Mr. Bullfrog," said she, not unkindly, yet with all the decision of her strong character, "let me advise you to overcome this foolish weakness, and prove yourself, to the best of your ability, as good a husband as I will be a wife. You have discovered, perhaps, some little imperfections in your bride. Well, what did you expect? Women are not angels. If they were, they would go to heaven for husbands; or, at least, be more difficult in their choice on earth."

"But why conceal those imperfections?" interposed I, tremulously.

"Now, my love, are not you a most unreasonable little man?" said Mrs. Bullfrog, patting me on the cheek. "Ought a woman to disclose her frailties earlier than the wedding day? Few husbands, I assure you, make the discovery in such good season, and still fewer complain that these trifles are concealed too long. Well, what a strange man you are! Poh! you are joking."

"But the suit for breach of promise!" groaned I.

"Ah, and is that the rub?" exclaimed my wife. "Is it possible that you view that affair in an objectionable light? Mr. Bullfrog, I never could have dreamed it! Is it an objection that I have triumphantly defended myself against slander and vindicated my purity in a court of justice? Or do you complain because your wife has shown the proper spirit of a woman, and punished the villain who trifled with her affections?"

"But," persisted I, shrinking into a corner of the coach, however, —for I did not know precisely how much contradiction the proper spirit of a woman would endure, —"but, my love, would it not have been more dignified to treat the villain with the silent contempt he merited?"

"That is all very well, Mr. Bullfrog," said my wife, slyly; "but, in that case, where would have been the five thousand dollars which are to stock your dry goods store?"

"Mrs. Bullfrog, upon your honor," demanded I, as if my life hung upon her words, "is there no mistake about those five thousand dollars?"

"Upon my word and honor there is none," replied she. "The jury gave me every cent the rascal had; and I have kept it all for my dear Bullfrog."

"Then, thou dear woman," cried I, with an overwhelming gush of tenderness, "let me fold thee to my heart. The basis of matrimonial bliss is secure, and all thy little defects and frailties are forgiven. Nay, since the result has been so fortunate, I rejoice at the wrongs which drove thee to this blessed lawsuit. Happy Bullfrog that I am!"

75

Sunday at Home

Every Sabbath morning in the summer-time I thrust back the curtain to watch the sunrise stealing down a steeple which stands opposite my chamber window. First the weathercock begins to flash; then a fainter lustre gives the spire an airy aspect; next it encroaches on the tower and causes the index of the dial to glisten like gold as it points to the gilded figure of the hour. Now the loftiest window gleams, and now the lower. The carved framework of the portal is marked strongly out. At length the morning glory in its descent from heaven comes down the stone steps one by one, and there stands the steeple glowing with fresh radiance, while the shades of twilight still hide themselves among the nooks of the adjacent buildings. Methinks though the same sun brightens it every fair morning, yet the steeple has a peculiar robe of brightness for the Sabbath.

By dwelling near a church a person soon contracts an attachment for the edifice. We naturally personify it, and conceive its massy walls and its dim emptiness to be instinct with a calm and meditative and somewhat melancholy spirit. But the steeple stands foremost in our thoughts, as well as locally. It impresses us as a giant with a mind comprehensive and discriminating enough to care for the great and small concerns of all the town. Hourly, while it speaks a moral to the few that think, it reminds thousands of busy individuals of their separate and most secret affairs. It is the steeple, too, that flings abroad the hurried and irregular accents of general alarm; neither have gladness and festivity found a better utterance than by its tongue; and when the dead are slowly passing to their home, the steeple has a melancholy voice to bid them welcome. Yet, in spite of this connection with human interests, what a moral loneliness on week-days broods round about its stately height! It has no kindred with the houses above which it towers; it looks down into the narrow thoroughfare—the lonelier because the crowd are elbowing their passage at its base. A glance at the body of the church deepens this impression. Within, by the light of distant windows, amid refracted shadows we discern the vacant pews and empty galleries, the silent organ, the voiceless pulpit and the clock which tells to solitude how time is passing. Time—where man lives not—what is it but eternity? And in the church, we might suppose, are garnered up throughout the week all thoughts and feelings that have reference to eternity, until the holy day comes round again to let them forth. Might not, then, its more appropriate site be in the outskirts of the town, with space for old trees to wave around it and throw their solemn shadows over a quiet green? We will say more of this hereafter.

But on the Sabbath I watch the earliest sunshine and fancy that a holier brightness marks the day when there shall be no buzz of voices on the Exchange nor traffic in the shops, nor crowd nor business anywhere but at church. Many have fancied so. For my own part, whether I see it scattered down among tangled woods, or beaming broad across the fields, or hemmed in between brick buildings, or tracing out the figure of the casement on my chamber floor, still I recognize the Sabbath sunshine. And ever let me recognize it! Some illusions—and this among them—are the shadows of great truths. Doubts may flit around me or seem to close their evil wings and settle down, but so long as I imagine that the earth is hallowed and the light of heaven retains its sanctity on the Sabbath—while that blessed sunshine lives within me—never can my soul have lost the instinct of its faith. If it have gone astray, it will return again.

I love to spend such pleasant Sabbaths from morning till night behind the curtain of my open window. Are they spent amiss? Every spot so near the church as to be visited by the circling shadow of the steeple should be deemed consecrated ground to-day. With stronger truth be it said that a devout heart may consecrate a den of thieves, as an evil one may convert a temple to the same. My heart, perhaps, has no such holy, nor, I would fain trust, such impious, potency. It must suffice that, though my form be absent, my inner man goes constantly to church, while many whose bodily presence fills the accustomed seats have left their souls at home. But I am there even before my friend the sexton. At length he comes—a man of kindly but sombre aspect, in dark gray clothes, and hair of the same mixture. He comes and applies his key to the wide portal. Now my thoughts may go in among the dusty pews or ascend the pulpit without sacrilege, but soon come forth again to enjoy the music of the bell. How glad, yet solemn too! All the steeples in town are talking together aloft in the sunny air and rejoicing among themselves while their spires point heavenward. Meantime, here are the children assembling to the Sabbath-school, which is kept somewhere within the church. Often, while looking at the arched portal, I have been gladdened by the sight of a score of these little girls and boys in pink, blue, yellow and crimson frocks bursting suddenly forth into the sunshine like a swarm of gay butterflies that had been shut up in the solemn gloom. Or I might compare them to cherubs haunting that holy place.

About a quarter of an hour before the second ringing of the bell individuals of the congregation begin to appear. The earliest is invariably an old woman in black whose bent frame and rounded shoulders are evidently laden with some heavy affliction which she is eager to rest upon the altar. Would that the Sabbath came twice as often, for the sake of that sorrowful old soul! There is an elderly man, also, who arrives in good season and leans against the corner of the tower, just within the line of its shadow, looking downward with a darksome brow. I sometimes fancy that the old woman is the happier of the two. After these, others drop in singly and by twos and threes, either disappearing through the doorway or taking their stand in its vicinity. At last, and always with an unexpected sensation, the bell turns in the steeple overhead and throws out an irregular clangor, jarring the tower to its foundation. As if there were magic in the sound, the sidewalks of the street, both up and down along, are immediately thronged with two long lines of people, all converging hitherward and streaming into the church. Perhaps the far-off roar of a coach draws nearer—a deeper thunder by its contrast with the surrounding stillness—until it sets down the wealthy worshippers at the portal among their humblest brethren. Beyond that entrance—in theory, at least—there are no distinctions of earthly rank; nor, indeed, by the goodly apparel which is flaunting in the sun would there seem to be such on the hither side. Those pretty girls! Why will they disturb my pious meditations? Of all days in the week, they should strive to look least fascinating on the Sabbath, instead of heightening their mortal loveliness, as if to rival the blessed angels and keep our thoughts from heaven. Were I the minister himself, I must needs look. One girl is white muslin from the waist upward and black silk downward to her slippers; a second blushes from top-knot to shoe-tie, one universal scarlet; another shines of a pervading yellow, as if she had made a garment of the sunshine. The greater part, however, have adopted a milder cheerfulness of hue. Their veils, especially when the wind raises them, give a lightness to the general effect and make them appear like airy phantoms as they flit up the steps and vanish into the sombre doorway. Nearly all—though it is very strange that I should know it—wear white stockings, white as snow, and neat slippers laced crosswise with black ribbon pretty high above the ankles. A white stocking is infinitely more effective than a black one.

Here comes the clergyman, slow and solemn, in severe simplicity, needing no black silk gown to denote his office. His aspect claims my reverence, but cannot win my love. Were I to picture Saint Peter keeping fast the gate of Heaven and frowning, more stern than pitiful, on the wretched applicants, that face should be my study. By middle age, or sooner, the creed has generally wrought upon the heart or been attempered by it. As the minister passes into the church the bell holds its iron tongue and all the low murmur of the congregation dies away. The gray sexton looks up and down the street and then at my window-curtain, where through the small peephole I half fancy that he has caught my eye. Now every loiterer has gone in and the street lies asleep in the quiet sun, while a feeling of loneliness comes over me, and brings also an uneasy sense of neglected privileges and duties. Oh, I ought to have gone to church! The bustle of the rising congregation reaches my ears. They are standing up to pray. Could I bring my heart into unison with those who are praying in yonder church and lift it heavenward with a fervor of supplication, but no distinct request, would not that be the safest kind of prayer? —"Lord, look down upon me in mercy!" With that sentiment gushing from my soul, might I not leave all the rest to him?

Hark! the hymn! This, at least, is a portion of the service which I can enjoy better than if I sat within the walls, where the full choir and the massive melody of the organ would fall with a weight upon me. At this distance it thrills through my frame and plays upon my heart-strings with a pleasure both of the sense and spirit. Heaven be praised! I know nothing of music as a science, and the most elaborate harmonies, if they please me, please as simply as a nurse's lullaby. The strain has ceased, but prolongs itself in my mind with fanciful echoes till I start from my reverie and find that the sermon has commenced. It is my misfortune seldom to fructify in a regular way by any but printed sermons. The first strong idea which the preacher utters gives birth to a train of thought and leads me onward step by step quite out of hearing of the good man's voice unless he be indeed a son of thunder. At my open window, catching now and then a sentence of the 'parson's saw', I am as well situated as at the foot of the pulpit stairs. The broken and scattered fragments of this one discourse will be the texts of many sermons preached by those colleague pastors—colleagues, but often disputants—my Mind and Heart. The former pretends to be a scholar and perplexes me with doctrinal points; the latter takes me on the score of feeling;

and both, like several other preachers, spend their strength to very little purpose. I, their sole auditor, cannot always understand them.

Suppose that a few hours have passed, and behold me still behind my curtain just before the close of the afternoon service. The hour-hand on the dial has passed beyond four o'clock. The declining sun is hidden behind the steeple and throws its shadow straight across the street; so that my chamber is darkened as with a cloud. Around the church door all is solitude, and an impenetrable obscurity beyond the threshold. A commotion is heard. The seats are slammed down and the pew doors thrown back; a multitude of feet are trampling along the unseen aisles, and the congregation bursts suddenly through the portal. Foremost scampers a rabble of boys, behind whom moves a dense and dark phalanx of grown men, and lastly a crowd of females with young children and a few scattered husbands. This instantaneous outbreak of life into loneliness is one of the pleasantest scenes of the day. Some of the good people are rubbing their eyes, thereby intimating that they have been wrapped, as it were, in a sort of holy trance by the fervor of their devotion. There is a young man, a third-rate coxcomb, whose first care is always to flourish a white handkerchief and brush the seat of a tight pair of black silk pantaloons which shine as if varnished. They must have been made of the stuff called 'everlasting', or perhaps of the same piece as Christian's garments in the *Pilgrim's Progress*, for he put them on two summers ago and has not yet worn the gloss off. I have taken a great liking to those black silk pantaloons. But now, with nods and greetings among friends, each matron takes her husband's arm and paces gravely homeward, while the girls also flutter away after arranging sunset walks with their favored bachelors. The Sabbath eve is the eve of love. At length the whole congregation is dispersed. No; here, with faces as glossy as black satin, come two sable ladies and a sable gentleman, and close in their rear the minister, who softens his severe visage and bestows a kind word on each. Poor souls! To them the most captivating picture of bliss in heaven is "There we shall be white!"

All is solitude again. But hark! A broken warbling of voices, and now, attuning its grandeur to their sweetness, a stately peal of the organ. Who are the choristers? Let me dream that the angels who came down from heaven this blessed morn to blend themselves with the worship of the truly good are playing and singing their farewell to the earth. On the wings of that rich melody they were borne upward.

This, gentle reader, is merely a flight of poetry. A few of the singing-men and singing-women had lingered behind their fellows and raised their voices fitfully and blew a careless note upon the organ. Yet it lifted my soul higher than all their former strains. They are gone—the sons and daughters of Music—and the gray sexton is just closing the portal. For six days more there will be no face of man in the pews and aisles and galleries, nor a voice in the pulpit, nor music in the choir. Was it worth while to rear this massive edifice to be a desert in the heart of the town and populous only for a few hours of each seventh day? Oh, but the church is a symbol of religion. May its site, which was consecrated on the day when the first tree was felled, be kept holy for ever, a spot of solitude and peace amid the trouble and vanity of our week-day world! There is a moral, and a religion too, even in the silent walls. And may the steeple still point heavenward and bedecked with the hallowed sunshine of the Sabbath morn!

O Henry

(1862-1910)

76

The Cop and the Anthem

On his bench in Madison Square Soapy moved uneasily. When wild geese honk high of nights, and when women without sealskin coats grow kind to their husbands, and when Soapy moves uneasily on his bench in the park, you may know that winter is near at hand.

A dead leaf fell in Soapy's lap. That was Jack Frost's card. Jack is kind to the regular denizens of Madison Square, and gives fair warning of his annual call. At the corners of four streets he hands his pasteboard to the North Wind, footman of the mansion of All Outdoors, so that the inhabitants thereof may make ready.

Soapy's mind became cognisant of the fact that the time had come for him to resolve himself into a singular Committee of Ways and Means to provide against the coming rigour. And therefore he moved uneasily on his bench.

The hibernatorial ambitions of Soapy were not of the highest. In them there were no considerations of Mediterranean cruises, of soporific Southern skies drifting in the Vesuvian Bay. Three months on the Island was what his soul craved. Three months of assured board and bed and congenial company, safe from Boreas and bluecoats, seemed to Soapy the essence of things desirable.

For years the hospitable Blackwell's had been his winter quarters. Just as his more fortunate fellow New Yorkers had bought their tickets to Palm Beach and the Riviera each winter, so Soapy had made his humble arrangements for his annual hegira to the Island. And now the time was come. On the previous night three Sabbath newspapers, distributed beneath his coat, about his ankles and over his lap, had failed to repulse the cold as he slept on his bench near the spurting fountain in the ancient square. So the Island loomed big and timely in Soapy's mind. He scorned the provisions made in the name of charity for the city's dependents. In Soapy's opinion the Law was more benign than Philanthropy. There was an endless round of institutions, municipal and eleemosynary, on which he might set out and receive lodging and food accordant with the simple life. But to one of Soapy's proud spirit the gifts of charity are encumbered. If not in coin you must pay in humiliation of spirit for every benefit received at the hands of philanthropy. As Caesar had his Brutus, every bed of charity must have its toll of a bath, every loaf of bread its compensation of a private and personal inquisition. Wherefore it is better to be a guest of the law, which though conducted by rules, does not meddle unduly with a gentleman's private affairs.

Soapy, having decided to go to the Island, at once set about accomplishing his desire. There were many easy ways of doing this. The pleasantest was to dine luxuriously at some expensive restaurant; and then, after declaring insolvency, be handed over quietly and without uproar to a policeman. An accommodating magistrate would do the rest.

Soapy left his bench and strolled out of the square and across the level sea of asphalt, where Broadway and Fifth Avenue flow together. Up Broadway he turned, and halted at a glittering cafe, where are gathered together nightly the choicest products of the grape, the silkworm and the protoplasm.

Soapy had confidence in himself from the lowest button of his vest upward. He was shaven, and his coat was decent and his neat black, ready-tied four-in-hand had been presented to him by a lady missionary on Thanksgiving Day. If he could reach a table in the restaurant unsuspected success would be his. The portion of him that would show above the table would raise no doubt in the waiter's mind. A roasted mallard duck, thought Soapy, would be about the thing—with a bottle of Chablis, and then Camembert, a demi-tasse and a cigar. One dollar for the cigar would be enough. The total would not be so high as to call forth any supreme manifestation of revenge from the cafe management; and yet the meat would leave him filled and happy for the journey to his winter refuge.

But as Soapy set foot inside the restaurant door the head waiter's eye fell upon his frayed trousers and decadent shoes. Strong and ready hands turned him about and conveyed him in silence and haste to the sidewalk and averted the ignoble fate of the menaced mallard.

Soapy turned off Broadway. It seemed that his route to the coveted island was not to be an epicurean one. Some other way of entering limbo must be thought of.

At a corner of Sixth Avenue electric lights and cunningly displayed wares behind plate-glass made a shop window conspicuous. Soapy took a cobblestone and dashed it through the glass. People came running around the corner, a policeman in the lead. Soapy stood still, with his hands in his pockets, and smiled at the sight of brass buttons.

"Where's the man that done that?" inquired the officer excitedly.

"Don't you figure out that I might have had something to do with it?" said Soapy, not without sarcasm, but friendly, as one greets good fortune.

The policeman's mind refused to accept Soapy even as a clue. Men who smash windows do not remain to parley with the law's minions. They take to their heels. The policeman saw a man half way down the block running to catch a car. With drawn club he joined in the pursuit. Soapy, with disgust in his heart, loafed along, twice unsuccessful.

On the opposite side of the street was a restaurant of no great pretensions. It catered to large appetites and modest purses. Its crockery and atmosphere were thick; its soup and napery thin. Into this place Soapy took his accusive shoes and telltale trousers without challenge. At a table he sat and consumed beefsteak, flapjacks, doughnuts and pie. And then to the waiter be betrayed the fact that the minutest coin and himself were strangers.

"Now, get busy and call a cop," said Soapy. "And don't keep a gentleman waiting."

"No cop for youse," said the waiter, with a voice like butter cakes and an eye like the cherry in a Manhattan cocktail. "Hey, Con!"

Neatly upon his left ear on the callous pavement two waiters pitched Soapy. He arose, joint by joint, as a carpenter's rule opens, and beat the dust from his clothes. Arrest seemed but a rosy dream. The Island seemed very far away. A policeman who stood before a drug store two doors away laughed and walked down the street.

Five blocks Soapy travelled before his courage permitted him to woo capture again. This time the opportunity presented what he fatuously termed to himself a 'cinch'. A young woman of a modest and pleasing guise was standing before a show window gazing with sprightly interest at its display of shaving mugs and inkstands, and two yards from the window a large policeman of severe demeanour leaned against a water plug.

It was Soapy's design to assume the role of the despicable and execrated "masher." The refined and elegant appearance of his victim and the contiguity of the conscientious cop encouraged him to believe that he would soon feel the pleasant official clutch upon his arm that would insure his winter quarters on the right little, tight little isle.

Soapy straightened the lady missionary's readymade tie, dragged his shrinking cuffs into the open, set his hat at a killing cant and sidled toward the young woman. He made eyes at her, was taken with sudden coughs and 'hems', smiled, smirked and went brazenly through the impudent and contemptible litany of the 'masher'. With half an eye Soapy saw that the policeman was watching him fixedly. The young woman moved away a few steps, and again bestowed her absorbed attention upon the shaving mugs. Soapy followed, boldly stepping to her side, raised his hat and said:

"Ah there, Bedelia! Don't you want to come and play in my yard?"

The policeman was still looking. The persecuted young woman had but to beckon a finger and Soapy would be practically en route for his insular haven. Already he imagined he could feel the cozy warmth of the station-house. The young woman faced him and, stretching out a hand, caught Soapy's coat sleeve.

Sure, Mike," she said joyfully, "if you'll blow me to a pail of suds. I'd have spoke to you sooner, but the cop was watching."

With the young woman playing the clinging ivy to his oak Soapy walked past the policeman overcome with gloom. He seemed doomed to liberty.

At the next corner he shook off his companion and ran. He halted in the district where by night are found the lightest streets, hearts, vows and librettos.

Women in furs and men in greatcoats moved gaily in the wintry air. A sudden fear seized Soapy that some dreadful enchantment had rendered him immune to arrest. The thought brought a little of panic upon it, and when he came upon another policeman lounging grandly in front of a transplendent theatre he caught at the immediate straw of 'disorderly conduct'.

On the sidewalk Soapy began to yell drunken gibberish at the top of his harsh voice. He danced, howled, raved and otherwise disturbed the welkin.

The policeman twirled his club, turned his back to Soapy and remarked to a citizen.

"'Tis one of them Yale lads celebratin' the goose egg they give to the Hartford College. Noisy; but no harm. We've instructions to leave them be."

Disconsolate, Soapy ceased his unavailing racket. Would never a policeman lay hands on him? In his fancy the Island seemed an unattainable Arcadia. He buttoned his thin coat against the chilling wind.

In a cigar store he saw a well-dressed man lighting a cigar at a swinging light. His silk umbrella he had set by the door on entering. Soapy stepped inside, secured the umbrella and sauntered off with it slowly. The man at the cigar light followed hastily.

"My umbrella," he said, sternly.

"Oh, is it?" sneered Soapy, adding insult to petit larceny. "Well, why don't you call a policeman? I took it. Your umbrella! Why don't you call a cop? There stands one on the corner."

The umbrella owner slowed his steps. Soapy did likewise, with a presentiment that luck would again run against him. The policeman looked at the two curiously.

"Of course," said the umbrella man—"that is—well, you know how these mistakes occur—I—if it's your umbrella I hope you'll excuse me–I picked it up this morning in a restaurant—If you recognise it as yours, why—I hope you'll—"

"Of course it's mine," said Soapy, viciously.

The ex-umbrella man retreated. The policeman hurried to assist a tall blonde in an opera cloak across the street in front of a street car that was approaching two blocks away.

Soapy walked eastward through a street damaged by improvements. He hurled the umbrella wrathfully into an excavation. He muttered against the men who wear helmets and carry clubs. Because he wanted to fall into their clutches, they seemed to regard him as a king who could do no wrong.

At length Soapy reached one of the avenues to the east where the glitter and turmoil was but faint. He set his face down this toward Madison Square, for the homing instinct survives even when the home is a park bench.

But on an unusually quiet corner Soapy came to a standstill. Here was an old church, quaint and rambling and gabled. Through one violet-stained window a soft light glowed, where, no doubt, the organist loitered over the keys, making sure of his mastery of the coming Sabbath anthem. For there drifted out to Soapy's ears sweet music that caught and held him transfixed against the convolutions of the iron fence.

The moon was above, lustrous and serene; vehicles and pedestrians were few; sparrows twittered sleepily in the eaves—for a little while the scene might have been a country churchyard. And the anthem that the organist played cemented Soapy to the iron fence, for he had known it well in the days when his life contained such things as mothers and roses and ambitions and friends and immaculate thoughts and collars.

The conjunction of Soapy's receptive state of mind and the influences about the old church wrought a sudden and wonderful change in his soul. He viewed with swift horror the pit into which he had tumbled, the degraded days, unworthy desires, dead hopes, wrecked faculties and base motives that made up his existence.

And also in a moment his heart responded thrillingly to this novel mood. An instantaneous and strong impulse moved him to battle with his desperate fate. He would pull himself out of the mire; he would make a man of himself again; he would conquer the evil that had taken possession of him. There was time; he was comparatively young yet; he would resurrect his old eager ambitions and pursue them without faltering. Those solemn but sweet organ notes had set up a revolution in him. To-morrow he would go into the roaring downtown district and find work. A fur importer had once offered him a place as driver. He would find him to-morrow and ask for the position. He would be somebody in the world. He would—

Soapy felt a hand laid on his arm. He looked quickly around into the broad face of a policeman.

"What are you doin' here?" asked the officer.

"Nothin'," said Soapy.

"Then come along," said the policeman.

"Three months on the Island," said the Magistrate in the Police Court the next morning.

The Prisoner of Zembla

So the king fell into a furious rage, so that none durst go near him for fear, and he gave out that since the Princess Ostla had disobeyed him there would be a great tourney, and to the knight who should prove himself of the greatest valor he would give the hand of the princess.

And he sent forth a herald to proclaim that he would do this.

And the herald went about the country making his desire known, blowing a great tin horn and riding a noble steed that pranced and gambolled; and the villagers gazed upon him and said: "Lo, that is one of them tin horn gamblers concerning which the chroniclers have told us."

And when the day came, the king sat in the grandstand, holding the gage of battle in his band, and by his side sat the Princess Ostla, looking very pale and beautiful, but with mournful eyes from which she scarce could keep the tears. And the knights which came to the tourney gazed upon the princess in wonder at her beauty, and each swore to win so that he could marry her and board with the king. Suddenly the heart of the princess gave a great bound, for she saw among the knights one of the poor students with whom she had been in love.

The knights mounted and rode in a line past the grandstand, and the king stopped the poor student, who had the worst horse and the poorest caparisons of any of the knights and said:

"Sir Knight, prithee tell me of what that marvellous shacky and rusty-looking armor of thine is made?"

"Oh, king," said the young knight, "seeing that we are about to engage in a big fight, I would call it scrap iron, wouldn't you?"

"Ods Bodkins!" said the king. "The youth hath a pretty wit."

About this time the Princess Ostla, who began to feel better at the sight of her lover, slipped a piece of gum into her mouth and closed her teeth upon it, and even smiled a little and showed the beautiful pearls with which her mouth was set. Whereupon, as soon as the knights perceived this, 217 of them went over to the king's treasurer and settled for their horse feed and went home.

"It seems very hard," said the princess, "that I cannot marry when I chews."

But two of the knights were left, one of them being the princess' lover.

"Here's enough for a fight, anyhow," said the king. "Come hither, O knights, will ye joust for the hand of this fair lady?"

"We joust will," said the knights.

The two knights fought for two hours, and at length the princess' lover prevailed and stretched the other upon the ground. The victorious knight made his horse caracole before the king, and bowed low in his saddle.

On the Princess Ostla's cheeks was a rosy flush; in her eyes the light of excitement vied with the soft glow of love; her lips were parted, her lovely hair unbound, and she grasped the arms of her chair and leaned forward with heaving bosom and happy smile to hear the words of her lover.

"You have foughten well, sir knight," said the king. "And if there is any boon you crave you have but to name it."

"Then," said the knight, "I will ask you this: I have bought the patent rights in your kingdom for Schneider's celebrated monkey wrench, and I want a letter from you endorsing it."

"You shall have it," said the king, "but I must tell you that there is not a monkey in my kingdom."

With a yell of rage the victorious knight threw himself on his horse and rode away at a furious gallop.

The king was about to speak, when a horrible suspicion flashed upon him and he fell dead upon the grandstand.

"My God!" he cried. "He has forgotten to take the princess with him!"

78

The Cactus

The most notable thing about Time is that it is so purely relative. A large amount of reminiscence is, by common consent, conceded to the drowning man; and it is not past belief that one may review an entire courtship while removing one's gloves.

That is what Trysdale was doing, standing by a table in his bachelor apartments. On the table stood a singular-looking green plant in a red earthen jar. The plant was one of the species of cacti, and was provided with long, tentacular leaves that perpetually swayed with the slightest breeze with a peculiar beckoning motion.

Trysdale's friend, the brother of the bride, stood at a sideboard complaining at being allowed to drink alone. Both men were in evening dress. White favors like stars upon their coats shone through the gloom of the apartment.

As he slowly unbuttoned his gloves, there passed through Trysdale's mind a swift, scarifying retrospect of the last few hours. It seemed that in his nostrils was still the scent of the flowers that had been banked in odorous masses about the church, and in his ears the lowpitched hum of a thousand well-bred voices, the rustle of crisp garments, and, most insistently recurring, the drawling words of the minister irrevocably binding her to another.

From this last hopeless point of view he still strove, as if it had become a habit of his mind, to reach some conjecture as to why and how he had lost her. Shaken rudely by the uncompromising fact, he had suddenly found himself confronted by a thing he had never before faced–his own innermost, unmitigated, arid unbedecked self. He saw all the garbs of pretence and egoism that he had worn now turn to rags of folly. He shuddered at the thought that to others, before now, the garments of his soul must have appeared sorry and threadbare. Vanity and conceit? These were the joints in his armor. And how free from either she had always been——But why——

As she had slowly moved up the aisle toward the altar he had felt an unworthy, sullen exultation that had served to support him. He had told himself that her paleness was from thoughts of another than the man to whom she was about to give herself. But even that poor consolation had been wrenched from him. For, when he saw that swift, limpid, upward look that she gave the man when he took her hand, he knew himself to be forgotten. Once that same look had been raised to him, and he had gauged its meaning. Indeed, his conceit had crumbled; its last prop was gone. Why had it ended thus? There had been no quarrel between them, nothing——

For the thousandth time he remarshalled in his mind the events of those last few days before the tide had so suddenly turned.

She had always insisted upon placing him upon a pedestal, and he had accepted her homage with royal grandeur. It had been a very sweet incense that she had burned before him; so modest (he told himself); so childlike and worshipful, and (he would once have sworn) so sincere. She had invested him with an almost supernatural number of high attributes and excellencies and talents, and he had absorbed the oblation as a desert drinks the rain that can coax from it no promise of blossom or fruit.

As Trysdale grimly wrenched apart the seam of his last glove, the crowning instance of his fatuous and tardily mourned egoism came vividly back to him. The scene was the night when he had asked her to come up on his pedestal with him and share his greatness. He could not, now, for the pain of it, allow his mind to dwell upon the memory of her convincing beauty that night—the careless wave of her hair, the tenderness and virginal charm of her looks and words. But they had been enough, and they had brought him to speak. During their conversation she had said:

"And Captain Carruthers tells me that you speak the Spanish language like a native. Why have you hidden this accomplishment from me? Is there anything you do not know?"

Now, Carruthers was an idiot. No doubt he (Trysdale) had been guilty (he sometimes did such things) of airing at the club some old, canting Castilian proverb dug from the hotchpotch at the back of dictionaries. Carruthers, who was one of his incontinent admirers, was the very man to have magnified this exhibition of doubtful erudition.

But, alas! the incense of her admiration had been so sweet and flattering. He allowed the imputation to pass without denial. Without protest, he allowed her to twine about his brow this spurious bay of Spanish scholarship. He let it grace his conquering head, and, among its soft convolutions, he did not feel the prick of the thorn that was to pierce him later.

How glad, how shy, how tremulous she was! How she fluttered like a snared bird when he laid his mightiness at her feet! He could have sworn, and he could swear now, that unmistakable consent was in her eyes, but, coyly, she would give him no direct answer. "I will send you my answer to-morrow," she said; and he, the indulgent, confident victor, smilingly granted the delay. The next day he waited, impatient, in his rooms for the word. At noon her groom came to the door and left the strange cactus in the red earthen jar. There was no note, no message, merely a tag upon the plant bearing a barbarous foreign or botanical name. He waited until night, but her answer did not come. His large pride and hurt vanity kept him from seeking her. Two evenings later they met at a dinner. Their greetings were conventional, but she looked at him, breathless, wondering, eager. He was courteous, adamant, waiting her explanation. With womanly swiftness she took her cue from his manner, and turned to snow and ice. Thus, and wider from this on, they had drifted apart. Where was his fault? Who had been to blame? Humbled now, he sought the answer amid the ruins of his self-conceit. If—

The voice of the other man in the room, querulously intruding upon his thoughts, aroused him.

"I say, Trysdale, what the deuce is the matter with you? You look unhappy as if you yourself had been married instead of having acted merely as an accomplice. Look at me, another accessory, come two thousand miles on a garlicky, cockroachy banana steamer all the way from South America to connive at the sacrifice—please to observe how lightly my guilt rests upon my shoulders. Only little sister I had, too, and now she's gone. Come now! take something to ease your conscience."

"I don't drink just now, thanks," said Trysdale.

"Your brandy," resumed the other, coming over and joining him, "is abominable. Run down to see me some time at Punta Redonda, and try some of our stuff that old Garcia smuggles in. It's worth the, trip. Hallo! here's an old acquaintance. Wherever did you rake up this cactus, Trysdale?"

"A present," said Trysdale, "from a friend. Know the species?"

"Very well. It's a tropical concern. See hundreds of 'em around Punta every day. Here's the name on this tag tied to it. Know any Spanish, Trysdale?"

"No," said Trysdale, with the bitter wraith of a smile—"Is it Spanish?"

"Yes. The natives imagine the leaves are reaching out and beckoning to you. They call it by this name—Ventomarme. Name means in English, 'Come and take me.'"

Oliver Wendell Holmes

(1841-1935)

79

A Visit to the Asylum for Aged and Decayed Punsters

Having just returned from a visit to this admirable Institution in company with a friend who is one of the Directors, we propose giving a short account of what we saw and heard. The great success of the Asylum for Idiots and Feeble-minded Youth, several of the scholars from which have reached considerable distinction, one of them being connected with a leading Daily Paper in this city, and others having served in the State and National Legislatures, was the motive which led to the foundation of this excellent charity. Our late distinguished townsman, Noah Dow, Esquire, as is well known, bequeathed a large portion of his fortune to this establishment— 'being thereto moved,' as his will expressed it, 'by the desire of *N. Dowing* some public Institution for the benefit of Mankind.' Being consulted as to the Rules of the Institution and the selection of a Superintendent, he replied, that 'all Boards must construct their own Platforms of operation. Let them select *anyhow* and he should be pleased.' N.E. Howe, Esq., was chosen in compliance with this delicate suggestion.

The Charter provides for the support of 'One hundred aged and decayed Gentlemen-Punsters.' On inquiry if there way no provision for *females*, my friend called my attention to this remarkable psychological fact, namely:

THERE IS NO SUCH THING AS A FEMALE PUNSTER.

This remark struck me forcibly, and on reflection I found that *I never knew nor heard of one*, though I have once or twice heard a woman make a *single detached* pun, as I have known a hen to crow.

On arriving at the south gate of the Asylum grounds, I was about to ring, but my friend held my arm and begged me to rap with my stick, which I did. An old man with a very comical face presently opened the gate and put out his head.

"So you prefer *Cane* to *A bell*, do you?" he said—and began chuckling and coughing at a great rate.

My friend winked at me.

"You're here still, Old Joe, I see," he said to the old man.

"Yes, yes—and it's very odd, considering how often I've *bolted*, nights."

He then threw open the double gates for us to ride through.

"Now," said the old man, as he pulled the gates after us, "you've had a long journey."

"Why, how is that, Old Joe?" said my friend.

"Don't you see?" he answered; "there's the *East hinges* on the one side of the gate, and there's the *West hinges* on t'other side—haw! haw! haw!"

We had no sooner got into the yard than a feeble little gentleman, with a remarkably bright eye, came up to us, looking very serious, as if something had happened.

"The town has entered a complaint against the Asylum as a gambling establishment," he said to my friend, the Director.

"What do you mean?" said my friend.

"Why, they complain that there's a *lot o' rye* on the premises," he answered, pointing to a field of that grain—and hobbled away, his shoulders shaking with laughter, as he went.

On entering the main building, we saw the Rules and Regulations for the Asylum conspicuously posted up. I made a few extracts which may be interesting:

SECT. I. OF VERBAL EXERCISES.

5. Each Inmate shall be permitted to make Puns freely from

eight in the morning until ten at night, except during Service in the Chapel and Grace before Meals.

6. At ten o'clock the gas will be turned off, and no further Puns, Conundrums, or other play on words will be allowed to be uttered, or to be uttered aloud.

9. Inmates who have lost their faculties and cannot any longer make Puns shall be permitted to repeat such as may be selected for them by the Chaplain out of the work of *Mr. Joseph Miller.*

10. Violent and unmanageable Punsters, who interrupt others when engaged in conversation, with Puns or attempts at the same, shall be deprived of their *Joseph Millers*, and, if necessary, placed in solitary confinement.

SECT. III. OF DEPORTMENT AT MEALS.

4. No Inmate shall make any Pun, or attempt at the same, until the Blessing has been asked and the company are decently seated.

7. Certain Puns having been placed on the *Index Expurgatorius* of the Institution, no Inmate shall be allowed to utter them, on pain of being debarred the perusal of *Punch* and *Vanity Fair*, and, if repeated, deprived of his *Joseph Miller.*

Among these are the following:

Allusions to *Attic salt*, when asked to pass the salt-cellar.

Remarks on the Inmates being *mustered*, etc., etc.

Associating baked beans with the *bene*-factors of the Institution.

Saying that beef-eating is *befitting*, etc., etc.

The following are also prohibited, excepting to such Inmates as may have lost their faculties and cannot any longer make Puns of their own:

'——your own *hair* or a wig;' 'it will be *long enough*,' etc., etc.; 'little of its age,' etc., etc.; also, playing upon the following words: _hos_pital; *mayor*; *pun*; *pitied*; *bread*; *sauce*, etc., etc., etc. *See* INDEX EXPURGATORIUS, *printed for use of Inmates.*

The subjoined Conundrum is not allowed: Why is Hasty Pudding like the Prince? Because it comes attended by its *sweet*; nor this variation to it, *to wit*: Because the *'lasses runs after it.*

The Superintendent, who went round with us, had been a noted punster in his time, and well known in the business world, but lost his customers by making too free with their names—as in the famous story he set afloat in '29 *of four Jerries* attaching to the names of a noted Judge, an eminent Lawyer, the Secretary of the Board of Foreign Missions, and the well-known Landlord at Springfield. One of the *four Jerries*, he added, was of gigantic magnitude. The play on words was brought out by an accidental remark of Solomons, the well-known Banker. "*Capital punishment!*" the Jew was overheard saying, with reference to the guilty parties. He was understood, as saying, *A capital pun is meant*, which led to an investigation and the relief of the greatly excited public mind.

The Superintendent showed some of his old tendencies, as he went round with us.

"Do you know"—he broke out all at once—" why they don't take steppes in Tartary for establishing Insane Hospitals?"

We both confessed ignorance.

"Because there are *nomad* people to be found there," he said, with a dignified smile.

He proceeded to introduce us to different Inmates. The first was a middle-aged, scholarly man, who was seated at a table with a *Webster's Dictionary* and a sheet of paper before him.

"Well, what luck to-day, Mr. Mowzer?" said the Superintendent.

"Three or four only," said Mr. Mowzer. "Will you hear 'em now—now I'm here?"

We all nodded.

"Don't you see Webster *ers* in the words cent_er_ and theat_er_?

"If he spells leather *lether*, and feather *fether*, isn't there danger that he'll give us a *bad spell of weather*?

"Besides, Webster is a resurrectionist; he does not allow *u* to rest quietly in the *mould*.

"And again, because Mr. Worcester inserts an illustration in his text, is that any reason why Mr. Webster's publishers should hitch one on in their appendix? It's what I call a *Connect-a-cut* trick.

"Why is his way of spelling like the floor of an oven? Because it is *under bread*."

"Mowzer!" said the Superintendent, "that word is on the Index!"

"I forgot," said Mr. Mowzer; "please don't deprive me of *Vanity Fair* this one time, sir."

"These are all, this morning. Good day, gentlemen." Then to the Superintendent: "Add you, sir!"

The next Inmate was a semi-idiotic-looking old man. He had a heap of block-letters before him, and, as we came up, he pointed, without saying a word, to the arrangements he had made with them on the table. They were evidently anagrams, and had the merit of transposing the letters of the words employed without addition or subtraction. Here are a few of them:

TIMES. SMITE! POST. STOP!
TRIBUNE. TRUE NIB. WORLD. DR. OWL.
ADVERTISER. { RES VERI DAT. { IS TRUE. READ!
ALLOPATHY. ALL O' TH' PAY. HOMOEOPATHY. O,
THE ——! O! O, MY! PAH!

The mention of several New York papers led to two or three questions. Thus: Whether the Editor of *The Tribune* was *H.G. Really*? If the complexion of his politics were not accounted for by his being *an eager* person himself? Whether Wendell *Fillips* were not a reduced copy of John *Knocks*? Whether a New York *Feuilletoniste* is not the same thing as a *Fellow down East*?

At this time a plausible-looking, bald-headed man joined us, evidently waiting to take a part in the conversation.

"Good morning, Mr. Riggles," said the Superintendent, "Anything fresh this morning? Any Conundrum?"

"I haven't looked at the cattle," he answered, dryly.

"Cattle? Why cattle?"

"Why, to see if there's any *corn under 'em*!" he said; and immediately asked, "Why is Douglas like the earth?"

We tried, but couldn't guess.

"Because he was *flattened out at the polls*!" said Mr. Riggles.

"A famous politician, formerly," said the Superintendent. "His grandfather was a *seize-Hessian-ist* in the Revolutionary War. By the way, I hear the *freeze-oil* doctrines don't go down at New Bedford."

The next Inmate looked as if he might have been a sailor formerly.

"Ask him what his calling was," said the Superintendent.

"Followed the sea," he replied to the question put by one of us. "Went as mate in a fishing-schooner."

"Why did you give it up?"

"Because I didn't like working for *two mast-ers*," he replied.

Presently we came upon a group of elderly persons, gathered about a venerable gentleman with flowing locks, who was propounding questions to a row of Inmates.

"Can any Inmate give me a motto for M. Berger?" he said.

Nobody responded for two or three minutes. At last one old man, whom I at once recognized as a Graduate of our University (Anno 1800) held up his hand.

"Rem *a cue* tetigit."

"Go to the head of the class, Josselyn," said the venerable patriarch.

The successful Inmate did as he was told, but in a very rough way, pushing against two or three of the Class.

"How is this?" said the Patriarch.

"You told me to go up *jostlin'*," he replied.

The old gentlemen who had been shoved about enjoyed the pun too much to be angry.

Presently the Patriarch asked again:

"Why was M. Berger authorized to go to the dances given to the Prince?"

The Class had to give up this, and he answered it himself:

"Because every one of his carroms was a *tick-it* to the ball."

"Who collects the money to defray the expenses of the last campaign in Italy?" asked the Patriarch.

Here again the Class failed.

"The war-cloud's rolling *Dun*," he answered.

"And what is mulled wine made with?"

Three or four voices exclaimed at once:

"*Sizzle-y* Madeira!"

Here a servant entered, and said, "Luncheon-time." The old gentlemen, who have excellent appetites, dispersed at once, one of them politely asking us if we would not stop and have a bit of bread and a little mite of cheese.

"There is one thing I have forgotten to show you," said the Superintendent, "the cell for the confinement of violent and unmanageable Punsters."

We were very curious to see it, particularly with reference to the alleged absence of every object upon which a play of words could possibly be made.

The Superintendent led us up some dark stairs to a corridor, then along a narrow passage, then down a broad flight of steps into another passageway, and opened a large door which looked out on the main entrance.

"We have not seen the cell for the confinement of 'violent and unmanageable' Punsters," we both exclaimed.

"This is the *sell!*" he exclaimed, pointing to the outside prospect.

My friend, the Director, looked me in the face so good-naturedly that I had to laugh.

"We like to humor the Inmates," he said. "It has a bad effect, we find, on their health and spirits to disappoint them of their little pleasantries. Some of the jests to which we have listened are not new to me, though I dare say you may not have heard them often before. The same thing happens in general society, with this additional disadvantage, that there is no punishment provided for 'violent and unmanageable' Punsters, as in our Institution."

We made our bow to the Superintendent and walked to the place where our carriage was waiting for us. On our way, an exceedingly decrepit old man moved slowly toward us, with a perfectly blank look on his face, but still appearing as if he wished to speak.

"Look!" said the Director—"that is our Centenarian."

The ancient man crawled toward us, cocked one eye, with which he seemed to see a little, up at us, and said:

"Sarvant, young Gentlemen. Why is a—a—a—like a—a—a—? Give it up? Because it's a—a—a—a—."

He smiled a pleasant smile, as if it were all plain enough.

"One hundred and seven last Christmas," said the Director. "Of late years he puts his whole Conundrums in blank—but they please him just as well."

We took our departure, much gratified and instructed by our visit, hoping to have some future opportunity of inspecting the Records of this excellent Charity and making extracts for the benefit of our Readers.

Oscar Wilde
(1854-1900)

80

The Model Millionaire

Unless one is wealthy there is no use in being a charming fellow. Romance is the privilege of the rich, not the profession of the unemployed. The poor should be practical and prosaic. It is better to have a permanent income than to be fascinating. These are the great truths of modern life which Hughie Erskine never realised. Poor Hughie! Intellectually, we must admit, he was not of much importance. He never said a brilliant or even an ill-natured thing in his life. But then he was wonderfully good-looking, with his crisp brown hair, his clear-cut profile, and his grey eyes. He was as popular with men as he was with women and he had every accomplishment except that of making money. His father had bequeathed him his cavalry sword and a History of the Peninsular War in fifteen volumes. Hughie hung the first over his looking-glass, put the second on a shelf between Ruff's Guide and Bailey's Magazine, and lived on two hundred a year that an old aunt allowed him. He had tried everything. He had gone on the Stock Exchange for six months; but what was a butterfly to do among bulls and bears? He had been a tea-merchant for a little longer, but had soon tired of pekoe and souchong. Then he had tried selling dry sherry. That did not answer; the sherry was a little too dry. Ultimately he became nothing, a delightful, ineffectual young man with a perfect profile and no profession.

To make matters worse, he was in love. The girl he loved was Laura Merton, the daughter of a retired Colonel who had lost his temper and his digestion in India, and had never found either of them again. Laura adored him, and he was ready to kiss her shoe-strings. They were the handsomest couple in London, and had not a penny-piece between them. The Colonel was very fond of Hughie, but would not hear of any engagement.

"Come to me, my boy, when you have got ten thousand pounds of your own, and we will see about it," he used to say; and Hughie looked very glum in those days, and had to go to Laura for consolation.

One morning, as he was on his way to Holland Park, where the Mertons lived, he dropped in to see a great friend of his, Alan Trevor. Trevor was a painter. Indeed, few people escape that nowadays. But he was also an artist, and artists are rather rare. Personally he was a strange rough fellow, with a freckled face and a red ragged beard. However, when he took up the brush he was a real master, and his pictures were eagerly sought after. He had been very much attracted by Hughie at first, it must be acknowledged, entirely on account of his personal charm. "The only people a painter should know," he used to say, "are people who are bête and beautiful, people who are an artistic pleasure to look at and an intellectual repose to talk to. Men who are dandies and women who are darlings rule the world, at least they should do so." However, after he got to know Hughie better, he liked him quite as much for his bright, buoyant spirits and his generous, reckless nature, and had given him the permanent entrée to his studio.

When Hughie came in he found Trevor putting the finishing touches to a wonderful life-size picture of a beggar-man. The beggar himself was standing on a raised platform in a corner of the studio. He was a wizened old man, with a face like wrinkled parchment, and a most piteous expression. Over his shoulders was flung a coarse brown cloak, all tears and tatters; his thick boots were patched and cobbled, and with one hand he leant on a rough stick, while with the other he held out his battered hat for alms.

"What an amazing model!" whispered Hughie, as he shook hands with his friend.

"An amazing model?" shouted Trevor at the top of his voice; "I should think so! Such beggars as he are not to be met with every day. A trouvaille, mon cher; a living Velasquez! My stars! what an etching Rembrandt would have made of him!"

"Poor old chap!" said Hughie, "how miserable he looks! But I suppose, to you painters, his face is his fortune?"

"Certainly," replied Trevor, "you don't want a beggar to look happy, do you?"

"How much does a model get for sitting?" asked Hughie, as he found himself a comfortable seat on a divan.

"A shilling an hour."

"And how much do you get for your picture, Alan?"

"Oh, for this I get two thousand!"

"Pounds?"

"Guineas. Painters, poets, and physicians always get guineas."

"Well, I think the model should have a percentage," cried Hughie, laughing; "they work quite as hard as you do."

"Nonsense, nonsense! Why, look at the trouble of laying on the paint alone, and standing all day long at one's easel! It's all very well, Hughie, for you to talk, but I assure you that there are moments when Art almost attains to the dignity of manual labour. But you mustn't chatter; I'm very busy. Smoke a cigarette, and keep quiet."

After some time the servant came in, and told Trevor that the frame-maker wanted to speak to him.

"Don't run away, Hughie," he said, as he went out, "I will be back in a moment."

The old beggar-man took advantage of Trevor's absence to rest for a moment on a wooden bench that was behind him. He looked so forlorn and wretched that Hughie could not help pitying him, and felt in his pockets to see what money he had. All he could find was a sovereign and some coppers. "Poor old fellow," he thought to himself, "he wants it more than I do, but it means no hansoms for a fortnight"; and he walked across the studio and slipped the sovereign into the beggar's hand.

The old man started, and a faint smile flitted across his withered lips. "Thank you, sir," he said, "thank you."

Then Trevor arrived, and Hughie took his leave, blushing a little at what he had done. He spent the day with Laura, got a charming scolding for his extravagance, and had to walk home.

That night he strolled into the Palette Club about eleven o'clock, and found Trevor sitting by himself in the smoking-room drinking hock and seltzer.

"Well, Alan, did you get the picture finished all right?" he said, as he lit his cigarette.

"Finished and framed, my boy!" answered Trevor; "and, by the bye, you have made a conquest. That old model you saw is quite devoted to you. I had to tell him all about you—who you are, where you live, what your income is, what prospects you have—"

"My dear Alan," cried Hughie, "I shall probably find him waiting for me when I go home. But of course you are only joking. Poor old wretch! I wish I could do something for him. I think it is dreadful that any one should be so miserable. I have got heaps of old clothes at home—do you think he would care for any of them? Why, his rags were falling to bits."

"But he looks splendid in them," said Trevor. "I wouldn't paint him in a frock coat for anything. What you call rags I call romance. What seems poverty to you is picturesqueness to me. However, I'll tell him of your offer."

"Alan," said Hughie seriously, "you painters are a heartless lot."

"An artist's heart is his head," replied Trevor; "and besides, our business is to realise the world as we see it, not to reform it as we know it. À chacun son métier. And now tell me how Laura is. The old model was quite interested in her."

"You don't mean to say you talked to him about her?" said Hughie.

"Certainly I did. He knows all about the relentless colonel, the lovely Laura, and the £10,000."

"You told that old beggar all my private affairs?" cried Hughie, looking very red and angry.

"My dear boy," said Trevor, smiling, "that old beggar, as you call him, is one of the richest men in Europe. He could buy all London to-morrow without overdrawing his account. He has a house in every capital, dines off gold plate, and can prevent Russia going to war when he chooses."

"What on earth do you mean?" exclaimed Hughie.

"What I say," said Trevor. "The old man you saw to-day in the studio was Baron Hausberg. He is a great friend of mine, buys all my pictures and that sort of thing, and gave me a commission a month ago to paint him as a beggar. Que voulez-vous? La fantaisie d'un millionnaire! And I must say he made a magnificent figure in his rags, or perhaps I should say in my rags; they are an old suit I got in Spain."

"Baron Hausberg!" cried Hughie. "Good heavens! I gave him a sovereign!" and he sank into an armchair the picture of dismay.

"Gave him a sovereign!" shouted Trevor, and he burst into a roar of laughter. "My dear boy, you'll never see it again. Son affaire c'est l'argent des autres."

"I think you might have told me, Alan," said Hughie sulkily, "and not have let me make such a fool of myself."

"Well, to begin with, Hughie," said Trevor, "it never entered my mind that you went about distributing alms in that reckless way. I can understand your kissing a pretty model, but your giving a sovereign to an ugly one—by Jove, no! Besides, the fact is that I really was not at home to-day to any one; and when you came in I didn't know whether Hausberg would like his name mentioned. You know he wasn't in full dress."

"What a duffer he must think me!" said Hughie.

"Not at all. He was in the highest spirits after you left; kept chuckling to himself and rubbing his old wrinkled hands together. I couldn't make out why he was so interested to know all about you; but I see it all now. He'll invest your sovereign for you, Hughie, pay you the interest every six months, and have a capital story to tell after dinner."

"I am an unlucky devil," growled Hughie. "The best thing I can do is to go to bed; and, my dear Alan, you mustn't tell any one. I shouldn't dare show my face in the Row."

"Nonsense! It reflects the highest credit on your philanthropic spirit, Hughie. And don't run away. Have another cigarette, and you can talk about Laura as much as you like."

However, Hughie wouldn't stop, but walked home, feeling very unhappy, and leaving Alan Trevor in fits of laughter.

The next morning, as he was at breakfast, the servant brought him up a card on which was written, "Monsieur Gustave Naudin, de la part de M. le Baron Hausberg." "I suppose he has come for an apology," said Hughie to himself; and he told the servant to show the visitor up.

An old gentleman with gold spectacles and grey hair came into the room, and said, in a slight French accent, "Have I the honour of addressing Monsieur Erskine?"

Hughie bowed.

"I have come from Baron Hausberg," he continued. "The Baron—"

"I beg, sir, that you will offer him my sincerest apologies," stammered Hughie.

"The Baron," said the old gentleman with a smile, "has commissioned me to bring you this letter"; and he extended a sealed envelope.

On the outside was written, "A wedding present to Hugh Erskine and Laura Merton, from an old beggar," and inside was a cheque for £10,000.

When they were married Alan Trevor was the best man, and the Baron made a speech at the wedding breakfast.

"Millionaire models," remarked Alan, "are rare enough; but, by Jove, model millionaires are rarer still!"

81

The Nightingale and the Rose

"She said that she would dance with me if I brought her red roses," cried the young Student; "but in all my garden there is no red rose."

From her nest in the holm-oak tree the Nightingale heard him, and she looked out through the leaves, and wondered.

"No red rose in all my garden!" he cried, and his beautiful eyes filled with tears. "Ah, on what little things does happiness depend! I have read all that the wise men have written, and all the secrets of philosophy are mine, yet for want of a red rose is my life made wretched."

"Here at last is a true lover," said the Nightingale. "Night after night have I sung of him, though I knew him not: night after night have I told his story to the stars, and now I see him. His hair is dark as the hyacinth-blossom, and his lips are red as the rose of his desire; but passion has made his face like pale ivory, and sorrow has set her seal upon his brow."

"The Prince gives a ball to-morrow night," murmured the young Student, "and my love will be of the company. If I bring her a red rose she will dance with me till dawn. If I bring her a red rose, I shall hold her in my arms, and she will lean her head upon my shoulder, and her hand will be clasped in mine. But there is no red rose in my garden, so I shall sit lonely, and she will pass me by. She will have no heed of me, and my heart will break."

"Here indeed is the true lover," said the Nightingale. "What I sing of, he suffers—what is joy to me, to him is pain. Surely Love is a wonderful thing. It is more precious than emeralds, and dearer than fine opals. Pearls and pomegranates cannot buy it, nor is it set forth in the marketplace. It may not be purchased of the merchants, nor can it be weighed out in the balance for gold."

"The musicians will sit in their gallery," said the young Student, "and play upon their stringed instruments, and my love will dance to the sound of the harp and the violin. She will dance so lightly that her feet will not touch the floor, and the courtiers in their gay dresses will throng round her. But with me she will not dance, for I have no red rose to give her"; and he flung himself down on the grass, and buried his face in his hands, and wept.

"Why is he weeping?" asked a little Green Lizard, as he ran past him with his tail in the air.

"Why, indeed?" said a Butterfly, who was fluttering about after a sunbeam.

"Why, indeed?" whispered a Daisy to his neighbour, in a soft, low voice.

"He is weeping for a red rose," said the Nightingale.

"For a red rose?" they cried; "how very ridiculous!" and the little Lizard, who was something of a cynic, laughed outright.

But the Nightingale understood the secret of the Student's sorrow, and she sat silent in the oak-tree, and thought about the mystery of Love.

Suddenly she spread her brown wings for flight, and soared into the air. She passed through the grove like a shadow, and like a shadow she sailed across the garden.

In the centre of the grass-plot was standing a beautiful Rose-tree, and when she saw it she flew over to it, and lit upon a spray.

"Give me a red rose," she cried, "and I will sing you my sweetest song."

But the Tree shook its head.

"My roses are white," it answered; "as white as the foam of the sea, and whiter than the snow upon the mountain. But go to my brother who grows round the old sun-dial, and perhaps he will give you what you want."

So the Nightingale flew over to the Rose-tree that was growing round the old sun-dial.

"Give me a red rose," she cried, "and I will sing you my sweetest song."

But the Tree shook its head.

"My roses are yellow," it answered; "as yellow as the hair of the mermaiden who sits upon an amber throne, and yellower than the daffodil that blooms in the meadow before the mower comes with his scythe. But go to my brother who grows beneath the Student's window, and perhaps he will give you what you want."

So the Nightingale flew over to the Rose-tree that was growing beneath the Student's window.

"Give me a red rose," she cried, "and I will sing you my sweetest song."

But the Tree shook its head.

"My roses are red," it answered, "as red as the feet of the dove, and redder than the great fans of coral that wave and wave in the ocean-cavern. But the winter has chilled my veins, and the frost has nipped my buds, and the storm has broken my branches, and I shall have no roses at all this year."

"One red rose is all I want," cried the Nightingale, "only one red rose! Is there no way by which I can get it?"

"There is a way," answered the Tree; "but it is so terrible that I dare not tell it to you."

"Tell it to me," said the Nightingale, "I am not afraid."

"If you want a red rose," said the Tree, "you must build it out of music by moonlight, and stain it with your own heart's-blood. You must sing to me with your breast against a thorn. All night long you must sing to me, and the thorn must pierce your heart, and your life-blood must flow into my veins, and become mine."

"Death is a great price to pay for a red rose," cried the Nightingale, "and Life is very dear to all. It is pleasant to sit in the green wood, and to watch the Sun in his chariot of gold, and the

Moon in her chariot of pearl. Sweet is the scent of the hawthorn, and sweet are the bluebells that hide in the valley, and the heather that blows on the hill. Yet Love is better than Life, and what is the heart of a bird compared to the heart of a man?"

So she spread her brown wings for flight, and soared into the air. She swept over the garden like a shadow, and like a shadow she sailed through the grove.

The young Student was still lying on the grass, where she had left him, and the tears were not yet dry in his beautiful eyes.

"Be happy," cried the Nightingale, "be happy; you shall have your red rose. I will build it out of music by moonlight, and stain it with my own heart's-blood. All that I ask of you in return is that you will be a true lover, for Love is wiser than Philosophy, though she is wise, and mightier than Power, though he is mighty. Flame-coloured are his wings, and coloured like flame is his body. His lips are sweet as honey, and his breath is like frankincense."

The Student looked up from the grass, and listened, but he could not understand what the Nightingale was saying to him, for he only knew the things that are written down in books.

But the Oak-tree understood, and felt sad, for he was very fond of the little Nightingale who had built her nest in his branches.

"Sing me one last song," he whispered; "I shall feel very lonely when you are gone."

So the Nightingale sang to the Oak-tree, and her voice was like water bubbling from a silver jar.

When she had finished her song the Student got up, and pulled a note-book and a lead-pencil out of his pocket.

"She has form," he said to himself, as he walked away through the grove—"that cannot be denied to her; but has she got feeling? I am afraid not. In fact, she is like most artists; she is all style, without any sincerity. She would not sacrifice herself for others. She thinks merely of music, and everybody knows that the arts are selfish. Still, it must be admitted that she has some beautiful notes in her voice. What a pity it is that they do not mean anything, or do any practical good." And he went into his room, and lay down on his little pallet-bed, and began to think of his love; and, after a time, he fell asleep.

And when the Moon shone in the heavens the Nightingale flew to the Rose-tree, and set her breast against the thorn. All night long she sang with her breast against the thorn, and the cold crystal Moon leaned down and listened. All night long she sang, and the thorn went deeper and deeper into her breast, and her life-blood ebbed away from her.

She sang first of the birth of love in the heart of a boy and a girl. And on the top-most spray of the Rose-tree there blossomed a marvellous rose, petal following petal, as song followed song. Pale was it, at first, as the mist that hangs over the river—pale as the feet of the morning, and silver as the wings of the dawn. As the shadow of a rose in a mirror of silver, as the shadow of a rose in a water-pool, so was the rose that blossomed on the topmost spray of the Tree.

But the Tree cried to the Nightingale to press closer against the thorn. "Press closer, little Nightingale," cried the Tree, "or the Day will come before the rose is finished."

So the Nightingale pressed closer against the thorn, and louder and louder grew her song, for she sang of the birth of passion in the soul of a man and a maid.

And a delicate flush of pink came into the leaves of the rose, like the flush in the face of the bridegroom when he kisses the lips of the bride. But the thorn had not yet reached her heart, so the rose's heart remained white, for only a Nightingale's heart's-blood can crimson the heart of a rose.

And the Tree cried to the Nightingale to press closer against the thorn. "Press closer, little Nightingale," cried the Tree, "or the Day will come before the rose is finished."

So the Nightingale pressed closer against the thorn, and the thorn touched her heart, and a fierce pang of pain shot through her. Bitter, bitter was the pain, and wilder and wilder grew her song, for she sang of the Love that is perfected by Death, of the Love that dies not in the tomb.

And the marvellous rose became crimson, like the rose of the eastern sky. Crimson was the girdle of petals, and crimson as a ruby was the heart.

But the Nightingale's voice grew fainter, and her little wings began to beat, and a film came over her eyes. Fainter and fainter grew her song, and she felt something choking her in her throat.

Then she gave one last burst of music. The white Moon heard it, and she forgot the dawn, and lingered on in the sky. The red rose heard it, and it trembled all over with ecstasy, and opened its petals to the cold morning air. Echo bore it to her purple cavern in the hills, and woke the sleeping shepherds from their dreams. It floated through the reeds of the river, and they carried its message to the sea.

"Look, look!" cried the Tree, "the rose is finished now"; but the Nightingale made no answer, for she was lying dead in the long grass, with the thorn in her heart.

And at noon the Student opened his window and looked out.

"Why, what a wonderful piece of luck!" he cried; "here is a red rose! I have never seen any rose like it in all my life. It is so beautiful that I am sure it has a long Latin name"; and he leaned down and plucked it.

Then he put on his hat, and ran up to the Professor's house with the rose in his hand.

The daughter of the Professor was sitting in the doorway winding blue silk on a reel, and her little dog was lying at her feet.

"You said that you would dance with me if I brought you a red rose," cried the Student. "Here is the reddest rose in all the world. You will wear it to-night next your heart, and as we dance together it will tell you how I love you."

But the girl frowned.

"I am afraid it will not go with my dress," she answered; "and, besides, the Chamberlain's nephew has sent me some real jewels, and everybody knows that jewels cost far more than flowers."

"Well, upon my word, you are very ungrateful," said the Student angrily; and he threw the rose into the street, where it fell into the gutter, and a cart-wheel went over it.

"Ungrateful!" said the girl. "I tell you what, you are very rude; and, after all, who are you? Only a Student. Why, I don't believe you have even got silver buckles to your shoes as the Chamberlain's nephew has"; and she got up from her chair and went into the house.

"What a silly thing Love is," said the Student as he walked away. "It is not half as useful as Logic, for it does not prove anything, and it is always telling one of things that are not going to happen, and making one believe things that are not true. In fact, it is quite unpractical, and, as in this age to be practical is everything, I shall go back to Philosophy and study Metaphysics."

So he returned to his room and pulled out a great dusty book, and began to read.

82

The Sphinx Without a Secret

One afternoon I was sitting outside the Café de la Paix, watching the splendour and shabbiness of Parisian life, and wondering over my vermouth at the strange panorama of pride and poverty that was passing before me, when I heard some one call my name. I turned round, and saw Lord Murchison. We had not met since we had been at college together, nearly ten years before, so I was delighted to come across him again, and we shook hands warmly. At Oxford we had been great friends. I had liked him immensely, he was so handsome, so high-spirited, and so honourable. We used to say of him that he would be the best of fellows, if he did not always speak the truth, but I think we really admired him all the more for his frankness. I found him a good deal changed. He looked anxious and puzzled, and seemed to be in doubt about something. I felt it could not be modern scepticism, for Murchison was the stoutest of Tories, and believed in the Pentateuch as firmly as he believed in the House of Peers; so I concluded that it was a woman, and asked him if he was married yet.

"I don't understand women well enough," he answered.

"My dear Gerald," I said, "women are meant to be loved, not to be understood."

"I cannot love where I cannot trust," he replied.

"I believe you have a mystery in your life, Gerald," I exclaimed; "tell me about it."

"Let us go for a drive," he answered, "it is too crowded here. No, not a yellow carriage, any other colour—there, that dark green one will do"; and in a few moments we were trotting down the boulevard in the direction of the Madeleine.

"Where shall we go to?" I said.

"Oh, anywhere you like!" he answered—"to the restaurant in the Bois; we will dine there, and you shall tell me all about yourself."

"I want to hear about you first," I said. "Tell me your mystery."

He took from his pocket a little silver-clasped morocco case, and handed it to me. I opened it. Inside there was the photograph of a woman. She was tall and slight, and strangely picturesque with her large vague eyes and loosened hair. She looked like a clairvoyante, and was wrapped in rich furs.

"What do you think of that face?" he said; "is it truthful?"

I examined it carefully. It seemed to me the face of some one who had a secret, but whether that secret was good or evil I could not say. Its beauty was a beauty moulded out of many mysteries—the beauty, in fact, which is psychological, not plastic—and the faint smile that just played across the lips was far too subtle to be really sweet.

"Well," he cried impatiently, "what do you say?"

"She is the Gioconda in sables," I answered. "Let me know all about her."

"Not now," he said; "after dinner," and began to talk of other things.

When the waiter brought us our coffee and cigarettes I reminded Gerald of his promise. He rose from his seat, walked two or three times up and down the room, and, sinking into an armchair, told me the following story:—

"One evening," he said, "I was walking down Bond Street about five o'clock. There was a terrific crush of carriages, and the traffic was almost stopped. Close to the pavement was standing a little yellow brougham, which, for some reason or other, attracted my attention. As I passed by there looked out from it the face I showed you this afternoon. It fascinated me immediately. All that night I kept thinking of it, and all the next day. I wandered up and down that wretched Row, peering into every carriage, and waiting for the yellow brougham; but I could not find ma belle inconnue, and at last I began to think she was merely a dream. About a week afterwards I was dining with Madame de Rastail. Dinner was for eight o'clock; but at half-past eight we were still waiting in the drawing-room. Finally the servant threw open the door, and announced Lady Alroy. It was the woman I had been looking for. She came in very slowly, looking like a moonbeam in grey lace, and, to my intense delight, I was asked to take her in to dinner. After we had sat down, I remarked quite innocently, "I think I caught sight of you in Bond Street some time ago, Lady Alroy." She grew very pale, and said to me in a low voice, "Pray do not talk so loud; you may be overheard." I felt miserable at having made such a bad beginning, and plunged recklessly into the subject of the French plays. She spoke very little, always in the same low musical voice, and seemed as if she was afraid of some one listening. I fell passionately, stupidly in love, and the indefinable atmosphere of mystery that surrounded her excited my most ardent curiosity. When she was going away, which she did very soon after dinner, I asked her if I might call and see her. She hesitated for a moment, glanced round to see if any one was near us, and then said, "Yes; to-morrow at a quarter to five." I begged Madame de Rastail to tell me about her; but all that I could learn was that she was a widow with a beautiful house in Park Lane, and as some scientific bore began a dissertation on widows, as exemplifying the survival of the matrimonially fittest, I left and went home.

"The next day I arrived at Park Lane punctual to the moment, but was told by the butler that Lady Alroy had just gone out. I went down to the club quite unhappy and very much puzzled, and after long consideration wrote her a letter, asking if I might be allowed to try my chance some other afternoon. I had no answer for several days, but at last I got a little note saying she would be at home on Sunday at four and with this extraordinary postscript: 'Please do not write to me here again; I will explain when I see you.' On

Sunday she received me, and was perfectly charming; but when I was going away she begged of me, if I ever had occasion to write to her again, to address my letter to 'Mrs. Knox, care of Whittaker's Library, Green Street.' 'There are reasons,' she said, 'why I cannot receive letters in my own house.'

"All through the season I saw a great deal of her, and the atmosphere of mystery never left her. Sometimes I thought that she was in the power of some man, but she looked so unapproachable, that I could not believe it. It was really very difficult for me to come to any conclusion, for she was like one of those strange crystals that one sees in museums, which are at one moment clear, and at another clouded. At last I determined to ask her to be my wife: I was sick and tired of the incessant secrecy that she imposed on all my visits, and on the few letters I sent her. I wrote to her at the library to ask her if she could see me the following Monday at six. She answered yes, and I was in the seventh heaven of delight. I was infatuated with her: in spite of the mystery, I thought then—in consequence of it, I see now. No; it was the woman herself I loved. The mystery troubled me, maddened me. Why did chance put me in its track?"

"You discovered it, then?" I cried.

"I fear so," he answered. "You can judge for yourself."

"When Monday came round I went to lunch with my uncle, and about four o'clock found myself in the Marylebone Road. My uncle, you know, lives in Regent's Park. I wanted to get to Piccadilly, and took a short cut through a lot of shabby little streets. Suddenly I saw in front of me Lady Alroy, deeply veiled and walking very fast. On coming to the last house in the street, she went up the steps, took out a latch-key, and let herself in. 'Here is the mystery,' I said to myself; and I hurried on and examined the house. It seemed a sort of place for letting lodgings. On the doorstep lay her handkerchief, which she had dropped. I picked it up and put it in my pocket. Then I began to consider what I should do. I came to the conclusion that I had no right to spy on her, and I drove down to the club. At six I called to see her. She was lying on a sofa, in a tea-gown of silver tissue looped up by some strange moonstones that she always wore. She was looking quite lovely. 'I am so glad to see you,' she said; 'I have not been out all day.' I stared at her in amazement, and pulling the handkerchief out of my pocket, handed it to her. 'You dropped this in Cumnor Street this afternoon, Lady Alroy,' I said very calmly. She looked at me in terror but made no attempt to take the handkerchief. 'What were you doing there?' I asked. 'What right have you to question me?' she answered. 'The right of a man who loves you,' I replied; 'I came here to ask you to be my wife.' She hid her face in her hands, and burst into floods of tears. 'You must tell me,' I continued. She stood up, and, looking me straight in the face, said, 'Lord Murchison, there is nothing to tell you.'—'You went to meet some one,' I cried; 'this is your mystery.' She grew dreadfully white, and said, 'I went to meet no one.'—'Can't you tell the truth?' I exclaimed. 'I have told it,' she replied. I was mad, frantic; I don't know what I said, but I said terrible things to her. Finally I rushed out of the house. She wrote me a letter the next day; I sent it back unopened, and started for Norway with Alan Colville. After a month I came back, and the first thing I saw in the Morning Post was the death of Lady Alroy. She had caught a chill at the Opera, and had died in five days of congestion of the lungs. I shut myself up and saw no one. I had loved her so much, I had loved her so madly. Good God! how I had loved that woman!"

"You went to the street, to the house in it?" I said.

"Yes," he answered.

"One day I went to Cumnor Street. I could not help it; I was tortured with doubt. I knocked at the door, and a respectable-looking woman opened it to me. I asked her if she had any rooms to let. 'Well, sir,' she replied, 'the drawing-rooms are supposed to be let; but I have not seen the lady for three months, and as rent is owing on them, you can have them.'—'Is this the lady?' I said, showing the photograph. 'That's her, sure enough,' she exclaimed; 'and when is she coming back, sir?'—'The lady is dead,' I replied. 'Oh sir, I hope not!' said the woman; 'she was my best lodger. She paid me three guineas a week merely to sit in my drawing-rooms now and then.' 'She met some one here?' I said; but the woman assured me that it was not so, that she always came alone, and saw no one. 'What on earth did she do here?' I cried. 'She simply sat in the drawing-room, sir, reading books, and sometimes had tea,' the woman answered. I did not know what to say, so I gave her a sovereign and went away. Now, what do you think it all meant? You don't believe the woman was telling the truth?"

"I do."

"Then why did Lady Alroy go there?"

"My dear Gerald," I answered, "Lady Alroy was simply a woman with a mania for mystery. She took these rooms for the pleasure of going there with her veil down, and imagining she was a heroine. She had a passion for secrecy, but she herself was merely a Sphinx without a secret."

"Do you really think so?"

"I am sure of it," I replied.

He took out the morocco case, opened it, and looked at the photograph. "I wonder?" he said at last.

83

A Selfish Giant

Every afternoon, as they were coming from school, the children used to go and play in the Giant's garden.

It was a large lovely garden, with soft green grass. Here and there over the grass stood beautiful flowers like stars, and there were twelve peach-trees that in the spring-time broke out into delicate blossoms of pink and pearl, and in the autumn bore rich fruit. The birds sat on the trees and sang so sweetly that the children used to stop their games in order to listen to them. "How happy we are here!" they cried to each other.

One day the Giant came back. He had been to visit his friend the Cornish ogre, and had stayed with him for seven years. After the seven years were over he had said all that he had to say, for his conversation was limited, and he determined to return to his own castle. When he arrived he saw the children playing in the garden.

"What are you doing here?" he cried in a very gruff voice, and the children ran away.

"My own garden is my own garden," said the Giant; "any one can understand that, and I will allow nobody to play in it but myself." So he built a high wall all round it, and put up a notice-board.

> **TRESPASSERS
> WILL BE
> PROSECUTED**

He was a very selfish Giant.

The poor children had now nowhere to play. They tried to play on the road, but the road was very dusty and full of hard stones, and they did not like it. They used to wander round the high wall when their lessons were over, and talk about the beautiful garden inside. "How happy we were there," they said to each other.

Then the Spring came, and all over the country there were little blossoms and little birds. Only in the garden of the Selfish Giant it was still winter. The birds did not care to sing in it as there were no children, and the trees forgot to blossom. Once a beautiful flower put its head out from the grass, but when it saw the notice-board it was so sorry for the children that it slipped back into the ground again, and went off to sleep. The only people who were pleased were the Snow and the Frost. "Spring has forgotten this garden," they cried, "so we will live here all the year round." The Snow covered up the grass with her great white cloak, and the Frost painted all the trees silver. Then they invited the North Wind to stay with them, and he came. He was wrapped in furs, and he roared all day about the garden, and blew the chimney-pots down. "This is a delightful spot," he said, "we must ask the Hail on a visit." So the Hail came. Every day for three hours he rattled on the roof of the castle till he broke most of the slates, and then he ran round and round the garden as fast as he could go. He was dressed in grey, and his breath was like ice.

"I cannot understand why the Spring is so late in coming," said the Selfish Giant, as he sat at the window and looked out at his cold white garden; "I hope there will be a change in the weather."

But the Spring never came, nor the Summer. The Autumn gave golden fruit to every garden, but to the Giant's garden she gave none. "He is too selfish," she said. So it was always Winter there, and the North Wind, and the Hail, and the Frost, and the Snow danced about through the trees.

One morning the Giant was lying awake in bed when he heard some lovely music. It sounded so sweet to his ears that he thought it must be the King's musicians passing by. It was really only a little linnet singing outside his window, but it was so long since he had heard a bird sing in his garden that it seemed to him to be the most beautiful music in the world. Then the Hail stopped dancing over his head, and the North Wind ceased roaring, and a delicious perfume came to him through the open casement. "I believe the Spring has come at last," said the Giant; and he jumped out of bed and looked out.

What did he see?

He saw a most wonderful sight. Through a little hole in the wall the children had crept in, and they were sitting in the branches of the trees. In every tree that he could see there was a little child. And the trees were so glad to have the children back again that they had covered themselves with blossoms, and were waving their arms gently above the children's heads. The birds were flying about and twittering with delight, and the flowers were looking up through the green grass and laughing. It was a lovely scene, only in one corner it was still winter. It was the farthest corner of the garden, and in it was standing a little boy. He was so small that he could not reach up to the branches of the tree, and he was wandering all round it, crying bitterly. The poor tree was still quite covered with frost and snow, and the North Wind was blowing and roaring above it. "Climb up! little boy," said the Tree, and it bent its branches down as low as it could; but the boy was too tiny.

And the Giant's heart melted as he looked out. "How selfish I have been!" he said; "now I know why the Spring would not come here. I will put that poor little boy on the top of the tree, and then I will knock down the wall, and my garden shall be the children's playground for ever and ever." He was really very sorry for what he had done.

So he crept downstairs and opened the front door quite softly, and went out into the garden. But when the children saw him they were so frightened that they all ran away, and the garden became winter again. Only the little boy did not run, for his eyes were so full of tears that he did not see the Giant coming. And the Giant stole up behind him and took him gently in his hand, and put him up into the tree. And the tree broke at once into blossom, and the birds came and sang on it, and the little boy stretched out his two arms and flung them round the Giant's neck, and kissed him. And the other children, when they saw that the Giant was not wicked any longer, came running back, and with them came the Spring. "It is your garden now, little children," said the Giant, and he took a great axe and knocked down the wall. And when the people were going to market at twelve o'clock they found the Giant playing with the children in the most beautiful garden they had ever seen.

All day long they played, and in the evening they came to the Giant to bid him good-bye.

"But where is your little companion?" he said: "the boy I put into the tree." The Giant loved him the best because he had kissed him.

"We don't know," answered the children; "he has gone away."

"You must tell him to be sure and come here to-morrow," said the Giant. But the children said that they did not know where he lived, and had never seen him before; and the Giant felt very sad.

Every afternoon, when school was over, the children came and played with the Giant. But the little boy whom the Giant loved was never seen again. The Giant was very kind to all the children, yet he longed for his first little friend, and often spoke of him. "How I would like to see him!" he used to say.

Years went over, and the Giant grew very old and feeble. He could not play about any more, so he sat in a huge armchair, and watched the children at their games, and admired his garden. "I have many beautiful flowers," he said; "but the children are the most beautiful flowers of all."

One winter morning he looked out of his window as he was dressing. He did not hate the Winter now, for he knew that it was merely the Spring asleep, and that the flowers were resting.

Suddenly he rubbed his eyes in wonder, and looked and

looked. It certainly was a marvellous sight. In the farthest corner of the garden was a tree quite covered with lovely white blossoms. Its branches were all golden, and silver fruit hung down from them, and underneath it stood the little boy he had loved.

Downstairs ran the Giant in great joy, and out into the garden. He hastened across the grass, and came near to the child. And when he came quite close his face grew red with anger, and he said, "Who hath dared to wound thee?" For on the palms of the child's hands were the prints of two nails, and the prints of two nails were on the little feet.

"Who hath dared to wound thee?" cried the Giant; "tell me, that I may take my big sword and slay him."

"Nay!" answered the child; "but these are the wounds of Love."

"Who art thou?" said the Giant, and a strange awe fell on him, and he knelt before the little child.

And the child smiled on the Giant, and said to him, "You let me play once in your garden, to-day you shall come with me to my garden, which is Paradise."

And when the children ran in that afternoon, they found the Giant lying dead under the tree, all covered with white blossoms.

Rabindranath Tagore

(1861-1941)

84

Saved

Gouri was the beautiful, delicately nurtured child of an old and wealthy family. Her husband, Paresh, had recently by his own efforts improved his straitened circumstances. So long as he was poor, Gouri's parents had kept their daughter at home, unwilling to surrender her to privation; so she was no longer young when at last she went to her husband's house. And Paresh never felt quite that she belonged to him. He was an advocate in a small western town, and had no close kinsman with him. All his thought was about his wife, so much so that sometimes he would come home before the rising of the Court. At first Gouri was at a loss to understand why he came back suddenly. Sometimes, too, he would dismiss one of the servants without reason; none of them ever suited him long. Especially if Gouri desired to keep any particular servant because he was useful, that man was sure to be got rid of forthwith. The high-spirited Gouri greatly resented this, but her resentment only made her husband's behaviour still stranger.

At last when Paresh, unable to contain himself any longer, began in secret to cross-question the maid about her, the whole thing reached his wife's ears. She was a woman of few words; but her pride raged within like a wounded lioness at these insults, and this mad suspicion swept like a destroyer's sword between them.

Paresh, as soon as he saw that his wife understood his motive, felt no more delicacy about taxing Gouri to her face; and the more his wife treated it with silent contempt, the more did the fire of his jealousy consume him.

Deprived of wedded happiness, the childless Gouri betook herself to the consolations of religion. She sent for Paramananda Swami, the young preacher of the Prayer-House hard by, and, formally acknowledging him as her spiritual preceptor, asked him to expound the Gita to her. All the wasted love and affection of her woman's heart was poured out in reverence at the feet of her Guru.

No one had any doubts about the purity of Paramananda's character. All worshipped him. And because Paresh did not dare to hint at any suspicion against him, his jealousy ate its way into his heart like a hidden cancer.

One day some trifling circumstance made the poison overflow. Paresh reviled Paramananda to his wife as a hypocrite, and said: 'Can you swear that you are not in love with this crane that plays the ascetic?'

Gouri sprang up like a snake that has been trodden on, and, maddened by his suspicion, said with bitter irony: 'And what if I am?' At this Paresh forthwith went off to the Court-house, and locked the door on her.

In a white heat of passion at this last outrage, Gouri got the door open somehow, and left the house.

Paramananda was poring over the scriptures in his lonely room in the silence of noon. All at once, like a flash of lightning out of a cloudless sky, Gouri broke in upon his reading.

'You here?' questioned her Guru in surprise.

'Rescue me, O my lord Guru,' said she, 'from the insults of my home life, and allow me to dedicate myself to the service of your feet.'

With a stern rebuke, Paramananda sent Gouri back home. But I wonder whether he ever again took up the snapped thread of his reading.

Paresh, finding the door open, on his return home, asked: 'Who has been here?'

'No one!' his wife replied. 'I have been to the house of my Guru.'

'Why?' asked Paresh, pale and red by turns.

'Because I wanted to.'

From that day Paresh had a guard kept over the house, and behaved so absurdly that the tale of his jealousy was told all over the town.

The news of the shameful insults that were daily heaped on his disciple disturbed the religious meditations of Paramananda. He felt he ought to leave the place at once; at the same time he could not make up his mind to forsake the tortured woman. Who can say how the poor ascetic got through those terrible days and nights?

At last one day the imprisoned Gouri got a letter. 'My child,' it ran, 'it is true that many holy women have left the world to devote themselves to God. Should it happen that the trials of this world are driving your thoughts away from God, I will with God's help rescue his handmaid for the holy service of his feet. If you desire, you may meet me by the tank in your garden at two o'clock to-morrow afternoon.'

Gouri hid the letter in the loops of her hair. At noon next day when she was undoing her hair before her bath she found that the letter was not there. Could it have fallen on to the bed and got into her husband's hands, she wondered. At first, she felt a kind of fierce pleasure in thinking that it would enrage him; and then she could not bear to think that this letter, worn as a halo of deliverance on her head, might be defiled by the touch of insolent hands.

With swift steps she hurried to her husband's room. He lay groaning on the floor, with eyes rolled back and foaming mouth. She detached the letter from his clenched fist, and sent quickly for a doctor.

The doctor said it was a case of apoplexy. The patient had died before his arrival.

That very day, as it happened, Paresh had an important appointment away from home. Paramananda had found this out, and accordingly had made his appointment with Gouri. To such a depth had he fallen!

When the widowed Gouri caught sight from the window of her Guru stealing like a thief to the side of the pool, she lowered her eyes as at a lightning flash. And in that flash she saw clearly what a fall his had been.

The Guru called: 'Gouri.'

'I am coming,' she replied.

When Paresh's friends heard of his death, and came to assist in the last rites, they found the dead body of Gouri lying beside that of her husband. She had poisoned herself. All were lost in admiration of the wifely loyalty she had shown in her sati, a loyalty rare indeed in these degenerate days.

85

The Cabuliwallah

My five years old daughter Mini cannot live without chattering. I really believe that in all her life she has not wasted a minute in silence. Her mother is often vexed at this, and would stop her prattle, but I would not. To see Mini quiet is unnatural, and I cannot bear it long. And so my own talk with her is always lively.

One morning, for instance, when I was in the midst of the seventeenth chapter of my new novel, my little Mini stole into the room, and putting her hand into mine, said: "Father! Ramdayal the door-keeper calls a crow a krow! He doesn't know anything, does he?"

Before I could explain to her the differences of language in this world, she was embarked on the full tide of another subject. "What do you think, Father? Bhola says there is an elephant in the clouds, blowing water out of his trunk, and that is why it rains!"

And then, darting off anew, while I sat still making ready some reply to this last saying: "Father! what relation is Mother to you?"

With a grave face I contrived to say: "Go and play with Bhola, Mini! I am busy!"

The window of my room overlooks the road. The child had seated herself at my feet near my table, and was playing softly, drumming on her knees. I was hard at work on my seventeenth

479

chapter, where Pratap Singh, the hero, had just caught Kanchanlata, the heroine, in his arms, and was about to escape with her by the third-story window of the castle, when all of a sudden Mini left her play, and ran to the window, crying: "A Cabuliwallah! a Cabuliwallah!" Sure enough in the street below was a Cabuliwallah, passing slowly along. He wore the loose, soiled clothing of his people, with a tall turban; there was a bag on his back, and he carried boxes of grapes in his hand.

I cannot tell what were my daughter's feelings at the sight of this man, but she began to call him loudly. "Ah!" I thought, "he will come in, and my seventeenth chapter will never be finished!" At which exact moment the Cabuliwallah turned, and looked up at the child. When she saw this, overcome by terror, she fled to her mother's protection and disappeared. She had a blind belief that inside the bag, which the big man carried, there were perhaps two or three other children like herself. The pedlar meanwhile entered my doorway and greeted me with a smiling face.

So precarious was the position of my hero and my heroine, that my first impulse was to stop and buy something, since the man had been called. I made some small purchases, and a conversation began about Abdurrahman, the Russians, the English, and the Frontier Policy.

As he was about to leave, he asked: "And where is the little girl, sir?"

And I, thinking that Mini must get rid of her false fear, had her brought out.

She stood by my chair, and looked at the Cabuliwallah and his bag. He offered her nuts and raisins, but she would not be tempted, and only clung the closer to me, with all her doubts increased.

This was their first meeting.

One morning, however, not many days later, as I was leaving the house, I was startled to find Mini, seated on a bench near the door, laughing and talking, with the great Cabuliwallah at her feet. In all her life, it appeared, my small daughter had never found so patient a listener, save her father. And already the corner of her little sari was stuffed with almonds and raisins, the gift of her visitor. "Why did you give her those?" I said, and taking out an eight-anna bit, I handed it to him. The man accepted the money without demur, and slipped it into his pocket.

Alas, on my return an hour later, I found the unfortunate coin had made twice its own worth of trouble! For the Cabuliwallah had given it to Mini; and her mother, catching sight of the bright round object, had pounced on the child with: "Where did you get that eight-anna bit?"

"The Cabuliwallah gave it me," said Mini cheerfully.

"The Cabuliwallah gave it you!" cried her mother much shocked. "O Mini! how could you take it from him?"

I, entering at the moment, saved her from impending disaster, and proceeded to make my own inquiries.

It was not the first or second time, I found, that the two had met. The Cabuliwallah had overcome the child's first terror by a judicious bribery of nuts and almonds, and the two were now great friends.

They had many quaint jokes, which afforded them much amusement. Seated in front of him, looking down on his gigantic frame in all her tiny dignity, Mini would ripple her face with laughter and begin: "O Cabuliwallah! Cabuliwallah! what have you got in your bag?"

And he would reply, in the nasal accents of the mountaineer: "An elephant!" Not much cause for merriment, perhaps; but how they both enjoyed the fun! And for me, this child's talk with a grown-up man had always in it something strangely fascinating.

Then the Cabuliwallah, not to be behindhand, would take his turn: "Well, little one, and when are you going to the father-in-law's house?"

Now most small Bengali maidens have heard long ago about the father-in-law's house; but we, being a little new-fangled, had kept these things from our child, and Mini at this question must have been a trifle bewildered. But she would not show it, and with ready tact replied: "Are you going there?"

Amongst men of the Cabuliwallah's class, however, it is well known that the words father-in-law's house have a double meaning.

It is a euphemism for jail, the place where we are well cared for, at no expense to ourselves. In this sense would the sturdy pedlar take my daughter's question. "Ah," he would say, shaking his fist at an invisible policeman, "I will thrash my father-in-law!" Hearing this, and picturing the poor discomfited relative, Mini would go off into peals of laughter, in which her formidable friend would join.

These were autumn mornings, the very time of year when kings of old went forth to conquest; and I, never stirring from my little corner in Calcutta, would let my mind wander over the whole world. At the very name of another country, my heart would go out to it, and at the sight of a foreigner in the streets, I would fall to weaving a network of dreams, —the mountains, the glens, and the forests of his distant home, with his cottage in its setting, and the free and independent life of far-away wilds. Perhaps the scenes of travel conjure themselves up before me and pass and repass in my imagination all the more vividly, because I lead such a vegetable existence that a call to travel would fall upon me like a thunder-bolt. In the presence of this Cabuliwallah I was immediately transported to the foot of arid mountain peaks, with narrow little defiles twisting in and out amongst their towering heights. I could see the string of camels bearing the merchandise, and the company of turbanned merchants carrying some their queer old firearms, and some their spears, journeying downward towards the plains. I could see—. But at some such point Mini's mother would intervene, imploring me to "beware of that man."

Mini's mother is unfortunately a very timid lady. Whenever she hears a noise in the street, or sees people coming towards the house, she always jumps to the conclusion that they are either thieves, or drunkards, or snakes, or tigers, or malaria, or cockroaches, or caterpillars. Even after all these years of experience, she is not able to overcome her terror. So she was full of doubts about the Cabuliwallah, and used to beg me to keep a watchful eye on him.

I tried to laugh her fear gently away, but then she would turn round on me seriously, and ask me solemn questions:—

Were children never kidnapped?

Was it, then, not true that there was slavery in Cabul?

Was it so very absurd that this big man should be able to carry off a tiny child?

I urged that, though not impossible, it was highly improbable. But this was not enough, and her dread persisted. As it was indefinite, however, it did not seem right to forbid the man the house, and the intimacy went on unchecked.

Once a year in the middle of January Rahmun, the Cabuliwallah, was in the habit of returning to his country, and as the time approached he would be very busy, going from house to house collecting his debts. This year, however, he could always find time to come and see Mini. It would have seemed to an outsider that there was some conspiracy between the two, for when he could not come in the morning, he would appear in the evening.

Even to me it was a little startling now and then, in the corner of a dark room, suddenly to surprise this tall, loose-garmented, much bebagged man; but when Mini would run in smiling, with her "O Cabuliwallah! Cabuliwallah!" and the two friends, so far apart in age, would subside into their old laughter and their old jokes, I felt reassured.

One morning, a few days before he had made up his mind to go, I was correcting my proof sheets in my study. It was chilly weather. Through the window the rays of the sun touched my feet, and the slight warmth was very welcome. It was almost eight o'clock, and the early pedestrians were returning home with their heads covered. All at once I heard an uproar in the street, and, looking out, saw Rahmun being led away bound between two policemen, and behind them a crowd of curious boys. There were blood-stains on the clothes of the Cabuliwallah, and one of the policemen carried a knife. Hurrying out, I stopped them, and inquired what it all meant. Partly from one, partly from another, I gathered that a certain neighbour had owed the pedlar something for a Rampuri shawl, but had falsely denied having bought it, and that in the course of the quarrel Rahmun had struck him. Now, in the heat of his excitement, the prisoner began calling his enemy all sorts of names, when suddenly in a verandah of my house appeared my little Mini, with her usual exclamation: "O Cabuliwallah!

Cabuliwallah!" Rahmun's face lighted up as he turned to her. He had no bag under his arm to-day, so she could not discuss the elephant with him. She at once therefore proceeded to the next question: "Are you going to the father-in-law's house?" Rahmun laughed and said: "Just where I am going, little one!" Then, seeing that the reply did not amuse the child, he held up his fettered hands. "Ah!" he said, "I would have thrashed that old father-in-law, but my hands are bound!"

On a charge of murderous assault, Rahmun was sentenced to some years' imprisonment.

Time passed away and he was not remembered. The accustomed work in the accustomed place was ours, and the thought of the once free mountaineer spending his years in prison seldom or never occurred to us. Even my light-hearted Mini, I am ashamed to say, forgot her old friend. New companions filled her life. As she grew older, she spent more of her time with girls. So much time indeed did she spend with them that she came no more, as she used to do, to her father's room. I was scarcely on speaking terms with her.

Years had passed away. It was once more autumn and we had made arrangements for our Mini's marriage. It was to take place during the Puja Holidays. With Durga returning to Kailas, the light of our home also was to depart to her husband's house, and leave her father's in the shadow.

The morning was bright. After the rains, there was a sense of ablution in the air, and the sun-rays looked like pure gold. So bright were they, that they gave a beautiful radiance even to the sordid brick walls of our Calcutta lanes. Since early dawn that day the wedding-pipes had been sounding, and at each beat my own heart throbbed. The wail of the tune, Bhairavi, seemed to intensify my pain at the approaching separation. My Mini was to be married that night.

From early morning noise and bustle had pervaded the house. In the courtyard the canopy had to be slung on its bamboo poles; the chandeliers with their tinkling sound must be hung in each room and verandah. There was no end of hurry and excitement. I was sitting in my study, looking through the accounts, when some one entered, saluting respectfully, and stood before me. It was Rahmun the Cabuliwallah. At first I did not recognise him. He had no bag, nor the long hair, nor the same vigour that he used to have. But he smiled, and I knew him again.

"When did you come, Rahmun?" I asked him.

"Last evening," he said, "I was released from jail."

The words struck harsh upon my ears. I had never before talked with one who had wounded his fellow, and my heart shrank within itself when I realised this; for I felt that the day would have been better-omened had he not turned up.

"There are ceremonies going on," I said, "and I am busy. Could you perhaps come another day?"

At once he turned to go; but as he reached the door he hesitated, and said: "May I not see the little one, sir, for a moment?" It was his belief that Mini was still the same. He had pictured her running to him as she used, calling "O Cabuliwallah! Cabuliwallah!" He had imagined too that they would laugh and talk together, just as of old. In fact, in memory of former days he had brought, carefully wrapped up in paper, a few almonds and raisins and grapes, obtained somehow from a countryman; for his own little fund was dispersed.

I said again: "There is a ceremony in the house, and you will not be able to see any one to-day."

The man's face fell. He looked wistfully at me for a moment, then said "Good morning," and went out.

I felt a little sorry, and would have called him back, but I found he was returning of his own accord. He came close up to me holding out his offerings with the words: "I brought these few things, sir, for the little one. Will you give them to her?"

I took them and was going to pay him, but he caught my hand and said: "You are very kind, sir! Keep me in your recollection. Do not offer me money! —You have a little girl: I too have one like her in my own home. I think of her, and bring fruits to your child—not to make a profit for myself."

Saying this, he put his hand inside his big loose robe, and brought out a small and dirty piece of paper. With great care he unfolded this, and smoothed it out with both hands on my table. It bore the impression of a little hand. Not a photograph. Not a drawing. The impression of an ink-smeared hand laid flat on the paper. This touch of his own little daughter had been always on his heart, as he had come year after year to Calcutta to sell his wares in the streets.

Tears came to my eyes. I forgot that he was a poor Cabuli fruit-seller, while I was—. But no, what was I more than he? He also was a father.

That impression of the hand of his little Pārbati in her distant mountain home reminded me of my own little Mini.

I sent for Mini immediately from the inner apartment. Many difficulties were raised, but I would not listen. Clad in the red silk of her wedding-day, with the sandal paste on her forehead, and adorned as a young bride, Mini came, and stood bashfully before me.

The Cabuliwallah looked a little staggered at the apparition. He could not revive their old friendship. At last he smiled and said: "Little one, are you going to your father-in-law's house?"

But Mini now understood the meaning of the word "father-in-law," and she could not reply to him as of old. She flushed up at the question, and stood before him with her bride-like face turned down.

I remembered the day when the Cabuliwallah and my Mini had first met, and I felt sad. When she had gone, Rahmun heaved a deep sigh, and sat down on the floor. The idea had suddenly come to him that his daughter too must have grown in this long time, and that he would have to make friends with her anew. Assuredly he would not find her as he used to know her. And besides, what might not have happened to her in these eight years?

The marriage-pipes sounded, and the mild autumn sun streamed round us. But Rahmun sat in the little Calcutta lane, and saw before him the barren mountains of Afghanistan.

I took out a bank-note and gave it to him, saying: "Go back to your own daughter, Rahmun, in your own country, and may the happiness of your meeting bring good fortune to my child!"

Having made this present, I had to curtail some of the festivities. I could not have the electric lights I had intended, nor the military band, and the ladies of the house were despondent at it. But to me the wedding-feast was all the brighter for the thought that in a distant land a long-lost father met again with his only child.

86

My Fair Neighbour

My feelings towards the young widow who lived in the next house to mine were feelings of worship; at least, that is what I told to my friends and myself. Even my nearest intimate, Nabin, knew nothing of the real state of my mind. And I had a sort of pride that I could keep my passion pure by thus concealing it in the inmost recesses of my heart. She was like a dew-drenched sephali-blossom, untimely fallen to earth. Too radiant and holy for the flower-decked marriage-bed, she had been dedicated to Heaven.

But passion is like the mountain stream, and refuses to be enclosed in the place of its birth; it must seek an outlet. That is why I tried to give expression to my emotions in poems; but my unwilling pen refused to desecrate the object of my worship.

It happened curiously that just at this time my friend Nabin was afflicted with a madness of verse. It came upon him like an earthquake. It was the poor fellow's first attack, and he was equally unprepared for rhyme and rhythm. Nevertheless he could not refrain, for he succumbed to the fascination, as a widower to his second wife.

So Nabin sought help from me. The subject of his poems was the old, old one, which is ever new: his poems were all addressed to the beloved one. I slapped his back in jest, and asked him: 'Well, old chap, who is she?'

Nabin laughed, as he replied: 'That I have not yet discovered!'

I confess that I found considerable comfort in bringing help to my friend. Like a hen brooding on a duck's egg, I lavished all the warmth of my pent-up passion on Nabin's effusions. So vigorously did I revise and improve his crude productions, that the larger part of each poem became my own.

Then Nabin would say in surprise: 'That is just what I wanted to say, but could not. How on earth do you manage to get hold of all these fine sentiments?'

Poet-like, I would reply: 'They come from my imagination; for, as you know, truth is silent, and it is imagination only which waxes eloquent. Reality represses the flow of feeling like a rock; imagination cuts out a path for itself.'

And the poor puzzled Nabin would say: 'Y-e-s, I see, yes, of course'; and then after some thought would murmur again: 'Yes, yes, you are right!'

As I have already said, in my own love there was a feeling of reverential delicacy which prevented me from putting it into words. But with Nabin as a screen, there was nothing to hinder the flow of my pen; and a true warmth of feeling gushed out into these vicarious poems.

Nabin in his lucid moments would say: 'But these are yours! Let me publish them over your name.'

'Nonsense!' I would reply. 'They are yours, my dear fellow; I have only added a touch or two here and there.'

And Nabin gradually came to believe it.

I will not deny that, with a feeling akin to that of the astronomer gazing into the starry heavens, I did sometimes turn my eyes towards the window of the house next door. It is also true that now and again my furtive glances would be rewarded with a vision. And the least glimpse of the pure light of that countenance would at once still and clarify all that was turbulent and unworthy in my emotions.

But one day I was startled. Could I believe my eyes? It was a hot summer afternoon. One of the fierce and fitful nor'-westers was threatening. Black clouds were massed in the north-west corner of the sky; and against the strange and fearful light of that background my fair neighbour stood, gazing out into empty space. And what a world of forlorn longing did I discover in the far-away look of those lustrous black eyes! Was there then, perchance, still some living volcano within the serene radiance of that moon of mine? Alas! that look of limitless yearning, which was winging its way through the clouds like an eager bird, surely sought—not heaven— but the nest of some human heart!

At the sight of the unutterable passion of that look I could hardly contain myself. I was no longer satisfied with correcting crude poems. My whole being longed to express itself in some worthy action. At last I thought I would devote myself to making widow-remarriage popular in my country. I was prepared not only to speak and write on the subject, but also to spend money on its cause.

Nabin began to argue with me. 'Permanent widowhood,' said he, 'has in it a sense of immense purity and peace; a calm beauty like that of the silent places of the dead shimmering in the wan light of the eleventh moon. Would not the mere possibility of remarriage destroy its divine beauty?'

Now this sort of sentimentality always makes me furious. In time of famine, if a well-fed man speaks scornfully of food, and advises a starving man at point of death to glut his hunger on the fragrance of flowers and the song of birds, what are we to think of him? I said with some heat: 'Look here, Nabin, to the artist a ruin may be a beautiful object; but houses are built not only for the contemplation of artists, but that people may live therein; so they have to be kept in repair in spite of artistic susceptibilities. It is all very well for you to idealise widowhood from your safe distance, but you should remember that within widowhood there is a sensitive human heart, throbbing with pain and desire.'

I had an impression that the conversion of Nabin would be a difficult matter, so perhaps I was more impassioned than I need have been. I was somewhat surprised to find at the conclusion of my little speech that Nabin after a single thoughtful sigh completely agreed with me. The even more convincing peroration which I felt I might have delivered was not needed!

After about a week Nabin came to me, and said that if I would help him he was prepared to lead the way by marrying a widow himself.

I was overjoyed. I embraced him effusively, and promised him any money that might be required for the purpose. Then Nabin told me his story.

I learned that Nabin's loved one was not an imaginary being. It appeared that Nabin, too, had for some time adored a widow from a distance, but had not spoken of his feelings to any living soul. Then the magazines in which Nabin's poems, or rather my poems, used to appear had reached the fair one's hands; and the poems had not been ineffective.

Not that Nabin had deliberately intended, as he was careful to explain, to conduct love-making in that way. In fact, said he, he had no idea that the widow knew how to read. He used to post the magazine, without disclosing the sender's name, addressed to the widow's brother. It was only a sort of fancy of his, a concession to his hopeless passion. It was flinging garlands before a deity; it is not the worshipper's affair whether the god knows or not, whether he accepts or ignores the offering.

And Nabin particularly wanted me to understand that he had no definite end in view when on diverse pretexts he sought and made the acquaintance of the widow's brother. Any near relation of the loved one needs must have a special interest for the lover.

Then followed a long story about how an illness of the brother at last brought them together. The presence of the poet himself naturally led to much discussion of the poems; nor was the discussion necessarily restricted to the subject out of which it arose.

After his recent defeat in argument at my hands, Nabin had mustered up courage to propose marriage to the widow. At first he could not gain her consent. But when he had made full use of my eloquent words, supplemented by a tear or two of his own, the fair one capitulated unconditionally. Some money was now wanted by her guardian to make arrangements.

'Take it at once,' said I.

'But,' Nabin went on, 'you know it will be some months before I can appease my father sufficiently for him to continue my allowance. How are we to live in the meantime?' I wrote out the necessary cheque without a word, and then I said: 'Now tell me who she is. You need not look on me as a possible rival, for I swear I will not write poems to her; and even if I do I will not send them to her brother, but to you!'

'Don't be absurd,' said Nabin; 'I have not kept back her name because I feared your rivalry! The fact is, she was very much perturbed at taking this unusual step, and had asked me not to talk about the matter to my friends. But it no longer matters, now that everything has been satisfactorily settled. She lives at No. 19, the house next to yours.'

If my heart had been an iron boiler it would have burst. 'So she has no objection to remarriage?' I simply asked.

'Not at the present moment,' replied Nabin with a smile.

'And was it the poems alone which wrought the magic change?'

'Well, my poems were not so bad, you know,' said Nabin, 'were they?'

I swore mentally.

But at whom was I to swear? At him? At myself? At Providence? All the same, I swore.

87

The River Stairs

If you wish to hear of days gone by, sit on this step of mine, and lend your ears to the murmur of the rippling water.

The month of Ashwin (September) was about to begin. The river was in full flood. Only four of my steps peeped above the surface. The water had crept up to the low-lying parts of the bank, where the kachu plant grew dense beneath the branches of the mango grove. At that bend of the river, three old brick-heaps towered above the water around them. The fishing-boats, moored to the trunks of the bābla trees on the bank, rocked on the heaving flow-tide at dawn. The path of tall grasses on the sandbank had caught the newly risen sun; they had just begun to flower, and were not yet in full bloom.

The little boats puffed out their tiny sails on the sunlit river. The Brahmin priest had come to bathe with his ritual vessels. The women arrived in twos and threes to draw water. I knew this was the time of Kusum's coming to the bathing-stairs.

But that morning I missed her. Bhuban and Swarno mourned at the ghāt. They said that their friend had been led away to her husband's house, which was a place far away from the river, with strange people, strange houses, and strange roads.

In time she almost faded out of my mind. A year passed. The women at the ghāt now rarely talked of Kusum. But one evening I was startled by the touch of the long familiar feet. Ah, yes, but those feet were now without anklets, they had lost their old music.

Kusum had become a widow. They said that her husband had worked in some far-off place, and that she had met him only once or twice. A letter brought her the news of his death. A widow at eight years old, she had rubbed out the wife's red mark from her forehead, stripped off her bangles, and come back to her old home by the Ganges. But she found few of her old playmates there. Of them, Bhuban, Swarno, and Amala were married, and gone away; only Sarat remained, and she too, they said, would be wed in December next.

As the Ganges rapidly grows to fulness with the coming of the rains, even so did Kusum day by day grow to the fulness of beauty and youth. But her dull-coloured robe, her pensive face, and quiet manners drew a veil over her youth, and hid it from men's eyes as in a mist. Ten years slipped away, and none seemed to have noticed that Kusum had grown up.

One morning such as this, at the end of a far-off September, a tall, young, fair-skinned Sanyasi, coming I know not whence, took shelter in the Shiva temple, in front of me. His arrival was noised abroad in the village. The women left their pitchers behind, and crowded into the temple to bow to the holy man.

The crowd increased day by day. The Sanyasi's fame rapidly spread among the womenkind. One day he would recite the Bhágbat, another day he would expound the Gita, or hold forth upon a holy book in the temple. Some sought him for counsel, some for spells, some for medicines.

So months passed away. In April, at the time of the solar eclipse, vast crowds came here to bathe in the Ganges. A fair was held under the bābla tree. Many of the pilgrims went to visit the Sanyasi, and among them were a party of women from the village where Kusum had been married.

It was morning. The Sanyasi was counting his beads on my steps, when all of a sudden one of the women pilgrims nudged

another, and said: 'Why! He is our Kusum's husband!' Another
parted her veil a little in the middle with two fingers and cried out:
'Oh dear me! So it is! He is the younger son of the Chattergu family
of our village!' Said a third, who made little parade of her veil: 'Ah!
he has got exactly the same brow, nose, and eyes!' Yet another
woman, without turning to the Sanyasi, stirred the water with her
pitcher, and sighed: 'Alas! That young man is no more; he will not
come back. Bad luck to Kusum!'

But, objected one, 'He had not such a big beard'; and another,
'He was not so thin'; or 'He was most probably not so tall.' That
settled the question for the time, and the matter spread no further.

One evening, as the full moon arose, Kusum came and sat
upon my last step above the water, and cast her shadow upon me.

There was no other at the ghāt just then. The crickets were
chirping about me. The din of brass gongs and bells had ceased
in the temple—the last wave of sound grew fainter and fainter,
until it merged like the shade of a sound in the dim groves of
the farther bank. On the dark water of the Ganges lay a line of
glistening moonlight. On the bank above, in bush and hedge, under
the porch of the temple, in the base of ruined houses, by the side
of the tank, in the palm grove, gathered shadows of fantastic shape.
The bats swung from the chhatim boughs. Near the houses the
loud clamour of the jackals rose and sank into silence.

Slowly the Sanyasi came out of the temple. Descending a few
steps of the ghāt he saw a woman sitting alone, and was about to
go back, when suddenly Kusum raised her head, and looked behind
her. The veil slipped away from her. The moonlight fell upon her
face, as she looked up.

The owl flew away hooting over their heads. Starting at the
sound, Kusum came to herself and put the veil back on her head.
Then she bowed low at the Sanyasi's feet.

He gave her blessing and asked: 'Who are you?'

She replied: 'I am called Kusum.'

No other word was spoken that night. Kusum went slowly
back to her house which was hard by. But the Sanyasi remained
sitting on my steps for long hours that night. At last when the

moon passed from the east to the west, and the Sanyasi's shadow, shifting from behind, fell in front of him, he rose up and entered the temple.

Henceforth I saw Kusum come daily to bow at his feet. When he expounded the holy books, she stood in a corner listening to him. After finishing his morning service, he used to call her to himself and speak on religion. She could not have understood it all; but, listening attentively in silence, she tried to understand it. As he directed her, so she acted implicitly. She daily served at the temple—ever alert in the god's worship—gathering flowers for the puja, and drawing water from the Ganges to wash the temple floor.

The winter was drawing to its close. We had cold winds. But now and then in the evening the warm spring breeze would blow unexpectedly from the south; the sky would lose its chilly aspect; pipes would sound, and music be heard in the village after a long silence. The boatmen would set their boats drifting down the current, stop rowing, and begin to sing the songs of Krishna. This was the season.

Just then I began to miss Kusum. For some time she had given up visiting the temple, the ghāt, or the Sanyasi.

What happened next I do not know, but after a while the two met together on my steps one evening.

With downcast looks, Kusum asked: 'Master, did you send for me?'

'Yes, why do I not see you? Why have you grown neglectful of late in serving the gods?'

She kept silent.

'Tell me your thoughts without reserve.'

Half averting her face, she replied: 'I am a sinner, Master, and hence I have failed in the worship.'

The Sanyasi said: 'Kusum, I know there is unrest in your heart.'

She gave a slight start, and, drawing the end of her sári over her face, she sat down on the step at the Sanyasi's feet, and wept.

He moved a little away, and said: 'Tell me what you have in your heart, and I shall show you the way to peace.'

She replied in a tone of unshaken faith, stopping now and then for words: 'If you bid me, I must speak out. But, then, I cannot explain it clearly. You, Master, must have guessed it all. I adored one as a god, I worshipped him, and the bliss of that devotion filled my heart to fullness. But one night I dreamt that the lord of my heart was sitting in a garden somewhere, clasping my right hand in his left, and whispering to me of love. The whole scene did not appear to me at all strange. The dream vanished, but its hold on me remained. Next day when I beheld him he appeared in another light than before. That dream-picture continued to haunt my mind. I fled far from him in fear, and the picture clung to me. Thenceforth my heart has known no peace, —all has grown dark within me!'

While she was wiping her tears and telling this tale, I felt that the Sanyasi was firmly pressing my stone surface with his right foot.

Her speech done, the Sanyasi said:

'You must tell me whom you saw in your dream.'

With folded hands, she entreated: 'I cannot.'

He insisted: 'You must tell me who he was.'

Wringing her hands she asked: 'Must I tell it?'

He replied: 'Yes, you must.'

Then crying, 'You are he, Master!' she fell on her face on my stony bosom, and sobbed.

When she came to herself, and sat up, the Sanyasi said slowly: 'I am leaving this place to-night that you may not see me again. Know that I am a Sanyasi, not belonging to this world. You must forget me.'

Kusum replied in a low voice: 'It will be so, Master.'

The Sanyasi said: 'I take my leave.'

Without a word more Kusum bowed to him, and placed the dust of his feet on her head. He left the place.

The moon set; the night grew dark. I heard a splash in the water. The wind raved in the darkness, as if it wanted to blow out all the stars of the sky.

88

Raja and Rani

Bipin Kisore was born 'with a golden spoon in his mouth'; hence he knew how to squander money twice as well as how to earn it. The natural result was that he could not live long in the house where he was born.

He was a delicate young man of comely appearance, an adept in music, a fool in business, and unfit for life's handicap. He rolled along life's road like the wheel of Jagannath's car. He could not long command his wonted style of magnificent living.

Luckily, however, Raja Chittaranjan, having got back his property from the Court of Wards, was intent upon organising an Amateur Theatre Party. Captivated by the prepossessing looks of Bipin Kisore and his musical endowments, the Raja gladly 'admitted him of his crew.'

Chittaranjan was a B.A. He was not given to any excesses. Though the son of a rich man, he used to dine and sleep at appointed hours and even at appointed places. And he suddenly became enamoured of Bipin like one unto drink. Often did meals cool and nights grow old while he listened to Bipin and discussed with him the merits of operatic compositions. The Dewan remarked that the only blemish in the otherwise perfect character of his master was his inordinate fondness for Bipin Kisore.

Rani Basanta Kumari raved at her husband, and said that he was wasting himself on a luckless baboon. The sooner she could do away with him, the easier she would feel.

The Raja was much pleased in his heart at this seeming jealousy of his youthful wife. He smiled, and thought that women-folk know only one man upon the earth—him whom they love; and never think of other men's deserts. That there may be many whose merits deserve regard, is not recorded in the scriptures of women. The only good man and the only object of a woman's favours is he who has blabbered into her ears the matrimonial incantations. A little moment behind the usual hour of her husband's meals is a world of anxiety to her, but she never cares a brass button if her husband's dependents have a mouthful or not. This inconsiderate partiality of the softer sex might be cavilled at, but to Chittaranjan it did not seem unpleasant. Thus, he would often indulge in hyperbolic laudations of Bipin in his wife's presence, just to provoke a display of her delightful fulminations.

But what was sport to the 'royal' couple, was death to poor Bipin. The servants of the house, as is their wont, took their cue from the Rani's apathetic and wilful neglect of the wretched hanger-on, and grew more apathetic and wilful still. They contrived to forget to look after his comforts, to Bipin's infinite chagrin and untold sufferings.

Once the Rani rebuked the servant Puté, and said: 'You are always shirking work; what do you do all through the day?' 'Pray, madam, the whole day is taken up in serving Bipin Babu under the Maharaja's orders,' stammered the poor valet.

The Rani retorted: 'Your Bipin Babu is a great Nawab, eh?' This was enough for Puté. He took the hint. From the very next day he left Bipin Babu's orts as they were, and at times forgot to cover the food for him. With unpractised hands Bipin often scoured his own dishes and not unfrequently went without meals. But it was not in him to whine and report to the Raja. It was not in him to lower himself by petty squabblings with menials. He did not mind it; he took everything in good part. And thus while the Raja's favours grew, the Rani's disfavour intensified, and at last knew no bounds.

Now the opera of Subhadraharan was ready after due rehearsal. The stage was fitted up in the palace court-yard. The Raja acted the part of 'Krishna,' and Bipin that of 'Arjuna.' Oh, how sweetly he sang! how beautiful he looked! The audience applauded in transports of joy.

The play over, the Raja came to the Rani and asked her how she liked it. The Rani replied: 'Indeed, Bipin acted the part of "Arjuna" gloriously! He does look like the scion of a noble family. His voice is rare!' The Raja said jocosely: 'And how do I look? Am I not fair? Have I not a sweet voice?' 'Oh, yours is different case!' added the Rani, and again fell to dilating on the histrionic abilities of Bipin Kisore.

The tables were now turned. He who used to praise, now began to deprecate. The Raja, who was never weary of indulging in high-sounding panegyrics of Bipin before his consort, now suddenly fell reflecting that, after all, unthinking people made too much of Bipin's actual merits. What was extraordinary about his appearance or voice? A short while before he himself was one of those unthinking men, but in a sudden and mysterious way he developed symptoms of thoughtfulness!

From the day following, every good arrangement was made for Bipin's meals. The Rani told the Raja: 'It is undoubtedly wrong to lodge Bipin Babu with the petty officers of the Raj in the Kachari; for all he now is, he was once a man of means.' The Raja ejaculated curtly: 'Ha!' and turned the subject. The Rani proposed that there might be another performance on the occasion of the first-rice ceremony of the 'royal' weanling. The Raja heard and heard her not.

Once on being reprimanded by the Raja for not properly laying his cloth, the servant Puté replied: 'What can I do? According to the Rani's behests I have to look after Bipin Babu and wait on him the livelong day.' This angered the Raja, and he exclaimed, highly nettled: 'Pshaw! Bipin Babu is a veritable Nawab, I see! Can't he cleanse his own dishes himself?' The servant, as before, took his cue, and Bipin lapsed back into his former wretchedness.

The Rani liked Bipin's songs—they were sweet—there was

no gainsaying it. When her husband sat with Bipin to the wonted discourses of sweet music of an evening, she would listen from behind the screen in an adjoining room. Not long afterwards, the Raja began again his old habit of dining and sleeping at regular hours. The music came to an end. Bipin's evening services were no more needed.

Raja Chittaranjan used to look after his zemindari affairs at noon. One day he came earlier to the zenana, and found his consort reading something. On his asking her what she read, the Rani was a little taken aback, but promptly replied: 'I am conning over a few songs from Bipin Babu's song-book. We have not had any music since you tired abruptly of your musical hobby.' Poor woman! it was she who had herself made no end of efforts to eradicate the hobby from her husband's mind.

On the morrow the Raja dismissed Bipin—without a thought as to how and where the poor fellow would get a morsel henceforth!

Nor was this the only matter of regret to Bipin. He had been bound to the Raja by the dearest and most sincere tie of attachment. He served him more for affection than for pay. He was fonder of his friend than of the wages he received. Even after deep cogitation, Bipin could not ascertain the cause of the Raja's sudden estrangement. ''Tis Fate! all is Fate!' Bipin said to himself. And then, silently and bravely, he heaved a deep sigh, picked up his old guitar, put it up in the case, paid the last two coins in his pocket as a farewell bakshish to Puté, and walked out into the wide wide world where he had not a soul to call his friend.

89

The Postmaster

The postmaster first took up his duties in the village of Ulapur. Though the village was a small one, there was an indigo factory near by, and the proprietor, an Englishman, had managed to get a post office established.

Our postmaster belonged to Calcutta. He felt like a fish out of water in this remote village. His office and living-room were in a dark thatched shed, not far from a green, slimy pond, surrounded on all sides by a dense growth.

The men employed in the indigo factory had no leisure; moreover, they were hardly desirable companions for decent folk. Nor is a Calcutta boy an adept in the art of associating with others. Among strangers he appears either proud or ill at ease. At any rate, the postmaster had but little company; nor had he much to do.

At times he tried his hand at writing a verse or two. That the movement of the leaves and the clouds of the sky were enough to fill life with joy—such were the sentiments to which he sought to give expression. But God knows that the poor fellow would have felt it as the gift of a new life, if some genie of the Arabian Nights had in one night swept away the trees, leaves and all, and replaced them with a macadamised road, hiding the clouds from view with rows of tall houses.

The postmaster's salary was small. He had to cook his own meals, which he used to share with Ratan, an orphan girl of the village, who did odd jobs for him.

When in the evening the smoke began to curl up from the village cowsheds, and the cicalas chirped in every bush; when the mendicants of the Baül sect sang their shrill songs in their daily meeting-place, when any poet, who had attempted to watch the movement of the leaves in the dense bamboo thickets, would have felt a ghostly shiver run down his back, the postmaster would light his little lamp, and call out "Ratan."

Ratan would sit outside waiting for this call, and, instead of coming in at once, would reply, "Did you call me, sir?"

"What are you doing?" the postmaster would ask.

"I must be going to light the kitchen fire," would be the answer.

And the postmaster would say: "Oh, let the kitchen fire be for awhile; light me my pipe first."

At last Ratan would enter, with puffed-out cheeks, vigorously blowing into a flame a live coal to light the tobacco. This would give the postmaster an opportunity of conversing. "Well, Ratan," perhaps he would begin, "do you remember anything of your mother?" That was a fertile subject. Ratan partly remembered, and partly didn't. Her father had been fonder of her than her mother; him she recollected more vividly. He used to come home in the evening after his work, and one or two evenings stood out more clearly than others, like pictures in her memory. Ratan would sit on the floor near the postmaster's feet, as memories crowded in upon her. She called to mind a little brother that she had— and how on some bygone cloudy day she had played at fishing with him on the edge of the pond, with a twig for a make-believe fishing-rod. Such little incidents would drive out greater events from her mind. Thus, as they talked, it would often get very late, and the postmaster would feel too lazy to do any cooking at all. Ratan would then hastily light the fire, and toast some unleavened bread, which, with the cold remnants of the morning meal, was enough for their supper.

On some evenings, seated at his desk in the corner of the big empty shed, the postmaster too would call up memories of his own home, of his mother and his sister, of those for whom in his exile his heart was sad—memories which were always haunting him, but which he could not talk about with the men of the factory, though he found himself naturally recalling them aloud in the presence of the simple little girl. And so it came about that the girl would allude to his people as mother, brother, and sister, as if she had known them all her life. In fact, she had a complete picture of each one of them painted in her little heart.

One noon, during a break in the rains, there was a cool soft breeze blowing; the smell of the damp grass and leaves in the hot sun felt like the warm breathing of the tired earth on one's body. A persistent bird went on all the afternoon repeating the burden of its one complaint in Nature's audience chamber.

The postmaster had nothing to do. The shimmer of the freshly washed leaves, and the banked-up remnants of the retreating rain-clouds were sights to see; and the postmaster was watching them and thinking to himself: "Oh, if only some kindred soul were near—just one loving human being whom I could hold near my heart!" This was exactly, he went on to think, what that bird was trying to say, and it was the same feeling which the murmuring leaves were striving to express. But no one knows, or would believe, that such an idea might also take possession of an ill-paid village postmaster in the deep, silent mid-day interval of his work.

The postmaster sighed, and called out "Ratan." Ratan was then sprawling beneath the guava-tree, busily engaged in eating unripe guavas. At the voice of her master, she ran up breathlessly, saying: "Were you calling me, Dada?" "I was thinking," said the postmaster, "of teaching you to read." And then for the rest of the afternoon he taught her the alphabet.

Thus, in a very short time, Ratan had got as far as the double consonants.

It seemed as though the showers of the season would never end. Canals, ditches, and hollows were all overflowing with water. Day and night the patter of rain was heard, and the croaking of frogs. The village roads became impassable, and marketing had to be done in punts.

One heavily clouded morning, the postmaster's little pupil had been long waiting outside the door for her call, but, not hearing it as usual, she took up her dog-eared book, and slowly entered the room. She found her master stretched out on his bed, and, thinking that he was resting, she was about to retire on tip-toe, when she suddenly heard her name—"Ratan!" She turned at once and asked: "Were you sleeping, Dada?" The postmaster in a plaintive voice said: "I am not well. Feel my head; is it very hot?"

In the loneliness of his exile, and in the gloom of the rains, his ailing body needed a little tender nursing. He longed to remember the touch on the forehead of soft hands with tinkling bracelets, to imagine the presence of loving womanhood, the nearness of mother and sister. And the exile was not disappointed. Ratan ceased to be a little girl. She at once stepped into the post of mother, called in the village doctor, gave the patient his pills at the proper intervals, sat up all night by his pillow, cooked his gruel for him, and every now and then asked: "Are you feeling a little better, Dada?"

It was some time before the postmaster, with weakened body, was able to leave his sick-bed. "No more of this," said he with decision. "I must get a transfer." He at once wrote off to Calcutta an application for a transfer, on the ground of the unhealthiness of the place.

Relieved from her duties as nurse, Ratan again took up her old place outside the door. But she no longer heard the same old call. She would sometimes peep inside furtively to find the postmaster sitting on his chair, or stretched on his bed, and staring absent-mindedly into the air. While Ratan was awaiting her call, the postmaster was awaiting a reply to his application. The girl read her old lessons over and over again—her great fear was lest, when the call came, she might be found wanting in the double consonants. At last, after a week, the call did come one evening. With an overflowing heart Ratan rushed into the room with her—"Were you calling me, Dada?"

The postmaster said: "I am going away to-morrow, Ratan."

"Where are you going, Dada?"

"I am going home."

"When will you come back?"

"I am not coming back."

Ratan asked no other question. The postmaster, of his own accord, went on to tell her that his application for a transfer had been rejected, so he had resigned his post and was going home.

For a long time neither of them spoke another word. The lamp went on dimly burning, and from a leak in one corner of the thatch water dripped steadily into an earthen vessel on the floor beneath it.

After a while Ratan rose, and went off to the kitchen to prepare the meal; but she was not so quick about it as on other days. Many new things to think of had entered her little brain. When the postmaster had finished his supper, the girl suddenly asked him: "Dada, will you take me to your home?"

The postmaster laughed. "What an idea!" said he; but he did not think it necessary to explain to the girl wherein lay the absurdity.

That whole night, in her waking and in her dreams, the postmaster's laughing reply haunted her—"What an idea!"

On getting up in the morning, the postmaster found his bath ready. He had stuck to his Calcutta habit of bathing in water drawn and kept in pitchers, instead of taking a plunge in the river as was the custom of the village. For some reason or other, the girl could not ask him about the time of his departure, so she had fetched the water from the river long before sunrise, that it should be ready as early as he might want it. After the bath came a call for Ratan. She entered noiselessly, and looked silently into her master's face for orders. The master said: "You need not be anxious about my going away, Ratan; I shall tell my successor to look after you." These words were kindly meant, no doubt: but inscrutable are the ways of a woman's heart!

Ratan had borne many a scolding from her master without complaint, but these kind words she could not bear. She burst out weeping, and said: "No, no, you need not tell anybody anything at all about me; I don't want to stay on here."

The postmaster was dumbfounded. He had never seen Ratan like this before.

The new incumbent duly arrived, and the postmaster, having given over charge, prepared to depart. Just before starting he called Ratan and said: "Here is something for you; I hope it will keep you for some little time." He brought out from his pocket the whole of his month's salary, retaining only a trifle for his travelling expenses. Then Ratan fell at his feet and cried: "Oh, Dada, I pray you, don't give me anything, don't in any way trouble about me," and then she ran away out of sight.

The postmaster heaved a sigh, took up his carpet bag, put his umbrella over his shoulder, and, accompanied by a man carrying his many-coloured tin trunk, he slowly made for the boat.

When he got in and the boat was under way, and the rain-swollen river, like a stream of tears welling up from the earth, swirled and sobbed at her bows, then he felt a pain at heart; the grief-stricken face of a village girl seemed to represent for him the great unspoken pervading grief of Mother Earth herself. At one time he had an impulse to go back, and bring away along with him that lonesome waif, forsaken of the world. But the wind had just filled the sails, the boat had got well into the middle of the turbulent current, and already the village was left behind, and its outlying burning-ground came in sight.

So the traveller, borne on the breast of the swift-flowing river, consoled himself with philosophical reflections on the numberless meetings and partings going on in the world—on death, the great parting, from which none returns.

But Ratan had no philosophy. She was wandering about the post office in a flood of tears. It may be that she had still a lurking hope in some corner of her heart that her Dada would return, and that is why she could not tear herself away. Alas for our foolish human nature! Its fond mistakes are persistent. The dictates of reason take a long time to assert their own sway. The surest proofs meanwhile are disbelieved. False hope is clung to with all one's might and main, till a day comes when it has sucked the heart dry and it forcibly breaks through its bonds and departs. After that comes the misery of awakening, and then once again the longing to get back into the maze of the same mistakes.

90

Subha

When the girl was given the name of Subhashini, who could have guessed that she would prove dumb? Her two elder sisters were Sukeshini and Suhasini, and for the sake of uniformity her father named his youngest girl Subhashini. She was called Subha for short.

Her two elder sisters had been married with the usual cost and difficulty, and now the youngest daughter lay like a silent weight upon the heart of her parents. All the world seemed to think that, because she did not speak, therefore she did not feel; it discussed her future and its own anxiety freely in her presence. She had understood from her earliest childhood that God had sent her like a curse to her father's house, so she withdrew herself from ordinary people and tried to live apart. If only they would all forget her she felt she could endure it. But who can forget pain? Night and day her parents' minds were aching on her account. Especially her mother looked upon her as a deformity in herself. To a mother a daughter is a more closely intimate part of herself than a son can be; and a fault in her is a source of personal shame. Banikantha, Subha's father, loved her rather better than his other daughters; her mother regarded her with aversion as a stain upon her own body.

If Subha lacked speech, she did not lack a pair of large dark eyes, shaded with long lashes; and her lips trembled like a leaf in response to any thought that rose in her mind.

When we express our thought in words, the medium is not found easily. There must be a process of translation, which is often inexact, and then we fall into error. But black eyes need no translating; the mind itself throws a shadow upon them. In them thought opens or shuts, shines forth or goes out in darkness, hangs steadfast like the setting moon or like the swift and restless lightning illumines all quarters of the sky. They who from birth have had no other speech than the trembling of their lips learn a language of the eyes, endless in expression, deep as the sea, clear as the heavens, wherein play dawn and sunset, light and shadow. The dumb have a lonely grandeur like Nature's own. Wherefore the other children almost dreaded Subha and never played with her. She was silent and companionless as noontide.

The hamlet where she lived was Chandipur. Its river, small for a river of Bengal, kept to its narrow bounds like a daughter of the middle class. This busy streak of water never overflowed its banks, but went about its duties as though it were a member of every family in the villages beside it. On either side were houses and banks shaded with trees. So stepping from her queenly throne, the river-goddess became a garden deity of each home, and forgetful of herself performed her task of endless benediction with swift and cheerful foot.

Banikantha's house looked out upon the stream. Every hut and stack in the place could be seen by the passing boatmen. I know not if amid these signs of worldly wealth any one noticed the little girl who, when her work was done, stole away to the waterside and sat there. But here Nature fulfilled her want of speech and spoke for her. The murmur of the brook, the voice of the village folk, the songs of the boatmen, the crying of the birds and rustle of trees mingled and were one with the trembling of her heart. They became one vast wave of sound which beat upon her restless soul. This murmur and movement of Nature were the dumb girl's language; that speech of the dark eyes, which the long lashes shaded, was the language of the world about her. From the trees, where the cicalas chirped, to the quiet stars there was nothing but signs and gestures, weeping and sighing. And in the deep mid-noon, when the boatmen and fisher-folk had gone to their dinner, when the villagers slept and birds were still, when the ferry-boats were idle, when the great busy world paused in its toil and became suddenly a lonely, awful giant, then beneath the vast impressive heavens there were only dumb Nature and a dumb girl, sitting very silent, —one under the spreading sunlight, the other where a small tree cast its shadow.

But Subha was not altogether without friends. In the stall were two cows, Sarbbashi and Panguli. They had never heard their names from her lips, but they knew her footfall. Though she had no words, she murmured lovingly and they understood her gentle murmuring better than all speech. When she fondled them or scolded or coaxed them, they understood her better than men could do. Subha would come to the shed and throw her arms round Sarbbashi's neck; she would rub her cheek against her friend's, and Panguli would turn her great kind eyes and lick her face. The girl paid them three regular visits every day and others that were irregular. Whenever she heard any words that hurt her, she would come to these dumb friends out of due time. It was as though they guessed her anguish of spirit from her quiet look of sadness. Coming close to her, they would rub their horns softly against her arms, and in dumb, puzzled fashion try to comfort her. Besides these two, there were goats and a kitten; but Subha had not the same equality of friendship with them, though they showed the same attachment. Every time it got a chance, night or day, the kitten would jump into her lap, and settle down to slumber, and show its appreciation of an aid to sleep as Subha drew her soft fingers over its neck and back.

Subha had a comrade also among the higher animals, and it is hard to say what were the girl's relations with him; for he could speak, and his gift of speech left them without any common language. He was the youngest boy of the Gosains, Pratap by name, an idle fellow. After long effort, his parents had abandoned the hope that he would ever make his living. Now losels have this advantage, that, though their own folk disapprove of them, they are generally popular with every one else. Having no work to chain them, they become public property. Just as every town needs an open space where all may breathe, so a village needs two or three gentlemen of leisure, who can give time to all; then, if we are lazy and want a companion, one is to hand.

Pratap's chief ambition was to catch fish. He managed to waste a lot of time this way, and might be seen almost any afternoon so employed. It was thus most often that he met Subha. Whatever he was about, he liked a companion; and, when one is catching fish, a silent companion is best of all. Pratap respected Subha for her taciturnity, and, as every one called her Subha, he showed his affection by calling her Su. Subha used to sit beneath a tamarind, and Pratap, a little distance off, would cast his line. Pratap took with him a small allowance of betel, and Subha prepared it for him. And I think that, sitting and gazing a long while, she desired ardently to bring some great help to Pratap, to be of real aid, to prove by any means that she was not a useless burden to the world. But there was nothing to do. Then she turned to the Creator in prayer for some rare power, that by an astonishing miracle she might startle Pratap into exclaiming: "My! I never dreamt our Su could have done this!"

Only think, if Subha had been a water nymph, she might have risen slowly from the river, bringing the gem of a snake's crown to the landing-place. Then Pratap, leaving his paltry fishing, might dive into the lower world, and see there, on a golden bed in a palace of silver, whom else but dumb little Su, Banikantha's child? Yes, our Su, the only daughter of the king of that shining city of jewels! But that might not be, it was impossible. Not that anything is really impossible, but Su had been born, not into the royal house of Patalpur, but into Banikantha's family, and she knew no means of astonishing the Gosains' boy.

Gradually she grew up. Gradually she began to find herself. A new inexpressible consciousness like a tide from the central places of the sea, when the moon is full, swept through her. She saw herself, questioned herself, but no answer came that she could understand.

Once upon a time, late on a night of full moon, she slowly opened her door and peeped out timidly. Nature, herself at full moon, like lonely Subha, was looking down on the sleeping earth. Her strong young life beat within her; joy and sadness filled her being to its brim; she reached the limits even of her own illimitable loneliness, nay, passed beyond them. Her heart was heavy, and she could not speak. At the skirts of this silent troubled Mother there stood a silent troubled girl.

The thought of her marriage filled her parents with an anxious care. People blamed them, and even talked of making them outcasts. Banikantha was well off; they had fish-curry twice daily; and consequently he did not lack enemies. Then the women interfered, and Bani went away for a few days. Presently he returned and said: "We must go to Calcutta."

They got ready to go to this strange country. Subha's heart was heavy with tears, like a mist-wrapt dawn. With a vague fear that had been gathering for days, she dogged her father and mother like a dumb animal. With her large eyes wide open, she scanned their faces as though she wished to learn something. But not a word did they vouchsafe. One afternoon in the midst of all this, as Pratap was fishing, he laughed: "So then, Su, they have caught your bridegroom, and you are going to be married! Mind you don't forget me altogether!" Then he turned his mind again to his fish. As a stricken doe looks in the hunter's face, asking in silent agony: "What have I done to you?" so Subha looked at Pratap. That day she sat no longer beneath her tree. Banikantha, having finished his nap, was smoking in his bedroom when Subha dropped down at his feet and burst out weeping as she gazed towards him. Banikantha tried to comfort her, and his cheek grew wet with tears.

It was settled that on the morrow they should go to Calcutta. Subha went to the cow-shed to bid farewell to her childhood's comrades. She fed them with her hand; she clasped their necks; she looked into their faces, and tears fell fast from the eyes which spoke for her. That night was the tenth of the moon. Subha left her room, and flung herself down on her grassy couch beside her dear river. It was as if she threw her arms about Earth, her strong silent mother, and tried to say: "Do not let me leave you, mother. Put your arms about me, as I have put mine about you, and hold me fast."

One day in a house in Calcutta, Subha's mother dressed her up with great care. She imprisoned her hair, knotting it up in laces, she hung her about with ornaments, and did her best to kill her natural beauty. Subha's eyes filled with tears. Her mother, fearing they would grow swollen with weeping, scolded her harshly, but the tears disregarded the scolding. The bridegroom came with a friend to inspect the bride. Her parents were dizzy with anxiety and fear when they saw the god arrive to select the beast for his sacrifice. Behind the stage, the mother called her instructions aloud, and increased her daughter's weeping twofold, before she sent her into the examiner's presence. The great man, after scanning her a long time, observed: "Not so bad."

He took special note of her tears, and thought she must have a tender heart. He put it to her credit in the account, arguing that the heart, which to-day was distressed at leaving her parents, would presently prove a useful possession. Like the oyster's pearls, the child's tears only increased her value, and he made no other comment.

The almanac was consulted, and the marriage took place on an auspicious day. Having delivered over their dumb girl into another's hands, Subha's parents returned home. Thank God! Their caste in this and their safety in the next world were assured! The bridegroom's work lay in the west, and shortly after the marriage he took his wife thither.

In less than ten days every one knew that the bride was dumb! At least, if any one did not, it was not her fault, for she deceived no one. Her eyes told them everything, though no one understood her. She looked on every hand, she found no speech, she missed the faces, familiar from birth, of those who had understood a dumb girl's language. In her silent heart there sounded an endless, voiceless weeping, which only the Searcher of Hearts could hear.

Rudyard Kipling

(1865-1936)

91

How the Leopard Got His Spots

In the days when everybody started fair, Best Beloved, the Leopard lived in a place called the High Veldt. "Member it wasn't the Low Veldt, or the Bush Veldt, or the Sour Veldt, but the 'sclusively bare, hot, shiny High Veldt, where there was sand and sandy-coloured rock and 'sclusively tufts of sandy-yellowish grass. The Giraffe and the Zebra and the Eland and the Koodoo and the Hartebeest lived there; and they were 'sclusively sandy-yellow-brownish all over; but the Leopard, he was the 'sclusivest sandiest-yellowish-brownest of them all—a greyish-yellowish catty-shaped kind of beast, and he matched the 'sclusively yellowish-greyish-brownish colour of the High Veldt to one hair. This was very bad for the Giraffe and the Zebra and the rest of them; for he would lie down by a 'sclusively yellowish-greyish-brownish stone or clump of grass, and when the Giraffe or the Zebra or the Eland or the Koodoo or the Bush-Buck or the Bonte-Buck came by he would surprise them out of their jumpsome lives. He would indeed! And, also, there was an Ethiopian with bows and arrows (a 'sclusively greyish-brownish-yellowish man he was then), who lived on the High Veldt with the Leopard; and the two used to hunt together—the Ethiopian with his bows and arrows, and the Leopard 'sclusively with his teeth and claws—till the Giraffe and the Eland and the Koodoo and the

Quagga and all the rest of them didn't know which way to jump, Best Beloved. They didn't indeed!

After a long time—things lived for ever so long in those days—they learned to avoid anything that looked like a Leopard or an Ethiopian; and bit by bit—the Giraffe began it, because his legs were the longest—they went away from the High Veldt. They scuttled for days and days and days till they came to a great forest, 'sclusively full of trees and bushes and stripy, speckly, patchy-blatchy shadows, and there they hid: and after another long time, what with standing half in the shade and half out of it, and what with the slippery-slidy shadows of the trees falling on them, the Giraffe grew blotchy, and the Zebra grew stripy, and the Eland and the Koodoo grew darker, with little wavy grey lines on their backs like bark on a tree trunk; and so, though you could hear them and smell them, you could very seldom see them, and then only when you knew precisely where to look. They had a beautiful time in the 'sclusively speckly-spickly shadows of the forest, while the Leopard and the Ethiopian ran about over the 'sclusively greyish-yellowish-reddish High Veldt outside, wondering where all their breakfasts and their dinners and their teas had gone. At last they were so hungry that they ate rats and beetles and rock-rabbits, the Leopard and the Ethiopian, and then they had the Big Tummy-ache, both together; and then they met Baviaan—the dog-headed, barking Baboon, who is Quite the Wisest Animal in All South Africa.

Said Leopard to Baviaan (and it was a very hot day), "Where has all the game gone?"

And Baviaan winked. He knew.

Said the Ethiopian to Baviaan, "Can you tell me the present habitat of the aboriginal Fauna?" (That meant just the same thing, but the Ethiopian always used long words. He was a grown-up.)

And Baviaan winked. He knew.

Then said Baviaan, "The game has gone into other spots; and my advice to you, Leopard, is to go into other spots as soon as you can."

And the Ethiopian said, "That is all very fine, but I wish to know whither the aboriginal Fauna has migrated."

Then said Baviaan, "The aboriginal Fauna has joined the aboriginal Flora because it was high time for a change; and my advice to you, Ethiopian, is to change as soon as you can."

That puzzled the Leopard and the Ethiopian, but they set off to look for the aboriginal Flora, and presently, after ever so many days, they saw a great, high, tall forest full of tree trunks all 'sclusively speckled and sprottled and spotted, dotted and splashed and slashed and hatched and cross-hatched with shadows. (Say that quickly aloud, and you will see how very shadowy the forest must have been.)

"What is this," said the Leopard, "that is so 'sclusively dark, and yet so full of little pieces of light?"

"I don't know, said the Ethiopian, "but it ought to be the aboriginal Flora. I can smell Giraffe, and I can hear Giraffe, but I can't see Giraffe."

"That's curious," said the Leopard. "I suppose it is because we have just come in out of the sunshine. I can smell Zebra, and I can hear Zebra, but I can't see Zebra."

"Wait a bit, said the Ethiopian. "It's a long time since we've hunted 'em. Perhaps we've forgotten what they were like."

"Fiddle!" said the Leopard. "I remember them perfectly on the High Veldt, especially their marrow-bones. Giraffe is about seventeen feet high, of a 'sclusively fulvous golden-yellow from head to heel; and Zebra is about four and a half feet high, of a 'sclusively grey-fawn colour from head to heel."

"Umm," said the Ethiopian, looking into the speckly-spickly shadows of the aboriginal Flora-forest. "Then they ought to show up in this dark place like ripe bananas in a smokehouse."

But they didn't. The Leopard and the Ethiopian hunted all day; and though they could smell them and hear them, they never saw one of them.

"For goodness' sake," said the Leopard at tea-time, "let us wait till it gets dark. This daylight hunting is a perfect scandal."

So they waited till dark, and then the Leopard heard something breathing sniffily in the starlight that fell all stripy through the branches, and he jumped at the noise, and it smelt like Zebra, and it felt like Zebra, and when he knocked it down it kicked like Zebra, but he couldn't see it. So he said, "Be quiet, O you person without any form. I am going to sit on your head till morning, because there is something about you that I don't understand."

Presently he heard a grunt and a crash and a scramble, and the Ethiopian called out, "I've caught a thing that I can't see. It smells like Giraffe, and it kicks like Giraffe, but it hasn't any form."

"Don't you trust it," said the Leopard. "Sit on its head till the morning—same as me. They haven't any form—any of 'em."

So they sat down on them hard till bright morning-time, and then Leopard said, "What have you at your end of the table, Brother?"

The Ethiopian scratched his head and said, "It ought to be 'sclusively a rich fulvous orange-tawny from head to heel, and it ought to be Giraffe; but it is covered all over with chestnut blotches. What have you at your end of the table, Brother?"

And the Leopard scratched his head and said, "It ought to be 'sclusively a delicate greyish-fawn, and it ought to be Zebra; but it is covered all over with black and purple stripes. What in the world have you been doing to yourself, Zebra? Don't you know that if you were on the High Veldt I could see you ten miles off? You haven't any form."

"Yes," said the Zebra, "but this isn't the High Veldt. Can't you see?"

"I can now," said the Leopard. "But I couldn't all yesterday. How is it done?"

"Let us up," said the Zebra, "and we will show you."

They let the Zebra and the Giraffe get up; and Zebra moved away to some little thorn-bushes where the sunlight fell all stripy, and Giraffe moved off to some tallish trees where the shadows fell all blotchy.

"Now watch," said the Zebra and the Giraffe. "This is the way it's done. One—two—three! And where's your breakfast?"

Leopard stared, and Ethiopian stared, but all they could see were stripy shadows and blotched shadows in the forest, but never a sign of Zebra and Giraffe. They had just walked off and hidden themselves in the shadowy forest.

"Hi! Hi!" said the Ethiopian. "That's a trick worth learning. Take a lesson by it, Leopard. You show up in this dark place like a bar of soap in a coal-scuttle."

"Ho! Ho!" said the Leopard. "Would it surprise you very much to know that you show up in this dark place like a mustard-plaster on a sack of coals?"

"Well," calling names won't catch dinner, said the Ethiopian. "The long and the little of it is that we don't match our backgrounds. I'm going to take Baviaan's advice. He told me I ought to change; and as I've nothing to change except my skin I'm going to change that."

"What to?" said the Leopard, tremendously excited.

"To a nice working blackish-brownish colour, with a little purple in it, and touches of slaty-blue. It will be the very thing for hiding in hollows and behind trees."

So he changed his skin then and there, and the Leopard was more excited than ever; he had never seen a man change his skin before.

"But what about me?" he said, when the Ethiopian had worked his last little finger into his fine new black skin.

"You take Baviaan's advice too. He told you to go into spots."

"So I did," said the Leopard. I went into other spots as fast as I could. I went into this spot with you, and a lot of good it has done me."

"Oh," said the Ethiopian, "Baviaan didn't mean spots in South Africa. He meant spots on your skin."

"What's the use of that?" said the Leopard.

"Think of Giraffe," said the Ethiopian. "Or if you prefer stripes, think of Zebra. They find their spots and stripes give them per-feet satisfaction."

"Umm," said the Leopard. "I wouldn't look like Zebra—not for ever so."

"Well, make up your mind," said the Ethiopian, "because I'd

hate to go hunting without you, but I must if you insist on looking like a sun-flower against a tarred fence."

"I'll take spots, then," said the Leopard; "but don't make 'em too vulgar-big. I wouldn't look like Giraffe—not for ever so."

"I'll make 'em with the tips of my fingers," said the Ethiopian. "There's plenty of black left on my skin still. Stand over!'

Then the Ethiopian put his five fingers close together (there was plenty of black left on his new skin still) and pressed them all over the Leopard, and wherever the five fingers touched they left five little black marks, all close together. You can see them on any Leopard's skin you like, Best Beloved. Sometimes the fingers slipped and the marks got a little blurred; but if you look closely at any Leopard now you will see that there are always five spots—off five fat black finger-tips.

"Now you are a beauty!" said the Ethiopian. "You can lie out on the bare ground and look like a heap of pebbles. You can lie out on the naked rocks and look like a piece of pudding-stone. You can lie out on a leafy branch and look like sunshine sifting through the leaves; and you can lie right across the centre of a path and look like nothing in particular. Think of that and purr!'

"But if I'm all this," said the Leopard, "why didn't you go spotty too?"

"Oh, plain black's best for a nigger," said the Ethiopian. "Now come along and we'll see if we can't get even with Mr. One-Two-Three-Where's-your-Breakfast!'

So they went away and lived happily ever afterward, Best Beloved. That is all.

Oh, now and then you will hear grown-ups say, "Can the Ethiopian change his skin or the Leopard his spots?" I don't think even grown-ups would keep on saying such a silly thing if the Leopard and the Ethiopian hadn't done it once—do you? But they will never do it again, Best Beloved. They are quite contented as they are.

92

The Amir's Homily

His Royal Highness Abdur Rahman, Amir of Afghanistan, G.C.S.I., and trusted ally of Her Imperial Majesty the Queen of England and Empress of India, is a gentleman for whom all right-thinking people should have a profound regard. Like most other rulers, he governs not as he would but as he can, and the mantle of his authority covers the most turbulent race under the stars. To the Afghan neither life, property, law, nor kingship are sacred when his own lusts prompt him to rebel. He is a thief by instinct, a murderer by heredity and training, and frankly and bestially immoral by all three. None the less he has his own crooked notions of honour, and his character is fascinating to study. On occasion he will fight without reason given till he is hacked in pieces; on other occasions he will refuse to show fight till he is driven into a corner. Herein he is as unaccountable as the gray wolf, who is his blood-brother.

And these men His Highness rules by the only weapon that they understand—the fear of death, which among some Orientals is the beginning of wisdom. Some say that the Amir's authority reaches no farther than a rifle bullet can range; but as none are quite certain when their king may be in their midst, and as he alone holds every one of the threads of Government, his respect is increased among men. Gholam Hyder, the Commander-in-chief of the Afghan army, is feared reasonably, for he can impale; all Kabul city fears the Governor of Kabul, who has power of life and death through all the wards; but the Amir of Afghanistan, though outlying tribes pretend otherwise when his back is turned, is dreaded beyond chief and governor together. His word is red law; by the gust of his passion falls the leaf of man's life, and his favour is terrible. He has suffered many things, and been a hunted fugitive before he came to the throne, and he understands all the classes of his people. By the custom of the East any man or woman having a complaint to make, or an enemy against whom to be avenged, has the right of speaking face to face with the king at the daily public audience. This is personal government, as it was in the days of Harun al Raschid of blessed memory, whose times exist still and will exist long after the English have passed away.

The privilege of open speech is of course exercised at certain personal risk. The king may be pleased, and raise the speaker to honour for that very bluntness of speech which three minutes later brings a too imitative petitioner to the edge of the ever ready blade. And the people love to have it so, for it is their right.

It happened upon a day in Kabul that the Amir chose to do his day's work in the Baber Gardens, which lie a short distance from the city of Kabul. A light table stood before him, and round the table in the open air were grouped generals and finance ministers according to their degree. The Court and the long tail of feudal chiefs—men of blood, fed and cowed by blood—stood in an irregular semicircle round the table, and the wind from the Kabul orchards blew among them. All day long sweating couriers dashed in with letters from the outlying districts with rumours of rebellion, intrigue, famine, failure of payments, or announcements of treasure on the road; and all day long the Amir would read the dockets, and pass such of these as were less private to the officials whom they directly concerned, or call up a waiting chief for a word of explanation. It is well to speak clearly to the ruler of Afghanistan. Then the grim head, under the black astrachan cap with the diamond star in front, would nod gravely, and that chief would return to his fellows. Once that afternoon a woman clamoured for divorce against her husband, who was bald, and the Amir, hearing both sides of the case, bade her pour curds over the bare scalp, and lick them off, that the hair might grown again, and she be contented. Here the Court laughed, and the woman withdrew, cursing her king under her breath.

But when twilight was falling, and the order of the Court was a little relaxed, there came before the king, in custody, a trembling haggard wretch, sore with much buffeting, but of stout enough build, who had stolen three rupees—of such small matters does His Highness take cognisance.

'Why did you steal?' said he; and when the king asks questions they do themselves service who answer directly.

'I was poor, and no one gave. Hungry, and there was no food.'

'Why did you not work?'

'I could find no work, Protector of the Poor, and I was starving.'

'You lie. You stole for drink, for lust, for idleness, for anything but hunger, since any man who will may find work and daily bread.'

The prisoner dropped his eyes. He had attended the Court before, and he knew the ring of the death-tone.

'Any man may get work. Who knows this so well as I do? for I too have been hungered—not like you, bastard scum, but as any honest man may be, by the turn of Fate and the will of God.'

Growing warm, the Amir turned to his nobles all arow and thrust the hilt of his sabre aside with his elbow.

'You have heard this Son of Lies? Hear me tell a true tale. I also was once starved, and tightened my belt on the sharp belly-pinch. Nor was I alone, for with me was another, who did not fail me in my evil days, when I was hunted, before ever I came to this throne. And wandering like a houseless dog by Kandahar, my money melted, melted, melted till—' He flung out a bare palm before the audience. 'And day upon day, faint and sick, I went back to that one who waited, and God knows how we lived, till on a day I took our best lihaf—silk it was, fine work of Iran, such as no needle now works, warm, and a coverlet for two, and all that we had. I brought it to a money-lender in a bylane, and I asked for three rupees upon it. He said to me, who am now the King, "You are a thief. This is worth three hundred." "I am no thief," I answered, "but a prince of good blood, and I am hungry."—"Prince of wandering beggars," said that money-lender, "I have no money with me, but go to my house with my clerk and he will give you two rupees eight annas, for that is all I will lend." So I went with the clerk to the house, and we talked on the way, and he gave me the money. We lived on it till it was spent, and we fared hard. And then that clerk said, being a young man of a good heart, "Surely the money-lender will lend yet more on that lihaf," and he offered me two rupees. These I refused, saying, "Nay; but get me some work." And he got me work, and I, even I, Abdur Rahman, Amir of Afghanistan, wrought day by day as a coolie, bearing burdens, and labouring of my hands, receiving four annas wage a day for my sweat and backache. But he, this bastard son of naught, must steal! For a year and four months I worked, and none dare say that I lie, for I have a witness, even that clerk who is now my friend.'

Then there rose in his place among the Sirdars and the nobles one clad in silk, who folded his hands and said, 'This is the truth of God, for I, who, by the favour of God and the Amir, am such as you know, was once clerk to that money-lender.'

There was a pause, and the Amir cried hoarsely to the prisoner, throwing scorn upon him, till he ended with the dread 'Dar arid,' which clinches justice.

So they led the thief away, and the whole of him was seen no more together; and the Court rustled out of its silence, whispering, 'Before God and the Prophet, but this is a man!'

93

The Butterfly That Stamped

This, O my Best Beloved, is a story—a new and a wonderful story—a story quite different from the other stories—a story about The Most Wise Sovereign Suleiman-bin-Daoud—Solomon the Son of David.

There are three hundred and fifty-five stories about Suleiman-bin-Daoud; but this is not one of them. It is not the story of the Lapwing who found the Water; or the Hoopoe who shaded Suleiman-bin-Daoud from the heat. It is not the story of the Glass Pavement, or the Ruby with the Crooked Hole, or the Gold Bars of Balkis. It is the story of the Butterfly that Stamped.

Now attend all over again and listen!

Suleiman-bin-Daoud was wise. He understood what the beasts said, what the birds said, what the fishes said, and what the insects said. He understood what the rocks said deep under the earth when they bowed in towards each other and groaned; and he understood what the trees said when they rustled in the middle of the morning. He understood everything, from the bishop on the bench to the hyssop on the wall, and Balkis, his Head Queen, the Most Beautiful Queen Balkis, was nearly as wise as he was.

Suleiman-bin-Daoud was strong. Upon the third finger of the right hand he wore a ring. When he turned it once, Afrits and

Djinns came Out of the earth to do whatever he told them. When he turned it twice, Fairies came down from the sky to do whatever he told them; and when he turned it three times, the very great angel Azrael of the Sword came dressed as a water-carrier, and told him the news of the three worlds, Above—Below—and Here.

And yet Suleiman-bin-Daoud was not proud. He very seldom showed off, and when he did he was sorry for it. Once he tried to feed all the animals in all the world in one day, but when the food was ready an Animal came out of the deep sea and ate it up in three mouthfuls. Suleiman-bin-Daoud was very surprised and said, 'O Animal, who are you?' And the Animal said, 'O King, live for ever! I am the smallest of thirty thousand brothers, and our home is at the bottom of the sea. We heard that you were going to feed all the animals in all the world, and my brothers sent me to ask when dinner would be ready.' Suleiman-bin-Daoud was more surprised than ever and said, 'O Animal, you have eaten all the dinner that I made ready for all the animals in the world.' And the Animal said, 'O King, live for ever, but do you really call that a dinner? Where I come from we each eat twice as much as that between meals.' Then Suleiman-bin-Daoud fell flat on his face and said, 'O Animal! I gave that dinner to show what a great and rich king I was, and not because I really wanted to be kind to the animals. Now I am ashamed, and it serves me right. Suleiman-bin-Daoud was a really truly wise man, Best Beloved. After that he never forgot that it was silly to show off; and now the real story part of my story begins.

He married ever so many wifes. He married nine hundred and ninety-nine wives, besides the Most Beautiful Balkis; and they all lived in a great golden palace in the middle of a lovely garden with fountains. He didn't really want nine-hundred and ninety-nine wives, but in those days everybody married ever so many wives, and of course the King had to marry ever so many more just to show that he was the King.

Some of the wives were nice, but some were simply horrid, and the horrid ones quarrelled with the nice ones and made them horrid too, and then they would all quarrel with Suleiman-bin-

Daoud, and that was horrid for him. But Balkis the Most Beautiful never quarrelled with Suleiman-bin-Daoud. She loved him too much. She sat in her rooms in the Golden Palace, or walked in the Palace garden, and was truly sorry for him.

Of course if he had chosen to turn his ring on his finger and call up the Djinns and the Afrits they would have magicked all those nine hundred and ninety-nine quarrelsome wives into white mules of the desert or greyhounds or pomegranate seeds; but Suleiman-bin-Daoud thought that that would be showing off. So, when they quarrelled too much, he only walked by himself in one part of the beautiful Palace gardens and wished he had never been born.

One day, when they had quarrelled for three weeks—all nine hundred and ninety-nine wives together—Suleiman-bin-Daoud went out for peace and quiet as usual; and among the orange trees he met Balkis the Most Beautiful, very sorrowful because Suleiman-bin-Daoud was so worried. And she said to him, 'O my Lord and Light of my Eyes, turn the ring upon your finger and show these Queens of Egypt and Mesopotamia and Persia and China that you are the great and terrible King.' But Suleiman-bin-Daoud shook his head and said, 'O my Lady and Delight of my Life, remember the Animal that came out of the sea and made me ashamed before all the animals in all the world because I showed off. Now, if I showed off before these Queens of Persia and Egypt and Abyssinia and China, merely because they worry me, I might be made even more ashamed than I have been.'

And Balkis the Most Beautiful said, 'O my Lord and Treasure of my Soul, what will you do?'

And Suleiman-bin-Daoud said, 'O my Lady and Content of my Heart, I shall continue to endure my fate at the hands of these nine hundred and ninety-nine Queens who vex me with their continual quarrelling.'

So he went on between the lilies and the loquats and the roses and the cannas and the heavy-scented ginger-plants that grew in the garden, till he came to the great camphor-tree that was called the Camphor Tree of Suleiman-bin-Daoud. But Balkis hid among the tall irises and the spotted bamboos and the red lillies behind the camphor-tree, so as to be near her own true love, Suleiman-bin-Daoud.

Presently two Butterflies flew under the tree, quarrelling.

Suleiman-bin-Daoud heard one say to the other, 'I wonder at your presumption in talking like this to me. Don't you know that if I stamped with my foot all Suleiman-bin-Daoud's Palace and this garden here would immediately vanish in a clap of thunder.'

Then Suleiman-bin-Daoud forgot his nine hundred and ninety-nine bothersome wives, and laughed, till the camphor-tree shook, at the Butterfly's boast. And he held out his finger and said, 'Little man, come here.'

The Butterfly was dreadfully frightened, but he managed to fly up to the hand of Suleiman-bin-Daoud, and clung there, fanning himself. Suleiman-bin-Daoud bent his head and whispered very softly, 'Little man, you know that all your stamping wouldn't bend one blade of grass. What made you tell that awful fib to your wife?—for doubtless she is your wife.'

The Butterfly looked at Suleiman-bin-Daoud and saw the most wise King's eye twinkle like stars on a frosty night, and he picked up his courage with both wings, and he put his head on one side and said, 'O King, live for ever. She is my wife; and you know what wives are like.'

Suleiman-bin-Daoud smiled in his beard and said, 'Yes, I know, little brother.'

'One must keep them in order somehow, said the Butterfly, and she has been quarrelling with me all the morning. I said that to quiet her.'

And Suleiman-bin-Daoud said, 'May it quiet her. Go back to your wife, little brother, and let me hear what you say.'

Back flew the Butterfly to his wife, who was all of a twitter behind a leaf, and she said, 'He heard you! Suleiman-bin-Daoud himself heard you!'

'Heard me!' said the Butterfly. 'Of course he did. I meant him to hear me.'

'And what did he say? Oh, what did he say?'

'Well,' said the Butterfly, fanning himself most importantly, 'between you and me, my dear—of course I don't blame him, because his Palace must have cost a great deal and the oranges are just ripening,—he asked me not to stamp, and I promised I wouldn't.'

'Gracious!' said his wife, and sat quite quiet; but Suleiman-bin-Daoud laughed till the tears ran down his face at the impudence of the bad little Butterfly.

Balkis the Most Beautiful stood up behind the tree among the red lilies and smiled to herself, for she had heard all this talk. She thought, 'If I am wise I can yet save my Lord from the persecutions of these quarrelsome Queens,' and she held out her finger and whispered softly to the Butterfly's Wife, 'Little woman, come here.' Up flew the Butterfly's Wife, very frightened, and clung to Balkis's white hand.

Balkis bent her beautiful head down and whispered, 'Little woman, do you believe what your husband has just said?'

The Butterfly's Wife looked at Balkis, and saw the most beautiful Queen's eyes shining like deep pools with starlight on them, and she picked up her courage with both wings and said, 'O Queen, be lovely for ever. You know what men-folk are like.'

And the Queen Balkis, the Wise Balkis of Sheba, put her hand to her lips to hide a smile and said, 'Little sister, I know.'

'They get angry,' said the Butterfly's Wife, fanning herself quickly, 'over nothing at all, but we must humour them, O Queen. They never mean half they say. If it pleases my husband to believe that I believe he can make Suleiman-bin-Daoud's Palace disappear by stamping his foot, I'm sure I don't care. He'll forget all about it to-morrow.'

'Little sister,' said Balkis, 'you are quite right; but next time he begins to boast, take him at his word. Ask him to stamp, and see what will happen. We know what men-folk are like, don't we? He'll be very much ashamed.'

Away flew the Butterfly's Wife to her husband, and in five minutes they were quarrelling worse than ever.

'Remember!' said the Butterfly. 'Remember what I can do if I stamp my foot.'

'I don't believe you one little bit,' said the Butterfly's Wife. 'I should very much like to see it done. Suppose you stamp now.'

'I promised Suleiman-bin-Daoud that I wouldn't,' said the Butterfly, 'and I don't want to break my promise.'

'It wouldn't matter if you did,' said his wife. 'You couldn't bend a blade of grass with your stamping. I dare you to do it,' she said. Stamp! Stamp! Stamp!'

Suleiman-bin-Daoud, sitting under the camphor-tree, heard every word of this, and he laughed as he had never laughed in his life before. He forgot all about his Queens; he forgot all about the Animal that came out of the sea; he forgot about showing off. He just laughed with joy, and Balkis, on the other side of the tree, smiled because her own true love was so joyful.

Presently the Butterfly, very hot and puffy, came whirling back under the shadow of the camphor-tree and said to Suleiman, 'She wants me to stamp! She wants to see what will happen, O Suleiman-bin-Daoud! You know I can't do it, and now she'll never believe a word I say. She'll laugh at me to the end of my days!'

'No, little brother,' said Suleiman-bin-Daoud, 'she will never laugh at you again,' and he turned the ring on his finger—just for the little Butterfly's sake, not for the sake of showing off,—and, lo and behold, four huge Djinns came out of the earth!

'Slaves,' said Suleiman-bin-Daoud, 'when this gentleman on my finger' (that was where the impudent Butterfly was sitting) 'stamps his left front forefoot you will make my Palace and these gardens disappear in a clap of thunder. When he stamps again you will bring them back carefully.'

'Now, little brother,' he said, 'go back to your wife and stamp all you've a mind to.'

Away flew the Butterfly to his wife, who was crying, 'I dare you to do it! I dare you to do it! Stamp! Stamp now! Stamp!' Balkis saw the four vast Djinns stoop down to the four corners of the gardens with the Palace in the middle, and she clapped her hands softly and said, 'At last Suleiman-bin-Daoud will do for the sake of a Butterfly what he ought to have done long ago for his own sake, and the quarrelsome Queens will be frightened!'

The the butterfly stamped. The Djinns jerked the Palace and the gardens a thousand miles into the air: there was a most awful thunder-clap, and everything grew inky-black. The Butterfly's Wife fluttered about in the dark, crying, 'Oh, I'll be good! I'm so sorry I spoke. Only bring the gardens back, my dear darling husband, and I'll never contradict again.'

The Butterfly was nearly as frightened as his wife, and Suleiman-bin-Daoud laughed so much that it was several minutes before he found breath enough to whisper to the Butterfly, 'Stamp again, little brother. Give me back my Palace, most great magician.'

'Yes, give him back his Palace,' said the Butterfly's Wife, still flying about in the dark like a moth. 'Give him back his Palace, and don't let's have any more horrid magic.'

'Well, my dear,' said the Butterfly as bravely as he could, 'you see what your nagging has led to. Of course it doesn't make any difference to me—I'm used to this kind of thing—but as a favour to you and to Suleiman-bin-Daoud I don't mind putting things right.'

So he stamped once more, and that instant the Djinns let down the Palace and the gardens, without even a bump. The sun shone on the dark-green orange leaves; the fountains played among the pink Egyptian lilies; the birds went on singing, and the Butterfly's Wife lay on her side under the camphor-tree waggling her wings and panting, 'Oh, I'll be good! I'll be good!'

Suleiman-bin-Daolld could hardly speak for laughing. He leaned back all weak and hiccoughy, and shook his finger at the Butterfly and said, 'O great wizard, what is the sense of returning to me my Palace if at the same time you slay me with mirth!'

Then came a terrible noise, for all the nine hundred and ninety-nine Queens ran out of the Palace shrieking and shouting and calling for their babies. They hurried down the great marble steps below the fountain, one hundred abreast, and the Most Wise Balkis went statelily forward to meet them and said, 'What is your trouble, O Queens?'

They stood on the marble steps one hundred abreast and shouted, 'What is our trouble? We were living peacefully in our golden palace, as is our custom, when upon a sudden the Palace disappeared, and we were left sitting in a thick and noisome darkness; and it thundered, and Djinns and Afrits moved about in the darkness! That is our trouble, O Head Queen, and we are most extremely troubled on account of that trouble, for it was a troublesome trouble, unlike any trouble we have known.'

Then Balkis the Most Beautiful Queen—Suleiman-bin-Daoud's Very Best Beloved—Queen that was of Sheba and Sable and the Rivers of the Gold of the South—from the Desert of Zinn to the Towers of Zimbabwe—Balkis, almost as wise as the Most Wise Suleiman-bin-Daoud himself, said, 'It is nothing, O Queens! A Butterfly has made complaint against his wife because she quarrelled with him, and it has pleased our Lord Suleiman-bin-Daoud to teach her a lesson in low-speaking and humbleness, for that is counted a virtue among the wives of the butterflies.'

Then up and spoke an Egyptian Queen—the daughter of a Pharoah—and she said, 'Our Palace cannot be plucked up by the roots like a leek for the sake of a little insect. No! Suleiman-bin-Daoud must be dead, and what we heard and saw was the earth thundering and darkening at the news.'

Then Balkis beckoned that bold Queen without looking at her, and said to her and to the others, 'Come and see.'

They came down the marble steps, one hundred abreast, and beneath his camphor-tree, still weak with laughing, they saw the Most Wise King Suleiman-bin-Daoud rocking back and forth with a Butterfly on either hand, and they heard him say, 'O wife of my brother in the air, remember after this, to please your husband in all things, lest he be provoked to stamp his foot yet again; for he has said that he is used to this magic, and he is most eminently a great magician—one who steals away the very Palace of Suleiman-bin-Daoud himself. Go in peace, little folk!' And he kissed them on the wings, and they flew away.

Then all the Queens except Balkis—the Most Beautiful and Splendid Balkis, who stood apart smiling—fell flat on their faces, for they said, 'If these things are done when a Butterfly is displeased with his wife, what shall be done to us who have vexed our King with our loud-speaking and open quarrelling through many days?'

Then they put their veils over their heads, and they put their hands over their mouths, and they tiptoed back to the Palace most mousy-quiet.

Then Balkis—The Most Beautiful and Excellent Balkis—went forward through the red lilies into the shade of the camphor-tree and laid her hand upon Suleiman-bin-Daoud's shoulder and said, 'O my Lord and Treasure of my Soul, rejoice, for we have taught the Queens of Egypt and Ethiopia and Abyssinia and Persia and India and China with a great and a memorable teaching.'

And Suleiman-bin-Daoud, still looking after the Butterflies where they played in the sunlight, said, 'O my Lady and Jewel of my Felicity, when did this happen? For I have been jesting with a Butterfly ever since I came into the garden.' And he told Balkis what he had done.

Balkis—The tender and Most Lovely Balkis—said, 'O my Lord and Regent of my Existence, I hid behind the camphor-tree and saw it all. It was I who told the Butterfly's Wife to ask the Butterfly to stamp, because I hoped that for the sake of the jest my Lord would make some great magic and that the Queens would see it and be frightened.' And she told him what the Queens had said and seen and thought.

Then Suleiman-bin-Daoud rose up from his seat under the camphor-tree, and stretched his arms and rejoiced and said, 'O my Lady and Sweetener of my Days, know that if I had made a magic against my Queens for the sake of pride or anger, as I made that feast for all the animals, I should certainly have been put to shame. But by means of your wisdom I made the magic for the sake of a jest and for the sake of a little Butterfly, and—behold—it has also delivered me from the vexations of my vexatious wives! Tell me, therefore, O my Lady and Heart of my Heart, how did you come to be so wise?' And Balkis the Queen, beautiful and tall, looked up into Suleiman-bin-Daoud's eyes and put her head a little on one side, just like the Butterfly, and said, 'First, O my Lord, because I loved you; and secondly, O my Lord, because I know what women-folk are.'

Then they went up to the Palace and lived happily ever afterwards.

But wasn't it clever of Balkis?

THERE was never a Queen like Balkis,
From here to the wide world's end;
But Balkis talked to a butterfly
As you would talk to a friend.

There was never a King like Solomon,
Not since the world began;
But Solomon talked to a butterfly
As a man would talk to a man.

She was Queen of Sabaea—
And he was Asia's Lord—
But they both of 'em talked to butterflies
When they took their walks abroad!

S T Semyonov

(1868-1922)

94

The Servant

BY S T SEMYONOV

I

Gerasim returned to Moscow just at a time when it was hardest to find work, a short while before Christmas, when a man sticks even to a poor job in the expectation of a present. For three weeks the peasant lad had been going about in vain seeking a position.

He stayed with relatives and friends from his village, and although he had not yet suffered great want, it disheartened him that he, a strong young man, should go without work.

Gerasim had lived in Moscow from early boyhood. When still a mere child, he had gone to work in a brewery as bottle-washer, and later as a lower servant in a house. In the last two years he had been in a merchant's employ, and would still have held that position, had he not been summoned back to his village for military duty. However, he had not been drafted. It seemed dull to him in the village, he was not used to the country life, so he decided he would rather count the stones in Moscow than stay there.

Every minute it was getting to be more and more irksome for him to be tramping the streets in idleness. Not a stone did he leave

539

unturned in his efforts to secure any sort of work. He plagued all of his acquaintances, he even held up people on the street and asked them if they knew of a situation—all in vain.

Finally Gerasim could no longer bear being a burden on his people. Some of them were annoyed by his coming to them; and others had suffered unpleasantness from their masters on his account. He was altogether at a loss what to do. Sometimes he would go a whole day without eating.

II

One day Gerasim betook himself to a friend from his village, who lived at the extreme outer edge of Moscow, near Sokolnik. The man was coachman to a merchant by the name of Sharov, in whose service he had been for many years. He had ingratiated himself with his master, so that Sharov trusted him absolutely and gave every sign of holding him in high favour. It was the man's glib tongue, chiefly, that had gained him his master's confidence. He told on all the servants, and Sharov valued him for it.

Gerasim approached and greeted him. The coachman gave his guest a proper reception, served him with tea and something to eat, and asked him how he was doing.

"Very badly, Yegor Danilych," said Gerasim. "I've been without a job for weeks."

"Didn't you ask your old employer to take you back?"

"I did."

"He wouldn't take you again?"

"The position was filled already."

"That's it. That's the way you young fellows are. You serve your employers so-so, and when you leave your jobs, you usually have muddied up the way back to them. You ought to serve your masters so that they will think a lot of you, and when you come again, they will not refuse you, but rather dismiss the man who has taken your place."

"How can a man do that? In these days there aren't any employers like that, and we aren't exactly angels, either."

"What's the use of wasting words? I just want to tell you about myself. If for some reason or other I should ever have to leave this place and go home, not only would Mr. Sharov, if I came back, take me on again without a word, but he would be glad to, too."

Gerasim sat there downcast. He saw his friend was boasting, and it occurred to him to gratify him.

"I know it," he said. "But it's hard to find men like you, Yegor Danilych. If you were a poor worker, your master would not have kept you twelve years."

Yegor smiled. He liked the praise.

"That's it," he said. "If you were to live and serve as I do, you wouldn't be out of work for months and months."

Gerasim made no reply.

Yegor was summoned to his master.

"Wait a moment," he said to Gerasim. "I'll be right back."

"Very well."

III

Yegor came back and reported that inside of half an hour he would have to have the horses harnessed, ready to drive his master to town. He lighted his pipe and took several turns in the room. Then he came to a halt in front of Gerasim.

"Listen, my boy," he said, "if you want, I'll ask my master to take you as a servant here."

"Does he need a man?"

"We have one, but he's not much good. He's getting old, and it's very hard for him to do the work. It's lucky for us that the neighbourhood isn't a lively one and the police don't make a fuss about things being kept just so, else the old man couldn't manage to keep the place clean enough for them."

"Oh, if you can, then please do say a word for me, Yegor Danilych. I'll pray for you all my life. I can't stand being without work any longer."

"All right, I'll speak for you. Come again to-morrow, and in the meantime take this ten-kopek piece. It may come in handy."

"Thanks, Yegor Danilych. Then you will try for me? Please do me the favour."

"All right. I'll try for you."

Gerasim left, and Yegor harnessed up his horses. Then he put on his coachman's habit, and drove up to the front door. Mr. Sharov stepped out of the house, seated himself in the sleigh, and the horses galloped off. He attended to his business in town and returned home. Yegor, observing that his master was in a good humour, said to him:

"Yegor Fiodorych, I have a favour to ask of you."

"What is it?"

"There's a young man from my village here, a good boy. He's without a job."

"Well?"

"Wouldn't you take him?"

"What do I want him for?"

"Use him as man of all work round the place."

"How about Polikarpych?"

"What good is he? It's about time you dismissed him."

"That wouldn't be fair. He has been with me so many years. I can't let him go just so, without any cause."

"Supposing he has worked for you for years. He didn't work for nothing. He got paid for it. He's certainly saved up a few dollars for his old age."

"Saved up! How could he? From what? He's not alone in the world. He has a wife to support, and she has to eat and drink also."

"His wife earns money, too, at day's work as charwoman."

"A lot she could have made! Enough for kvas."

"Why should you care about Polikarpych and his wife? To tell you the truth, he's a very poor servant. Why should you throw your money away on him? He never shovels the snow away on time, or does anything right. And when it comes his turn to be night watchman, he slips away at least ten times a night. It's too cold for him. You'll see, some day, because of him, you will have trouble with the police. The quarterly inspector will descend on us, and it won't be so agreeable for you to be responsible for Polikarpych."

"Still, it's pretty rough. He's been with me fifteen years. And to treat him that way in his old age—it would be a sin."

"A sin! Why, what harm would you be doing him? He won't starve. He'll go to the almshouse. It will be better for him, too, to be quiet in his old age."

Sharov reflected.

"All right," he said finally. "Bring your friend here. I'll see what I can do."

"Do take him, sir. I'm so sorry for him. He's a good boy, and he's been without work for such a long time. I know he'll do his work well and serve you faithfully. On account of having to report for military duty, he lost his last position. If it hadn't been for that, his master would never have let him go."

IV

The next evening Gerasim came again and asked:

"Well, could you do anything for me?"

"Something, I believe. First let's have some tea. Then we'll go see my master."

Even tea had no allurements for Gerasim. He was eager for a decision; but under the compulsion of politeness to his host, he gulped down two glasses of tea, and then they betook themselves to Sharov.

Sharov asked Gerasim where he had lived before and what work he could do. Then he told him he was prepared to engage him as man of all work, and he should come back the next day ready to take the place.

Gerasim was fairly stunned by the great stroke of fortune. So overwhelming was his joy that his legs would scarcely carry him. He went to the coachman's room, and Yegor said to him:

"Well, my lad, see to it that you do your work right, so that I shan't have to be ashamed of you. You know what masters are like. If you go wrong once, they'll be at you forever after with their fault-finding, and never give you peace."

"Don't worry about that, Yegor Danilych."

"Well—well."

Gerasim took leave, crossing the yard to go out by the gate. Polikarpych's rooms gave on the yard, and a broad beam of light from the window fell across Gerasim's way. He was curious to get a glimpse of his future home, but the panes were all frosted over, and it was impossible to peep through. However, he could hear what the people inside were saying.

"What will we do now?" was said in a woman's voice.

"I don't know, I don't know," a man, undoubtedly Polikarpych, replied. "Go begging, I suppose."

"That's all we can do. There's nothing else left," said the woman. "Oh, we poor people, what a miserable life we lead. We work and work from early morning till late at night, day after day, and when we get old, then it's, 'Away with you!'"

"What can we do? Our master is not one of us. It wouldn't be worth the while to say much to him about it. He cares only for his own advantage."

"All the masters are so mean. They don't think of any one but themselves. It doesn't occur to them that we work for them honestly and faithfully for years, and use up our best strength in their service. They're afraid to keep us a year longer, even though we've got all the strength we need to do their work. If we weren't strong enough, we'd go of our own accord."

"The master's not so much to blame as his coachman. Yegor Danilych wants to get a good position for his friend."

"Yes, he's a serpent. He knows how to wag his tongue. You wait, you foul-mouthed beast, I'll get even with you. I'll go straight to the master and tell him how the fellow deceives him, how he steals the hay and fodder. I'll put it down in writing, and he can convince himself how the fellow lies about us all."

"Don't, old woman. Don't sin."

"Sin? Isn't what I said all true? I know to a dot what I'm saying, and I mean to tell it straight out to the master. He should see with his own eyes. Why not? What can we do now anyhow? Where shall we go? He's ruined us, ruined us."

The old woman burst out sobbing.

Gerasim heard all that, and it stabbed him like a dagger. He realised what misfortune he would be bringing the old people, and it made him sick at heart. He stood there a long while, saddened, lost in thought, then he turned and went back into the coachman's room.

"Ah, you forgot something?"

"No, Yegor Danilych." Gerasim stammered out, "I've come—listen—I want to thank you ever and ever so much—for the way you received me—and—and all the trouble you took for me—but—I can't take the place."

"What! What does that mean?"

"Nothing. I don't want the place. I will look for another one for myself."

Yegor flew into a rage.

"Did you mean to make a fool of me, did you, you idiot? You come here so meek—'Try for me, do try for me'—and then you refuse to take the place. You rascal, you have disgraced me!"

Gerasim found nothing to say in reply. He reddened, and lowered his eyes. Yegor turned his back scornfully and said nothing more.

Then Gerasim quietly picked up his cap and left the coachman's room. He crossed the yard rapidly, went out by the gate, and hurried off down the street. He felt happy and lighthearted.

Stephen Leacock

(1869-1944)

95

My Financial Career

When I go into a bank I get rattled. The clerks rattle me; the wickets rattle me; the sight of the money rattles me; everything rattles me.

The moment I cross the threshold of a bank and attempt to transact business there, I become an irresponsible idiot.

I knew this beforehand, but my salary had been raised to fifty dollars a month and I felt that the bank was the only place for it.

So I shambled in and looked timidly round at the clerks. I had an idea that a person about to open an account must needs consult the manager.

I went up to a wicket marked "Accountant." The accountant was a tall, cool devil. The very sight of him rattled me. My voice was sepulchral.

"Can I see the manager?" I said, and added solemnly, "alone." I don't know why I said "alone."

"Certainly," said the accountant, and fetched him.

The manager was a grave, calm man. I held my fifty-six dollars clutched in a crumpled ball in my pocket.

"Are you the manager?" I said. God knows I didn't doubt it.

"Yes," he said.

"Can I see you," I asked, "alone?" I didn't want to say "alone" again, but without it the thing seemed self-evident.

The manager looked at me in some alarm. He felt that I had an awful secret to reveal.

"Come in here," he said, and led the way to a private room. He turned the key in the lock.

"We are safe from interruption here," he said; "sit down."

We both sat down and looked at each other. I found no voice to speak.

"You are one of Pinkerton's men, I presume," he said.

He had gathered from my mysterious manner that I was a detective. I knew what he was thinking, and it made me worse.

"No, not from Pinkerton's," I said, seeming to imply that I came from a rival agency.

"To tell the truth," I went on, as if I had been prompted to lie about it, "I am not a detective at all. I have come to open an account. I intend to keep all my money in this bank."

The manager looked relieved but still serious; he concluded now that I was a son of Baron Rothschild or a young Gould.

"A large account, I suppose," he said.

"Fairly large," I whispered. "I propose to deposit fifty-six dollars now and fifty dollars a month regularly."

The manager got up and opened the door. He called to the accountant.

"Mr. Montgomery," he said unkindly loud, "this gentleman is opening an account, he will deposit fifty-six dollars. Good morning."

I rose.

A big iron door stood open at the side of the room.

"Good morning," I said, and stepped into the safe.

"Come out," said the manager coldly, and showed me the other way.

I went up to the accountant's wicket and poked the ball of money at him with a quick convulsive movement as if I were doing a conjuring trick.

My face was ghastly pale.

"Here," I said, "deposit it." The tone of the words seemed to mean, "Let us do this painful thing while the fit is on us."

He took the money and gave it to another clerk.

He made me write the sum on a slip and sign my name in a book. I no longer knew what I was doing. The bank swam before my eyes.

"Is it deposited?" I asked in a hollow, vibrating voice.

"It is," said the accountant.

"Then I want to draw a cheque."

My idea was to draw out six dollars of it for present use. Someone gave me a chequebook through a wicket and someone else began telling me how to write it out. The people in the bank had the impression that I was an invalid millionaire. I wrote something on the cheque and thrust it in at the clerk. He looked at it.

"What! are you drawing it all out again?" he asked in surprise. Then I realized that I had written fifty-six instead of six. I was too far gone to reason now. I had a feeling that it was impossible to explain the thing. All the clerks had stopped writing to look at me.

Reckless with misery, I made a plunge.

"Yes, the whole thing."

"You withdraw your money from the bank?"

"Every cent of it."

"Are you not going to deposit any more?" said the clerk, astonished.

"Never."

An idiot hope struck me that they might think something had insulted me while I was writing the cheque and that I had changed my mind. I made a wretched attempt to look like a man with a fearfully quick temper.

The clerk prepared to pay the money.

"How will you have it?" he said.

"What?"

"How will you have it?"

"Oh"—I caught his meaning and answered without even trying to think—"in fifties."

He gave me a fifty-dollar bill.

"And the six?" he asked dryly.

"In sixes," I said.

He gave it me and I rushed out.

As the big door swung behind me I caught the echo of a roar of laughter that went up to the ceiling of the bank. Since then I bank no more. I keep my money in cash in my trousers pocket and my savings in silver dollars in a sock.

96

The New Food

I see from the current columns of the daily press that "Professor Plumb, of the University of Chicago, has just invented a highly concentrated form of food. All the essential nutritive elements are put together in the form of pellets, each of which contains from one to two hundred times as much nourishment as an ounce of an ordinary article of diet. These pellets, diluted with water, will form all that is necessary to support life. The professor looks forward confidently to revolutionizing the present food system."

Now this kind of thing may be all very well in its way, but it is going to have its drawbacks as well. In the bright future anticipated by Professor Plumb, we can easily imagine such incidents as the following:

The smiling family were gathered round the hospitable board. The table was plenteously laid with a soup-plate in front of each beaming child, a bucket of hot water before the radiant mother, and at the head of the board the Christmas dinner of the happy home, warmly covered by a thimble and resting on a poker chip. The expectant whispers of the little ones were hushed as the father, rising from his chair, lifted the thimble and disclosed a small pill of concentrated nourishment on the chip before him. Christmas turkey, cranberry sauce, plum pudding, mince pie—it was all there, all jammed into that little pill and only waiting to expand. Then the father with deep reverence, and a devout eye alternating between the pill and heaven, lifted his voice in a benediction.

At this moment there was an agonized cry from the mother.

"Oh, Henry, quick! Baby has snatched the pill!" It was too true. Dear little Gustavus Adolphus, the golden-haired baby boy, had grabbed the whole Christmas dinner off the poker chip and bolted it. Three hundred and fifty pounds of concentrated nourishment passed down the oesophagus of the unthinking child.

"Clap him on the back!" cried the distracted mother. "Give him water!"

The idea was fatal. The water striking the pill caused it to expand. There was a dull rumbling sound and then, with an awful bang, Gustavus Adolphus exploded into fragments!

And when they gathered the little corpse together, the baby lips were parted in a lingering smile that could only be worn by a child who had eaten thirteen Christmas dinners.

97

Borrowing a Match

You might think that borrowing a match upon the street is a simple thing. But any man who has ever tried it will assure you that it is not, and will be prepared to swear to the truth of my experience of the other evening.

I was standing on the corner of the street with a cigar that I wanted to light. I had no match. I waited till a decent, ordinary-looking man came along. Then I said:

"Excuse me, sir, but could you oblige me with the loan of a match?"

"A match?" he said, "why certainly." Then he unbuttoned his overcoat and put his hand in the pocket of his waistcoat. "I know I have one," he went on, "and I'd almost swear it's in the bottom pocket—or, hold on, though, I guess it may be in the top—just wait till I put these parcels down on the sidewalk."

"Oh, don't trouble," I said, "it's really of no consequence."

"Oh, it's no trouble, I'll have it in a minute; I know there must be one in here somewhere"—he was digging his fingers into his pockets as he spoke—"but you see this isn't the waistcoat I generally . . ."

I saw that the man was getting excited about it. "Well, never mind," I protested; "if that isn't the waistcoat that you generally— why, it doesn't matter."

"Hold on, now, hold on!" the man said, "I've got one of the cursed things in here somewhere. I guess it must be in with my watch. No, it's not there either. Wait till I try my coat. If that confounded tailor only knew enough to make a pocket so that a man could get at it!"

He was getting pretty well worked up now. He had thrown down his walking-stick and was plunging at his pockets with his teeth set. "It's that cursed young boy of mine," he hissed; "this comes of his fooling in my pockets. By Gad! perhaps I won't warm him up when I get home. Say, I'll bet that it's in my hip-pocket. You just hold up the tail of my overcoat a second till I . . ."

"No, no," I protested again, "please don't take all this trouble, it really doesn't matter. I'm sure you needn't take off your overcoat, and oh, pray don't throw away your letters and things in the snow like that, and tear out your pockets by the roots! Please, please don't trample over your overcoat and put your feet through the parcels. I do hate to hear you swearing at your little boy, with that peculiar whine in your voice. Don't—please don't tear your clothes so savagely."

Suddenly the man gave a grunt of exultation, and drew his hand up from inside the lining of his coat.

"I've got it," he cried. "Here you are!" Then he brought it out under the light.

It was a toothpick.

Yielding to the impulse of the moment I pushed him under the wheels of a trolley-car, and ran.

98

The Awful Fate of Melpomenus Jones

Some people—not you nor I, because we are so awfully self-possessed—but some people, find great difficulty in saying good-bye when making a call or spending the evening. As the moment draws near when the visitor feels that he is fairly entitled to go away he rises and says abruptly, "Well, I think I . . ." Then the people say, "Oh, must you go now? Surely it's early yet!" and a pitiful struggle ensues.

I think the saddest case of this kind of thing that I ever knew was that of my poor friend Melpomenus Jones, a curate—such a dear young man, and only twenty-three! He simply couldn't get away from people. He was too modest to tell a lie, and too religious to wish to appear rude. Now it happened that he went to call on some friends of his on the very first afternoon of his summer vacation. The next six weeks were entirely his own—absolutely nothing to do. He chatted awhile, drank two cups of tea, then braced himself for the effort and said suddenly:

"Well, I think I . . ."

But the lady of the house said, "Oh, no! Mr. Jones, can't you really stay a little longer?"

Jones was always truthful. "Oh, yes," he said, "of course, I—er—can stay."

"Then please don't go."

He stayed. He drank eleven cups of tea. Night was falling. He rose again.

"Well now," he said shyly, "I think I really . . ."

"You must go?" said the lady politely. "I thought perhaps you could have stayed to dinner . . ."

"Oh well, so I could, you know," Jones said, "if . . ."

"Then please stay, I'm sure my husband will be delighted."

"All right," he said feebly, "I'll stay," and he sank back into his chair, just full of tea, and miserable.

Papa came home. They had dinner. All through the meal Jones sat planning to leave at eight-thirty. All the family wondered whether Mr. Jones was stupid and sulky, or only stupid.

After dinner mamma undertook to "draw him out," and showed him photographs. She showed him all the family museum, several gross of them—photos of papa's uncle and his wife, and mamma's brother and his little boy, an awfully interesting photo of papa's uncle's friend in his Bengal uniform, an awfully well-taken photo of papa's grandfather's partner's dog, and an awfully wicked one of papa as the devil for a fancy-dress ball. At eight-thirty Jones had examined seventy-one photographs. There were about sixty-nine more that he hadn't. Jones rose.

"I must say good night now," he pleaded.

"Say good night!" they said, "why it's only half-past eight! Have you anything to do?"

"Nothing," he admitted, and muttered something about staying six weeks, and then laughed miserably.

Just then it turned out that the favourite child of the family, such a dear little romp, had hidden Mr. Jones's hat; so papa said that he must stay, and invited him to a pipe and a chat. Papa had the pipe and gave Jones the chat, and still he stayed. Every moment he meant to take the plunge, but couldn't. Then papa began to get very tired of Jones, and fidgeted and finally said, with jocular irony, that Jones had better stay all night, they could give him a shake-down. Jones mistook his meaning and thanked him with tears in his eyes, and papa put Jones to bed in the spare room and cursed him heartily.

After breakfast next day, papa went off to his work in the City, and left Jones playing with the baby, broken-hearted. His nerve was utterly gone. He was meaning to leave all day, but the thing had got on his mind and he simply couldn't. When papa came home in the evening he was surprised and chagrined to find Jones still there. He thought to jockey him out with a jest, and said he thought he'd have to charge him for his board, he! he! The unhappy young man stared wildly for a moment, then wrung papa's hand, paid him a month's board in advance, and broke down and sobbed like a child.

In the days that followed he was moody and unapproachable. He lived, of course, entirely in the drawing-room, and the lack of air and exercise began to tell sadly on his health. He passed his time in drinking tea and looking at the photographs. He would stand for hours gazing at the photographs of papa's uncle's friend in his Bengal uniform—talking to it, sometimes swearing bitterly at it. His mind was visibly failing.

At length the crash came. They carried him upstairs in a raging delirium of fever. The illness that followed was terrible. He recognized no one, not even papa's uncle's friend in his Bengal uniform. At times he would start up from his bed and shriek, "Well, I think I . . ." and then fall back upon the pillow with a horrible laugh. Then, again, he would leap up and cry, "Another cup of tea and more photographs! More photographs! Har! Har!"

At length, after a month of agony, on the last day of his vacation, he passed away. They say that when the last moment came, he sat up in bed with a beautiful smile of confidence playing upon his face, and said, "Well—the angels are calling me; I'm afraid I really must go now. Good afternoon."

And the rushing of his spirit from its prison-house was as rapid as a hunted cat passing over a garden fence.

Virginia Woolf

(1882-1941)

99

Solid Objects

The only thing that moved upon the vast semicircle of the beach was one small black spot. As it came nearer to the ribs and spine of the stranded pilchard boat, it became apparent from a certain tenuity in its blackness that this spot possessed four legs; and moment by moment it became more unmistakable that it was composed of the persons of two young men. Even thus in outline against the sand there was an unmistakable vitality in them; an indescribable vigour in the approach and withdrawal of the bodies, slight though it was, which proclaimed some violent argument issuing from the tiny mouths of the little round heads. This was corroborated on closer view by the repeated lunging of a walking-stick on the right-hand side. "You mean to tell me . . . You actually believe . . ." thus the walking-stick on the right-hand side next the waves seemed to be asserting as it cut long straight stripes upon the sand.

"Politics be damned!" issued clearly from the body on the left-hand side, and, as these words were uttered, the mouths, noses, chins, little moustaches, tweed caps, rough boots, shooting coats, and check stockings of the two speakers became clearer and clearer; the smoke of their pipes went up into the air; nothing was so solid, so living, so hard, red, hirsute and virile as these two bodies for miles and miles of sea and sandhill.

They flung themselves down by the six ribs and spine of the black pilchard boat. You know how the body seems to shake itself free from an argument, and to apologize for a mood of exaltation; flinging itself down and expressing in the looseness of its attitude a readiness to take up with something new—whatever it may be that comes next to hand. So Charles, whose stick had been slashing the beach for half a mile or so, began skimming flat pieces of slate over the water; and John, who had exclaimed "Politics be damned!" began burrowing his fingers down, down, into the sand. As his hand went further and further beyond the wrist, so that he had to hitch his sleeve a little higher, his eyes lost their intensity, or rather the background of thought and experience which gives an inscrutable depth to the eyes of grown people disappeared, leaving only the clear transparent surface, expressing nothing but wonder, which the eyes of young children display. No doubt the act of burrowing in the sand had something to do with it. He remembered that, after digging for a little, the water oozes round your finger-tips; the hole then becomes a moat; a well; a spring; a secret channel to the sea. As he was choosing which of these things to make it, still working his fingers in the water, they curled round something hard—a full drop of solid matter—and gradually dislodged a large irregular lump, and brought it to the surface. When the sand coating was wiped off, a green tint appeared. It was a lump of glass, so thick as to be almost opaque; the smoothing of the sea had completely worn off any edge or shape, so that it was impossible to say whether it had been bottle, tumbler or window-pane; it was nothing but glass; it was almost a precious stone. You had only to enclose it in a rim of gold, or pierce it with a wire, and it became a jewel; part of a necklace, or a dull, green light upon a finger. Perhaps after all it was really a gem; something worn by a dark Princess trailing her finger in the water as she sat in the stern of the boat and listened to the slaves singing as they rowed her across the Bay. Or the oak sides of a sunk Elizabethan treasure-chest had split apart, and, rolled over and over, over and over, its emeralds had come at last to shore. John turned it in his hands; he held it to the light; he held it so that its irregular mass blotted out the body and extended right arm of his friend. The green thinned and thickened slightly as it was held against the sky or against the body. It pleased him; it puzzled him; it was so hard, so concentrated, so definite an object compared with the vague sea and the hazy shore.

Now a sigh disturbed him—profound, final, making him aware that his friend Charles had thrown all the flat stones within reach, or had come to the conclusion that it was not worth while to throw them. They ate their sandwiches side by side. When they had done, and were shaking themselves and rising to their feet, John took the lump of glass and looked at it in silence. Charles looked at it too. But he saw immediately that it was not flat, and filling his pipe he said with the energy that dismisses a foolish strain of thought:

"To return to what I was saying——"

He did not see, or if he had seen would hardly have noticed, that John, after looking at the lump for a moment, as if in hesitation, slipped it inside his pocket. That impulse, too, may have been the impulse which leads a child to pick up one pebble on a path strewn with them, promising it a life of warmth and security upon the nursery mantelpiece, delighting in the sense of power and benignity which such an action confers, and believing that the heart of the stone leaps with joy when it sees itself chosen from a million like it, to enjoy this bliss instead of a life of cold and wet upon the high road. "It might so easily have been any other of the millions of stones, but it was I, I, I!"

Whether this thought or not was in John's mind, the lump of glass had its place upon the mantelpiece, where it stood heavy upon a little pile of bills and letters and served not only as an excellent paper-weight, but also as a natural stopping place for the young man's eyes when they wandered from his book. Looked at again and again half consciously by a mind thinking of something else, any object mixes itself so profoundly with the stuff of thought that it loses its actual form and recomposes itself a little differently in an ideal shape which haunts the brain when we least expect it. So John found himself attracted to the windows of curiosity shops when he was out walking, merely because he saw something which reminded him of the lump of glass. Anything, so long as it was an object of some kind, more or less round, perhaps with a dying flame deep sunk in its mass, anything—china, glass, amber, rock, marble—even the smooth oval egg of a prehistoric bird would do. He took, also, to keeping his eyes upon the ground, especially in the neighbourhood of waste land where the household refuse is thrown away. Such objects often occurred there—thrown away, of no use to anybody, shapeless, discarded. In a few months he had collected four or five specimens that took their place upon the mantelpiece. They were useful, too, for a man who is standing for Parliament upon the brink of a brilliant career has any number of papers to keep in order—addresses to constituents, declarations of policy, appeals for subscriptions, invitations to dinner, and so on.

One day, starting from his rooms in the Temple to catch a train in order to address his constituents, his eyes rested upon a remarkable object lying half-hidden in one of those little borders of grass which edge the bases of vast legal buildings. He could only touch it with the point of his stick through the railings; but he could see that it was a piece of china of the most remarkable shape, as nearly resembling a starfish as anything—shaped, or broken accidentally, into five irregular but unmistakable points. The colouring was mainly blue, but green stripes or spots of some kind overlaid the blue, and lines of crimson gave it a richness and lustre of the most attractive kind. John was determined to possess it; but the more he pushed, the further it receded. At length he was forced to go back to his rooms and improvise a wire ring attached to the end of a stick, with which, by dint of great care and skill, he finally drew the piece of china within reach of his hands. As he seized hold of it he exclaimed in triumph. At that moment the clock struck. It was out of the question that he should keep his appointment. The meeting was held without him. But how had the piece of china been broken into this remarkable shape? A careful examination put it beyond doubt that the star shape was accidental, which made it all the more strange, and it seemed unlikely that there should be another such in existence. Set at the opposite end of the mantelpiece from the lump of glass that had been dug from the sand, it looked like a creature from another world—freakish and fantastic as a harlequin. It seemed to be pirouetting through space, winking light like a fitful star. The contrast between the china so vivid and alert, and the glass so mute and contemplative, fascinated him, and wondering and amazed he asked himself how the two came to exist in the same world, let alone to stand upon the same narrow strip of marble in the same room. The question remained unanswered.

He now began to haunt the places which are most prolific of broken china, such as pieces of waste land between railway lines, sites of demolished houses, and commons in the neighbourhood of London. But china is seldom thrown from a great height; it is one of the rarest of human actions. You have to find in conjunction a very high house, and a woman of such reckless impulse and passionate prejudice that she flings her jar or pot straight from the window without thought of who is below. Broken china was to be found in plenty, but broken in some trifling domestic accident, without purpose or character. Nevertheless, he was often astonished as he came to go into the question more deeply, by the immense variety of shapes to be found in London alone, and there was still more cause for wonder and speculation in the differences of qualities and designs. The finest specimens he would bring home and place upon his mantelpiece, where, however, their duty was more and more of an ornamental nature, since papers needing a weight to keep them down became scarcer and scarcer.

He neglected his duties, perhaps, or discharged them absent-mindedly, or his constituents when they visited him were unfavourably impressed by the appearance of his mantelpiece. At any rate he was not elected to represent them in Parliament, and his friend Charles, taking it much to heart and hurrying to condole with him, found him so little cast down by the disaster that he could only suppose that it was too serious a matter for him to realize all at once.

In truth, John had been that day to Barnes Common, and there under a furze bush had found a very remarkable piece of iron. It was almost identical with the glass in shape, massy and globular, but so cold and heavy, so black and metallic, that it was evidently alien to the earth and had its origin in one of the dead stars or was itself the cinder of a moon. It weighed his pocket down; it weighed the mantelpiece down; it radiated cold. And yet the meteorite stood upon the same ledge with the lump of glass and the star-shaped china.

As his eyes passed from one to another, the determination to possess objects that even surpassed these tormented the young man. He devoted himself more and more resolutely to the search. If he had not been consumed by ambition and convinced that one day some newly-discovered rubbish heap would reward him, the disappointments he had suffered, let alone the fatigue and derision, would have made him give up the pursuit. Provided with a bag and a long stick fitted with an adaptable hook, he ransacked all deposits of earth; raked beneath matted tangles of scrub; searched all alleys and spaces between walls where he had learned to expect to find objects of this kind thrown away. As his standard became higher and his taste more severe the disappointments were innumerable, but always some gleam of hope, some piece of china or glass curiously marked or broken lured him on. Day after day passed. He was no longer young. His career—that is his political career—was a thing of the past. People gave up visiting him. He was too silent to be worth asking to dinner. He never talked to anyone about his serious ambitions; their lack of understanding was apparent in their behaviour.

He leaned back in his chair now and watched Charles lift the stones on the mantelpiece a dozen times and put them down emphatically to mark what he was saying about the conduct of the Government, without once noticing their existence.

"What was the truth of it, John?" asked Charles suddenly, turning and facing him. "What made you give it up like that all in a second?"

"I've not given it up," John replied.

"But you've not the ghost of a chance now," said Charles roughly.

"I don't agree with you there," said John with conviction. Charles looked at him and was profoundly uneasy; the most extraordinary doubts possessed him; he had a queer sense that they were talking about different things. He looked round to find some relief for his horrible depression, but the disorderly appearance of the room depressed him still further. What was that stick, and the old carpet bag hanging against the wall? And then those stones? Looking at John, something fixed and distant in his expression alarmed him. He knew only too well that his mere appearance upon a platform was out of the question.

"Pretty stones," he said as cheerfully as he could; and saying that he had an appointment to keep, he left John—for ever.

100

A Haunted House

Whatever hour you woke there was a door shutting. From room to room they went, hand in hand, lifting here, opening there, making sure—a ghostly couple.

"Here we left it," she said. And he added, "Oh, but here too!" "It's upstairs," she murmured. "And in the garden," he whispered. "Quietly," they said, "or we shall wake them."

But it wasn't that you woke us. Oh, no. "They're looking for it; they're drawing the curtain," one might say, and so read on a page or two. "Now they've found it," one would be certain, stopping the pencil on the margin. And then, tired of reading, one might rise and see for oneself, the house all empty, the doors standing open, only the wood pigeons bubbling with content and the hum of the threshing machine sounding from the farm. "What did I come in here for? What did I want to find?" My hands were empty. "Perhaps it's upstairs then?" The apples were in the loft. And so down again, the garden still as ever, only the book had slipped into the grass.

But they had found it in the drawing room. Not that one could ever see them. The window panes reflected apples, reflected roses; all the leaves were green in the glass. If they moved in the drawing room, the apple only turned its yellow side. Yet, the moment after, if the door was opened, spread about the floor, hung upon the walls, pendant from the ceiling—what? My hands were empty. The shadow of a thrush crossed the carpet; from the deepest wells of silence the wood pigeon drew its bubble of sound. "Safe, safe, safe," the pulse of the house beat softly. "The treasure buried; the room . . ." the pulse stopped short. Oh, was that the buried treasure?

A moment later the light had faded. Out in the garden then? But the trees spun darkness for a wandering beam of sun. So fine, so rare, coolly sunk beneath the surface the beam I sought always burnt behind the glass. Death was the glass; death was between us; coming to the woman first, hundreds of years ago, leaving the house, sealing all the windows; the rooms were darkened. He left it, left her, went North, went East, saw the stars turned in the Southern sky; sought the house, found it dropped beneath the Downs. "Safe, safe, safe," the pulse of the house beat gladly. "The Treasure yours."

The wind roars up the avenue. Trees stoop and bend this way and that. Moonbeams splash and spill wildly in the rain. But the beam of the lamp falls straight from the window. The candle burns stiff and still. Wandering through the house, opening the windows, whispering not to wake us, the ghostly couple seek their joy.

"Here we slept," she says. And he adds, "Kisses without number." "Waking in the morning—" "Silver between the trees—" "Upstairs—" "In the garden—" "When summer came—" "In winter snowtime—" The doors go shutting far in the distance, gently knocking like the pulse of a heart.

Nearer they come; cease at the doorway. The wind falls, the rain slides silver down the glass. Our eyes darken; we hear no steps beside us; we see no lady spread her ghostly cloak. His hands shield the lantern. "Look," he breathes. "Sound asleep. Love upon their lips."

Stooping, holding their silver lamp above us, long they look and deeply. Long they pause. The wind drives straightly; the flame stoops slightly. Wild beams of moonlight cross both floor and wall, and, meeting, stain the faces bent; the faces pondering; the faces that search the sleepers and seek their hidden joy.

"Safe, safe, safe," the heart of the house beats proudly. "Long years—" he sighs. "Again you found me." "Here," she murmurs, "sleeping; in the garden reading; laughing, rolling apples in the loft. Here we left our treasure—" Stooping, their light lifts the lids upon my eyes. "Safe! safe! safe!" the pulse of the house beats wildly. Waking, I cry "Oh, is this your buried treasure? The light in the heart."